ROCK HALL

by JOSEPH JOHN SZYMANSKI

iUniverse, Inc.
New York   Bloomington

ROCK HALL

iUniverse books may be ordered through booksellers or by contacting:

iUniverse
1663 Liberty Drive
Bloomington, IN 47403
www.iuniverse.com
1-800-Authors (1-800-288-4677)

Because of the dynamic nature of the Internet, any Web addresses or
links contained in this book may have changed since publication and
may no longer be valid. The views expressed in this work are solely those
of the author and do not necessarily reflect the views of the publisher,
and the publisher hereby disclaims any responsibility for them.

ISBN: 978-1-4502-3003-2 (sc)
ISBN: 978-1-4502-3058-2 (ebook)

Printed in the United States of America

iUniverse rev. date: 7/22/2010

Dedication

This regional novel is dedicated to my parents, Lola Muller and Joseph William Szymanski, children of Ella Hartman and Frank Muller, and Victoria and John Szymanski.

In the 1920's, my Muller and Szymanski grandparents owned small restaurants across the street from each other in the 700 and 800 blocks of South Bond Street in Fells Point (when no one called it *Fells Point*) in southeast Baltimore, Maryland (when everyone pronounced it *Bawlmer* or *Balamer, Murlin*).

None of my grandparents had an education above the eighth grade, and ran their businesses without any records, checking and savings accounts, or credit cards. Everything was on a cash basis for purchases delivered to their doorstep. No one talked about making a profit, even though they owned and occupied their buildings. As long as they had enough cash to pay their bills, they were content. Enjoyment came from working and the pleasure of seeing customers, who were mostly from the neighborhood.

The Muller family of German and Irish descent, produced eight daughters and one son and owned one of the best seafood restaurants in the city from the 1920's to the 50's, at 709 and

711 South Bond Street. Their specialty was blue crabs, clams and oysters, all fresh from the Chesapeake Bay.

At 709, a long stand-up bar stretched along one wall in the front half of the restaurant for customers who ordered beer and whiskey. In the middle room were about eight 6-foot long tables that accommodated at least 60 customers for lunch and dinner. In the back room, a small kitchen with four baths of boiling lard for deep-frying oysters and clams, hand-made into paddies with their own juices and covered with cracker-meal and seasoning by Mom Muller and two friends, Frances Donohoe and Alice Gerstung, the wife of Harry Gerstung of Gerstung's Bakery, Baltimore's best bakery.

At 711, a door opened to a long 13-foot wide passage for customers who made their way pass a cooler and barrels of oysters and clams and bushels of crabs waiting to be steamed over an open wood-burning hearth, to a door in the back kitchen of 709, where carry-out orders were placed.

The Szymanski family of Polish descent, produced three girls and four boys and owned a small tavern cattycorner to Muller's at 696-698 South Bond Street, and catered mostly to sailors and merchant seamen in town for a few days of leave before shipping out to ports all over the world.

As far as I can remember, the name *Szymanski* did not appear anywhere on the outside of the building. Only bold, capitalized letters spelled out **BAR**, in the leaded-glass transom over the front door. I guess everyone knew it was 'Szymanski's Bar' by being familiar with the family over the years.

The front room, about 13 by 25 feet, included a long bar, where customers would stand and slouch while eating or drinking. Positioned at each end of the huge liquor display directly behind the bar were two two-gallon glass jars containing the largest pickled pig's feet in Maryland. The pig's feet immersed in yellowish liquid inside the jars resembled specimens in a forensic lab.

In a much smaller room behind the bar was an open kitchen with about eight card tables that accommodated 32 customers who could watch and smell the homemade food being prepared nearby.

There was no menu; not even a chalk board to identify the soup and special of the day. Their specialty was food that 'stuck' to your bones, like sour beef, cooked with ginger snaps after being marinated for a day or two, and served with dumplings or potatoes. I loved that smell almost as much as their customers loved it.

My father left school at the age of 13 because his father, almost 50, needed help in the family business. For the next three years, he did some cooking, kept track of supplies, moved heavy kegs of beer into position behind the bar, and often entertained the seamen with his singing voice.

At the age of 15, he and an older brother, Andy, worked two jobs. In the afternoon they supported their father in the family business, then grabbed some shuteye before waking at 3 am and walking two miles to work for Southern Seafood. The owners of Southern Seafood, which opened in 1922 as an ice-making plant in Camden Yards, also occupied the largest stall inside the wholesale seafood market in the center of Baltimore. Both brothers were paid $1 per day to move barrels of oysters, clams and fish on and off trucks and horse-driven carts and pack everything in ice before it spoiled. Although both were teenagers who stood only 5-foot 8-inches, they quickly developed into young men with muscles of steel.

Andy worked continuously for Southern Seafood for 50 years and missed only 50 days due to sickness, for which he was docked in pay as an hourly employee. In 1976, Southern Seafood informed its 22 employees that they were selling their land and buildings for development of Camden Yards and a new baseball stadium for the city. When he clocked out on the last day of work, he received a final paycheck with no bonus, vacation pay, or even a *Thank You.*

Luckily, Andy's wife, Christina, had health coverage from her employment with the telephone company to cover unexpected health problems that plagued him in later years.

My father, after working five years for Southern Seafood without any health coverage, decided to apply for a job with the Baltimore City Police Department. So at 18, with the help of a local politician, he became a policeman and began working for $14 a week. He started in the traffic division and worked the swing shift, 7am - 3pm, 3pm - 11pm, 11pm - 7am.

For the first seven years he was a foot-patrolman, walking a beat alone, along the notorious block of burlesque houses of Baltimore Street, in one of the toughest neighborhoods only a few blocks from police headquarters and City Hall. Shootings and homicides were everyday occurrences, but the worst times were when he was ordered to a business or residence to settle domestic disputes, such as restraining a drunken husband who was beating his wife with a loaded pistol.

Around the age of 25 he married my mother, who had just turned 21. At 27, he was transferred to the motor pool and rode a motorcycle. For the next six years, he patrolled the old Baltimore-Washington highway until he was injured in a horrendous collision while in pursuit of a speeding car on the slick winter road.

With incredible skill and ingenuity, Dr. George H. Yeager, of the University of Maryland School of Medicine, performed one of the first vein-transplants to save his legs, but phlebitis and arteriosclerosis would plague him the rest of his life. His legs from the knee down appeared the color of purple because of poor circulation of blood. This condition meant that he had to be extremely careful of anyone or anything bumping into his legs, with daily baths, applications of special ointments, and change of dressings, all to reduce peritonitis, gangrene or other infections. His legs were always wrapped in a special elastic sleeve to reduce cardiovascular problems.

After his injury, he was reassigned to a desk job inside the traffic division, processing traffic citations until finally obtaining a medical discharge. During a career of almost 35 years on the police force, he never rose above the rank of a patrolman.

When I questioned him about why he was never promoted, he confessed with considerable urging that a police captain and lieutenant "had it in for him." These two corrupt officers had asked my father, during his first week on the police force, to go into a business store on Baltimore Street and pick up a brown paper bag from the owner. When he asked them what was inside the bag, they told him "that's none of your business. Just go inside and pick up the bag."

When he refused, they told him, "you'll regret it," and as long as they were his supervisors, always gave him the worst assignments under their control. He told me, "At least I can go to bed at night and not be afraid of someone coming to arrest me." Those officers also spread the word among other supervisors that my father was a "trouble-maker," which was not easy to overcome, despite having the respect of his fellow patrolmen who also walked a beat alone.

The bag probably contained 'kick-back' money taken by unscrupulous 'top-brass' police officers who were supposed to lead their men, and serve and protect the people. Instead, they turned a blind eye to prostitution, intoxication and disorder which included robbing customers who had too much to drink inside the noisy and smoky burlesque houses along Baltimore Street.

My father never had a credit card. He maintained a philosophy throughout his entire life: "If you can't pay cash for it, you don't need it." One glare from his face was enough to get his point across. He had a big heart, especially for the little guy, and wore his sentimentality out in the open. He cried at the happiest of times, telling us "It's good to be alive." His handshake and smile always left a good impression on everyone. He protected his family from ever hearing about his life on the police force until late in life, about five years before he died at the age of 95.

When I questioned him about his motorcycle accident and life-saving operation in which the doctors were close to amputating his legs, he simply shook his head and began crying. After wiping his eyes, I asked him if he ever felt any pain. He smiled and answered, "I've been to Hell and can take anything anyone dishes out to me."

At family gatherings, he and his brother-in-law, Andrew Muller, were the life of the party, with their impromptu skits that always included songs in which he sang the harmony. He was the most honest man I've ever known in my life.

During the 1950's one of the top scouts and coaches of amateur baseball in Baltimore was Sterling "Sheriff" Fowble, who lived nearby in our neighborhood of East Baltimore. During his 40 years of coaching 14-16 year-olds in amateur sandlot baseball, his best players were: Ron Swoboda, who signed with the New York Mets; Al Kaline of Southern High School, who signed with the Detroit Tigers, played in more games and hit more home runs than anyone in Tiger history and eventually entered the Hall of Fame; Jim Spencer of Patterson Park High School, who signed with the Boston Red Sox and rose to AAA with Louisville before an injury ended his career; my brother, Frank, who signed with the Cleveland Indians and played against Juan Marichal, Tommy Davis, and Felipe Alou; and a long list of other ballplayers who started their career under the tutelage of Sheriff on their way to the major leagues.

Sheriff told me that my father, in his teens, would have made a good baseball player if he had the same opportunities as *his* kids. He said that my father was a very good pitcher and hitter who once pitched a double hitter and hit a home run in each game, only to be chased all the way from the playing field to his parent's house on Bond Street by angry players on the losing team.

Finally, some words about my mother, who was the most influential and powerful member of the family, despite standing only 5 foot 2 inches and weighing less than 100 pounds. She loved school but at the end of the eighth grade was forced to work in the Muller family restaurant, seven days a week.

After their marriage, they bought a row house with white marble steps on Ellwood Avenue, across the street from Patterson Park. While my father worked as a policeman, she continued working in the family restaurant, cleaning the kitchen and scrubbing floors on her hands and knees, waiting on tables, and serving customers that often included Mayor Tommy DeAliceandro and Governor Theodor McKeldin. (I played the accordion for them and they were big tippers!)

She dedicated her entire life to her husband and three sons. Included in her work routine was the washing and ironing of seven white shirts a week, a fresh one that my father wore each day on the police force. She controlled the budget under the severest circumstances. Once, when I stole a nickel from the tin can of coins, I had my fingers held over the flames of the top burner of the kitchen stove. It was a lesson that stayed with me to this day.

At Christmas time, when the post office needed help sorting mail at their facilities around the city, she worked part-time in order to earn extra money to buy presents. She never missed a baseball game that my brother played anywhere in Baltimore.

When I was about 10 years old, she carried a 22-pound accordion three blocks to the Eastern Avenue electric trolley and up a flight of steps to the second floor of the Joseph Lopez Music Studio near Broadway, so that I could learn to play the accordion. The music lessons lasted two years.

After my brothers and I flew the nest, she volunteered at St. Patrick's School on Broadway, working without pay as a teacher's aide to her youngest sister, Frances, who taught kindergarten there. She worked her entire life, without complaint, and died at the age of 95.

Finally, as an afterthought, I'd like also to dedicate this novel to my personal heroes: Simon Wiesenthal, Robert Oppenheimer,

Werner von Braun, General George S. Patton Jr., and John F. and Robert F. Kennedy.

JOSEPH J. SZYMANSKI

P.S. I had the pleasure of playing baseball with Jim Spencer at Patterson Park High and for Sheriff Fowble's High AC (High's Ice Cream Athletic Club) in the 1950's, and playing against Al Kaline of Southern High. I was also the only infielder on Patterson's baseball teams of 1950 and 1951 to play with Danny Ganz, Butch Housekenect, Gil Thomas and Jim Spencer who all signed pro contracts after graduation.

Acknowledgement

My deepest gratitude is extended again to Michael 'Mike' McGrath who edited the manuscript at least four times, called my attention to the format for giving the dialogue a more natural sound and kept my spirits up during a year of torment from the writing process. I was always left with the question, "Why are so many new ideas coming after I've handed over the manuscript to Mike for his edit?"

Appreciation is also extended to Jeanie Woods, who managed to fit in an occasional line edit among her incredible schedule of activities that occupy her retirement.

In the jargon of watermen, Mike and Jeanie have always given me the *smart* of it!

And speaking of watermen, particularly those from Rock Hall, it was not my intent to ridicule them by writing some dialogue with slang, as Gordon Beard compiled in his book about the people of Baltimore speaking Baltimorese. (See *Glossary* at end of last chapter.)

On the contrary, watermen have my deepest respect because they are a dying breed who continue to carry on their chosen profession despite the pollution of the Bay and government regulations that hamper their workdays.

Lastly, my gratitude extends to Paul Gregory, legendary agent and producer, who gave me the confidence to continue after reading the prequel *BETTERTON* and called it "a solid storyline with strong characters that will make a good TV series."

JOSEPH J. SZYMANSKI

Preface

Before he went from Betterton to Iraq, a 24-year-old private in the Army told his mother and younger sister, "Take care of the Bay, and the Bay will take care of you." Three months later he died at the hands of a suicide bomber. His death was just another casualty in wartime, and unnoticed in his home town, despite the military Honor Guard that accompanied his body for burial in Betterton, a forgotten town on the Eastern Shore of Maryland.

His last words to them referred to the Chesapeake Bay of Maryland, the largest tributary in America. It was a simple statement by a naive youngster, but somewhat profound, coming from a breed of young watermen who carry on the tradition of making their living by fishing and crabbing on the Bay. His family's life was revealed briefly in the prequel, *BETTERTON*, published in 2009 as the first of a planned trilogy (see www. bettertonthebook.com). I suggest the reader have a good look at *BETTERTON* to grasp the essence and background of the main characters and settings portrayed herein.

The sequel, *ROCK HALL*, is a story of people living 26 miles south of Betterton. Both towns are situated in Kent County and have much in common. Starting with their size, Rock Hall is about 30% larger than Betterton at just under one-square mile in area. As for population, census figures indicate 30 percent more people living in Rock Hall than in Betterton. Percentages, however, can be misleading, since 30 percent translates to only 240 people. Rock Hall has approximately 800 permanent residents, whereas Betterton has 560.

More than 90 percent of all land in Kent County is agricultural, which is taxed at about 10 percent of the assessed value of residential land. From a socio-economic standpoint, less than 10% of the residents of Rock Hall and Betterton have a college or university degree. Of those who graduated from high school, less than 10% have ever taken a course in anything to advance their education, prepare them for a higher-paying job or give their children a better life. Finally, almost 90 percent of all working heads of families, of which half are single parents, earn less than $40,000 annually.

But one thing is certain among Rock Hall's permanent residents: They are fiercely independent and determined to keep their town exactly as it has been for the past 100 years, come hell or high water. They simply don't care one iota what anyone else thinks or does, as long as it doesn't change the look and feel of their town.

From a historic standpoint, between the 1780's and 1790's, General George Washington (born in 1732) and his crew supposedly sailed down the Potomac River, crossed the Chesapeake Bay, and landed at Rock Hall. After consuming some oysters, Washington eventually made his way to Philadelphia, the nation's capitol at that time.

Lieutenant Colonel Tench Tilghman, Aide-de-camp to General George Washington, and his crew repeated the trip in 1781. He was selected personally by Washington and entrusted to carry the documents of the American victory over the British, signed by General Lord Charles Cornwallis who surrendered at Yorktown, Virginia. After landing at Rock Hall, Tilghman began his legendary horseback ride from Rock Hall to the Continental Congress in Philadelphia.

From these historic early days to the present, hard-working watermen in their skipjacks and buy-boats prowled the Bay for fish, crabs, oysters and clams, which were brought into harbors like Rock Hall. After their catch was recorded, it was quickly packed in ice and shipped to seafood markets in Baltimore, Philadelphia and Wilmington.

Today Rock Hall has a sandy beach about the size of two basketball courts, roughly 50 by 200 feet, and the shore is free of sea nettles and jelly fish. But tourists don't come to play and lay on the sand. Most of them chow down on crab cakes, and those with boats haul them by trailers, off-load them into Rock Hall Harbor and motor or sail directly into the Bay. About 25% of the houses in Rock Hall are second homes, for weekends or summer vacations, then shuttered for the winter months.

When the Chesapeake Bay Bridge was completed in 1952, most vacationers preferred Ocean City, where beaches were more expansive and accompanied by every modern convenience imaginable. But there were always a few die-hards and sporting enthusiasts who came to Rock Hall for a summer of fun on the Bay, whether it was for fishing, crabbing or entering sailboat races on the weekends.

In the fictional novel *ROCK HALL* that takes place today, whether the permanent residents of Rock Hall like it or not, change is coming to the eastern shore of Maryland. It's unexpected, in the form of Mark Hopkins, a 26-year old handsome, rich, ambitious and intuitive former SEAL Lieutenant. He was one of the lucky ones who, after four years of combat in Iraq, came home all in one piece, except for the nightmares that continue to stir in his mind.

If he has any foibles, it's his tendency to act as a Monarch butterfly, never content to stay very long in one place, moving when the conditions are right from one beautiful woman or place to another, and not necessarily in search of something better. Psychiatrists, especially those from Vienna, would call him *flighty*.

As you begin reading *ROCK HALL*, you'll discover that it's not only about people living in a bayside town, but more about this former SEAL whose motto is: *You Can Be Better Than You Are.*

Whereas the previously-published book *BETTERTON* was about 50% fact and 50% fiction, it's sequel *ROCK HALL* is just the opposite. But don't ask me what parts are factual and what are fictional. At this moment it's still a blur in my mind. It's safe to say that the storyline and characters are strong but imaginary. While the names of people and businesses may seem familiar, they are all fictitious, and any resemblance to actual places or persons, living or dead, is entirely coincidental.

One final remark about watermen. Several months ago when I donated several copies of *BETTERTON* to the senior club in Rock Hall to sell at their Christmas luncheon, an elderly lady approached me to pick up her copy and wanted it autographed. I asked her why she was buying it, and she bent over to whisper into my ear, "My husband's a waterman and told me to buy it because he wants to know what shit you're writing about them!"

I was shocked at first, then realized the title page of my novels about small towns bordering the Chesapeake Bay, like Betterton and Rock Hall, should have the following precautionary notice: "Reading this book may be injurious to your mental health."

You may eventually reach the conclusion that *You Can Be Better than You Are.* Remember: Change is good. Change is healthy. Change is necessary for growth in body and spirit.

Joseph J. Szymanski

Chapter 1

It may be a brisk November-morning breeze blowing at 20 mph outside on the Chesapeake Bay, but inside Annette's Antiques, a porch-front home converted into an antiques store in Betterton, the breeze is anything but fresh. It's like the merchandise on display in the front showroom: Stagnant and covered with a layer of dust.

Around the middle of store a woman's hand grips an odorizer, thrusts it upward and above the merchandise and waves the spray in all directions for about three seconds. The person doing the spraying is the owner of the shop, Annette Welles, a stunning and vivacious 45-year old antiques dealer with a curvaceous body, supported by the most beautiful long legs in the world.

After she moves closer to a bay window and opens one of the side panels to let in some fresh air, the morning sunlight reveals more details of her 38-24-26 figure under a tight-fitting sweater and trousers.

"Oh, what a beautiful morning in Betterton," she says to herself. "If I didn't have to raise two kids as a single mother years ago, I'd probably be tap-dancing on stage with the Rockettes at the Radio Music Hall in New York City this morning, instead of dealing in antiques, which is not so bad when you think about it."

After moving away from the window, she walks over to a jewelry case, with a slight swagger in her shoulders and bouncy steps. Her features are high-definition movie-star quality, with a perpetual 'happy-go-lucky' smile on her face, which always leaves people asking themselves, "Why is she working in a small fishing village like Betterton when she could be in Hollywood making movies?"

"Let me *outa* here," squawks a parrot inside its covered cage in a far corner of the store.

"Mark, better remove the cover over Gertie's cage and do it before she has a nervous breakdown," Annette shouts across the room. "I can't wait to hear what she has to say this morning. She's always like a breath of fresh air in this dust bin."

"I was about to do just that, but decided to wait until you finished spraying a lavender scent," answers Mark Hopkins, a tall, handsome, muscular 27-year old, who's dressed in denim shirt and trousers, with the word 'SEAL' stenciled along one sleeve.

Mark removes the cover and folds it neatly as Gertie begins to ruffle some feathers and blurts out, "Another day, another dollar."

"Are you sure, Gertie? That's an old cliché. Today's dollar is not worth what it was yesterday. The economy's going down the drain and people have slowed down when it comes to buying art."

He rotates his shoulders to imitate Gertie's movement whose feathers continue to ruffle, then pours some fresh water into her trough attached to the cage.

"Gertie, you're just like me in the morning, getting the kinks out of your neck. For the first month or two after I first met your owner, Knute Runagrun, I thought he was a ventriloquist, putting words in your mouth. But since I've gotten to know you better, I realize you're one smart parrot who can speak for yourself. If I wasn't trying to make a buck in the art business as Annette's partner, I'd take you over to the Hippodrome in Baltimore and let you squawk on stage for big money, maybe get you a gig in the movies, too."

"*Bal-a-mer*? I heard it's a great place to live, work and play," squawks Gertie while nodding her head and pronouncing the name of the city in three distinct nasal syllables.

"Speaking of Baltimore," Annette exclaims while putting some books into an arts and crafts bookcase, "those tourists are not flocking to Betterton on the *New Bay Belle* ferry from Baltimore, as they did in the 1950's and 60's."

The glass doors of the bookcase reflect the morning sun beaming through the front bay window and cast shadows of their movement against the walls of the store.

"My mom and dad spent their childhood, taking the ferry on weekends, from the Inner Harbor, down the Patapsco River and across the Chesapeake Bay," he tells her.

"In the old days, hundreds of vacationers came to Betterton Beach," answers Annette, "with its hotels, restaurants and an amusement park that centered around a carousel of prancing horses carved by the Pennsylvania sculptor Herman Dentzel."

"That's ancient history," he replies slowly with a touch of regret in his voice. "All gone. Now, the only people you see in this bayside town on the eastern shore are watermen, and they're certainly not interested in antiques. Come to think of it, I haven't a clue what they're interested in."

While talking to one another, each is busy rearranging the clutter in the front showroom, where squeaks in the wood flooring seem to punctuate their dialogue.

Suddenly, some discordant musical notes are heard, sounds that drift from a corner table on which a kitten, with autumn-colored fur, is pulling the strings of a zither with its paws.

"I think you should take a few lessons from Reggie Perdue," he tells the kitten." "You're hitting some dominant 7th and 9th notes, like one's heard on Henry Mancini's theme for *Charade*."

The kitten looks up at him, stops plucking the strings of the zither, and yawns as if to say, 'Mancini? *Charade?* What the hell are you talking about?'

"Did you notice a new painting hanging on the back wall?" asks Mark with a loud voice so that his words carry over to Annette who's now moving things around in the middle of the store.

"As a matter of fact, I did. Where'd it come from and who painted it?"

"Take a good look at it and you tell me who is the artist?"

"It's a view of Central Park, New York City, signed in the lower right-hand "Anthony Benedetto." Never heard of him," she replies.

Oh, yes you have."

"When I say 'Never,' I mean 'Never." Are you pulling my leg? Are you telling me something that I know but don't know that I know it?" she asks with a puzzled look on her face and a play on words.

"Affirmative. Just trying to tease you a little," he exclaims. "Reggie dropped it off late last night. It's a gift from one of his celebrity recording stars, Tony Bennett, for us to sell, with the proceeds going to victims who lost a parent in Haiti's earthquake. The price is $5,000 and a bargain, believe me. In a fancy gallery in New York, Chicago or Los Angeles, it would be priced at $10,000 to $15,000."

Seconds later, a terrific bang vibrates the entire room.

"Frustration, that's what it is," utters Mark in a loud voice that echoes off the walls.

"What was that bang?" she asks.

"I dropped a four-foot bronze of a nude woman. It must weigh over 90 pounds. She sort of came to life momentarily and wiggled out of my grasp, like a slippery eel. Perhaps she thought I was getting too fresh by grabbing her around her..."

He pauses to see if any customers are nearby and says, "Breasts. Maybe she thought I was some kind of sex per-vert."

He walks over to a rack of vintage clothes, finds a shear beige-colored silk scarf and wraps it around the neck of the nude figure so that the ends drape down over her breasts.

"Wouldn't want to offend anyone by exposing too much of your beautiful body, my dear, especially in a conservative town like Betterton," he mutters.

"Are you talking to me, Mark?" she asks while moving behind a jewelry showcase whose top is the same height as her waist. "I think you said something about frustration. "

"Sorry if I'm a little jumpy this morning. I was up at 4, on my computer, in the middle of writing an email to a buddy in California, when the electricity went out to my quarters over the garage next door. Seems like there's more power outages in Betterton in one month than most big cities have in a year. Although the email was saved, by the time power was restored, I lost my train of thought and couldn't go back to sleep. It was important to get my ideas down while they were flowing out of my mind."

"I know the feeling. I was up at 5, reading a story about the plight of the Bay and the runoff of pesticides and fertilizers from farms that border the shore, killing everything, especially the crab grass. Without oxygen all sea life and vegetation die, and dead zones are created. The article said the government's going to spend another million dollars for another study of a previous study on the health of the Bay."

"So what else is new?" he asks with a shrug of his shoulders. "That's par for the course. The government has no solutions after all its studies and is spinning its wheels again. It distresses me that we can't hire execs from the private sector, like eBay and Apple, to help in the management of the Bay. What a challenge and opportunity to do good for so many people."

He looks at a grandfather's clock as it strikes a mixture of Westminster chimes totaling 11 o'clock.

"Right on time, which matches my Rolex. Speaking of time, wasn't there some rumors about those government facilities at

Edgewood Arsenal, inside Aberdeen Proving Ground, dumping their hazardous waste offshore?"

"Tommy told me many times," she admits, "that after a violent storm, he suspected that the soil around Edgewood and Aberdeen was stirred up and poured into the Susquehanna and eventually the Chesapeake Bay, killing fish and crabs as it made its way under the Bay Bridge. 'Anyone with a brain in their body could see the discoloration in the water,' he often told me."

"There's no way to hide hazardous waste and certainly not by piping it into the Bay and hoping it will dissolve quickly, without leaving any traces," Mark answers. "Those heavy metals sink to the bottom but can move with the tides and storms.

"Before he went off to Iraq," she continues, "Tommy said 'We should take care of the Bay, and the Bay would take care of us.' If he hadn't been killed by a suicide bomber six months ago, he'd be out on his boat, fishing or crabbing, trying to make a living as a waterman."

"Did he work the water alone?"

"All alone, but he was a member of a dying breed. Today, I bet there's no more than10 watermen from this area still working the Bay, a big drop from the 50's and 60's, long before you were born, Mark."

"And from what I've heard," he answers while examining a cobalt-blue Royal-Vienna vase, "over the past year the commercial watermen don't get much help from the government who restricts their fishing and crabbing to three days a week. That restriction forces them to over-fish and over-crab to make a decent living for their families, and if they get caught..."

"Those fines are severe, believe me," she exclaims by rubbing her thumb, forefinger and middle fingers together, in reference to the money it costs for violating the law. "Inspectors are always prowling around on their patrol boats and can spot a waterman a mile away with their binoculars, especially if he's in an area that's off-limits. Tommy got caught once, and once was enough."

"Watermen are frustrated," answers Mark with disgust in his voice, "but not as much as me. They can't make a decent living *on* the Bay and we can't make a decent living *by* the Bay."

He walks back again to the bronze nude, rolls it like a beer barrel about 10 feet to a position near the front bay window and says, "Screw this town. I don't care if it's conservative or not, I'm putting you right in the sunlight, where you belong, so that your best assets are on display."

Meanwhile, Annette, who stands five foot ten inches tall, is feeling full of vim and vigor, as usual. She moves over to Mark and the bronze nude, and glances at the model's bare breasts and impulsively unbuttons the top two buttons of her sweater. Some cleavage appears in her bodice, but at this point, it's not an intentional act on her part, that is, until she bends slightly backward, a gesture to uplift her bust line.

She looks again at the nude's breasts for comparison to hers and takes a handkerchief out of her back pocket to wipe some dust off the nude's shoulder.

"Looks like Annette's intends to turn 'dusting' into 'lusting,' or is that a stretch of my imagination?" Mark mutters to himself.

"I'll never look like her," Annette boasts, "no matter what exercise or diet I'm on, but at least I could feel like her, with that confident pose that says, 'Come on world. Show me what you can do and I'll show you what I can do!"

She twitches her head from side to side and upward as if to shake off any illusions about the similarities between her and the bronze nude, and continues, "By the way, Mark, did you read the newspaper this morning?"

"You know I never read the *Sun* until I've had one of your muffins with a cup of hot coffee, and you didn't make any yesterday."

"Sorry, but I got tied up with Richard, no pun intended. We're trying to decide on a wedding date, and the sooner the better." She ends her conversation by motioning toward the back of the showroom and tells him, "I think you may have a customer that needs your help."

Mark turns around and suddenly notices a short, stubby man in his 50's, wearing a weather-beaten pea coat, who's in the act of removing a picture with a heavy frame from the wall.

"Not too heavy for you, is it?" he asks while looking into his somber face. "I never realized you were in the shop. You'd make a good cat burglar tip-toeing on the roof of those mansions in Hitchcock's film, *To Catch a Thief.* Are you looking for anything in particular, or, as the local folks say, 'Anything I can do you for?' "

He laughs at himself and recalls the scolding he would get from his high school English teacher for ending a sentence with a preposition, but that's the way people in Betterton speak and, despite graduating from Johns Hopkins University with a degree in psychology, bad grammar is beginning to rub off onto him.

"Not really," the waterman replies. "Just browsing. I'm retired and got plenty of time on my hands now." He hangs the picture back again on its metal hanger.

"You appear to be much too young for a retiree," acknowledges Mark with a smile. "Are you from around here?"

"Born and raised in *Betterin*," he boasts, "*bin* a waterman all my life, and proud of it."

"You're the first person living in Betterton who's ever been inside our store, at least since I've been Annette's partner. I was just telling her that the people around here have absolutely no interest in antiques, and now I'll have to retract my statement."

"Well, *wit* me, I'm just *curyus*. As watermen 'round these parts say, 'that's the *smart* of it.' I'm simply browsing, really."

Mark raises his eyebrows upward, shakes his head in puzzlement and says to himself, "I'm used to the people in Baltimore speaking the slang of *Basic Baltimorese*, as Gordon Beard calls it, but never heard the expression *'the smart of it'* before. I'll have to file that one away."

"Did *ya* know," he asks Mark, "that *furty* years ago the *Chesspeak* Bay provided more crabs for people to *eht* than any other body of *warder* in the *whirl*?"

"Not sure that's true nowadays, based on what I've read and heard about the nitrogen and phosphorous pollution in the Bay, and federal cutbacks in workdays for commercial watermen."

"*Ya* sure are well-informed. Where *ya* from?"

"*Bal-ti-more*," answers Mark proudly, pronouncing it in three syllables.

"Oh, you're a foreigner, a chicken-necker."

Mark ignores his slur and asks, "Do you fish after the crab season is over?"

"When I first started out as a teenager helping my Pop. But, after he died, I inherited his boat and concentrated on crabbing, which always fascinated me. That is, up until a few years ago when it got to be too much work baiting six thousand feet of trotlines with clams. Yea, I have to admit that those crabs always fascinated me."

"Are you saying that you only crabbed on the Bay?"

"That's right. I am or was strictly a crabber. Some say a *crabby* old crabber 'cause I call 'em like I see 'em. When Pop told me about the deadly squall of '39, I stayed with crabs and left the fish and *ursters* to other watermen. Ever heard about the squall that took the lives of about a dozen *urstermen* from Cambridge?"

"I wasn't born then and neither were you."

"According to Pop, it was 15 minutes of Hell. *Febrarie* the third, at three in the afternoon. *Urystermen* from Crisfield were caught off-guard while out in the Bay with their skipjacks and skiffs loaded with *urysters*. They had no idea that northerly winds of 65 mph were sweeping across the Bay, from Annapolis to the Choptank River. With the snap of your fingers, the skies turned pitch-black with winds howling as the squall and its waterspout sucked water into its funnel and began spinning like a toy top. In less than 15 minutes, a dozen watermen were dead and no one knows how many vessels were overturned and disappeared.

Survivors said the squall cut a trough through the Bay so deep you could almost see the bottom."

He sneezes and blows his nose with a tattered handkerchief, then lowers his head to his chest and pauses to wipe a tear that begins to swell up in his eyes.

"Watermen are a brotherhood," he continues, "like policemen and firemen, and whenever one loses his life on the water, the memories stay with you for a lifetime. If you don't believe me, it's all in a new book, *Skipjack: the Story of America's Last Sailing Oystermen,* by Christopher White. That squall of '39 **was** 15 minutes of Hell. For me, life's too short to risk it for *urysters,* so I stayed with crabbing."

"That was a smart decision on your part because those oysters are heavy to move around."

"Bet you didn't know when crabs migrate, they can swim 35 miles in 48 hours?"

"That's almost as fast as Florence Chadwick swimming the English Channel."

"Whose Florence Chadwick?

"She swam the Channel from Calais to the shore of Dover, 21 miles, in about 14 hours in 1950."

"Didn't know Dover had a shore."

"It's not the Dover in Delaware you're probably thinking of. It's the one in England."

"Never *hoyd of it.*" He picks up a coffee mug with a wrap-around decal of a blue crab and continues, "How'd you like to be a female crab that moults 18 to 20 times in its lifetime, which averages about 3 years?"

"I heard that they're lucky to live one year, and grow faster in the fresh waters of the middle and upper Bay, but prefer salty waters for their love-making and spawning."

"Sooks, that's what they're called. They're sexually mature females, and guess what?"

"What?"

He pulls a clipping out of his tattered wallet and hands it to Mark, who reads it out loud, *"Blue crabs have a nuptial moult, with no coitus interuptus, locked into two lovers' embrace, for 5 to 12 hours."*

Mark sighs and begins laughing as he puts one arm on the waterman's shoulder and asks, "Love-making of 5 to 12 hours? I don't believe it. That's what I call giving everything for the sake of love."

"And when it comes to spawning, the eggs laid are not much bigger than a large pin head."

Mark shakes his head in astonishment at the waterman's knowledge, which is enhanced by his deep southern accent that forces Mark to listen closely to each word.

"How do you know when a sook is mature?" he asks curiously.

"Turn 'em over. The sook's apron on its belly is a semi-circular bell shape with a point at the top of its V-shaped apron. The normal female blue crab has a simple apron shaped like a V with no point."

"And the male?"

"It's called a Jimmy and has an apron with an inverted T."

"Can you tell a male from a female without turning it over to see its abdomen?"

"Abb-doo what?"

"Belly."

"Easy to tell the difference. Females have bright red pinchers at the end of its blue claws. Watermen call it *nail polish*. Males have a deep lapis-lazuli color along their arms with a red tip at the end of their pinchers."

"Astounding," Mark remarks.

"And did you know crabs are color-blind?"

"I think you're a living Wikipedia!"

"A what?"

"Forget it. I'll explain later. Continue with your lecture, professor."

"Crabs can crawl, swim and bite like hell. People think those crabs jump out of the water into your boat. You got to find them 'cause they're hiding in the shoals, eating and getting fat like me. Then there's the winds that kick up unexpectedly, especially the northwesterly ones, that blow the crabs off the bar of shallow waters into much deeper waters. When you mix in those summer thunder squalls and water spouts, that's when I do a lot of praying to the Lord. That's the *right smart of it.*"

"How long you been a waterman?"

"Don't know for sure, maybe 30 to 40 years. Like I said before, I was thirteen and learned it from my Pop, who learned it from his Pop. I wouldn't go into it today. Not many are handing down their boats to their kids either. The fleet's dwindling."

After the waterman moves his visor cap further back on his head, Mark takes a closer look at his muscular build and tanned face covered with wrinkles and dry skin. During their brief talk, he notices his unexpected twitch or nervous tick in his head and slumping posture with broad shoulders bent forward, probably the result of lifting heavy bushels of crabs. It's obvious that the wear and tear of his life on the Bay has taken its toll physically as well as mentally.

"I have to laugh," admits the waterman, "when I look down at that olive-green top shell, a sign of a healthy crab, and think about the *green ecologists* who want to save the Bay yet won't take up the battle with the Department of Environment and get stronger fines and maybe a jail sentence for farmers polluting the Bay."

"That was my suspicion too. There must be a better way to protect the Bay and the watermen. Must be tough to make a living for families. You have a family living here?"

"Not anymore."

"If you don't mind, I'd like to ask a few questions that have nothing to do with crabs or watermen."

"*Fire away.*"

"Have you ever been to Chadds Ford to see the paintings of Andrew Wyeth?"

"Where's Chadds *Furd*? Who's Wyeth?"

"Ever met a movie star? You know, Tallulah Bankhead's grave is at St. Paul's cemetery, about five miles outside Rock Hall. Did you ever meet her when she was living around these parts?"

"Who's *Tulla* Bankhead?"

"Ever been to the Hippodrome in Baltimore to see their stage shows?"

"What's the *Hippdrum*?"

"Ever been to a museum like the Winterthur in Delaware?"

"Huh? Why all the questions?" The waterman's feathers are ruffled by Mark's questions.

"Sorry. I'm just trying to make a point."

"What point? *Ya* tryin' to make fun of me?"

"Absolutely not. I meant no harm. I'm gathering information."

"OK. So I ain't educated."

"Never too late to make a start." Mark hesitates to see what the waterman says next, but no words come out of his mouth. "I'm waiting to see if you'll ask where or how to start. If you'd like a part-time job, as liaison..."

"Liaison?" he interrupts before Mark can complete the sentence.

"Look here, mate. you have brains, and I'd like to prove that *You Can Be Better Than You Are.* That's why I want you to keep in touch with me. You know the Bay as a waterman, a crabber who does more than simply put down his trot line and haul in the crabs for a living. You could be a liaison between the Bay and my plans for an institute to study and protect the Bay. But I'll tell you about it later. I heard someone coming up the front steps."

Rather than continue his conversation with the waterman, Mark looks over a rack of vintage clothes towards the front door, which swings open and bangs against the wall. He leans his body awkwardly to catch a glimpse of a tall, slender and elderly lady, wearing glasses and a long gray woolen coat and matching hat. The coat almost falls to her ankles. She looks to be in her early

13

80's and enters the store with the aid of an aluminum cane that thumps as it strikes the wooden-planked floor whenever she takes a step or two inside.

The waterman who was talking to Mark, quickly walks over to greet her and asks, "Aren't *ya* Miss Hufnagel?"

"Yes, I am," she answers surprisingly.

"Do *ya member* me?" he asks.

"My memory is not as good as it used to be," she replies apologetically. "I hope you'll forgive me for not recognizing you."

"Ya was my English teacher!"

"Maybe that's why I don't remember you," she explains, then pauses to say, "Were you one of my students at Patterton High in East Baltimore or at Kent High in Worton?"

"Kent High," he answers quickly.

"Ah, yes, now it comes back to me. You were the one who was always staring out the window, day dreaming about the Chesapeake Bay."

"That's right," he admits proudly as he draws his head and shoulders backward and thrusts his belly forward.

She turns to Mark and asks, "I hope you won't mind my looking around your shop, but I just moved into the senior living complex up the street and I'm looking for an inexpensive print to brighten up my kitchen."

"Have a look around," advises Mark. "I'm sure you'll find what you're looking for here." He pauses and begins laughing. "If we don't have it, you don't need it!"

A few minutes later she walks over to Mark and whispers, "You were right. I found precisely what I wanted. How much is this framed print of Van Gogh's *Sunflowers*?"

Mark takes her by one arm, and walks her to the front of the store where they can talk privately without anyone overhearing them. He tells her, "I can tell by the dust on the top edge that it needs a new home. The price is right, too. I want you to have it and every time you look at it, you'll think of someone who appreciates English teachers and all they've given us."

"I can't accept it," she tells him, "without paying something for it."

"Then," he counters, "donate whatever you think is fair to your church."

She leans over and gives him a little kiss on the side of his cheek.

"That's the nicest 'thank you' in the world," he answers. "When you have the time, please look up Manny Meyer, Maureen Greenspan and Jack Johnson at the senior complex? They're better known as 'Manny, Mo, and Jack,' and they helped to train my track team, the Betterton Breeze. Say hello and thanks from Mark Hopkins."

He opens the front door for her and watches as she walks slowly, with a cane in one hand and the framed print held tightly under the other arm, down the front pathway to the sidewalk, where a white mini-bus is parked at the curb.

After Mark straightens his shoulder blades and runs his fingers through his hair, he looks around the store and discovers that the waterman has disappeared as strangely as he first appeared.

He tries to re-connect his rambling comments to Annette about business in Betterton and repeats, "Frustration. That's what it is."

"I think I heard you say that the first time," she answers. "Are you still talking to me?"

"Now I am," he utters loudly, "and to this semi-nude bronze of Aphrodite." He walks over to where Annette's rearranging some jewelry in a showcase, and says, "Before I got side-tracked with our two visitors, I was referring to our antiques business. It's the middle of November, and as Shakespeare would say, 'Now is the winter of *our* discontent.'"

"You were a little heavy on your pronunciation of *our*."

"Well, since we're partners, what's mine is yours, including a share of the doom and gloom of business prospects. Winter's coming a little late this year, but tourists won't be coming, at least not to Betterton. They can see ice and snow around their homes in Philadelphia, Baltimore and Wilmington as easily as trudging through it here. Don't you agree?"

"Agree to what?" she murmurs.

"Agree that the prospects for the winter are looking dim and dimmer," he replies.

It's clear that neither one is paying serious attention to the other as they continue rearranging things inside the store, cluttered with so much stuff that it's always impossible to navigate from one area to another without bumping into and breaking something.

Annette turns away from the jewelry showcase and reaches up to a recorder on a shelf and lowers the volume on a CD of Steve Allen's theme song for *Picnic*.

"I love that theme song, written by Steve Allen, about a small town just like Betterton, " she tells Mark. "Reminds me of my first romance with an antiques dealer who played the piano when the shop was empty of customers."

In a quick flashback, she reminisces about meeting a dealer in Philadelphia, who offered her a job and lodging above his shop on Pine Street in the City of "Brotherly Love." Over a period of six months, she learned quite a bit about how to run an antiques business, but never expected to get pregnant. Although their partnership never reached the stage of marriage, it did produce a son, Tommy, who died six months ago in Iraq, at the age of 24.

Mark removes a guitar from the wall, which is covered with some cobwebs, and strums the strings haphazardly, causing a discordant sound.

"Ouch," replies Annette, as her flashback ends and she returns to reality. "That was Tommy's guitar, which is not for sale. I keep it here so people like Reggie can give it a workout, but your strumming reminds me of my second love."

"I'm all ears, Annette. Whatever you tell me stays right here," he admits.

"His name was Joseph Lopez, a young music teacher from Baltimore who had taken the *Bay Belle* ferry from 'Charm City' to Betterton for a weekend cruise. I was halfway up a ladder, hanging my sign "Annette's Antiques" over the front doorway when he helped me down. I took one look into his face, the color of mahogany with bright shiny eyes and curly dark hair, and was hooked. We spent that first day walking all over town and ending the night in a love nest on the outskirts of Betterton, 'splendor in the grass' as he called it. I'll never forget our first night together with the moonlight filtering through the branches and leaves of a giant Elm tree and shinning on his face. Under that moonlight, he looked like Othello, the dark-skinned Moorish general in Shakespeare's tragedy."

"Did the moonlight make you into Desdemona, his wife?"

"Ostensibly, yes. It was a night that I fell in love not knowing where it might lead. It truly was love at first sight."

"First impulses are often the best beginnings."

"He was 26, about as handsome a man as there was on Earth, with a million dollar smile and confident nature. He told me about being born in the Philippines, but studied the steel guitar in Hawaii. At the age of 24, he was offered free rent by a music-instrument distributor if he would move to East Baltimore, open a studio and sell accordions and guitars to Polish and German families who wanted their children to take lessons from him. So he opened one on the second floor of a storefront florist shop on Eastern Avenue near Broadway, an area with poor families who had a love for music. He gave lessons for $1 an hour, and always left five minutes at the end to play his electric steel guitar. He probably could have been a studio musician but didn't want to move to New York. Baltimore suited him perfectly."

"Good for him. Money was not his main concern. In a way, he was advocating my motto: *You Can Be Better Than You Are*."

"His studio," he said, "was about as simple as you can imagine, with promotional posters of accordion and guitar manufacturers hanging on the walls, and a few metal folding chairs in front of two music stands. His joy came from the satisfaction of watching a young child develop an appreciation for music while their mother or father sat quietly in the background."

"I wish I could have met and known him," replies Mark with sincerity.

"He also said it was almost always a mother who carried the 22-pound case with an accordion inside, up a stairway of at least 15 steps, and who occasionally dropped it halfway up so she could catch her breath. He was aware of the sound and rushed to grab the case with one hand and use the other to help her climb the remaining steps up to his studio."

"How long did your love affair go on, if you don't mind my asking?"

"Not long by today's standards. Three months to be exact. He followed the same routine, taking the ferry from Baltimore to Betterton every two weeks, and ending with a rendezvous in our love nest. But, despite our strong attraction to one another, our dates led only to one conclusion. I preferred living in a small town like Betterton, and he preferred the diversity of a big city like Baltimore."

"And?"

"After we broke up, he never knew that I was pregnant, and that Sandy would be born six months later."

"I can't begin to imagine the struggle and how tough it was for you to raise two children as a single mother," he admits.

"I was never short on confidence and independence, and never ever asked a cent to support my children. Pride can be painful, but we managed to survive. When they turned 21, they were on their own, and I ran my antiques shop with the belief that 'work cures all ills.'

Mark realizes what's mainly on his mind will be difficult to express since she is so good and very special. Nevertheless, stagnancy has no place here and Mark's ambitions are forcing him to move away from Betterton and to greener pastures.

"And what about your fiancé, Richard Wagner?" he asks.

"Must not forget Richard, who proposed to me 10 days and 10 hours ago."

"You remember it so precisely. That's why there's a wonderful glow on your face. I'm very happy for you. But I may have seen someone I know walking down the street towards Betterton Beach. Would you excuse me for a moment? I need a breath of fresh air anyway."

Mark removes an old Army telescope from a wall near the front door and steps onto the front porch. When he looks through the lens toward Betterton Beach, whatever he thought he saw has disappeared, but that doesn't stop him from moving the scope upward into the bay to catch a glimpse of a solitary waterman working the Bay. He pivots the scope 45 degrees to his left and, on the horizon, sees the outline of the Chesapeake Bay Bridge, or it could be his imagination taking over here.

He lowers the hand that holds the scope, takes a deep breath and reminisces about the first time he met Annette.

In a series of quick flashbacks, he recalls first being attracted to her daughter, Sandy, on the top deck of the *New Bay Belle* ferry. He told them about being honorably discharged as a second lieutenant and informing his father, owner of Bethlehem Steel, that he preferred not to join his firm as a junior executive. After four years of combat in Iraq and repeatedly facing the possibility of a suicide bomber, he wanted some peace and quiet, with blue skies overhead, possibly owning a farm filled with Canada geese everywhere and opportunities to strike it rich at a country auction.

After an hour on the top deck, they learned with careful probing that he was ambitious, persevering, intuitive and able to size up situations quickly. "They surmised that these traits were acquired from majoring in psychology at Johns Hopkins University, officer's candidate school and four years in the military as a Navy SEAL.

Halfway along the cruise and, while he was below deck to buy them some refreshments. Sandy's screams were heard, the result of being frightened by some skinheads who were teasing her and forced her backward, where she tripped over a railing. Moments later, he was plunging from the top deck into the Bay to save her life.

Not many swimmers would have reached her in the turbulent waters of the Bay, but Mark managed to grab her from going under for a third time. If he hadn't reached her in the next few seconds, her fall overboard would have been fatal.

Minutes later, Mark and Sandy were fished out of the Bay by Reggie Perdue, who was following the wake of the ferry in his family's luxury yacht, on his way home to Betterton. (Reggie's father was the founder of Perdue Farms, famous for its high-quality tender chicken.)

While everyone seemed deliriously happy when they finally set foot on the Betterton pier, Reggie learned that Sandy's brother was killed in Iraq and was on board the ferry as well, with an honor guard, Captain Harvey Kasoff, for burial at a small church cemetery three blocks up the hill from the pier-landing at Betterton Beach.

Annette was waiting anxiously at the pier to embrace her daughter and Mark, who introduced her to Reggie. It was an incredible moment where a rescue led to friendships that last a lifetime.

Several hours after the cemetery service, Annette asked Mark about his knowledge of antiques and experience at auctions. Subsequently, she offered him a job and the opportunity to live in her son's apartment over the garage. Without hesitation, he made it clear that he would not be interested in working *for* her, but willing to work *with* her, which subsequently led to an equal partnership in the antiques business.

During the next six months, Mark found several treasures at a country auction called Dixon's in Crumpton. Here, every Wednesday beginning at 8 in the morning, everything created on God's earth is consigned when the owner no longer needs it or heirs are selling off an estate.

Mark's most recent discovery was a rare Philadelphia lowboy that netted their partnership a profit of $74,000. Not a bad start. But that's all in the past, as he is convinced that there are bigger and better things that challenge him.

His flashback ends as he reads the temperature, 55 degrees, on a thermometer attached to an outside wall of Annette's Antiques.

Moments later, he's again in the front showroom, glancing down at a 12-inch high, bronze bust of Richard Wagner, the famous German composer, modeled by the French sculptor Gaston Leroux.

"Ever take a close look at the resemblance to your Richard?" he asks while raising it high into the air for her to see. "It's remarkable."

"Never gave it a close look. In fact, I can't remember where I got it. I guess that's the difference between being a dealer and collector. When you get down to it, I've never collected anything because there were too many bills to pay. Perhaps I should keep that bronze and see if I get the itch to collect like you and some of my customers."

At this moment Mark realizes that Annette is completely content to live in Betterton and operate her business as a hobby, making enough money to break even or show an occasional profit. On the other hand, he is ambitious and anxious to carve out a distinguished career in many fields. And buried deep in his psyche is the desire to do something for his fallen comrades who served in his SEAL squad in Iraq.

Their partnership appears to resemble a pair of individuals in which one sprints with all his might while the other jogs along, in the dust so to speak. But Mark feels very fortunate to be able to work with such a decent, gorgeous and good woman. Her happy-go-lucky attitude in the face of bad economic times always lifts his spirit whenever they're together. If she has any fault, it might be her habit of constantly moving things around in the shop, shuffling merchandise to the point where he can't find things when he wants to show something to a customer. When the shop is empty of customers, Mark often tries to imagine her on stage at the Radio Music Hall, tap-dancing with the Rockettes in a chorus line and showing everyone the most beautiful long legs in the world.

"Auk-shun, auk-shun" Gertie squawks from her cage in a far corner.

"I was thinking the same thing, Gertie girl. Must be telepathy, which is a first because I've heard about telepathy between humans but never between a human and a parrot," remarks Annette.

"Is Gertie telling us to sell some of this stuff at auction in Crumpton?" asks Mark.

"Ausgezeichnet, which means 'excellent' in German. When I first started in the antiques business on Pine Street in Philadelphia, my German-Jewish customers always said that when they spotted something special to buy," replies Annette while tapping her toes again. "We should pack some of this stale merchandise like those iridescent amber-colored carnival glass bowls and English porcelain figurines gathering dust over there in the corner," Annette declares with an outburst that surprises Mark.

"Might as well pack the old American Indian baskets and arrowheads, and those corroded brass portals salvaged from old boats, too" Mark declares.

"Pack all the stuff our customers tells us 'we'll pass on it, thank you' and sell it at Dixon's Auction in Crumpton," she utters.

"If that's what you want, we'll take enough clutter to pile on one 3- by 6-foot table inside their hanger. We have to change our goals and concentrate on buying and selling one high-quality piece, whether it's a painting or piece of furniture."

"Clear out whatever you think will give the store a fresh look. There's nothing here that I can't live without. It's time to begin some house-cleaning."

"Is that an order?" Mark asks.

"You're a former Navy SEAL Lieutenant and I'm a toe-tapping dancer that could have been on stage with the Rockettes at the Radio Music Hall in New York. You don't need any orders from me. Decide for yourself. You're on your own, son," she responds with a laugh. "Actually, you're like a son, very much like Tommy, but four years older and much wiser."

"In that case," Mark suggests, "get some cardboard boxes and we'll begin packing this stuff and loading it into your pickup. I'd like to be in bed and asleep by 9:30, which would give me seven hours of beauty sleep. Let's get cracking."

Chapter 2

At 5:30 am the next morning, Annette is gripping the steering wheel of her pick up while driving in complete darkness from Betterton to Crumpton.

Mark is seated in the passenger seat to her right, and enjoys a cup of hot coffee while acting as a lookout for deer who often burst out of the heavily-wooded areas along the 26-mile trip.

"You been driving this route so many times, you probably could drive it blind-folded," Mark tells her. "But for the sake of a deer, keep your speed below 35 mph in these wooded areas in case one is blinded or confused."

"Looking ahead," Annette responds, "I'll be happy if we don't find anything inside the hangar or outside in the fields to buy and bring back to Betterton. It'll be nice to move around a little more easily in the front showroom, for once in a blue moon. Now, where did that expression come from?" she asks facetiously.

"I haven't a clue, but I'll tell you later if I haven't already told you about a blue moon over a fjord in Bergen, Norway."

"Sounds romantic, Mark."

"Far from it. Our SEAL unit was on a mission to destroy some mines left over from the Nazi's when they occupied Norway. But that's in the past. We have to think about turning 'trash into cash' this morning."

"I'm looking forward to a fresh cup of coffee at the Amish deli inside the hangar," Annette tells him, "and maybe I'll splurge for one of their fabulous cinnamon buns, too."

Forty minutes later Annette backs her pickup truck in front of a double-door entryway at Dixon's Auction hangar.

"If you don't mind, Mark, you can begin unloading this stuff and set it inside while I go to the office and register for a consignor's table. Hopefully they'll assign us a table so that our stuff will be auctioned between 10 and 12, a good time where more dealers are bidding. We don't want a table at the beginning of the sale, at 8 am, 'cause many dealers are still on the road or busy unloading their stuff in the fields outside. That's why you got such a good buy on that Chippendale low-boy at 8:05 am six months ago."

"Ah, yes. good memories and a good profit, since I paid around $3,000 and sold it for $77,000. But you're only as good as your last best sale, and our better days are ahead of us."

"You're an optimist. It's good to be around you when you're in a groove and thinking positively. I've been worried that you haven't had your mind on the antiques business lately. You've have been thinking about something else."

"Very perceptive of you, Annette, but we'll talk about that later, perhaps during the drive back to Betterton."

While Annette heads over to Dixon's office, Mark begins to unload the pickup and stacks eight boxes carefully in a wide entryway.

Five minutes later, Annette is beaming as she tells him, "We have table 77. You always had luck with those 7's, so maybe we'll make a little profit from this clutter, which should be sold around noon." She surveys the complex inside and continues, "There must be over 2,000 things piled on 60 tables today."

"But Dixon's will sell it fast and probably be finished by 3 pm."

"When you open these boxes," Annette continues, "I may not have packed everything perfectly, especially a porcelain tea pot, so watch out that the top lid doesn't fall out. We don't want to chip any of the porcelain and glassware when we unpack it. They'll have enough chips by the time they're sold by the auctioneer, from mishandling by people inspecting everything before the auction."

Within 20 minutes the contents of eight boxes are unpacked and displayed on Table #77, which looks like a crystal and porcelain pyramid rising into the air. Larger and heavier things are positioned on the bottom under a three-tier table that Annette borrowed from a dealer friend who's setting up her stuff nearby. She attaches a note to the tier table that reads 'Table Not For Sale.'

"I feel like a big spender this morning," Mark tells her. "It's too early to begin looking at the tables inside or the junk in the fields outside, so let's have breakfast which is *on* me. After breakfast, we'll have plenty of time to see if we can find a gem or two."

A few minutes later, both are seated inside the Amish Restaurant, where at least eight young Amish girls in their late teens or early 20's, wearing black dresses with a black and white hat, move quickly and efficiently to serve customers lucky to find a table since there's always a line at the door.

Everything on the menu is delicious, and the quantity is high and prices low. Their breakfast specialty is corned beef flakes immersed in a gluey gravy over home-made biscuits, and a scrapple and egg sandwich that's at least 2-inches thick. Each is priced at $3.

During breakfast Annette tries to reconnect their conversation earlier when they were arranging their consignment on Table #77.

"As I said before, you really are an optimist," she remarks.

"It's contagious. I caught it from you," he answers. "That's what I enjoy most about being your partner in the antiques business. From the first time we met on top the *New Bay Belle* ferry, I sensed your inner confidence and independence, even though it was a painful time for you and Sandy with your son below deck. If I were twenty-five years older, I'd put a ring on your finger, because you are one gorgeous lady."

"How fresh you are or refreshing. Richard might have something to say about that. Actually, he's beat you to the punch. We're now trying to decide on a wedding date."

"You know it all started right here, inside Dixon's office next door. I was standing in line to pay for a guitar and model ship when Richard introduced himself to me. If that wasn't fate, what was it?"

"You and I have accomplished a lot in that time, haven't we?"

About an hour later, Mark and Annette are walking in the fields outside the hangar.

"Good for us to walk off that breakfast," Mark says while bending over to look closer at a pile of 35-mm cameras scattered on a blanket, which is spread out on the moist soil mixed with gravel. "At one time these Nikon and Minolta cameras would bring a good price, but not anymore. Today, people want digital cameras and I can't blame them. They're so easy to use and download. No more film to process."

Annette grabs his arm and says, "Do you see what I see over there?"

"Over where?" he asks.

"Two ladies fighting over a row of potted flowers," Annette tells him. "Neither one is able to form a pile or grouping of the pots they intend to bid on."

"It's an interesting situation there," he remarks, "because, after the consignor drops his consignment in a long row, in this case, a row of potted flowers, bidders, like those two ladies, can pull whatever they want out of the row and form a pile behind the row. Then, when the auctioneer in his golf cart reaches that consignor's row, he'll auction the pile formed behind the row separately. I think that's the way the auction goes on here."

Mark and Annette turn to each other as if reading each other's mind.

"What would you say if I proposed..." Mark tries to continue but can't get all the words out of his mouth easily; he's a little tongue-tied temporarily, like a relay in his brain that unexpectedly short-circuits.

"Proposed?" Annette asks while facing him directly. "Shouldn't you be on one knee when you make a proposal?"

"It's not that kind of proposal," he answers. "Let's hit the road and head back to the shop. There's something I want to talk over with you, if you don't mind."

"Whatever pleases you, Mark. There's nothing that sparks my interest here, so it's a good thing to go back home with an empty truck, a new first for me."

As Annette begins to drive slowly out of the Dixon complex, her pickup bounces after falling into a series of pot holes scattered around the grounds of the hangar.

"Hold tight, Mark, I seem to be hitting every pot hole here. Glad our truck is empty, otherwise we'd have damaged stuff in the bed of our pickup."

"Rough roads, like rough business, doesn't seem to bother you as much as it bothers me," Mark declares slightly frustrated.

"Oh my," utters Annette while glancing quickly in his direction. She senses something serious stirring inside him. "Let it out, Mark. Don't harbor anything that's bothering you."

During the 26-mile drive from Crumpton back to Betterton, Mark tries to explain what's been on his mind over the past three weeks.

"I'm still concerned about my implication in Vera's murder and the attitude of people in Betterton and Rock Hall who are familiar with the case, which is affecting our business," he admits reluctantly. "You recall my buying that model ship, *Gratitude,* at Dixon's?"

"You mean the one you sold five months ago to Bud and Vera Wayne, owners of Swan Point Marina in Rock Hall?"

"That's right. I can't forget the look in Bud's eyes when I showed him the dagger used to repair the stern of the model ship. Little did I know he would one night use it to kill his wife and implicate me in the killing. It took two trials to catch that bastard."

"I remember everything like it was yesterday," she acknowledges. "In the first trial, Bud walked out of the courtroom as a free man because the jury was not convinced that he was the murderer, based on the fact that the murder weapon, possibly the dagger that belonged to you, was not found, and he denied any knowledge of ever seeing it."

"A month later, after the dagger's worth, half a million dollars, was published in the *Kent News*, he retrieved it from somewhere along the shoreline near the Wildlife Refuge, where he had buried it."

"In the second trial he had no recourse other than to plead guilty to perjury and received a sentence of 22 years imprisonment, without the benefit of parole."

"The stain of my being implicated in Vera's murder will never fade away." he mutters painfully. "Memories of the trial, especially the testimony of police who discovered her sitting in the front seat of her Caddy with her throat cut from ear to ear and me passed out in the passenger seat still haunt me, horrible images that are embedded in my psyche forever."

The frustration mounting inside him eventually leads him to make a fist with his right hand and pound it against the dashboard, producing a thud with little resonance.

"Careful, Mark, you don't want to hurt yourself unnecessarily," Annette says.

"The stigma will always be there," he continues. "Perhaps it's just an excuse that the future of doing business in Betterton is looking dim and dimmer. From my perspective, it's obvious. Something has to give."

"Give?" she asks with a degree of suspicion as she turns for an instant to look at his face. "Maybe I've been a little blind and naive not to see you and me and Betterton in a brighter light. You're not thinking of ending our partnership, of leaving Betterton?"

"Life is not all peaches and cream," he utters with a snicker. "I never realized it until now that I'm full of clichés and crap. Nevertheless, Thanksgiving is approaching, a time for reflection. Our business is down and cannot get any lower. I'm also getting claustrophobia from living in the cramped apartment over the garage next door. That place will never make the pages of *House Beautiful* or *Architectural Digest*, even with slip-covers over the sofa. Plus I notice the curtains are always moving in the upstairs back window of Nellie's B&B next door. I think she's taking photos of people going in and out of my apartment. You should speak to her about it when you have a chance."

"Forget Nellie for the time being. About our business going down the drain, that's an exaggeration. Furthermore, appearance is important. If you give the appearance that everything is going well, then good things will happen. Maybe you're dwelling too much on the negative and should look at the positive, things you've discovered at auction and friends you've made here."

Mark tightens the belt on his trousers and pulls down the visor over the passenger's seat to look at himself in a small mirror attached to the visor. He doesn't like the scowl on his face and mutters to himself, "Don't take out your frustration and anger on Annette. Take a deep breath. and ease up. You're lucky to be alive. God's been good to you."

"Vera's murder was six months ago," Annette remarks. "You've been vindicated and the murderer is now in prison. People have short memories, if any, around here. You've been a joy to be around, and a fabulous partner in our business. I also thought you and Sandy would get hitched one of these days, and take over the shop, so I can spend more time with Richard. We're like two lovebirds in a new nest, looking forward to our wedding coming up on Christmas Eve."

"I'm not sure that Sandy has the slightest inclination of running an antiques shop," he answers. "She's a gifted artist and should continue to concentrate on her art, and not waste time waiting for tourists or old-time clients to buy something. The only way to make big money in the antiques business is to comb the auctions at Weschler's in Washington DC, Freeman's in Philly or Dixon's in Crumpton and hope you find a high-quality painting or piece of furniture."

"Is there another reason behind your decision to leave the nest?"

"I didn't want to bring it up, but you mentioned your upcoming wedding. When I think about our partnership, you'll be taking on the responsibilities of a wife and that's wonderful, believe me. It means I would be running the shop, and when I think of that, I have a problem that rattles my insides."

"Did you say *rattle*?"

"If I were going to start a business in antiques, I certainly wouldn't choose Betterton for its location. Why would I want to drop anchor in Betterton when there's nothing here? No hotels, motels, coffee houses, bars, schools, recreation centers, nothing in the way of history, culture or entertainment, plus an overall attitude of its residents that resent any change. There's also no heroes here on which to build something special, although I think Sandy could be a significant sculptor."

"Heroes? Never gave it a thought before. Maybe you could be a hero?"

"No, not me, surely not me, but Sandy has the potential to be one. She has the God-given talent to be an important sculptor and take her place alongside an exhibition of works by Rodin and Claudel. And before I forget it, consider her bronze of *Storm Cat* sold. I'm buying it, not because of my relationship with Sandy, but because it's a marvelous likeness of the Kentucky Derby winner. The price of $5,000, set by her sponsor and breeder, Tom

Bowman, is a steal. Not much markup when you consider the casting costs at least $3,500, which means they split $1,500 profit. Peanuts, really."

"You've given me an idea. Perhaps I should buy one, to go with the bronze of Richard Wagner. So you see, Mark, I've got that itch to collect from you."

"Sometimes, there are treasures right in front of you if you take the time to open your eyes," he admits.

"Getting back to tourists," Annette declares, "if pollution of the Bay continues in the direction it's now headed, then first-time tourists will find another place to visit."

"Don't get me wrong here, but it seems as if Betterton is becoming a ghost town through which people drive inland to Chestertown, Middletown, or Wilmington. And frankly, Rock Hall is not much better. It's about one block in which almost half of the businesses and buildings are now up for sale. My life is worth more than sitting inside an antiques shop in a decaying bayside town. I like the idea of going to auctions and meeting other dealers and collectors."

"Can't blame you. If I were twenty years younger, I'd do the same thing."

"Please try to understand where I'm coming from," he smiles because he's ending a sentence with a preposition again. "Don't misinterpret my anger and take it personally. You're the last person in the world that I would ever want to hurt. No words can express how grateful I am for the opportunity you've given me."

"You mean this is the end of the beginning?"

"Yes, now it's time to take a new tack with my sails, become a private dealer, where I'm free to travel and meet serious collectors and do whatever I can do to help veterans who served in the military and need a little boost in their life. Being tied down and running a shop primarily for tourists is not for me. Time is too short and precious. Simply put, I need the stimulation of educated people who are interested in science and fine art."

After pausing to catch his breath, he realizes that she is stunned and speechless.

"I have my eyes on a farm, about 50 acres outside Rock Hall, near the Wildlife Refuge on the right side of Eastern Neck Island Road facing the Bay," he continues. "It's not even for sale, but I expect to talk to the owner soon. If I'm able to get it, lots of ideas are floating around in my head, and I'll have to spend all my time there."

As Mark and Annette enter the rear door of her shop in Betterton, the Westminster grandfather's clock begins to chime, indicating 11 am, and the telephone rings on an extension mounted on a rear wall.

Since Mark opened the door for her to enter first, Annette picks up the phone, listens for a moment and hands it to him.

"It's Winfrid Strong, the DA in Chestertown," she tells him.

"Would you mind coming as soon as possible to my office?" asks Strong. "I want to return your dagger, the one you brought back from Iraq. Now that the case against Bud Wayne is closed, it's your property and its value, $500,000, scares the hell out of me. The sooner you take possession and sign the release, the better I'll feel. How soon can you get here?"

"I'll be in your office in 30 minutes unless I hit a deer on the road," he answers.

"Don't do that. You could be arrested," Strong tells Mark.

Because it's a mild, sunny afternoon Mark drives his BMW convertible with the top down in the direction of Chestertown, 12 miles inland from Betterton. He enjoys the cool breeze rustling through his curly hair and slaps the side of his head with his right hand. He's *slap-happy*.

Further along the way, he is fully energized, inhales lots of fresh air, and admires different farms and forests along the roadside, with nothing but blue skies overhead. It's a glorious day until there's a bend in the road ahead, whereupon he turns the steering wheel and drives slowly downward along a stretch of huge trees lining both sides of a shady section.

A damp chill suddenly covers his body and causes him to shudder and tightly grip the steering wheel of his BMW. He lowers the speed of his car as his mind drifts into a quick flashback of a recent mission in Norway, with a small squad of divers under his command as a Navy SEAL Lieutenant.

A full moon is the only light illuminating a section along an outer fjord about two miles outside the harbor of Bergen, Norway. Mark is standing inside a large motorized craft with four SEALS, all wearing neoprene wetsuits. Their mission: Detonate four newly-discovered mines left over from the days of German occupation in World War II.

Mark holds a waterproof GPS console with a small monitor screen that shows the precise latitude and longitude of everything in the water, whether it's metal, mammal or human. Such missions are usually executed at night because rays of the sun are refracted in the water and interfere with a diver's electronic gauges.

"Let's go over it one last time," he cautions them. "Remember, time is important here. You have 30 minutes to find your specific mine, secure it with a harness and move it about 100 feet. When your mine is positioned on the circumference, according to your GPS settings and coordinates, send me a signal and wait 10 seconds for confirmation from me. If you don't get confirmation, do not, under any circumstances, arm the detonator. Leave the mine, get the hell out of there and return to Base 1. If you get confirmation, set the detonator for 40 minutes, get the hell out of there and return to Base 1. Check your oxygen levels again, and if you have enough air, shove off."

The first three mines are soon positioned perfectly around the circumference of a ring and the detonators are all confirmed. The fourth SEAL runs out of oxygen. It's his first mission in unknown waters and his nerves get the best of him, causing him to use up his oxygen quicker than normal. He moves his mine into its correct position, gets confirmation, and sets the detonator. Suddenly, when he can't read his GPS or compass, a condition he suspects has to do with the 'Bermuda Triangulation' effect. He becomes confused, disorientated and panics. Instead of swimming away from the ring of mines, he swims toward the center, where the percussion of an explosion could be fatal. Realizing he's lost, he cries out, "Can anybody hear me? Where in the hell am I?"

Mark immediately suspects that something has gone wrong and tells the helmsman of the craft, "It must be the Bermuda Triangulation where everything goes haywire. Send an SOS of our position to headquarters. I'm going in."

"It can't be done," the helmsman tells him while grabbing his arm. "You've got confirmation on three mines set to explode in 20 minutes. You can't make it to the fourth SEAL and get back in time. It can't be done."

"Let go of my arm and get out of my way," he screams. "Don't ever tell me it can't be done."

There's a splash in the water as he dives overboard, then complete silence.

For the next 15 minutes, an eerie feeling overtakes the helmsman as he looks and listens for any sign of life. Not even waves are bouncing up against the craft. Then, suddenly, one SEAL, and seconds later the second SEAL, followed by the third SEAL all pop up like submerged cork buoys.

After the three SEALS climb aboard, they peer out over the waters of the fjord, maintaining their rigid stance, holding their breath and waiting, waiting, waiting.

About five minutes later, there's a huge explosion 200 meters away, with waves that begin to rock the craft. Their heads drop to their chests and no one utters a word. They continue to hold their breath as the fingers of their hands clench into fists.

Finally, a GPS console is thrown into the center of the raft and four arms reach over the sides of the raft. It's Mark and the fourth SEAL. When they try to haul them aboard, Mark stops them and says, "Hold off. Give us a minute to catch our breath."

"How in the hell did you do it?" the helmsman asks while staring down into his face.

"I haven't a clue, except when I was ready to give up the search, I heard his screams and cried out, 'Over here, kid, or something like that.' Then I ordered him to follow me, put my life in God's hands and prayed for guidance," he answers slowly while still trying to catch his breath. "Although I used my instincts, I felt as if God was nudging me all the way."

When the flashback ends, Mark's fingers grip the steering wheel of his car as he blurts out, "Yes, it's good to be alive. Thanks be to God."

He gazes momentarily down at the speedometer on the dashboard. The pointer oscillates between 60 and 65 mph as he says to himself, "Better control my emotions and speed here. This is the moment when most drivers get a speeding ticket."

Twenty minutes later, he's pulling his car into a parking lot behind the DA's office.

"I can't tell you how happy I am to hand over that valuable dagger," the DA concedes. "The thought of someone breaking in and stealing it gave me nightmares. Who would have thought it was worth a half-million dollars?"

Mark signs a receipt for the return of the dagger, still sealed in an evidence bag. He walks over to a corner for privacy, tears the bag open and places the dagger in a sheath attached to a belt strapped around his waist, and pulls his shirt overtop.

When he returns to his BMW, he plops into the driver's seat and telephones Annette.

"Can you close up shop for two hours and have lunch with me at Waterman's in Rock Hall?" he asks.

"Why not, Mark, I don't see anyone breaking down my door to rush in and buy something. Should I meet you there?"

"No, stay put. I'll come to your shop and we'll drive in my car, if you have no objections."

"Fine. I'll be waiting in the front showroom," she replies.

An hour later, Mark parks his car outside Waterman's Restaurant in Rock Hall and escorts Annette inside for a quick lunch. After they settle into a corner table with a view of the harbor and Bay Bridge on the horizon, each orders one of their popular 12-ounce Maryland crab cakes with Old Bay seasoning, along with a side order of coleslaw and a bottle of Anchor Steam beer.

Over lunch, while both are enjoying a moment away from the shop, he thanks her for taking him on as an equal partner in her antiques business. He reiterates his hunger for something more, although his goals are not yet clearly defined. He mentions that the living quarters over the garage were a temporary expedient that he has outgrown.

"I'm still frustrated," he remarks between guzzles of his beer, "about the local people of Betterton who have not the slightest interest in art. I'll never be content to live in a town that has no desire or interest in attracting new business. I've reconciled, in my mind, the simple fact that the situation is hopeless, that you or I cannot engage any of the local residents in discussions about antiques. I've given up trying."

"I can see the frustration in your eyes," she acknowledges, "and the veins popping out of your neck. I suspect one more thing too, your attraction to the Chesapeake Bay. I saw that sparkle in your eyes every time we were together at Betterton Beach. You seemed mesmerized while gazing out at the sunset over the Bay Bridge."

"It's true. The proximity of the Bay and views of the Bridge have a special attraction for me. I expect to contact Judy Ridgefield, who has a marvelous decoy collection but is getting up in age, and see if we might work out a sale of her farm to me on a life-estate basis. It's a long shot, but who knows what might happen. Also, as a backup plan, I've let the word out among realtors in Rock Hall and hope one of them will find something near the

Wildlife Refuge along Eastern Neck Island Road, but only if the property is on the Bay side of the road. I want to be able to look out every morning, noon, and night, at the Chesapeake Bay, not the Chester River."

Annette, while disappointed, tells him, "Well, if you're going to dream, dream big. You're welcome to continue to live in the apartment for as long as you like. Give me an hour or two to tabulate our sales and your portion of the profit, ending our much-too-brief partnership. Are you sure you won't reconsider?"

Mark smiles, shakes his head from side to side several times and asks her to keep his decision to leave Betterton confidential until he can talk to Sandy and explain his plans. "I want news about my leaving Betterton to come right from my lips. Things happen in people's lives, and sometimes it changes them. It's that simple, and trust me, money does have something to do with it too. I'm thinking of the power that comes from money, and what it can do for veterans who served our country in combat."

Mark waves to the waitress and motions for the check, then looks Annette directly in her eyes, and says, "My father often told me stories about how Baltimore developed, from the Inner Harbor to Penn Station. He gave most of the credit to Mayor Donald Schaefer, and do you know how he did it?"

"No," she answers, "but I'd like to know."

"He began at 7 in the morning and hired a taxi cab. He'd ride all over the city, talking to the cabbie, listening to what he had to say about new construction that caused delays or changes in the cabby's routes. When there was a pause, he'd put his head out the open window and listen for the sounds of a jack hammer. That was music to his ears, because it meant change and improvement.

"Now, I ask you, when is the last time you ever saw the Mayor of Betterton walk around town or pop into our store to see what's going on? Never. Perhaps that's a bit unfair since I've been living here only six months. I couldn't even tell you the name of the mayor, or what he or she looks like."

"From what I've read in the *Kent News*," Annette answers, "their town meetings have no more than five or six residents showing up, and they spend more time arguing over a leaky pipe and high water bill than they do about bringing new business into Betterton."

After lunch, Annette is unusually quiet during the 26-mile drive back to Betterton until Mark asks her about Richard Wagner, her fiancé.

"Although the wedding is a month away," she declares, "we've already received the construction permits and hired Jack Johnson of the Senior Complex to construct the two-story addition that includes a grand room, 30 by 40 feet, for special exhibitions and occasions, and enough space to accommodate Richard's baby grand, with a new master bedroom overhead."

Mark says, "You're talking about a wing of 1,200 square feet upstairs. What are you going to do up there, play one-on-one basketball?"

"It's our first marriage, so we'll play it by ear, I guess," she says while blushing and grinning at the same time.

In the next half hour, they reminisce in a series of quick flashbacks how their partnership prospered, starting with his first purchase at Dixon's Auction in Crumpton, an acoustic guitar that he intended to repair and turnover for a profit.

While standing in line to get his invoice, he met Richard Wagner, a retired professor of music from Washington College, who eventually helped him install a transducer for better acoustics. Subsequently Mark introduced him to Annette, and love blossomed quickly between them.

The reminiscing ends as Mark parks his car beside his garage apartment at the rear of the property.

When they enter the back door of Annette's store, they find Knute Runagrun, the retired Norwegian tugboat captain, talking to his pet parrot, Gertie, who's learned some new words.

When Knute leans his 5-foot body closer to her birdcage, she squawks "*Good Show.*"

"You must've had an Englishman pay you a visit while I was away," Knute responds quickly. "Those Englishmen learned that expression when their teachers complimented them for work well done. I must confess, Gertie, that you have the accent down pat. *Good Show*, Gertie girl. The next thing I know, you'll be saying *Capital.*"

Gertie suddenly squawks out, "*Capital One*...have fun with *Capital One...Fund.*"

Knute pushes his captain's hat back above his forehead and turns it 45 degrees so that the brim is over one ear. He grins and replies, "Gertie always gets the last word in, just like Katharine Hepburn whenever she's talking to John Wayne in *True Grit.*"

After Mark laughs at Knute's and Gertie's antics, he excuses himself to visit Sandy inside her studio next door to the main house.

Annette takes a gentle hold of Knute's arm and walks him to a far corner of the shop. She turns around to face him directly, places a hand on his shoulders and asks, "Would you consider working longer hours to help out in the store since Mark will be leaving Betterton, possibly for Rock Hall?"

Knute is shocked and says, "A lot of water has flowed under the bridge, so to speak. I thought he was just getting settled here. He's accomplished so much in only six months, but I can understand his stretching out his wings."

"It would be a great gesture on your part since you already know the store and me. I'll have my hands full with the remodeling project and our upcoming wedding."

"You can count on me," he answers with a big smile. "Yes, I'd love to help out in any way I can and perhaps ask Mo Greenspan at the senior complex if she'd be interested in helping us, too. She's half my age, twice as pretty and much sweeter with people. Timing might be right since she's looking for something interesting and creative to do nowadays. She was a lawyer for a big firm in *Balamer*."

"That's music to my ears," she tells him. "The alternative would be to close the shop on certain days and reduce the hours on other days. I've realized my energy is not what it used to be and setbacks like Mark leaving for greener pastures make me a sick in the stomach."

"Don't worry your pretty little head. With winter approaching, spend your time with your contractor and husband, not necessarily in that order."

He laughs at the realization that he is taking over an antiques store after so many years at the helm of a tug boat.

"As far as money goes," she declares, "I can pay you by the hour or put you on salary, whatever pleases you."

"First, let me have a talk with Mo. We can work out the money later. Whatever you pay me won't put me in a higher tax bracket," he says facetiously while turning his captain's cap around so that the visor is now shading the back of his head.

Meanwhlle, Mark finds Sandy in her studio, adding some finishing touches to her latest sculpture.

He lets out a "Wow" when he gazes at a life-size clay model of 27-year old Liz Carter, who posed several months ago.

The model is a semi-nude, with both breasts exposed, firm and fully packed. Over one shoulder a Roman robe is draped and falls downward around her waist, while her right hand extends outward as if she's about to say something important. A touch of originality is the way Sandy turned the model's head 45 degrees to her right, as if something unexpectedly interrupted her words. The 5' 8" high clay model is based substantially on records of the life of Pompeia, the beautiful third wife of Julius Caesar.

Mark studies the surface texture applied by Sandy and realizes it's not the polished look of historical statues of ancient Rome that he has seen in reference books and museums. The surface, instead, has the look and feel of Auguste Rodin and Camille Claudel, two of Mark's favorite sculptors.

He remembers that Camille was one of Rodin's most-gifted students and invited to be a collaborator. She eventually became his lover, and despite his enticement and encouragement, was never able to pry him away from his marriage. Eventually Camille was tormented by demons coming from Rodin and conflicts with a mother jealous of her daughter's success, who relished in making life as miserable as possible for her. With great delight, her mother had her committed to a sanitarium, where she was confined to live out the last 30 years of her life as a tragic figure in art.

Mark also remembers reading about historians and experts who had difficulty in identifying their collaboration, such as where Rodin started a work and Claudel finished it, or vice versa.

But one thing is perfectly clear: Sandy has created something special, and for Mark to see immediately the resemblance to Auguste Rodin or Camille Claudel is quite an accomplishment for this promising 24-year old sculptor from Betterton.

"If you could spare an hour," he tells her, "I'd like to have a private talk on the beach."

His heart normally would be overflowing with emotion but at this moment, it's painful for him to face the truth about his decision to leave Betterton, and more importantly, the change in his feelings towards her.

"It sounds serious," she answers, thinking he might be ready to repeat his proposal of marriage from last September. "I'm at your service, sir."

She removes her soiled smock, hangs it on a hanger behind the garage door and brushes her hair in a mirror. On the way out of her studio, she remembers to cover the 5-foot high, model with several wet cloths to keep the clay surface from drying out.

In a quiet cove at Betterton Beach they find a shady spot and lean with their backs against a high bank of ground.

"I've been thinking about us and our future together," he begins to tell her while lowering his head and scrawling into the sand with his fingers. "There's no easy way for me to say it, but facts are facts and feelings are feelings. I've reached a decision, not an easy one to make, but here goes."

He pauses to take a deep breath and let's it out slowly while turning his head to look directly into her eyes.

"I'm going to flee my nest in Betterton, stretch my wings and fly to a farm near the Wildlife Refuge, if it's at all possible."

"What did you say? she asks with hesitation after each word. "What, but what about us?"

"We'll always have Paris," he answers facetiously, almost callously. "I always liked that line from *Casablanca*."

His meek attempt to lighten the serious mood fails to register with Sandy, who's in shock.

"Whatever's happened between us doesn't amount to *a hill of beans*," he answers sheepishly, then presses his right hand against his heart and massages it. "I'm sorry, Sandy. I was simply trying to make light of a serious situation. I don't want to hurt you because I still love you, but I'm not *in love* with you anymore."

"Is it something I've done to you?"

"No, Sandy, it's nothing you've done or haven't done."

"Something's happened to me, mostly because of my implication in Vera's murder and the frustration of living in Betterton. Our relationship lately is like a clock that loses a few seconds every minute, a few minutes every hour, a few hours every day. The love between us is still there, but not what it used to be."

Mark pauses as his eyes moisten. Sandy is the last person he would ever want to hurt.

The sound of two sea gulls flapping their wings overhead breaks the silence as tears begin to roll slowly down her cheeks.

"That's not the words I expected to hear from your lips," she answers after gathering some strength. "But you'll always be in my heart. Saving my life after I tripped over the railing of the ferry doesn't mean that you're beholden to me for the rest of my life. But, over the past weeks, I had the feeling that *your* heart was not in your work. Your mind seemed to be drifting away from me, too."

Mark puts one hand around her shoulder and, with the other, wipes away the tears falling down her cheeks with his handkerchief.

"When you rescued me in the Bay," she continues, "it turned out that you inadvertently rescued yourself. You found a new calling in the art world. But I think you're reaching for the stars."

"No, Sandy, 'the stars are reaching for me,' as Billy Wilder would say."

"Is your decision final?" she asks with trepidation in her voice.

"Yes, it's final. But this is more about life than about love. You'll always be close to my heart. I feel a big change is needed for me to flourish. It's possible that meeting the people of Rock Hall will bring the same attitudes and results as those from Betterton, but it certainly can't get any worse."

They rise and embrace, as if it might be for the last time as Sandy lifts her head and kisses him tenderly on his lips.

"I'll need that kiss," she whispers into his ear, "to carry me through my 'winter of discontent,' as Shakespeare called it."

"Sandy, I predict great things ahead for you. As your mother often told us, 'work cures all ills,' so pour yourself into your sculpture and paintings. I didn't want you to know it until later, but I'm taking part of you with me. I bought your bronze cast of *Storm Cat*, which will be the first piece in my new private collection of art."

"That merits another kiss," she tells him.

They walk slowly along Betterton beach and turn right at a path leading upward to Main Street.

When they reach Annette's shop, they give each other a kiss on the cheek and walk slowly to their respective quarters; Mark, to his apartment over the garage and Sandy, to her bedroom at the rear of the shop.

Chapter 3

The following day, around 9 in the morning, Mark is alone inside the front showroom of Annette's Antiques when he uses his cell phone to telephone Abigail Woods.

She is a former director of the Washington County Museum of Fine Arts in Hagerstown, retired but involved in so many projects that it's hard to keep track of her. Mark fortunately finds her in her condo in her hometown of Baltimore, near Johns Hopkins University where she got her Master's in Art History.

"How soon can you meet me in Betterton to discuss the sale of the jeweled dagger with you as exclusive agent?" he asks.

"You mean the one I discovered in those photos in your file on the model ship *Gratitude*, the one regrettably used in the murder of Vera Wayne? she asks bluntly.

"That's the one"

"Give me three hours and I should be in Betterton around noon today."

"Drive carefully and, if the traffic is heavy, take your time. I'm not going anywhere and neither is the dagger," he replies and hangs up the phone.

Precisely at noon, Abigail arrives at Annette's Antiques and is delighted to see Mark again.

"How nice of you to think of me. I haven't seen you since we worked together setting the trap for Bud Wayne and the subsequent two trials. I've told my mother how much I enjoyed working with you."

"Well, I never forgot you and the important part you played, especially in identifying the historic nature of the dagger and determining its incredible value as a rare antiquity."

"It's telepathy or extra-sensory perception, because earlier this week, my mother asked me, 'Whatever happened to that dagger worth $500,000?' "

"Perhaps I should also hire your mother to help us in selling it to a museum."

"That might be a bit difficult."

"Why is that?"

"My mother's dead. She died about 40 years ago right after I got my Master's at Hopkins."

"I'm sorry that she's not physically around anymore," he tells her after realizing that Abigail is actually talking to her mother's spirit. "I would have enjoyed meeting her."

"She's always with me. I get all my strength and will power from her."

"Wonderful. Now, let's get down to business and the order of the day. Are you ready to act as sole agent in the sale of my Baghdad dagger to a museum for $500,000?"

"You bet I am. Before I left my condo, I telephoned the insurance agent that I know from my days in the museum at Hagerstown to get his input on insuring it against fire, theft, or damage during the consignment period. Also you may be surprised that I've prepared a contract."

"No, Abigail, I'm not surprised at anything you do. You're always a step ahead of me."

"The contract stipulates that I will be the exclusive agent and paid a commission of 10% of the sale price after a sale is consummated, with a consignment period of 30 days."

"You've covered everything that's obvious, but left out two important conditions" he declares.

"And what are they?"

"First, a statement should be included in your bill of sale to the museum that they are buying only the dagger, and all rights to duplicate it, in the form of a replica or facsimile, are reserved by me. A copyright or trademark application should be filed with the Library of Congress to protect against any infringement here. Of course, the museum is free to publish photographs for posters or exhibition catalogs. This sale fits into the category of Intellectual Properties, and merits close scrutiny. If the museum wants to market a replica of the dagger, we'll discuss that possibility later."

She scratches her head and tells him, "I never thought about anyone making a copy of the dagger and selling it over the Internet. If you thought there were hackers on the Internet, there are twice as many inside companies in countries like China and India waiting to capitalize on Intellectual Properties, eager to produce a replica of the jeweled Baghdad dagger on their assembly line, for sale all over the world. I'll consult with experts to determine the best way to proceed and protect ourselves and the museum from infringement and anyone creating a phony or poorly-manufactured replica. We definitely need protection here. And what's the second factor you want included in the contract?"

"I want it clearly stipulated that the sale is final, and I'm selling it as an individual without any knowledge of the possibility of its being a historical treasure. After discovering it imbedded in the sand next to my fallen comrade, I removed it and brought it to America without any knowledge that it may be forbidden to take such an object of cultural heritage out of the country, during a war."

"Provided, of course, the combat in Iraq is classified as a war," she interjects.

"Politics aside," he continues, "if a museum buys it and later it is restituted to Iraq, the museum will bear full responsibility for loss of ownership and will not hold me liable for damages or return of the purchase money. Remember: the sale is final. Once payment is made, there is no 'buyer's remorse' for recourse."

"I get the picture. No need to explain it further. If you recall about six months ago, I was told by several appraisers in New York, specialists in Islamic artifacts, that the value was $500,000, and, at that time, had informal discussions with the director of a new historical museum, also in New York, about acquiring it as the first piece to enter their permanent collection. There's no such thing in the art world as a 'slam dunk' but I expect a sale should be completed within 30 days, provided there's no unforeseen development."

When Mark invites her for lunch, she apologizes and tells him, "I better get back to Baltimore and get "cracking," as you call it, on the work ahead. But give my regards to Sandy and tell her I'll drop in to see her next time I pay you a visit. I'm curious about how she's coming along with her sculpture of Liz as Pompeia."

"Before you go, do you like peaches?" Mark asks suddenly.

"I make the best peach pie in Baltimore," she responds proudly.

"On the back porch I have a half-bushel of peaches. You're welcome to take as many as you need. They're from a lady in Rock Hall, Eloise, who has the best pair of ..."

He pauses for a quick flashback, more like a photograph of Eloise passing slowly across his eyes. A few months ago she answered her back door, dressed in a nightgown with the bodice open and no brassiere to hold her enormous breasts in place. His first reaction was full of flattery because he sensed that she was more interested in him than in his appraising a beautiful bronze nude of Cleopatra. His flashback ends quickly when he scratches his hair furiously, the way Johnny Cammareri (Danny Aiello) did in *Moonstruck*, to stimulate his brain cells.

"You were saying, 'Pair of …'," she asks with a loud voice to shock him back to reality.

"Peach trees, I mean, she's got the best pair of peach trees." A devilish smile crosses his face as he walks with Abigail to the rear of the store and continues, "I pay her an occasional visit to pick up the sweetest peaches in the world. She picks them herself."

Under his breath, he says to himself, "I cannot picture her on a ladder picking peaches off a tree, but one of these days, I should find out how she does it."

"I'll take the entire half-bushel," Abigail declares, "and when I 'pay' you a visit, no pun intended, I'll bring you my award-winning peach pie with a touch of Jamaican rum added at the last minute of baking."

"Marvelous," he answers while walking her to the rear door where the peaches are ripening on a bench.

Next door, inside her studio with passages of Rimsky-Korsakov's *Scheherazade* playing in the background, Sandy stands under a single overhead spotlight. Her fingers are covered with clay as she adds some finishing touches to her life-size model, but her movements are much more forceful, thinking about Mark's decision to end their romance and move to the Rock Hall area.

"In difficult times, Mom always said that hard work is the best medicine," she tells the clay model as if were alive. "Not talking today? I've got to talk to somebody about you and there's no one better than Liz who posed for you. It's time to telephone her and let her see how beautiful you are."

When she takes a few steps backward to see the finished model from a distance of 12 feet, the clay sculpture looks similar to those in a museum exhibition.

From the porch outside the front door of her shop, Annette watches Mark as he puts the half bushel of peaches into the trunk of Abigail's car, then calls him by name and waves a check in her hand as an enticement to come back to the shop.

"I wasn't trying to show off. I merely wanted to catch your attention and settle our business before you disappear," she declares. "Are you sure you won't reconsider your decision to end our partnership?"

"Thanks, but no thanks," he says.

"In that case, here's a closing statement and a check for $42,000. It includes the profit from the sale of the low-boy to Lois Carnegie and other sales we've made together, less a deduction of $5,000 for your purchase of bronze cast of *Storm Cat*. You may be surprised that the stuff we sold at Crumpton brought a resounding $600, which is about $300 more than I expected. Shows you how fast Dixon's can tabulate their sales and have a check ready for the consignor to pick up at the end of the day."

Mark gives her a hug, and repeats one of his favorite sayings, "*This is not the end. This is not even the beginning of the end. But it is the end of the beginning.* No one said it better than Churchill. It's increasingly hard for me to be original nowadays. I think I said the same thing to Sandy recently."

"And how did she take it?" Annette asks, with emphasis on 'she.'

"About what I expected, under the circumstances."

"By the way, Mark, when you begin repeating yourself, do they haul you away to the funny farm in Sykesville, you know the asylum?"

"If I keep banging my head against a brick wall in Betterton, I deserve to go there. I may forget the people in Betterton, those who made my life a little miserable here, but I'll never forgive them."

"Forgive who?" she asks with alarm.

"The town's people. I'm also still teed off at the people in Betterton for not appreciating my kids, the Betterton Breeze, and what they've accomplished."

"That's all in the past, Mark. You and your Breeze team can hold your heads up high. Perhaps you can use them in some of your upcoming projects."

"Your check together with the proceeds of the dagger should give me a running start, don't you think?"

The telephone rings on an extension phone and after Annette answers it, her smile turns into sadness.

"Yes, I can hear everything perfectly," she answers. "I'll pass on the information to Mark who's standing a few feet away."

Annette pauses and lowers her chin to her chest.

"I'm sorry to have to tell you this, Mark, but one of my friends, a nurse at the Chester River Hospital in Chestertown, said that, a few minutes ago, Judy Ridgefield has been taken to the emergency room. She may have suffered a stroke."

"Is she alive?"

"Yes, so far. I know you'll want to see her since you often talked about her."

"I must get to the hospital immediately," he blurts out.

"I'll tell the hospital that you're on your way and that you're a relative so you can see her as soon as she's able to have visitors."

Before Annette can complete her last words, Mark races across the room and rushes out the front door.

Within the next few minutes, he's driving his BMW slightly above the speed limit on his way inward to Chestertown, praying that the Good Lord will look kindly on her and spare her any pain and suffering.

Twenty minutes later, Mark is standing in front of the head nurse in the reception room of the cardiology ward on the third floor of the hospital and tells her that he's a relative. By telling a fib, he expects to gain quick admittance.

She looks him over, from top to bottom, all 6-feet 4-inches, 220 pounds of his frame with muscles bulging under his shirt. and murmurs, "You must be kidding. Judy's barely five feet tall in stockings and weighs about 115 pounds. You sure don't look like a relative, and don't tell you were the black sheep of the family."

"Actually," he confesses apologetically, "I'm not a relative but a close friend."

She winks at him and says, "If it takes a lie to do someone some good, then go right in."

As he opens the door to her room and peers inside, he finds her awake and looking surprisingly refreshed and energized.

"I pressed the medic-alert on my key chain," she tells him with a welcoming smile, "and was lucky to get an ambulance quickly and all the stuff that goes with it, especially oxygen. A blockage in one artery was discovered by the cardiologist, Dr. Edward "Tim" Bartholomay, who inserted a metal stint in the clogged area during angioplasty."

As Judy finishes her sentence, Dr. Bartholomay appears without them knowing he's in the room. He overhears her conversation with Mark and tells her, "Now, you'll have to be careful when you walk through those security detectors at the airport!"

They share a good laugh as the doctor asks, "And how is Judy feeling today?"

"Like a million dollars after taxes," she admits, "a hundred percent better. When I get *outa* here, I'm *gonna* buy a piano and take some music lessons."

After Dr. Bartholomay checks her vital signs, he reads the paperwork on a clipboard attached to the footboard of her bed. As he begins to leave her room, he stops in his tracks.

"Did you say 'piano' lessons?" he asks somewhat astonished. "Any exercise will be beneficial to your heart, but don't overdue your rendition of *Chopsticks*."

She laughs as Dr. Bartholomay leaves the room and beckons Mark to move closer to her bed.

"A few days ago, after I ate something spicy, a sharp pain came up suddenly around my heart, but then went away. I didn't want to take any chances, so I asked for an emergency appointment to see my family doctor, Michael Peimer, who gave me a complete physical. All my vital signs appeared to be normal. Even the electrocardiogram (EKG) failed to disclose a blockage. Fortunately for me, Dr. Peimer put me on blood-thinners and other heart medication as a precaution."

"Well, you look marvelous, Judy. The Good Lord is watching over you."

"As much as I hate making changes, I know change is inevitable."

"You'll have to find out what caused the plaque buildup, won't you?"

"That's true. But I won't be able to move around the house like I'm used to and eventually, may not be able to live there anymore. I could end up in one of those medical-assisted care places."

"I wouldn't think too far ahead right now. You can wait until you're back on your feet again."

Sorry, Mark, but there's no time to waste. You may be surprised to know that you've been on my mind for the past week or more, as I thought about consigning some decoys for you to sell at Annette's Antiques."

"As I said before, all in due time, Judy. We've got to get you back on your feet. We can talk about business later."

"No, Mark, there's not a better time than now," she tells him while lifting her body higher against her headboard. "I heard through the grapevine that you're looking to buy a farm outside Rock Hall. Perhaps we should talk about *my* farm."

She notices how Mark's face lights up like a Christmas tree turned on for the first time and continues, "It probably sounds like a morbid thing to say, but I hate like hell to move out of my farmhouse. I'd prefer to die in my own bed, if you get my drift."

"Judy, Judy, Judy," Mark replies in his best imitation of Cary Grant, "you'll have many good years ahead of you if you follow your doctor's advice. Let's not speak anymore about dying in your home. But if you insist on talking about your farm, I have an idea you can toss around while recuperating from your surgery.

"Please proceed. Doctor Mark," she says facetiously.

"Since you have no children or haven't mentioned relatives or heirs, at some point in your life you'll have to sell your farm, and, as you told me, move into an assisted-living facility, with all the medical equipment and staff to help you."

"Go on, Mark."

"You could establish a trust in which you deed your farm to the trust for tax purposes But you'd still need money to pay for medical expenses."

"And?"

"Finally and better yet, you could sell the farm on a life-estate basis, which means you would get the money immediately from the sale of the farm and continue to live in your home for the remainder of your life. Of course, you'd be responsible for paying the taxes and utilities, but you won't have to worry about finances or money problems, at least as far as I can see."

Judy smiles, sighs a little and tells him, "I like the last one of those possibilities the best."

"In that case," Mark says with a touch of the jitters and butterflies suddenly stirring in his stomach, "what would you say to selling me your farm on a life-estate basis? I could live temporarily in a separate part of your house, and be available to look after your needs. But I would like to build an addition to your home for me and a young short-haired golden Labrador that I plan on adopting from the kennels of the Humane Society of Kent County."

She leans forward away from the pillows as Mark rearranges them on her bed to make her more comfortable.

"You'll have to give up some privacy in exchange for my living inside," he continues with increasing confidence, "but I'll be available, night and day, to look after your needs. You know, Judy, I've always taken care of my men when I was a Lieutenant in the military."

He pauses to search for something else to consider, then admits, "A good accountant or tax attorney can advise us on the best way to reduce any taxes. We'll cross that bridge when we come to it, if we come to it."

Smiles cover their faces as they ponder everything said. Under these circumstances it's clearly a win-win situation for the buyer and seller.

The following day, Mark is standing in the drawing room of his parent's home in Cylburn Park, Baltimore. He waits anxiously beside his mother for the arrival of his father, so he can bring them up to date on his life on the eastern shore. In the meantime, they're looking at various framed family photos setting on the Bosendorfer baby grand.

Mark picks up one of his father in a sterling-silver frame.

"That was your father's yearbook picture when he graduated first in his metallurgy class at Hopkins," Sara explains. "He just turned 21. Wasn't he handsome? Of all the photos here, it's strange that you selected this one."

"I love this shot," Mark answers, "because Dad reminds me of William Holden when he made *Picnic* with Kim Novak. That movie's one of my favorites. Dad was a handsome young man when he graduated from Hopkins."

"And very special on the inside too, like you, son," she admits while moving closer to him. She holds the photo close to his face to see their resemblance.

Suddenly, Mark's father, William II, walks heavy-footed into the room, dressed in a dark business suit ruffled and spotted with dirt and rust. With his head down, resting almost on his chest, he jerks his tie away from the collar of his shirt and drags his feet like he's carrying a 150-pound gorilla on his shoulders. The look on his face is no longer similar to the photographs displayed on the piano. The corners of his lips are tilted downward and his teeth are gripped tightly in a snarl.

When he finally raises his head and sees his loved ones waiting for him, the look of frustration and depression gradually disappears.

They each give him a kiss on his lips.

It may seem unusual for a son to give his father a kiss directly on his lips, but he's been doing it all his life, beginning as a child who always gave his father and mother a goodnight kiss before going to bed.

"I see that you brushed against some rusty pipes," Sara admonishes him in gentle tones."You've been talking to your men near those blast furnaces. At least I don't see any burn marks on your suit tonight."

"Better than brushing up against RL Stackhouse and his union thugs," he replies, "pressuring me to sell them the mill."

He mixes himself a cocktail of 12-year old Chevas Regal with a touch of water, and takes a seat in an antique French Aubusson-style upholstered arm chair near the fireplace.

Mark looks again at the photo and realizes how stress can age a man, especially when you're running a steel mill almost single-handedly. Now, his father's former erect posture is replaced by a hunched back. His speech has changed too; words are more difficult to formulate. Talking mostly with steel workers is not the language used in most businesses or in family discussions.

From his suit pocket William pulls out a newspaper clipping and shows them an article about a declining industry that cannot compete with foreign mills.

"It's mostly my fault," he admits in a stern voice. "I'm beginning to feel the strain of running the mill almost single-handedly. It's taking a heavy toll on me because I never could relinquish power or responsibility. It was my job, from the time I joined the firm as a metallurgist fresh *outa* Hopkins, to insure that every procedure for smelting steel was followed precisely when your grandfather passed the reins to me in the 70's."

"How many times have we told you to loosen those reins?" Sara asks with a degree of frustration.

"I appreciate all your concern, but someone has to quarterback the team and lead it down the field," answers William.

"But you're the coach, not the quarterback," Mark answers.

"And at what price?" asks Sara.

William leans forward in his chair, sighs and dismisses the concerns of his family.

"You've heard it a thousand times before," he utters, "so my telling it one more time won't hurt. I always liked the sound of my father's voice, especially when he told me I was now in charge of the mill. He was passing the torch of Bethlehem Steel to me, right here in this exact spot."

His mind switches to automatic pilot since he's at home and can relax with his family. He takes another sip of his cocktail and proceeds to recite again a short history of Bethlehem Steel.

"The site was about 100 acres, 10 miles east of Baltimore and on the northern shore of the Patapsco River as it enters the Chesapeake Bay. Thomas Sparrow received the land as a grant from Lord Baltimore in 1652. About 235 years later, around 1887, Fredrick Wood, working with Pennsylvania Steel of Pittsburgh and Bethlehem Iron of Baltimore, formed Bethlehem Steel."

Mark looks at his mother, smiles and tells her, "This story never get old."

"William Hopkins I was a silent partner of Charles Schwab, the mastermind behind Bethlehem Steel and one of Andrew Carnegie's top advisors. Andrew Mellon was the banker who supplied the money. I forgot what year they all split up, perhaps around 1890. Fast forward to the 1940's and 1950's when the plant employed over 31,000 workers, and was the biggest producer of steel in the world. Bethlehem Steel *was* the pride of Baltimore."

"For a few old die-hards, it's still the pride of Baltimore," his son admits.

"When I graduated from Hopkins at 21," William continues, "I was full of ambition and ideas about how to run a steel mill. But after I came on board, the company's success turned downward. It really was bad timing, with the advent of stronger labor unions, unfair labor practices and foreign competition."

He laughs at himself and swallows down the remains of his entire cocktail in one gulp.

"Although Hopkins gave me a good education in metallurgy," he continues, "I probably should have taken a course in business management because it was rough going after the war, with competition, as I said before, from foreign governments and unions taking a big bite out of our profits. Now, we're faced every day with struggles against union bosses, infiltrated with mafia thugs who want to increase the pay of workers, reduce the work week and raise the influence of the union by hiring more inspectors simply to handle grievances."

Mark, sitting with his mother in a love seat across from his father, reaches in his pocket and hands something to his father and says, "Do you remember giving me this…?"

It's a thin compass about two inches in diameter and a quarter of an inch thick.

"Yes, that was a long time ago, I think when you became a teenager," he answers.

"Do you remember what you told me when you gave it to me?"

"That's much too long ago," he admits. "I can't remember what I had for breakfast this morning."

"You told me," Mark admits, "this compass will help me to find my way home if I get lost. Well, it *was* easier to find my way home. But what did I find waiting inside? Mom alone, and when you finally showed up, you were tired and weary. Do you have any recollection of how many hours we were alone without you here?"

His father begins to notice a slight degree of resentment in Mark's disclosure.

"You always told me," Mark continues, "that time was important and time can never be recaptured once it's expended. Yet the mill was putting a stranglehold around you, and you didn't even know it. And what did it get you? You've aged way beyond how a man of 60 should look."

His father nods his head apologetically and in agreement with his son's feelings.

"Father, I love you more than you'll ever know, and that's why I decided to strike out for myself instead of joining you in the mill. Sooner or later, it will kill you. You have to back off and enjoy the benefits you've earned. Do something you've wanted to do for a long time. I can't read your mind. You could begin by taking Mom on a short trip, perhaps to Western Maryland or the eastern shore of Maryland and look up at blue skies instead of the metal roof of Bethlehem Steel. Why not work only four days a week, similar to what the unions are demanding for their workers?"

His father rises from his seat, puts his thumbs around his suspenders and pushes them outward, then let's go, creating a loud snap when they strike his chest.

Mark rises from his seat and stands in front of his father with his head resting on his chest.

Seconds later, his father raises his head, looks directly up at a 45-degree angle into Mark's blue eyes, grabs his higher shoulders and says, "Forgive me, son. I didn't realize it, but I should have known. You have a right to resent me for treating you and your mother that way. It wasn't a question of mill versus family. It was trying to do the best for both. It was my responsibility to carry on the tradition of the Hopkins legacy handed down by your grandfather. One day, whether you like it or not, you may be faced with similar challenges."

Mark gives his father a bear hug as his eyes grow moist and says, "There's not a hell of a lot of time left in our lives to share with each other. You've got to make a decision to relinquish some responsibilities. And do it while you're still able to make decisions."

After mixing another cocktail, William asks them to take a seat around a game table where he can explain some new developments that will affect them. He seems to be getting paranoid about being overheard, even in his own home.

"The pressure to compete with foreign firms is taking its toll on the steel industry and particularly our mill. Foreign governments are subsidizing their firms to enable them to manufacture and sell steel at lower prices. They're really taking a temporary loss with the intent to drive us out of business. After that, they can raise their prices and make a killing, because they'll be the sole source for the production and purchase of steel."

"Is there anything our government can do? Mark asks.

"Are you kidding? They turn a blind eye and tell us, 'That's your problem, the price you pay in a competitive business.' One solution, the easiest, would be to sell the mill. I've had meetings with two suitors who are ready to buy it. The first is RL Stackhouse, boss of the United Steel-Workers Union. The second is Salvi Solimeni of Mittal, the largest steel maker in the world, based in London. Salvi's the right-hand man of founder Lakshmi Mittal.

"Both of them will give me a big paycheck along with a seat on the board of directors, an honorary-emeritus position, purely for show."

"And I thought I had problems," says Mark. "I came here to meet with Mike Bloomburg and his junior partner, Lola Albright, to get their advice about a farm that I might buy on a life-estate basis, and establishing a trust with proceeds from the sale of the Baghdad dagger to a museum. And, are you ready for this?"

"Oh, no, Mark, don't tell us Sandy's pregnant?" asks Sara incredulously.

He bursts out laughing, and continues, "Close, Mom, but no brass ring. I'm thinking of having a baby."

A baby did you say? Now that's a first," replies William who busts out laughing. "Men can't have babies, at least as far as I know."

"Go ahead, have your laugh at my expense. At least I've managed to lift your spirits temporarily. Actually, I'm thinking of adopting Jaime, Vera's baby. There's something strange and wonderful about how that baby grabbed my finger and wouldn't let go when I first saw him in a basket at her marina in Rock Hall."

"All babies grab and hold tight," admits Sara.

"Maybe so, but this was decidedly different, believe me."

"Maybe it's something in the water of the Chesapeake Bay after you rescued Sandy," declares Sara, "but I see a wonderful glow in you, something I've never seen before. We're very pleased that you're enjoying your life on the Eastern Shore after being implicated in Vera's murder."

"When you finished your SEAL career," his father interjects, "for my own selfish reasons, I wanted you to join me and eventually take over the mill. You've made us very proud in your pursuit of art and antiques, and, more importantly, building relationships with people."

"Are you prepared for everything it takes to care for Jaime?" Sara asks while playing with her pearl necklace. "Infants take a lot of time and care. I know firsthand, being alone while your father was busy in the mill. You've got visits to the doctor and clinic, preparation of baby food, constantly checking the baby's vital signs, interruptions from whatever you're doing to find out why he's crying and why his temperature is climbing. Do you get the picture?"

"I'll arrange for a nanny to take care of some of his needs and mine too, especially if she's anything like Nora Arnezeder," Mark boasts. "Jaime will get the best care money can buy, plus a good education "

"Nora who?" ask his mother.

"One of the rising stars of the French cinema and one of the most beautiful women who co-starred in *Paris 36,*" Mark answers. "I'll bring a DVD of the film so you can see for yourself how lovely she is."

The doorbell rings, and the maid ushers Mike Bloomburg and Lola Albright into the drawing room.

A few minutes later, everyone is seated comfortably around a large antique Sheraton library table with a pattern of beautiful inlaid wood running around the perimeter top, which is supported by a double pedestal.

Mark makes certain that he sits next to Lola, a stunning package of beauty and brains, and at 26, already a rising star at

Mike Bloomburg's law firm. She graduated first in her class two years ago at the University of Baltimore law school.

"I want to hear every minutia of your advice," he explains, "and enjoy the scent of your perfume. Is it *Shalimar*?"

"It is *Shalimar*, Mark, Do you like it? I wear just a touch, otherwise it may cause a distraction with a client."

"I think you're per-fect," he answers in two syllables with a touch of Maurice Chevalier. "I mean, it's perfect."

William looks at Sara and says, "There goes our boy again, flirting as usual."

"I think it's nice when a young man pays a lady a compliment," Sara replies. "You used to pay me those compliments too, remember?"

"If you're referring to me, thank you. Compliments are always welcome. And I adore that painting by Alfred Munnings that hangs in your hall, just outside the library."

"It's my grandfather, on his favorite hunter, *Alert*," he replies. "He was Master of the fox hunts for over 30 years."

"It must have been heavenly, for him to ride his jumper whenever he could break away from the business of running his mill," she answers with a comforting smile.

"Do you ride?" he asks with some curiosity.

"When I can. Mike keeps me pretty busy, sometimes on the weekends."

"Perhaps we can ride together one of these days, before winter sets in."

"I'd like that, Mark," she replies, with a beguiling smile.

Mike Bloomburg finally interrupts and says, "As much as I enjoy listening to your talk about perfume, art, horses, and fox hunts, I think you should know that the clock is ticking for two top lawyers called with a sense of urgency by you, Mark, to discuss real estate, a living trust, and God knows what else. So, let's get cracking."

He hands Mark an orange-colored legal notepad identical to the one that Lois removes from her briefcase and says, "Lola, the meeting is all yours."

"Pardon me," interrupts Mark, "but before you begin, please keep in mind that there's no guarantee that the owner of Ridgefield Farms, Judy Ridgefield, is going to sell me her property. Nevertheless, everything you tell me today will be relayed to give her the benefit of your legal advice, too."

"No problem," Lola declares. "I see no reason why our firm can't represent the buyer and seller, provided everything is fully disclosed to all parties."

Lois begins her presentation slowly with factors to consider when a property is bought and sold on a life-estate basis, along with the possible tax benefits.

"If you, as buyer, plan on living in the house along with the seller, you can deduct all expenses for the care of the seller during her lifetime there. If you construct an addition for your sole use, then those expenses are not deductible nor are the utilities. However, if you add an office or gallery-showroom to exhibit art that you intend to sell, then all those expenses are deductible. If you upgrade the premises by installing energy-efficient HVAC and solar panels, conserving water runoff from rain and ponds, and for reducing the use of electricity at high-demand hours, all of these upgrades are deductible from your income taxes."

"Wonderful. Keep going, please. Can I deduct a maid or nanny to look after me?" he asks facetiously.

"Just pick up the phone and give me a little jingle," she whispers close to his ear. 'It won't cost you a cent."

Mark is pleased and impressed by Lola's preparation and demeanor. While making some notes, he senses a chemistry developing between them, starting in a friendly way that may lead to something serious later. The movement of her lips and hands is very sensuous and registers in his psyche.

He often nods his head in agreement and understanding as she stresses certain items indicated on her notepad. His mind drifts for a few seconds to compare Lola's beauty and brains to Liz Carter, the Pentagon major he met outside Penn Station six months ago, and subsequently to Sandy Welles.

"If a sale materializes," he asks Lola, "would you prepare the necessary documents for creating a trust and incorporating 'Ridgefield-Hopkins LLC' in Delaware, for possible tax benefits? The more money I can save in taxes, the more money I can spend doing good for veterans who need our help. I envision three projects under the umbrella of the parent Ridgefield-Hopkins LLC."

"Only three?" Lola asks teasingly.

"We'll start with three," he replies while laughing. "First, a lab for research of pollutants in the Chesapeake Bay. Second, a film studio for the production of scientific and art films. And third, an R&R lodge for families of Red Cross veterans, who served in combat."

"That's quite an undertaking," Mike answers.

"Like father, like son," interjects William who's enjoying his son's revelations.

"I envision a set of small sound stages," Mark continues, "linked like a caterpillar, standing four-feet above ground in case of high tides or winds of 165 mph like those of Hurricane *Isabel* that flooded Rock Hall in September 2003."

"And what happens if a butterfly emerges from the caterpillar?" asks Lola facetiously.

"Whatever emerges will benefit mankind. Personally, I'd love to make a small budget film like *Marty*. We're not looking to build a mini-Universal Studios, but I think it would be fun to run a small film production unit. Universities are giving courses in film-making with the latest computer-generated software and technology. Making a movie is easy. Making a good movie with a solid storyline and strong characters is another thing."

"You're certainly not short on ambition, Mark. We're all behind you 100 percent," interjects Mike Bloomburg.

Everyone, especially Mark, claps their hands in approval.

"If everything is planned properly," Mark concedes, "Ridgefield will give a boost to Kent County and the Eastern Neck Wildlife Refuge down the road from us. But I can already hear the screams and hollers coming from the Planning and Zoning Department of Kent County. When I asked why there were no wind turbines to capture the energy of constant high winds off the Bay and convert it into electricity, they made it clear by telling me, 'No wind mills. They spoil the view and could be hazardous to geese.' They fail to comprehend the need for new sources of energy required for future development, especially for chicken farmers like Perdue."

"That attitude is not new," interjects Mike. "Kent County is notorious for trying to keep agricultural land preserved for the farmers and hunters. It's corn and soybeans, deer and geese. At least the idea of a small complex to study the Bay and give veterans some R & R deserves some consideration."

Lola tells Mark, "Thanks, Mark. There goes my weekend of riding with you at Hunt Valley. I can foresee Mike pushing all this work on my desk when we get back to the office."

They all have a good laugh, and wish him good luck with his plans for Ridgefield.

The following morning around 10, Mark stands in the living room of Judy Ridgefield's farm house. It has a cathedral ceiling, like an old school house, and measures about 22 x 35 feet. Scattered on walls and shelves everywhere are at least 200 carved wooden decoys. He gives them a casual glance but is drawn to the front bay window where he admires a perfect view of the Chesapeake Bay and the Bay Bridge.

The sky is filled with geese flying in perfect formation, each school resembling the swept wing of a Stealth bomber. This brisk November morning seems special; his dream of owning a farm on the Bay may be on the verge of coming true.

"I wonder," he mutters, "if Ridgefield Farm will soon become my 'pot of gold' at the end of a rainbow."

Judy hands him a cup of coffee and waits to hear more of his thoughts. "Breathtaking views of the Bay," he says, "good for the soul and nourishment for creativity."

Judy returns to the kitchen, opens her oven and removes a tray of freshly-made blueberry muffins.

"Have a seat, take a load off your mind and bite into a muffin" she tells him. "Bet you didn't know that I won first prize in the *Murlin*-muffin-cook-off at Smith Island a thousand years ago, before I married my husband. Everyone always told me that he married me for my muffins, not for the love I could give him."

Mark bites into his muffin and tells her, "Never tasted anything like it before. My mother was always bragging about the muffins from Gerstungs' Bakery as being the best she ever tasted. I'll have to take one with me for her to taste.

"Speaking of Gerstung's, did you know that the old man, Harry Gerstung, built some cottages overlooking the bluffs of Betterton for weekend lodging of tourists?"

What? That's news to me.

"Of course, they're all closed up, been closed up for years since people are not coming there anymore for a weekend. But that's another story," she tells him with a wave of her hand as if that's all in the past.

"I'm aware of that, which is why I left Betterton in the first place," replies Mark.

"Since you visited me in the hospital a few days ago," she continues, "I've given a lot of thought to you and your ideas, and I am leaning towards a sale of my farm to you on a life-estate basis. Does this idea appeal to you?"

"Absolutely. I was hoping you would say that," he boasts. "I've consulted with my attorneys in Baltimore in case you decided to go in my direction. But I'll need a place to live, since I've ended my partnership with Annette in Betterton."

"This will be your new, 'old' home."

"In that case, we have to decide on a price that's fair to both of us," Mark declares. "Here's an index card. Write down the price you have in mind, and I'll do the same, then we'll compare numbers to see the difference, and how much we have to compromise."

Each takes a card and writes down a number.

When the cards are turned over, the numbers match exactly: $300,000.

They burst out laughing.

"We're off to a good start, Judy, or as Humphrey Bogart said in *Casablanca,* 'this could be the start of a beautiful friendship.' I love that line."

He gives her a big hug.

"I bet you know every line in that film, don't you?" she asks while looking directly into his eyes.

"Actually I do, mainly because I love the screenwriters who wrote the script, the Epstein brothers, Julius and… isn't that funny? I've forgotten the name of Julius' older brother."

"No matter, Mark. I love those lines too. Classic lines stick with you."

"Now I remember the name of the other brother. He was Philip. What a pair of gifted writers, whose words had a flair for the *dramatique* blended with the *comique.*"

Mark tries to show off his slight knowledge of French words, which are uttered with a touch of Maurice Chevalier, one of his favorite actors. Unfortunately, whether or not it's because of her hearing difficulty, Judy fails to get the gist of Mark's levity.

"The Epstein brothers wrote *Casablanca* in association with Howard Koch," he continues, "although it's almost impossible to know how to divide the credit. Bet you couldn't guess what his annotated screenplay fetched when it was sold at auction a few years ago?"

"You've got me there, Mark. I haven't a clue," she retorts. "Don't keep me in suspense."

"Would you believe it sold for $175,000?" he declares.

"My word, that's probably what it cost to make the movie."

"Getting back to our deal, I'll make myself comfortable in your Stickley rocking chair and write you a deposit."

He removes a check from his wallet, uses a book for support, and fills out the check. As he begins writing, his fingers begin to tremble.

"It's not every day that you buy your first home," Judy says "It happens only once in your lifetime."

He rises from his chair and tells her proudly, "Here's my check made payable to you, for $30,000, a deposit of 10% of the purchase price. My lawyers have prepared a contract for us as buyer and seller. If you agree to the conditions specified in the contract, we'll sign it now."

"She takes his check and begins to read the contract, with her eyes glancing back and forth at both pieces of paper.

"I never ever gave any thought to selling my farm, but frankly, I can't think of a better person to sell it to than to you."

"I'll deliver the contract personally to the escrow office of either John Davis or Alex Raisin in Chestertown. Since the buyer is the one who selects the escrow office, I'll flip a coin because they are two of the most qualified and nicest people in the world, not only for escrows, but for all legal matters relating to real estate. Annette introduced me to them several months ago and recommends them highly."

After she reads the contract twice, she borrows his pen to sign her name at the bottom of the page. She doesn't ask any questions as Mark leans over to grasp gently her right wrist to hold her hand steady. Her eighty years, plus her recent angioplasty and the idea of selling her jewel of a farm, all contribute to making her fingers a bit jittery.

"That's fine, Judy. Looks like a doctor's signature on a prescription," he remarks.

At the bottom of the sales contract, he adds his signature with a flourish, and makes a fist and thrusts it into the air. He freezes a moment, lifts his head upward, and whispers, "Thank you, Lord."

"Yes, you're right, Mark," says Judy. "Thank you, Lord, for sending someone like you to look after me."

"The escrow will be 30 days, sufficient time for processing everything, such as making a title search of the property and obtaining the Certificate of Title Insurance. This process should be a *'wham bam, thank you ma'am'* type of escrow. When it's time to sign the final papers, I'll pick you up and we'll drive together to Chestertown."

"Do you want to move in during escrow?"

"We'll make that decision after escrow opens. You'll continue to live in your home for the remainder of your lifetime, but title of ownership will pass to me. If you don't mind, I'd like to keep the 'Ridgefield' name. It's a good name, with some history attached to it."

"You might add your name to mine and call it 'Ridgefield Hopkins,'" she remarks with a degree of excitement in her voice.

"I'm perfectly pleased to keep it short and simple, something people can say anywhere, anytime that is easily recognized immediately. Perhaps in the next few days you can see if there's a room or two that I can live in here while an addition is constructed. I want you to have your privacy, but permit me live within arm's reach, so to speak, to look after your needs. I'll take good care of you, Judy, like I always took good care of my men in the military."

The telephone rings and Judy is reluctant to answer it until Mark urges her to pick up the phone.

"It might be important, Judy, perhaps your doctor," he bellows out.

"Hello, Hick," she answers and quickly presses the phone against her chest. "It's Hick Clark, one of the local realtors who always has his eyes, ears and nose in the air, like a golden retriever. He's resourceful, always looking for clients who want to buy or sell properties in Kent County."

She lifts the receiver again to her ear and says, "Yes, Hick, I can hear you better now. Must have been a flock of geese flying overhead that interrupted the signal. You know how poor telephone reception is here, at the end of Eastern Neck Island Road."

She pauses a long time to hear what he has to say, then abruptly tells him, "I've already found a buyer for my farm, and it will stay in the family. Rumors of my demise were premature, weren't they? It was a pleasure to get your call."

She hangs up and smiles broadly in Mark's direction.

During Judy's telephone conversation with Hick Clark, Mark again gazes around her living room and, from an end table on one side of a sofa, picks up a carved decoy by the Chestertown carver, Charlie Joiner.

Eventually he raises it into eye level and turns it in various positions to study the posture and texture of the carving.

"Wonderful quality, isn't it? My late husband and I have been friends and fans of Charlie for over 40 years."

Mark returns the decoy to its original location and continues, "Getting back to our business at hand, as quickly as possible after escrow is completed, I'd like to move in and begin the new addition on the side or back of your home, and complete it before winter sets in. Hopefully, Jack Johnson, who's living at the Senior Living Complex in Betterton, can begin construction of an addition as soon as escrow closes. Naturally, all of these costs will be my responsibility. And you might be surprised that I've decided to pay all the utilities and taxes from now to eternity."

"I thought it was 'from here to eternity,' and no, Mark," she replies, with sincerity in her voice, "I'm not surprised at all by your gesture to pay my part of the utilities and taxes. I suspect you always do the right thing. In the next few days, I'll study the rooms in the back, places that I've taken for granted and used as storage for things that I should probably sell at Crumpton. Furthermore, you have my permission to begin the addition *during* escrow."

"That's good news. I can ask Jack to get the necessary building and health permits, order materials, all the things you have to do to get a jump on the actual construction and finish before winter sets in. We'll upgrade all the electric heating and cooling at the same time. No more worries if all the kitchen appliances are plugged in at the same time."

"When I look at your deposit check, I feel as if I'm not really selling my home, but taking on a guest, permanently."

"I don't have much to move from Betterton because the apartment over the garage was furnished, if you want to call it furnished. I'll buy new bedding but the auction at Crumpton will have all the furnishings. Everything there can be bought for half-price but will come with some scratches. If I bought brand new items from a department store, by the time is was transported here, it would have loads of scratches anyway."

"Listening to you, Mark," she discloses, "makes me wish I was 30 years younger so that I could dive into art as you're doing. Being around you is like a breath of fresh air. Hope you won't mind my looking over your shoulder now and then. I like antiques when they're as old as an old battle-ax like me."

Judy picks up the tray of muffins from the kitchen counter and asks him, "Have another muffin?"

"I have to watch my figure. All my hormones are moving like pistons in a Mercedes," he tells her with a laugh. "Keep in mind that in the first few months, I'll be looking over your shoulder, learning your routine and habits. If the weather holds up, the 800-square-foot addition should be finished in less than three weeks."

"You're glowing like a glowworm," she says. "I can understand your excitement, after all, it *is* your first home."

"I see it all in my imagination: a master bedroom and private bath; an office for my computer and reference books; and perhaps a second bedroom for guests who want to spend the night here. Ridgefield will be my Shangri-la."

"I can hear the rumors flying around Betterton and Rock Hall," Judy concedes. "Rich widow and handsome former SEAL, all living under one roof. It'll do wonders for my image. Who knows? Might even get my name in the gossip column. All because of you. You really are, as I've said before, a breath of fresh air in this dust bin."

"A dust bin?" he asks quickly. "That's what Annette called her store, with its antiques covered with a layer of dust."

After Mark concludes his business with Judy, he's a little giddy as he lets the steering wheel slide in his fingers while driving his BMW down a dirt road leading away from the main house. If a policeman in a patrol car were following him, he would be given a citation for reckless driving. But not today, not on a farm that will soon bear his name on the property deed.

About 30 feet away from the black-top, two-lane Eastern Neck Island Road, Mark spots a four-foot-square, weather-beaten, wooden sign, that reads: *ANYONE DISTURBING THE PEACE WILL BE PROSECUTED.*

"I'll have to move you," he says loudly, "out of the cornfield, into a place of prominence, and paint a big yellow smiling face below the words."

After Mark arrives back in Betterton, he sees Jack Johnson, who's giving a final inspection to Annette's addition.

He calls him over to an area where they talk privately and tells him, "Shake my hand, Jack. I'm a homebuyer and you're the first to know it. As soon as you complete this remodel for Annette, I want you drive out to see Ridgefield. You're my contractor for an addition there."

'Congratulations, Mark. That's good news. I should be available sometime tomorrow. We can take a look at Ridgefield to see what you have in mind there. If you want to finish everything before winter sets in, how about getting your Betterton Breeze track team to help me? But you'll have to arrange that, not me."

"Leave it to me," he declares.

"After studying your project," Jack tells him, "I'll draw up the plans and get them to the planning and zoning people in Chestertown for the construction permits."

Chapter 4

Four weeks after taking possession of the dagger, Abigail arrives in Rock Hall to meet with Mark inside his newly remodeled addition to Judy's farmhouse.

"Welcome to Ridgefield and my Shangri-la," he boasts while helping her up the front steps leading to the porch. "Later on, Jack Johnson will install a handicap ramp on the side for easier access for everyone, including my golden retriever, Jen."

The moment Mark mentions her name, Jen rushes through an access door and rubs her body against Abigail's leg as a sign of welcome too.

Once inside his office, Mark moves a Charles and Ray Eames lounge chair and ottoman away from a corner and closer to his computer for her to rest her body.

"I'm going modern here but intend to blend antiques with modern art and furniture," he tells her. "Modern furniture like this Eames chair I picked up at Dixon's is easy on the eyes. Simple lines that remind me of my geometry and calculus classes. You don't have to worry about temperature and humidity affecting it like you would with an antique piece. And it's much easier to dust.

"The ottoman's very functional, especially to rest my arthritic knee that acts up occasionally."

She opens her purse, removes a beige-colored envelope and studies it before handing to him.

"I'd trade back my commission if you could give me a new knee that was pain-free when I move around," she utters with a laugh. "Here's a little something to tide you over until you buy your next painting."

"The proceeds from the sale of the jeweled dagger to a new museum in New York City?" he asks.

"That's right and thanks for letting me be your agent in this transaction. The sale was a little more complicated than I first envisioned, mainly because of the aspect of a possible restitution under the cultural heritage laws governing objects removed from a country during wartime."

"I assume, the issue was resolved, otherwise you wouldn't be handing me a check. Can you disclose any details?"

"The director, who wants to remain anonymous for the moment, had many long discussions with the head of the Historical Artifacts Agency (HAA) in Iraq. Both came to the following agreement before a sale was consummated: In exchange for signing a release of restitution and waiver of liability, the Iraqi government received one of the latest tower cranes, compliments of the board of trustees of the museum. Iraq apparently needs giant construction cranes that can lift 19 tons of materials."

"Excuse me for a moment, please," he tells her while leaving his office and walking into the living room to grab a cushion from the settee there. He stares for a long time at the cashier's check, in the amount of $450,000, made payable to Mark Hopkins, and tears begin to roll down his cheek.

"Damn it," he says. "I'd trade this check and all the money I have if I could bring Rusty back alive from Iraq."

After returning to his office, he puts the cushion under Abigail's knee.

"Better get as comfortable as possible because we have a lot to discuss. Would you like a glass of wine or cup of coffee?"

"Thanks, Mark, but I'm fine at the moment."

"From the moment you recognized, in my file photos, the dagger on my workbench beside the model ship *Gratitude*, my life has changed. It was you and only you who identified the historical importance and incredible value of the dagger, and it was you and only you who later made the crucial telephone call to trap Bud Wayne, who used it as the murder weapon to kill his wife."

"Those were some tense moments," she admits.

"When I study this check, I can't help but think about the cost of war and loss of life, and Rusty."

"Who was Rusty?" she asks.

"A member of my squad. We were sitting inside an armored vehicle on the outskirts of Baghdad when a suicide bomber fired a grenade missile at us. The explosion turned everything upside down and sideways, with everyone thrown outside into a large crater. Rusty, a nickname because he had hair the color of a rusty pipe, ended up on top of me when I came to. He must have died instantly from a broken neck. In the ground a few feet from his body was the dagger sticking halfway out of the sand, with its blade flashing in my eyes from reflections of the sun. Without much thought, I grabbed it and stuffed it inside my flak-jacket."

"Rusty may have saved your life," she murmurs.

"Several days after this tragedy, I had to prepare a casualty report and revisited the site again, with an interpreter who told me that many fierce battles were fought at this particular location, dating back several hundred years to when Sheiks were in power. He said 'It's like what you Americans call a freeway interchange, where roads crisscross in all directions.' He indicated that there were probably hundreds of relics buried in the sands, from ambitious Sheiks who wanted more land, more women, more treasures and fought bloody wars against neighboring tribes."

"It's almost like the dagger had a spirit inside it," she admits."Remember, I'm familiar with spirits."

"Very perceptive of you, because I reached the same conclusion. But the spirit is two-edged like the blade of that dagger. One good, one evil. So far, the evil edge is winning with the deaths of

Rusty and Vera. I cannot rest until I try to change the spirit into good, and I can begin today, with your help."

"What would you like me to do?"

He pauses to wipe some perspiration from his forehead and looks around his office, including photos on the wall and the *Storm Cat* bronze resting on a pedestal in a corner.

"I hate to admit it but it seems as if I feed off people and react to people like you. What would you say about us becoming collaborators and enter today into a partnership? You can even name your own salary. With your consent I'm handing you this check to open an account and the authority to sign checks against this account.

"I have in mind the creation of an R&R refuge for Red Cross military men and women who served in combat, and for their families, especially vets who have fallen on tough times, and need some mentoring and a little push upward in their lives."

"Go on, please."

"I envision a lodge at Ridgefield where these good people can stay for R&R. We'll be their hosts for a few weeks, like a time-share, but hopefully not more than a month."

"Collaborators? R&R Refuge? I'm with you so far" she answers.

"Open the main account in the name of Ridgefield-Hopkins, as the parent company or umbrella under which several sub-accounts will draw funds from, for accounting purposes. For example, we'll give the refuge a temporary designation 'MRCERV,' for Military Red Cross Entitlement Refuge for Vets."

"An interesting designation," she answers with an approving nod of her head. "I can see you've given this considerable thought."

"I have nothing but plenty of time to develop plans for Ridgefield, and, as I've said before, a program for mentoring vets who need help in finding their way back from combat."

"Seems similar to your mentoring those young men who became the Betterton Breeze," she replies.

"Exactly. If it worked for those kids, it can work for others. At least we'll give it a try."

"Anything else?"

"I'd like you to contact Lola Albright, our family attorney in Baltimore, who's familiar with my intention to form a limited liability corporation in Delaware, for tax benefits. Find out what information she needs to establish a trust, so that this money is not taxed as capital gains. It's a donation from me, in memory of my fallen comrades. As much as I love the government and the American way of life, I don't want the government taking 33%."

He reaches into his wallet and hands her Lola's business card.

"I've already had conversations. with Lola and her boss, Mike Bloomburg."

"I'm ahead of you, Mark," she replies. "I've watched you too, and often thought about how to get more involved in your life. Somehow, someway, you seem to be in the middle of combat, a combat of ideas, vibrant ideas. I'd like to be on your team and tag along for awhile until I run out of energy. You're 27 going on 21, and I'm 60 going on 75. When I retired as director of a museum, retirement seemed to be a wonderful relief from the daily workload. But frankly, now I'm bored out of my mind. I've always enjoyed new challenges and, from what you've told me so far, this is a wonderful situation for me. Your ideas and goals will definitely benefit some deserving veterans."

"Before you leave," he pauses, "I'd like you to contact Maureen 'Mo' Greenspan at the Senior Living Complex in Betterton. She's a retired attorney who can give you some help in preparing the necessary documents to adopt Jaime Wayne, Vera's one-year-old son."

"You're going to adopt a baby?

"Why not? There's something peculiar about Jaime and me. It started with the moment he grabbed my finger and wouldn't let go."

"All babies grab a finger and don't let go."

"That's exactly what my mother told me, but this was different. I felt an attraction right away, something I can't explain fully. It happened when I met Vera, Bud and Jaime inside their office at Swan Point Marina. So far, the identity of the real birth father is unknown and could possibly be either Pretty Boy Floyd or Bud Wayne. Or another man entirely. From what I've learned about her life, Vera often floated freely from bedroom to bedroom, if you get my drift."

"Keep going, Mark."

"This baby should not be abandoned, or left in the hands of any of the men I just mentioned. I believe I owe it to Vera. I can't explain it right now, but there's something about her and her baby that baffles me, and it's not the insurance money and trust she established before her death."

He pauses to wipe some perspiration from his forehead.

"If I hadn't bid on and bought that guitar, which included the model ship, then Vera would never had telephoned me about buying the ship. She never would've met me and might still be alive today. Fate played a dirty trick on her and on me since I was implicated in her murder."

"You can't continue to harbor those memories, otherwise, they'll spread like a cancer."

"That's easier said than done," he replies. "On the other hand, it was rumored that she was attracted to military men. Perhaps that's why she managed to drug me at the Saloon. Since her killer has been brought to justice, I don't hold a grudge against her or feel angry anymore about being implicated in her murder. She never found the right man who could fully satisfy all her needs. She was a lost soul."

"From what I've heard, all of them end up battered and bruised, but not murdered," admits Abigail.

"I recall something Paul Newman said about Liz Taylor," he tells her while he stretches his fingers and cracks his knuckles.

"And what was that?"

"Newman said, 'She was a *functioning voluptuary*.' I think the same expression applies to Vera. She was given up to luxurious or sensuous pleasures, at least that's my impression from our few encounters."

"Jaime will need the kind of care that you can give him," says Abigail, "such as a good education, a creative environment, better than anything he would get from a foster home or from baby-sitters who have other things on their mind besides baby-sitting."

"I'll also insure that his trust is never touched. You remember that he inherited $500,000, money from Vera's life insurance, which is now deposited in one of the local banks. Also, Vera left her home and soft-crab business, including her *sloughing shed*, to Jaime and the trust."

"What's a *sloughing shed*?" asks Abigail.

"While I'm certainly not an expert here, I've managed to learn a good deal from that Betterton waterman who came into our shop a while back and from Bonnie and Floyd who are now running Vera's soft-crab business."

"Don't keep me in suspense. Get on with it."

"Are you sure you want me to tell you?"

"For God's sake, yes. How many times do I have to tell you."

Both are teasing each other and obviously enjoying the repartee developing here.

"A *sloughing shed* or *pound*," he begins, "is a building with a concrete pad about 20 by 20 feet. Water is pumped directly from the river, Bay or from tanks outside the shed filled with Bay water, through a maze of pipes into at least eight 3- by 6- by 1-foot-high stainless tables called holding tanks."

"O.K. So much for the water. What's next?"

"Water flows into each tank and is re-circulated through filters to remove contaminants. Everything is designed so that a special specie of the blue crab called a *peeler* believes it's still swimming in the Bay."

"*Peeler?*" she asks, "I remember reading a few years ago "Beautiful Swimmers" by William Warner, who wrote about that red rim on the swimming paddle of the back fin of a peeler."

"You're getting ahead of me. Watermen first have to sort out or *cull* their catch. Using their hands or hand-tongs, they put large males, called *Jimmies,* into a bushel basket labeled #1, medium males and all females into #2, peelers into #3, and paper-shell (throwback) *culls* into #4."

"About those *peelers,*" she interrupts, "which I remember are both sexes, the waterman's eyes must be as sharp as an eagle to spot that red rim."

"Maybe not that sharp, but you get the idea. A waterman can sell his peelers to a *sloughing shed* business, like Bonnie and Floyd's, for $2 each, whereas a normal #1 Jimmy might sell for 50 cents."

"What happens after the peelers are sold?" she asks while sliding back in her lounge chair.

"They're put into a tank to swim freely until they undergo one of God's little miracles, a metamorphosis, a sloughing or shedding. The peeler backs out of the old shell, like outgrowing an old suit, and emerges with a larger shell."

"I think you're going to tell me that it's due to a special enzyme in the peeler."

"Abigail, you amaze me because you're always right. Do you remember how long it takes for peeler to slough?"

"You've got me here."

"About three days."

"And if I recall correctly, crabs grow a new shell at least five times before reaching maturity, don't they?

"Yes, but only the peeler grows a soft shell each time, whereas the others always grow a hard shell."

"Very interesting."

"Pay attention, because the tricky part is monitoring the tanks and removing each peeler within about two hours of final sloughing. Otherwise, the soft shell becomes hard.

"You're wearing me out. Does this story have a happy ending?"

"From a business standpoint, yes, because the peelers are removed from the tank, and placed in a cooler, with their face upward at an angle of 45 degrees to prevent fluid from escaping from its mouth and gills. If all goes well, they can live for 4 to 5 days, and sold wholesale for four times their purchase price."

"But watermen can't catch crabs all year, can they?"

"No they can't, so it's profitable about five to six months, as long as crabs are migrating in the Bay. It's a seasonal business because everything closes down in the winter."

Mark and Abigail both lean their heads back as if they gave each other a short lecture on *Callinectes sapidus,* Greek for beautiful swimmer.

"The last word here," he declares, "should go to Joseph Szymanski, known locally as the *Hemingway by the Bay,* a legend in his own mind, who occasionally gets a spark or two of originality. He claims '**a** *sloughing shed* **is a maternity ward where a peeler is reborn and gives birth to itself.**' "

"I thought we were speaking about Vera. How in the world did she get in a position of owning such a business?" Abigail asks and hopes the answer will end this discussion that slows up the storyline.

"It descended in her family until she was 27, became pregnant and married Bud. It's a screwy mess because it was rumored around town that she was sleeping with Floyd and Bud, off and on, if you get my drift. She married Bud, probably because he had a marina and money in the bank, whereas Floyd only had his good looks. She kept her old home that Floyd rented while he managed the soft-crab business, and they split the profits. Does that make sense to you?"

"Not really, but it has the makings of a good art film." she replies with a laugh. "And the next time I bite into one of those succulent soft crabs, sautéed in butter, and laid on a slice of whole wheat toast with a thin layer of mayonnaise, lettuce and tomato,

I'll have more appreciation of the *peeler*, and how it achieved metamorphosis!"

"As watermen say, *that's the smart of it*."

"I'm flabbergasted. Obviously, you've been rubbing shoulders with smart watermen, haven't you?"

"Only one waterman, which is enough to last for a lifetime. He never told me his name nor introduced himself and didn't ask for my name. His life was all about blue crabs and crabbing on the Chesapeake Bay."

"Too bad. He could have learned a lot from you."

"That's his loss, not mine."

"Getting back to reality and your intent to adopt Vera's baby, do you think that you can devote the time and energy required here? You certainly have a lot of things on your plate. You shouldn't take valuable time away from your talents as a private dealer in fine arts. I don't think you can have it all."

"I don't want it all. I just want to do the right thing. It may seem like a juggling act, but with proper planning and help from talented people like you, everything will fall into place. Do you have time for lunch?"

"I can't wait to bite into a soft crab sandwich but I'll take a rain check. Before I return to Baltimore, I promised to see Sandy. When I was here a month ago, she was just beginning her clay model of Liz, and I can't wait to see how far she has progressed."

Forty minutes later, Abigail is walking around the life-size clay model positioned in the middle of Sandy's studio next door to Annette's Antiques.

"The 26-mile drive from Rock Hall to your studio was worth it. You've created something special here," Abigail gushes with excitement, "and it should be seen in this stage by art lovers before you think about casting it in bronze. With your permission, I'd like to take some photos to show to Rebecca McLain, my successor and new director of the Washington County Museum in Hagerstown.

She's also the curator of an exhibition, in the planning stage, called *From Model to Casting - A Sculptor's Vision."*

"Is it good enough for that show?" Sandy asks.

"I wouldn't say it if I didn't believe in it and in you."

"Well," Sandy quickly answers, "I wouldn't want to take advantage of our friendship, but certainly, you can take all the pictures you want."

"That's not taking advantage of anything. What are friends for? If I didn't think it would enhance the show and let people see the process of transforming a live model into a clay model, I wouldn't get involved. It's that simple. All artists need a window of opportunity opened for them. In the end, the public will be the judge."

"Of course, I'm looking far ahead," interjects Sandy, "but if the director would like Liz and me to give a short talk about the modeling and sculpting process, we would love to be part of the exhibition."

Sandy watches Abigail study the model and take several quick pictures before switching off her digital camera.

"There's something that I'd like to tell you," declares Sandy as she finds a seat to make her comfortable, "because you've had years of experience running a museum in Hagerstown."

"You have my complete attention," she replies.

"I've always felt that since my rescue in the Bay by Mark, God has a special place for me and creative people like me. There's a moment in everyone's life or it should be a moment in everyone's life, when adversity is transformed into accomplishment, accomplishment that was unexpected, unreal, uncommon, unequaled.

"For me, it was transforming clay found here in the fields of Betterton into a living thing, a model of a beautiful semi-nude so realistic that it looks like it's alive. At some point during the handling of the clay, I felt as though my hands were no longer under my control. They were guided and moved by another force of energy, of creativity from God above."

Abigail is stunned by Sandy's revelations. She switches the camera back on again, and circles a second time around the clay model, popping shot after shot, close-up and long range. The flash of each shot makes the process seem like a *Harper's Bazaar* fashion photo-shoot in the Louvre by Richard Avedon.

"That's about the most intuitive, heart-warming account that I've ever heard," Abigail confesses. "You should immediately write it down in a diary, so that you have an accurate record of your intimate thoughts."

"This is another day of discovery," acknowledges Abigail, "like the day I recognized and identified the rarity of the Baghdad dagger in one of Mark's photographs."

It's now Thanksgiving, and gathered around the dining table inside Annette's home are Sandy, Richard, Mark, Abigail, Reggie, Stash and Elle, with Annette as hostess. Four men, four women, 'The Magnificent Eight,' Annette calls them.

Annette opens an antique medicine cabinet off to one side of the room and removes a bottle of Robert Mondavi's best private-estate Burgundy wine. She opens it with her face glowing and circles around the table to fill the glass of each guest.

Eventually, she lifts her glass to toast everyone around the table, especially Mark.

"If this Navy SEAL sitting across from me hadn't rescued Sandy in the Chesapeake Bay six months ago," she admits, "became a trusted friend and partner in the antiques business, whose first purchase at Dixon's was an acoustic guitar, I never would've met the man I'm about to marry on Christmas Eve. Here's to you, Mark, with thanks from Sandy, Richard and me."

"Don't forget me," cries out Richard Wagner, grandson of the famous German Composer. "If I hadn't been distracted and missed out on biding for that guitar, but ended up buying its amplifier, if I hadn't been standing in line to pay my bill at Dixon's positioned directly behind Mark, I never would have met him, exchanged phone numbers and come to the antiques shop where

I met the lady I'm about to marry." He pauses and asks, "Is that two or three 'if's?' "

"And how about me?" asks Reggie. "If I hadn't been trailing the *New Bay Belle* ferry and caught sight of Sandy and Mark falling from the top deck into the Bay, and rescued them all by myself, none of us would be here for this glorious Thanksgiving dinner. Let's make a toast to the Good Lord, who brought us together, and hopefully will keep us together."

"Amen!" they exclaim in unison.

"I realize that you've set your wedding date," says Mark, "but no one has talked about where you're being married and your reception."

"Since snow and ice are always blanketing this area, it would make sense for us to limit unnecessary travel," answers Annette. "So we've decided to have it all in one place, inside our new addition. The space can easily accommodate about 20 guests. We'll have the civil wedding ceremony and reception in the same room" she declares while raising both hands with index and middle fingers crossed, a sign of good luck.

"But we'll have a surprise," Richard interjects with a touch of braggadocio. "We've made arrangements with the Amish farmer nearby to borrow his horse and sleigh to take everyone on a nice ride around Betterton. Now that's something special, don't you think? Actually, it was Sandy's idea."

"I was thinking about those old Currier and Ives prints," admits Sandy. "It seemed like a perfect thing for the holidays, especially on Christmas Eve."

The next Wednesday, Mark rises at 5 a.m. and brews himself a pot of finely-ground Chock-full-o'-Nuts coffee. He looks at the label and immediately images of Jackie Robinson, a vice president of the coffee company, flash through his mind, especially the way Jackie jockeyed off first base to antagonize the pitcher on the mound of a baseball game. Whenever he was on base, he was transformed into a cheetah with lightning bolts of power and speed.

Around 1957, after his playing days with the Brooklyn Dodgers were over, Jackie was made a senior vice president of Chock-full-o'-Nuts, founded in Brooklyn in 1926. Mark believed this brand simply tasted better because Jackie was associated with the company and was a fierce competitor who stood for excellence, whether it was on a baseball field or in the front office.

In the 1950's not many African-Americans were front-office executives, but Jackie was something special. So was his older brother Matthew 'Mack' Robinson, who ran the 200-meter dash in the 1936 Summer Olympics in Berlin and won the silver medal, only 12 inches behind gold-medalist Jesse Owens.

Whereas Jesse became an instant celebrity and eventually a legend in his lifetime, Mack became a custodian, a street sweeper, in the Sanitation Department of the City of Pasadena, California.

As Mark continues to sip his coffee, he glances out the bay window of the living room and watches about a one-inch layer of rain water completely cover the ground between his house and car. He hesitates about driving this Wednesday morning to the auction in Crumpton. After all, it is a 40-minute trip in a gentle rain that has fallen all night, which means flooding of the roads. He contemplates the upcoming action and suspects that it might be a good opportunity to make the drive there since not many bidders are expected to attend under these weather conditions.

However, past experience from attending auctions in Baltimore in inclement weather always produced the opposite result, where everyone had the same idea that no one would show up and the chances of bidding against a mob of bidders were favorable. In all these cases, however, the opposite occurred because everyone weathered the storm and flocked to the auction.

After Mark completes the 40-minute drive from Rock Hall to Crumpton, he parks his BMW about 50 feet from the front door of the hangar. By the time he sets foot inside the hangar, his shoes are soaked with water and mud from sloshing in puddles everywhere in the parking lot.

The building is cold and damp, and the three furnaces are just starting to burn the large chunks of wood piled nearby.

As Mark walks around Table #1, he overhears several dealers talking and their words are muffled somewhat by the damp air too. It reminds him of the sounds of words spoken in an underground bunker, always difficult to comprehend.

At the far end of the table he notices a German painting leaning against a small stool. It's an oil on canvas, an interior scene, with two figures. There's a young Bavarian man dressed in his lederhosen and green felt hat who looks down and smiles at a beautiful young farm girl - called a Madchen - dressed in a dirndl and seated in a chair while knitting. The smile on her beautiful face indicates that she's fully aware of the attention coming from an admirer.

The painting is only about 18 inches high and 12 inches wide, but it's framed in an antique 4-inch wide, ornate, composition frame weighing at least 20 pounds. It's probably a work painted around 1890-93 and is signed "E. Rau."

Mark quickly sizes up the situation. If he can buy this painting for under $2,000, it would be a steal since the artist is Emil Rau, whose paintings of this size would easily fetch $5,000 to $12,000 at the auctions in New York. He's also not very comfortable walking around the concrete floor with shoes and socks soaking wet. Since this is a good environment in which to catch a cold or the flu, he decides that if he wins the bidding for $2,000 or less, he'll call it a day. Otherwise, he'll check out the other 60 tables to see what might be worth buying for inventory.

Mark glances down at his watch just as an announcement blasts over the loud speakers, "Inside tables to auction in five minutes."

He keeps his position at the far end of Table #1, directly in front of the Rau painting. Precisely at 8 a.m., the 28-year old grandson of the founder of Dixon's auction, Dylan Dixon, climbs into his position on the mobile auction vehicle with a young lady beside him to record the sale. He squirms a little because the vehicle holds only two people, and both are sitting on a hard wooden bench.

"Remember everyone," he begins his spiel, "when I say 'Sold,' you own it. Take it immediately from our helpers Dave Bloom and Rick Nelson, so it won't get damaged in handling. Never leave it alone, otherwise someone will pick it up and walk off with it. Alright Dave, what's your first item up for bid?"

Dave thrusts high in the air several sterling silver bowls from Kirk and Company of Baltimore.

Several dealers battle it out but pay only the price based on the scrap weight of silver, which is currently about $15 an ounce. Obviously, these dealers have already weighed the pieces beforehand with the small scales that they carry in their jackets.

On the other side of the table, Rick Nelson grabs a chair off the table and hoists it into the air and shouts "Wicker Chair." It's actually a Windsor chair, but who cares, when it brings only $30, a bargain.

In a matter of less than 10 minutes, Dylan has sold over 35 items stacked on Table #1, and finally Dave Bloom holds up the German painting and shouts out, "Oil painting in frame."

The bidding starts at $20 and Mark patiently lets the bidding around the table escalate in $20 increments to $100, then watches two bidders bidding in $25 increments take it up to $500. He enters the fray at $600 and battles one determined lady dressed in an Eskimo coat with her hood pulled forward to hide her face from everyone except the eyes of the auctioneer. The increments increase now to $50, and Dylan takes Mark's bid for $1,000, and asks, "Eleven hundred, anyone?" He seems to hesitate forever before pounding his fist downward on a wooden shelf.

"It's yours for one thousand," Dylan says while pointing to Mark.

"Mark Hopkins 21661," he shouts at the top of his lungs.

"Easy lad." Dylan tells him while laughing. "A deaf man could hear you!"

"Good luck with it," says Dave Bloom as he hands Mark the painting like a quarterback extending his arms to hand off the football to his charging halfback.

Mark takes it with both hands since the frame is heavy, and immediately walks away from the congested table in a direction towards the Amish Deli, where the aisles are empty of people at this early morning hour. He gazes down at his watch, and it's only fifteen minutes past 8 in the morning.

He intends to take the painting to his car, but when he opens the exit door of the hangar, it's still drizzling outside along with some gusts of wind blowing in every direction. He realizes that such a wonderful painting should not be carried directly into the rain without some protection. In such instances he is permitted to store things in Dave Bloom's stall near the exit door.

So he walks into the stall and notices that no one is around to watch what he intends to do with the painting. He quickly stands it on its longest edge on a top shelf about five feet off the ground, in a far corner of the stall. Finally, he places a large portrait against the painting in an effort to hide it from sight. His next thought is to find some protective material, such as paper, plastic, or blanket to wrap the painting for transport to his car.

Mark leaves the stall and walks toward the auctioneer, who is now positioned on Table #2. He moves around the back of the mobile auction vehicle and notices a large Hudson Bay blanket on Table #3.

About 15 minutes later, Dave Bloom is holding up the blanket, and Mark opens the bidding at $20, and eventually wins it with a bid of $40. Dave hands him the blanket, and Mark rushes back to Dave's storage stall. He walks through the stall, and when he pulls the large portrait away from the wall, the painting is gone. It's stolen, a felony theft because its value is $1,000 or more.

Mark is stunned and sick to his stomach. He's completely dumbfounded that the possibility of theft in broad daylight never crossed his mind. Only 15 minutes have elapsed from the time he first placed it on a top shelf in the far corner of the stall. Obviously someone must have seen him take the painting into Dave's stall. He also suspects that the thief was a dealer who opened the stall's rear door and walked directly into the falling rain and wind gusts, conditions that will surely damage the painting.

Mark spends ten minutes outside in the rain, trying to look inside all the parked vehicles, but realizes that almost all of them have smoky glass windows that make it impossible to see what's inside. The thief probably drove away as fast as he stole the painting.

With little recourse, he informs the auctioneer about the theft and offers a reward of $1,000.

Dylan interrupts the auction and makes an immediate announcement about the theft, the reward offered, and turns to Mark whispers, "I told you to be careful, didn't I?"

Mark walks over to the Dixon front office and informs Miss Vicky, the office manager, of the theft and that he'll contact the sheriff to file a report.

An hour later Deputy Steenken of the Queen Anne's County Sheriff's Office arrives, and both men move to a quiet corner of the hangar. Mark quickly recalls as many details as he can remember, and the deputy writes everything down on a theft report and assigns a case number. Mark signs the report, receives a copy for his records, and thanks the deputy for his help.

Still feeling depressed, Mark has one more thought here and walks back to Miss Vicky.

"Would you kindly ask Dylan," he pleads, "to contact the consignor of the stolen painting to see if he or she might have a photo or any records that will help in the investigation?"

As he leaves the office and walks across the hangar, Mark is angry at himself for not being more vigilant.

"Dylan warned me," he tells himself, "so it's partly my fault. Going home empty-handed is one thing, but going home with a bill for a $1,000 purchase with nothing to show for it is another thing. If that painting is ever put up for auction or exhibited in a museum, we'll catch the crook. If it hangs in someone's home, we'll never get the chance for a recovery. The only benefit for me is that the purchase price can be deducted when I file my next income tax return."

After he finally reaches the exit door and opens it, the gloom and doom feelings inside him persist despite a complete change in the weather. Outside the hangar vehicles and people are moving in the mud, but under bright sunshine.

"If it hadn't been raining at 8:15 this morning," he mutters to himself, "the painting would be safely inside my car, and I would be one happy buyer. Was it fate or the devil that stretched out his hand and stole my painting from under my nose?"

When Mark settles into his office chair at Ridgefield, he begins the process of sending an email to all the auction houses on the east coast, alerting the heads of the Department of 19th Century European Paintings of the theft, and then contacts the Art Loss Register to file a request for a registration that will distribute news about the theft over the Internet. The entire process will be more complicated because no photograph is presently available.

Then he remembers that in The Netherlands there is the famous Rijksbureau voor Kunsthistorische Documentatie in The Hague, better known as the 'RKD,' that houses over three million photographs of paintings from Old Masters to Contemporary works in all mediums. Perhaps a photograph of the Rau painting may be available in one of their photographic files on the artist, provided the painting has appeared at auction or exhibition. Otherwise, with no photograph available, a verbal description will have to suffice.

By the time Mark switches on his HP pavilion desk-top computer, he's no longer feeling sorry for himself. It's not like he lost a friend or colleague, or suffered a heart attack. It's only a thousand dollar painting, and perhaps a lesson will be learned from this incident at Crumpton that will benefit him for the rest of his life.

For the remainder of the day, he will feed information into the computer, surf the Internet, including eBay, for auction houses, restorers, galleries, and any place where paintings are marketed.

Chapter 5

Meanwhile, back in Betterton, Liz surprises Sandy by knocking on her studio door, unannounced.

Completely caught off guard, Sandy gives her a big hug and escorts her to the middle of her studio.

"Here it is," she tells Liz slowly with pride in each word. "When I telephoned and invited you to see *our* creation, you couldn't give me an exact time when you'd be able to come and now here you're, face to face with yourself in clay. As much as I like the clay model, you're still the most beautiful woman I've ever seen. I hope you as Pompeia will please you as much as it does me."

When Liz has a chance to digest the pose and feeling expressed by the life-size clay model of a semi-nude woman, she is speechless momentarily.

"Oh, I can't believe it. Do I really look like that woman, standing with a garment wrapped around her waist, the voluptuous third wife of Julius Caesar?"

Liz begins to walk slowly around the model and pauses to touch the cheek, lips and hair of her head.

"Do you have a chair for me to sit in before I fall down?

Sandy finds one of those Hollywood folding chairs, the ones that have the name of the director, actor or actress stenciled on the back strapping.

Is drooling permitted?" Liz asks. "Can I gush a little? Oh, it's beautiful, as if it could come to life at any moment. It seems that there's a spirit stirring inside it. Although the image is of me, this is really more about you and your talents as a sculptor. Words like 'fabulous,' 'amazing,' 'incredible,' pop into my mind. Need I go on?"

"Go on. I need all the compliments I can get today," Sandy utters. "It's been awhile since I've seen Mark, and I'm beginning to miss him more than I thought I could ever miss anyone."

"Oh, that's a surprise. If it's not imposing on my part, would it help to talk about it?"

"Not really. He felt restrained here in Betterton, and wanted to stretch his wings. Although it wasn't a big surprise when he decided to leave Betterton, it was a shock when he left me, but not because of another girl. He bought himself a farm near the Eastern Neck Wildlife Refuge outside Rock Hall."

She pauses after Liz puts her arm around her.

"What you need is a new man in your life," Liz advises, "and if that's not possible, pour yourself wholeheartedly into your work."

"That's precisely what my mother always said," Sandy responds. "But work does not cure everything. Work cannot and will never take the place of a man to lean on when you need support. You didn't know that I could have become his fiancé when he proposed six months ago. In a strange way, Mark was too good to be true and always setting his sights on something bigger and better. It sounds ridiculous, but Mark is a Monarch butterfly, always fluttering around, setting down for a moment, then abruptly moving on to a different spot."

"Each of us has a little of the characteristics of a butterfly in our psyche. Perhaps Mark has more than others. Everyone has a tendency to move to new and better feeding grounds. If you're ambitious and creative, you can't be stagnant. You're inclined to migrate. It's part of maturity."

As soon as Liz completes her last word, the phone rings and Reggie is on the line, wanting to talk to Mark. Sandy reluctantly explains the situation, and repeats the exact same words she told Liz moments ago.

"I hope things are going better for you than for me," she suddenly blurts out. "How is your love life, if you don't mind me getting personal?"

"Ruth and I have split up, too," he tells her. "She was flying east and west with American Airlines, and I was driving north and south for recording dates in New York."

"Timing is right for you, Reggie. I've got someone in my studio that you should meet, and I don't mean my clay model. This lady is 'too good to be true,' believe me. If you can dash over here in the next few minutes, I'll introduce you to Liz Carter, a major at the Pentagon who posed for me."

While Reggie drives from his secluded estate a few miles outside of Betterton, Sandy hangs up her smock and brushes her hair in a small mirror.

"Reggie's on his way over to meet you. In the meantime, I'll bring you up to date with Abigail Woods, whom you've already met. She has taken photos of the model and intends to show them to the new director of the Washington County Museum in Hagerstown, with the hope that it might be included in an upcoming exhibition."

"Maybe it'll make you and me two new stars in the art world," Liz says facetiously.

Ten minutes later, Reggie knocks at the garage door, and Sandy is excited to introduce him to Liz. It's love at first sight, which doesn't surprise anyone, since they have much in common: talent, sensitivity, and a love of music.

"I studied piano in my teens at the Peabody Conservatory in Baltimore," Liz tells Reggie, "but gravitated into metallurgy at

Hopkins. The money earned in science far out-weighed anything I could ever hope to make playing the piano. Of course, if you're a studio musician like yourself, you can make a pretty good living, can't you?"

Reggie is almost speechless but says to himself, "Ruth was beautiful, but Liz is breathtaking and electrified. She takes my breath away. I've never met anyone so sensitive, intelligent and so quick to make friends."

Minutes later, he's walking her up the steps to his 4,000 square-foot concrete home, based on Prairie design by Frank Lloyd Wright that features low exterior horizontal lines and open interior spaces. The home is Reggie's sanctuary, where he can study and rehearse for recording dates in New York. He finds inspiration whenever he gazes through windows at the forest that surrounds it, with a small pond nearby, reminiscent of a Robert Frost poem.

Once inside the grand room with its cathedral ceiling and leaded-glass panels, he claps his hands to turn on the Bose supersonic sound system that sends a slight shiver up Liz's spine. It's a recording that Reggie made with Les Paul, purely instrumental, the theme from the film *The Sandpiper*.

It doesn't take long for Liz to relax completely, starting with the genteel way Reggie removes her coat and takes her hand as he shows her around his music studio.

Every wall is accented only with photos of celebrities whose records included him as a backup guitarist.

"You won't find any original paintings hanging on the walls because I know nothing about art. I've led a very sheltered and shallow life," he confesses.

"When I get to know you better, perhaps we can visit a gallery or two. It's never too late to start a collection. It all starts with an itch," she admits with a laugh.

Liz is fascinated, then impressed by his charm, and eventually lured and hooked by his frankness and friendliness.

They seem to move in complete harmony, almost in slow motion and will spend the rest of the day and night together.

Inside Reggie's master bedroom, they mate, but not as long as a Chesapeake Bay male and female blue crab that can take up to 12 hours to make love.

Almost with a snap of the fingers, it's now Christmas Eve and the wedding day for Annette and Richard. Nearly six inches of snow blanket the entire Eastern Shore of Maryland. Yet inside Annette's newly-constructed addition, everyone is feeling excited, warm and cozy. It's like peering inside a ski lodge in New England; with guests dressed in country-casual, après-ski-type winter apparel, lightweight and very colorful. It's also a holiday time, in which friends and relatives can share God's blessings and the joy of two middle-aged friends about to walk down the marital aisle for the first time.

About 20 guests are invited, including Sandy; Mark with Abigail; Jesse with three members of his Breeze track team; Knute with the three seniors Manny, Mo and Jack; Lois with Clowie; Stash Piotrowski with his wife, Elle; Mike Bloomburg with his colleague, Lola Albright, and her newly-hired apprentice, Little Mac Bride; and finally, Reggie with Liz.

Most of the women are outfitted in turtleneck sweaters and slacks, which obviously cannot compare to the apparel worn by the bride, Annette Welles, who is dressed in an off-white, long-sleeved, satin blouse with orange polka dots and matching slacks, and white leather shoes with small cleats on the toe and heel. The groom is outfitted in Bavarian-green flannel trousers with a wide red stripe up the sides, with suspenders over his beige-colored turtle-neck shirt and white bow tie. He's chosen this outfit to pay homage to his great grandfather, the famous German composer, Richard Wagner.

The civil wedding ceremony, presided over by Mark Mumford, Clerk of the Circuit Court and Justice of the Peace for Kent

County, begins precisely at noon in the left-half of the new wing of the couple's home.

"Dearly Beloved," Mumford begins as he surveys the guests gathered in a semi-circle, "we are called here today to witness the bonds of matrimony between this handsome man and this beautiful woman. If anyone can show 'just cause' why this union shall not occur, let them come forth now or forever bury their cause along the shores of the Chesapeake Bay."

Mumford pauses to wink at the guests.

"Do you, Annette Welles," Mumford asks as he leans slightly towards her, "take Richard Wagner, to be your lawful wedded husband, to have and to hold from this day forward, for better, for worse, for richer, for poorer, in sickness and health, to love and to cherish, until death you do part?"

"I do," answers Annette with an incredible smile that lasts 10 seconds or more.

"Do you, Richard Wagner, "Mumford asks as he turns toward him and nods with his head, "take Annette Welles, to be your lawful wedded wife, to have and to hold from this day forward, for better, for worse, for richer, for poorer, in sickness and health, to love and to cherish, until death you do part?"

"I do," repeats Richard as he takes his right hand to his lips and blows a short kiss in Annette's direction.

"And now, Richard, you may place the wedding ring on Annette's finger."

'With this ring I thee wed," he tells her.

"And now, Annette, you may place the wedding ring on Richard's finger."

"With this ring I thee wed," she tells him.

"You have declared your consent to be married," Mumford declares with a step backward. "May the Good Lord strengthen your consent and fill you both with his blessings. What God has joined, let no one divide."

Mumford leans his head forward to pronounce, "You may now kiss each other. The bonds of holy matrimony are complete and official."

"I've been dreaming about this day from the moment I first met you," Richard tells her followed by a kiss they will remember for a lifetime.

"The feeling is mutual," says Annette while still in his embrace. "I loved you from the first moment I met you."

After the wedding ceremony is completed, the decorative six-panel screens that divided the room and concealed the reception section are removed.

The entire wing, 1,200 square feet, is now open for the reception.

Mark notices that Lola is standing directly under mistletoe attached to a chandelier and walks over with the intention of giving her a kiss.

When he faces her, however, her eyes are paralyzed for a second or two, as if her mind is telling her, 'You've waited a long time for this moment. Carpe Diem. Seize the Day.'

"You're under arrest," she blurts out in a parody of reading someone their Miranda rights. "You have the right to remain silent, the right to retain counsel, namely me, but if you choose to kiss me, the act may be used in evidence against you."

They begin laughing and are unaware that others seem to enjoy their impromptu antics.

"This is a warm-up kiss," she tells him. "I'd like to have a word with you privately when you have a moment."

"Per-fect," he answers quickly and pronounces it in two syllables. "Let's wait for our sleigh ride after the reception when we'll have some privacy. Can't wait to hear what's on your mind."

After Lola gives Mark a short kiss on his lips followed by a hug, she walks him over to Little Mac.

"I think you know each other, don't you?" she asks Little Mac.

"We certainly do," answers Mark ahead of Little Mac. "I was the first to see him outside Penn Station, the first to recognize a special talent waiting to bust out of his body. What's going on here? The last time I saw you, you were working for the *Sun* and covering the track meet at the Harvest Moon Fest. How did you get an invitation for the wedding?"

"You'll have to talk to Mike about that," Little Mac tells him.

"I know you won't believe it," Mike Bloomburg chimes in, "but I met him outside Penn Station too, learned that he was a writer, a good writer, and offered him a job as a paralegal for our firm. Based on his performance, I'm sponsoring him, at least for his first year, of law school at the University of Baltimore. He's working under Lola, and we're very pleased so far."

Eventually everyone settles into their seats around a long table positioned near a baby grand piano.

Mark rises from his seat and taps his champagne glass gently with a knife to get their attention.

"With your permission," he begins, "I'd like to be the first to propose..."

He accidentally glances at Lola sitting at the end of the table when he pauses, leaving her the impression that he's conveying a subliminal message here.

"A toast to Annette and Richard," he continues after a slight pause. "Everyone knows it was love at first sight and first bite after Richard was invited for lunch and tasted one of her homemade crab cakes. Everyone could see, over a short period of time, a glow radiating from their faces. It was chemistry personified, like an atomic reaction with all those atoms and molecules stirring around in their bodies, being bombarded, splitting, and releasing all that energy."

Reggie rises after Mark completes his toast, turns directly to the bride and groom, and continues, "I'm better with a guitar in my hands but here's my wish for you: May the Good Lord watch over you and protect you in the years ahead, and may all your ups and downs in life be gentle ones, like the words written on your wedding cake."

Eventually, everyone leaves their seat to form a line at a buffet of assorted seafood prepared by Manny Meyer, former short-order cook at Muller's Restaurant on Bond Street in East Baltimore.

Heated trays include broiled Maryland crab cakes, baked rockfish almandine, crispy oyster paddies deep fried in lard, where a card hangs from the tray that reads 'Cardiac Patients Beware' and four vegetables. At the end of the buffet are assorted rolls made from a recipe of Harry Gerstung of Gerstung's Bakery, where Manny also worked part-time before retirement.

After dinner comes the ceremonial cutting of the wedding cake, designed by Sandy, which shows a man and woman skiing down a slope on the outside of three layers, graduated with the largest being the base. Engraved in the icing of the top layer: 'May All Your Ups and Downs Be Gentle Ones.'

For entertainment, Reggie walks over to his Paul Reed Smith (PRS) acoustic electric guitar, propped in a corner near the piano.

"To start things off," he announces, "it would be apropos if all of us sang one of the most popular Christmas songs ever written, by one of the most noted songwriters in the American songbook, Israel Baline."

He pauses to see a puzzled look cross everyone's face.

"Israel Baline?" Annette asks.

"Well," answers Reggie, "you probably know him better as Irving Berlin." As he begins to play *White Christmas* Stash takes out his Horner harmonica and Elle takes a position at the baby grand to form a trio while everyone sings along.

Reggie's signature technique of stretching simple chords into dominant 7th and 9ths is the main reason why he's a highly respected studio musician, always in demand in New York recordings for vocalists like Tony Bennett, Johnny Mathis and Natalie Cole.

After the song ends followed by a medley of Christmas ballads, Annette asks all the single ladies to form a group behind her for the tossing of the flower bouquet. As the eligible ladies jostle in a fun-loving way for a front position, Annette suddenly tosses her floral bouquet over her shoulder.

It bounces off Sandy's outstretched hands into Liz's lap, reminiscent of a basket catch by the great Willie Mays.

As everyone begins to tease her, Liz looks in the direction of Reggie, with an affectionate and enticing smile. Perhaps Reggie is really the new man in her life.

In an attempt to save the best for last, Richard announces a special surprise for everyone, especially his new bride. He raises the lid of his baby grand, and plays a new concerto that he's been working on for over a year.

For the next three minutes, he plays the piano with the gusto of Arthur Rubinstein and ends with a crescendo. It's not until he pounds the climatic chord that he manages to release an incredible smile and begins to laugh at himself.

"At no time did my fingers leave my hands." he declares. "I never thought I'd get through it today."

After everyone applauds and congratulates Richard for his original concerto, Sandy switches on a CD of a recording of Henry Mancini's *Meglio Stasera*, known as *It Had Better Be Tonight,* with lyrics by Johnny Mercer, composed for the film *The Pink Panther*, introduced so beautifully by Fran Jeffries, in her film debut.

It's one of Sandy's favorite songs and the vibrant Latin tempo gets everyone dancing and interacting with each other. The music lasts almost six minutes with automatic looping of the melody. It's a fitting conclusion as everyone forms a conga line that snakes around the room and allows them to release their inhibitions one last time.

It's not a surprise that the four members of Mark's track team, The Betterton Breeze, stand out here. When Mark and Sandy first met them, they were always dancing to hip-hop music from a radio one of them carried around everywhere.

The best is reserved for last, however, as Annette surprises everyone, except for her daughter, Sandy, by toe-tapping Mancini's Latin arrangement in the same fantastic manner as Fran Jeffries danced in the film. Even Richard is flabbergasted but very proud of his new bride.

"I never knew she had it in her," he professes to everyone within hearing distance. "When I first met her, she was stunningly beautiful. Little did I know she had musical talent waiting to burst out if given the chance."

After the Mancini recording ends, it's about 3 in the afternoon and guests pair-off for a short one-horse, two-seater sleigh ride in the snowy back roads around Betterton.

A camera is passed among the guests to pop a picture or two in memory of the occasion.

When it comes to Mark and Lola's turn in the sleigh, he lifts her up into her seat, grabs the reins and tells the horse, "Giddy-up, Nellie."

"Seems like you right at home and completely in command of the situation," she replies.

"I've been around horses all my life," he tells her, "as far back as I can remember, starting with pony rides in Hunt Valley. Until now, I never realized how much I've missed being around them."

"Do you miss being around me, too?" she asks tenderly, then looks around to make sure no one else is on board.

"What's going on, Lola? What's on your mind?"

"Just want to be sure we're alone, except for Nellie."

"I guarantee she won't tell a soul. This sounds serious."

"That depends on you."

"You have me in suspense. Tell me what's on your mind. We're already half way around town, which is about two square blocks."

"All right. Since you asked for it, I think I'm falling in love with you."

Mark pulls the reins to slow up Nellie's gait and looks at Lola whose face is aglow with a blush on her cheeks. He pauses to inhale a deep breath and let's it out slowly.

"You're very special to me and important to my family. I've thought a lot about you and me, more than you'll ever know. But, and it's a big 'but,' it wouldn't be fair for us to get serious at this moment. I'm still trying to get my feet on the ground at Ridgefield."

"So, for the time being, we'll be good friends?" she asks with regret.

"Very good friends, maybe even lovers, if that's what you want, but not beholding to one another at this moment in time."

"In that case, better give me a kiss to hold me over during 'the winter of my discontent.'"

Mark ties the reins to a fitting on the front of the sleigh and permits Nellie to trot the rest of the trip on 'automatic pilot,' since she's very familiar with the route. He reaches over and gives Lola a kiss that seems to last 30 seconds.

When their sleigh ride is over, the wedding reception is over too.

Mike is waiting by his car with Little Mac at his side. After Lola walks from the sleigh to his car, she is noticeably sad but only for a moment.

"That was something special, wasn't it?" Mike asks her.

"It certainly was, in more ways than you'll ever know," she answers.

Mark watches their car pull away from the curb, with heavy grayish-white fumes coming out of the exhaust pipe, as it heads back in the direction of Chestertown.

Abigail and Mark enter their car for the drive back to Ridgefield and wave goodbye to Sandy who climbs the stairs to her new 'old' apartment over the garage.

Mark never lets the speedometer get above 35 miles an hour because of patches of ice and snow on the road. Inside their vehicle both are surprisingly silent as they reflect on a very special and beautiful Christmas Eve wedding and reception, one that they'll remember for a lifetime.

The next day is Christmas, and Mark spends the entire time with his mother and father at Cylburn in Baltimore. The three of them seem to sense a change in the air and spend almost the entire day relaxing and poring over scrap books of their lives. This is a time for reflection and soul-searching, with lots of questions but very few answers. It's a dilemma, especially for William who tries to balance family responsibilities with those of the steel mill.

The following mid-morning, Mark is back at Ridgefield and laying down an oriental carpet in his bedroom, which is completely furnished with purchases from Dixon's auction in Crumpton, at a discount of at least 50% below the retail price.

He walks into the adjoining room, his office, and glances at the calendar on a wall.

"Only a few days until New Years," he exclaims to no one in particular, "and I don't even have a date. I must be doing something wrong, knowing all these beautiful girls like Lola, Sandy and Ruth. All short-term relationships. What's going on here? What's the matter with me?"

He plops down into a leather chair, gets comfortable, swivels it 360 degrees slowly around his office and looks at shelves stacked with books on art, artists and antiques.

"This is going to be my think-tank, my private sanctuary, where I can relax and bounce things off the walls and establish priorities. The old adage, *Plan Your Work Before You Work Your Plan,* applies here and now."

He hangs a small painting, titled *Bird Whistling in Winter,* by Harvey Otis Young, on a wall above and to the right of his computer monitor. It's almost within arm's reach so that he can see the bird close-up, and even talk to it, like talking to Gertie, the squawking parrot that Knute Runagrun brought to Annette's Antiques many months ago. The only difference here is that the bird in the painting doesn't talk back.

He walks around the room and admires the black and white photos of his Breeze track team that hang on one wall.

"I love these photographs of The Betterton Breeze winning the mile relay at the Harvest Fest in Rock Hall. Look at Jessie, extending his chest across the finish line, timed perfectly by Manny with his camera."

On the opposite wall are framed photos of his life, starting with his first lesson in swimming where his father let go of him to see if he would float in the pool. The caption below the photo reads: "When he went under the water, his mother cried out, 'For heaven's sake, don't let him drown until we can find out what he can do with his life!' "

There are several large photos of him running track for Hopkins, along with those taken of Annette and Sandy in Betterton and of Dixon's auction.

"Good memories," he says to himself, "that will serve me when I think how far I've come in such a short time."

On Friday afternoon, Mark telephones his mother in Baltimore.

"It just occurred to me that I haven't been to antique row on Howard Street for a few years," he tells her. "I have a hunch that there's something inside one of those stores for me. Tomorrow, around noon, I'm planning to drive over to Baltimore."

"You have a premonition?" Sara asks curiously. "By all means, you should always follow a hunch, like betting on a horse not expected to win at Pimlico."

"If I don't get mugged while I'm there, I'd like to invite you and Dad for dinner at Haussner's Restaurant at 6. No need to make a reservation, because they don't take them. We'll just have to wait in line after we get there."

"Wonderful news, son," she answers quickly. "I can't wait to tell your father. He's been working Saturdays at the mill, trying to catch up on some paperwork. I'll tell him about your invitation as soon as he walks in the door. Until tomorrow, may God watch over you."

After Mark hangs up the phone, he checks his wallet to see if he has a few checks in case he finds something to buy on Howard Street.

"I know one dealer, Jimmy Judd, who'll be happy to see me and try to entice me into buying something. His line is always, 'buy and give,' meaning buy a piece of art and give it to someone, so they'll remember you every time they look at it."

The next morning around 10:30, Mark carries a cup of coffee in one hand as he opens the door of his BMW. He straps himself into a custom-fitted leather seat that grips his body like a racecar, and soon he's driving along Eastern Neck Island Road into Rock Hall. He turns right at the only blinking yellow light in town, onto route 20, and heads in the direction of Chestertown, 12 miles away. Time goes by quickly as he listens repeatedly to a CD of Reggie in a New York recording studio, as a backup guitarist on Les Paul's re-recording of *How High The Moon*.

After reaching Chestertown, he turns right onto route 213, passes Washington College, where he anchored the mile relay in a win for Hopkins five years ago. He nods his head with pride, reminiscing about the track meet against the Shoremen, who were considered superior with Ells Boyd, Hank Mazurski, Mickey DiMaggio and Lew Buckley running their tails off.

"Now, why would I remember those guys?" he asks himself. "Guess it's because the Blue Jays of Hopkins pulled off an upset."

He drives down a hill that curves gradually to the left, crosses over the decaying concrete and steel Chester River Bridge with its antiquated drawbridge that looks as if it will plunge into the river at any moment.

Once over the bridge, he's now in Queen Anne's County. Thirty minutes later he passes Centreville, an historic town and government seat of Queen Anne's County. Within another 30 minutes, he's passing cars on route 50 and 301, heading south.

Coming into his view is the concrete bridge over Kent Narrows onto Kent Island, situated on about 2,000 acres, with creek and coves galore. The island stretches laterally like a giant claw, for about 10 miles.

When he glances to the right and left sides of the road, he notices hundreds of four-story buildings clustered and sprouting up like mushrooms. It's over a thousand condos packed into one square mile. Most of the buildings were built after 1952, when the first span of the Chesapeake Bay Bridge was completed; the second span wasn't completed until 1973.

"Why can't the people of Kent County," he exclaims, "get it into their miniscule brains that a small increase in development, certainly not anywhere approaching this level, is good for decaying hamlets like Betterton and Rock Hall. People would be flocking there, like Canada geese, for the chance to live near the Bay."

He turns his thoughts and attention to the traffic of big rigs whose drivers must be on a tight schedule as they pass him on both sides of the freeway.

"Doubling the size of Rock Hall," he continues talking to himself, "represents an additional 900 people to the census records."

He grips the steering wheel of his BMW much tighter in a fit of anger.

"I give up," he concludes."It's like banging my head against a brick wall. They *want* their small towns? They've *got* their small towns. Maybe that's why Ocean City is so popular. It's only 100 miles away and booming. And the women are hot, but not as hot as in Annapolis."

He scratches his head and shakes it from side to side.

"Now, why in the hell am I thinking about Annapolis? Maybe it's because of the night we celebrated the end of a special SEAL seminar, when I was blindfolded, forced to wear head gear over my ears, and delivered to a room for a sexual encounter with a sizzling sexpot. That whole night seemed unreal. Or was it a figment of my imagination?"

The entrance to the Chesapeake Bay Bridge, is approaching, which takes him into Prince George's County. In a matter of 1 ½ hours, he's navigated through three counties in Maryland, with more to come.

Surprisingly, the traffic heading north on Route 97 towards Baltimore is not too bad, with no congestion, accidents or breakdowns so far, but plenty of patrol cars with their lights flashing along the right side of the freeway.

"Speeding tickets are expensive," he tells himself, "and those cops write them faster than you can say *Jackie Robinson*. Better forget about Annapolis and concentrate completely on the road to Charm City."

When he arrives at antique row on Howard Street in Baltimore, he finds a parking spot in the middle of the block, directly in front of Judd's Antiques.

He walks a few steps into a vestibule and pushes a doorbell. Seconds later, a buzzer sounds, releasing the lock. He steps inside and surveys the clutter everywhere, just like Annette's Antiques, but better quality clutter.

"Well, Mom, look who's just walked in," says Jimmy Judd from the far end of the store. He's dressed in his Oxford button-down white shirt with the sleeves rolled up and a pleasing smile on his handsome face

"Good to see you again, Jimmy, and you too, Catherine," Mark says buoyantly. "I see you're still keeping the books for your son," he yells in a louder voice since she's slightly hard of hearing at 90 years of age.

"I've been doing it for 60 years, first for my husband and now Jimmy. What else would I be doing at my age? And don't ask me how old I am," she responds with a tease while adjusting her vintage hat and collar of a dark two-piece suit.

"I haven't seen you for years," Jimmy remarks, "especially at the local auctions around town. What brings you to Charm City?"

"I've been away," Mark replies with a broader smile, "in Iraq, off and on for four years, and, are you ready for this?"

"Ready for what?' he asks.

"I'm now a private dealer in the art business, known as Mark Hopkins, agent triple seven."

"Welcome to the game, or should I call it a racket?" bellows Jimmy.

"Ditto," shouts Catherine as she plops down into her seat.

"I like the look on your face, Mark," Jimmy acknowledges. "You should and will do well in the art business because you have good instincts. I still remember when you beat me out of a Renoir painting up for auction many years ago.

"It's nice to see you prospering here," says Mark. "You're one of the last of the Mohicans along antique row."

"Over the past 10 years," answers Jimmy, "we've seen an increase in crime that discourages customers from shopping here. It's mostly about drugs. Now, as we get up in age, over 39, way over 39, we're thinking about moving down the street and renting a stall in a larger building. We don't want to close up entirely and walk away because we love what we're doing."

"That would be a shame," interjects Catherine, "a shame on the city for not using the police force to protect this area which is vital to the city. I remember when people came from four states to shop along antique row and walk to Lexington Market for lunch."

After exchanging memories and examining the inventory on display in Judd's Antiques, Mark tells them that he wants to pay a brief visit to Thames Antiques, about 15 stores down the street from them.

"The last time I saw Thames," admits Mark, "he was gloating over a watercolor of Indians camped near a lake by Alfred Jacob Miller, that he picked up from an itinerant beggar who knocked on his door and wanted some money to buy a fifth of whiskey. Guess I shouldn't blame him for gloating."

"You're not jealous, are you?" asks Jimmy. "Your time will come eventually."

"Perhaps I am jealous," answers Mark. "Those opportunities never happen to me, I mean, someone literally handing you a fabulous piece of art. Where I'm living now, you have to dig, dig, and dig, and most of the time, come up only with clay."

A minute later, Mark is ringing the bell at Thames Antiques. When the buzzer releases the lock, he steps inside but has difficulty in surveying the clutter because there's not a light on in the shop.

"Whatya want?" asks Thames, the 50-year old owner, who remains seated at his desk in the middle of the shop.

"Would it be too much trouble to turn on a light or two? asks Mark.

"Help yourself. Turn on all the lights you need," Thames orders.

After Mark switches on two large table lamps, a layer of dust over all the clutter is evident and much worse than inside Annette's Antiques. Here, Thames probably never handled a feathered duster or dust cloth in his lifetime. Or maybe he keeps it that way intentionally, because antique dealers like to see the dust. It means the stuff has been sitting in its spot for a while, and perhaps a lower price is possible.

"I doubt if you remember me," Mark utters, "but I've been in your store many times before I went in the Navy. Been down to see Jimmy Judd and his mother"

"Can't say I do," he answers. "Them and me are the last dealers on *Harrid* Street. *Ya* looking for *anythink* special?"

"No, not really. Just browsing. Do you mind?"

"Help *yurselp*," he replies while leaning his beer belly onto his desktop. "Watch out so *ya* don't slip or trip over *somethink*. This place is getting stuffed, like me. I'm planning to go to the

Quairyum at the *Inna Harber* at 2 to see their new *inner-restin* expo, and have a slice of lemon *moran pie* in Lexington Market."

"Speaking of interesting," Mark asks, "any interesting paintings come your way lately?"

"What *ya* see is what *ya* get. I don't hide *anythink*. It's all out *dare*. Look *'rown, Ya* might spot *somethink*."

Mark navigates carefully through the maze of stuff cluttered everywhere and finds himself near a back wall. As he tries to lean forward and get a closer look at an old print of Mount Vernon Place, his foot bangs against a framed painting standing vertically on the ground, between two showcases of costume jewelry. Because Thames is something of a miser who wants to keep his expenses down, he hardly ever turns on any lights in his shop. A buyer really has to strain his or her eyes to inspect anything here. On the contrary, maybe that's Thames' way of adding suspense to the art of discovering a gem within the clutter.

Mark carefully pulls the framed painting towards him, holds it at eye level and has a closer look at it near a lamp that provides just enough light to see what he wants to see.

"What do you know about this piece?"

"*Nothink*" groans Thames.

"And how much is it?"

"10,000 clams, ah, bucks," exclaims Thames.

Mark doesn't know quite how to react here. Perhaps Thames is playing games, or throwing out a price to get a laugh, or wanting some reaction or response from a customer.

"I probably could buy his entire store for that price," Mark says to himself. "It's typical of an unsophisticated dealer to throw out a price simply to see if it strikes a bell with a potential buyer."

Mark pauses for about 10 seconds and begins to walk towards Thames.

"I'll take it!" exclaims Mark in a loud voice. "Write up an invoice for me."

"Show me the money, first!" Thames answers by pronouncing the word 'money' in two distinct syllables and raises his right hand into the air and rubs the thumb and two forefingers together to give him a clear sign to come up with the payment before he writes out an invoice.

Mark opens his wallet and removes a check. He looks around for a spot in the shop, somewhere, anywhere, just a one-by-one-foot area should be sufficient. He finally moves a few porcelain figures on an old table and clears a space. He fills out his check for $10,000 made payable to Thames Antiques and hands it to him.

"And here's my Maryland Trader's License Number," Mark informs him, "so that there's no added sales tax. It's for resale."

After Thames hands Mark his receipt, he never thanks him for the purchase. Not even a 'good luck' and 'come back again' or 'why don't you look around for something else to buy.' He, however, pauses to have a closer look at Mark's address.

"Rock Hall? Where in the hell is Rock Hall?" he asks.

"Down on the Eastern Shore of Maryland, near Chestertown and Washington College."

"Never heard of it," he says with a smirk.

After folding the receipt and placing it in his wallet, Mark asks, "Can you tell me how and where you got it?"

"A black guy knocked at my back door, said he had some things in his truck that he wanted to sell, so I picked out the painting. That was it."

"I hope it wasn't stolen," Mark utters with raised eyebrows.

"Don't ask, don't tell, that's my credo," echoes Thames. "If it turns out that it's stolen, bring it back, and I'll give you back *ya* money."

"Would you write that on the front of the receipt, and sign it?" asks Mark, as he removes the receipt from his wallet and hands it back to Thames.

"I would and will," answers Thames.

Mark leaves Thames' store, walks a half block back to his car and places the painting in the trunk of his BMW. While he drives along Howard Street, heading north over the rusted steel frame of the Howard Street Bridge, he is full of excitement. He can hardly control himself and his BMW.

"Knowledge is power and money in the bank," he brags outloud. "After I saw the subject matter and brushstroke, I realized it was something special. Then, in the lower right-hand corner was the signature of the artist, clearly signed in block letters, with a date of 1878. I knew immediately that I hit the jackpot."

In another 15 minutes, he is pulling his car into the long circular driveway of his parent's home at 4915 Greenspring Avenue. The home sits in the middle of a small park called Cylburn Park, which, in the old days, was considered the keystone of magnificent estates ringing the city of Baltimore.

It was the home of Mark's great-grandfather, William Hopkins Sr., the brains behind Bethlehem Steel, who, with money flowing in, thanks to the industrial revolution, bragged to everyone that he made the best steel in the world, had the most beautiful wife, the fastest horses and the grandest home in Baltimore.

Mark pauses to look up at the tall central tower, designed in a simplified Second empire style by the architect of City Hall, George A. Frederick. The foundation skirt was built of gneiss, a stone quarried from Bare Hills, nearby. Landscaping around the mansion was the creation of the Olmsted brothers. Everyone connected with the building of the mansion is included in 'Who's Who in America.'

Mark removes the painting from the trunk of his car and rings the front door bell. A maid welcomes him inside a small vestibule with a mosaic marble floor, and a leaded-glass transom and mirrors on one wall beside a row of hooks on which to hang your coat. He walks down the main hall with its cathedral ceiling and parquet floors of oak, maple and black walnut, laid out in a diamond pattern. He turns left into the drawing room and sets the painting on a wide ledge against a row of leather-bound books, in the far corner, next to a Philadelphia grandfather's clock.

He looks closely again at the impressionist painting.

"If I pat myself on my back," he says while laughing, "I'm sure to get a broken arm, but timing is everything. And this beauty is destined for distinction. It belongs in a museum."

About this time his mother walks into the drawing room, and greets him tenderly with a kiss and hug.

"I thought I heard the doorbell ring. Missed you, son, although it only been a few days since you were here. You look very excited. Do you care to share it or am I misreading something?"

"Yes, I'm excited for many reasons, especially to be with you again, and all in one piece. No mugging along Howard Street, but a little sparing inside one of the antique stores. I'll wait until Dad gets here and explain everything. Is he still under pressure at the mill?"

"You know him. A thousand horses couldn't slow him down. I'm afraid to think what might be in store for him, for me and for you."

William walks unexpectedly into the room and his spirits are lifted considerably.

"Wonderful that we can be together again. Would anyone like a cocktail, besides me?"

After no one answers, he mixes himself a cocktail of scotch on the rocks, and tells them, "As Chuck Thompson would say at those Orioles games, 'How 'bout that!' "

"I think he said, 'Ain't the beer cold,' according to his biographer, Gordon Beard," Mark says as a matter of record to correct his father's remark.

"A new 'old' home is not all that I own," he tells them.

He walks to the corner of the drawing room, picks up the painting that he just bought at Thames Antiques, and holds it up so they can get a good look at it. "What do you think of this?" he asks them.

His mother and father join arms, as they admire it together from a distance of a few feet. A glitter of satisfaction begins to cover their faces.

"That could hang on the wall of any museum in America or Europe, couldn't it?" asks Sara.

"Or Walters Art Gallery nearby," boasts William. "It's remarkable, poetic, relaxing to look at it. That was always my criteria in buying a good painting. It had to be relaxing to the eyes and mind. What's going on here? Are you giving it to us?"

"Sorry, Dad, this baby is going to auction in London. I think it's one of the best paintings ever painted by Albert Edelfelt, the Finnish impressionist, who trained in Antwerp and at the French Academy in Paris. I've only seen one of his paintings on exhibition, but studied photographs of his works in Finland and Russia, as well as European and British museums. His portraits are so captivating that, once you've seen one close-up, you never forget it. Never dreamed that I would ever have an opportunity to own one of his paintings."

"I love the pose," says his mother. "An attractive young girl, dressed in all her white finery, with chapeau of lace, reading a book, under a tree, with dapples of sunlight streaming through the leaves. Looks like a scene out of the pages of Margaret Mitchell's *Gone With The Wind*, but painted about 60 years before she wrote her masterpiece. Now, how can you get anything better than that?"

"It's about 22 by 26 inches," acknowledges his father who spreads his hand along the sides of the painting to take a quick measurement. "Where did you find it, and don't tell me you discovered it at Crumpton?"

"No, Dad, it was purely by accident when I dropped in to see a dealer along Howard Street. It didn't come cheaply, though."

"Are you going to tell us how much it cost? his mother asks.

"Take a guess," he replies.

"$25,000," answers his father.

His mother refuses to hazard a guess and puts one hand over her mouth.

"A cool $10,000, not exactly a bargain price since it came from a crummy shop where everything inside was covered with dust," Mark growls with a touch of disdain, "I had to control my emotions inside Thames Antiques for fear the owner might realize its tremendous value."

"Sounds as if you're upset, perhaps envious, that the dealer could squeeze $10,000 out of you. You and I know that, when you're involved in buying something and confident about its value, the risk is lower, and there's a big reward ahead. Personally, I think you've got something here that's worth ten times what you paid for it."

"I agree too. Congratulations," echoes his mother, while giving him a gentle kiss on his cheek.

"Well I didn't exactly steal it like a pirate, nor did Thames lure me with his brash demeanor. Wish I could keep it but I'll need the money for my project at Ridgefield."

He takes the painting in one hand over to a corner of the drawing room and places it inside a 7-foot high, antique Dutch armoire, normally used to store expensive linens. He locks the door and spends a few seconds to look at the key, which he weighs it in his hand momentarily, then hands it to his mother for safe-keeping.

"I'll take a digital photo of it tomorrow morning," he explains. "If you don't mind, I'd like to leave it here temporarily while planning my next step, which includes contacting Christie's and Sotheby's in London, two of the biggest auction houses in the world. This beauty may need a light cleaning of the dirt or grime and old varnish although collectors prefer to bid on paintings that are untouched by a conservator.

"If the experts at the auction houses in London feel it should be cleaned before auction, they have some of the best restorers and conservators in the world who could bring the painting back to its original state."

He pauses and raises both hands with clenched fists, like a boxer who just won a tough fight for the championship. He walks closer to them and puts his arms around their shoulders.

"This whole afternoon, starting with my drive over the Bay Bridge and finding this gem of a painting, gives me a good appetite for a dinner at Haussner's. Let's freshen-up and meet down here in about 20 minutes. We'll take one car. I plan on spending the night here and driving back to Rock Hall in the morning."

Chapter 6

An hour later, Mark drives his father's '83 Mercedes 500 along Eastern Avenue in East Baltimore, turns left on Clinton Street, and pulls into a small parking lot opposite Haussner's and behind Michael and Ann Yeager's Music Store.

"No line tonight," he remarks as they're walking across Clinton Street. "Maybe their business is down since Mrs. Haussner passed away, and her daughter and son-in law are running things, or it could be customers want healthier foods with lower cholesterol and entrees without heavy gravies."

After taking a few steps inside the main dining room, they gaze at all the incredible art and antiques decorating every foot of space imaginable. Although they dined there many times over the years, the thrill of sitting in the splendor of fine art is always something special.

Stephen George, co-owner and maitre d', leads them to a table near one of their favorite paintings, Arthur John Elsley's "I'se Biggest!" in which a smiling girl of four, in a dress with frills, stands on a large book and measures her height against a St. Bernard sitting behind her with its nose held high in the air.

The history of Haussner's Restaurant is one of giant proportions. William 'Willy' Haussner, a great-grandson to a baroness, was born in 1894 in Roth, Bavaria, near Nurnberg, Germany. He trained as a Master Chef and immigrated in 1925 to America to work for a reformed Mennonite family in Peoria, Illinois. Within three months, he moved to Baltimore to live with his brother, Karl, and the following year, opened a small food market on the 13-foot wide ground floor of a two-story row house on the corner of Eastern Avenue and Clinton Street. Nine years later, he bought three row houses across the street which he converted into a restaurant.

In 1935, he married Frances Wilke three weeks after meeting her. She was born in Bontkirchen, north of Dusseldorf, Germany in 1909, one of three children who all came to Baltimore in 1924. She helped her father and brother run their first grocery store on Preston and Ensor Streets, in the center of Baltimore, which was soon expanded into 12 locations around the city.

Frances is credited with having a collector's itch, and with her husband's support, began an incredible quest to acquire fine paintings, sculpture of marble and bronze, and antiques of all kinds. The itch lasted for over 30 years, and some dealers suspected that their purchases were probably tax-deductible since they enhanced the atmosphere and reputation for fine dining.

Every dealer in Baltimore, Philadelphia and New York was aware of the Haussner's appetite for art and telephoned them whenever they found a good piece to sell them. Occasionally each would browse the auctions or a familiar shop alone, and owners scurried to lay out the welcome mat by showing them something special, something they were reserving for them. That is, until Willy died in 1963. By then, there was no room anywhere for additional works of art, including their private residence in Homewood and farm in Western Maryland.

Frances, with the support of her only daughter, Francie, and her husband, Stephen George, carried on the well-earned reputation as Baltimore's best restaurant until the matriarch died in 1999.

Mark pulls out a chair so that his mother can sit between them, and does the same for his father.

"Enjoy your dinner," Stephen says while handing each one a menu. "A waitress will be with you momentarily."

Within a minute later, an attractive middle-aged brunette, dressed in an immaculate white uniform with a black lace apron, sets a basket of freshly-baked and assorted muffins and rolls in the middle of their table.

"Would you like to have something from the bar?" she asks with a smile.

Mark orders a frosted glass of his favorite beer, Anchor Steam, brewed in San Francisco since 1896, and tasting every bit as good, if not better, than the German imports that Haussner's has in kegs behind the bar.

His father orders a bottle of Burgundy vintner's reserve from Kendall Jackson in Napa Valley.

"For this occasion, all our beverages are imported from California tonight. For your mother and me, I chose Kendall-Jackson, not only because it's a good vineyard, but because the owner, Jess Jackson, also co-owns one of the most exciting thoroughbreds in racing today. She's a filly named Rachel Alexandra, bigger than some of the stallions that she runs against. I love her spirit and gallantry. It inspires and invigorates me when I'm feeling low at the mill. The wine is very good, but that filly is fantastic."

"Awesome," interjects his mother with a sense of pride, "to see that filly cross the finish line ahead of the best thoroughbreds running today."

After perusing the menu and its more than 50 entrees, Mark orders the seafood combination platter, which includes a crab cake, a finger-sized lobster, fried oysters and clams, and scallops sautéed in butter, with side dishes of creamed spinach and Brussels Sprouts.

He shakes his head in wonderment.

"I know of no other restaurant where you can select two side dishes from a list of 27 vegetables," exclaims Mark. "Never knew there was that number of vegetables in the world, but they're here, on the menu. It always makes the choice difficult but satisfying."

"Age before beauty," interjects Sara with a laugh. "You should have let me order first."

"I guess I'm still used to being a Navy officer, where rank has its privileges. Forgive me, mom. What are you ordering?"

"I'd like the roast goose with stuffed dressing, sauerkraut, and creamed cauliflower," she answers with a smack of her lips. "Being with the two men in my life arouses my appetite too."

"I think I'll settle for the sauerbraten, with Tyrolean potato dumplings and buttered carrots," boasts his father. "My cardiologist will have fits, but this is a special night."

Over the course of the next hour, all three enjoy a reunion, with happy spirits flowing easily. Their enjoyment of the dinner and satisfaction of being together combine to form a memorable experience.

"Since I'm now a private dealer in art and learning more about paintings and their prices at auction, I discovered that story-telling paintings, like this one by Elsley hanging on the wall behind our table, are growing in popularity. I would bet that Haussner never paid more than a few thousand dollars for it in the 1940's, and today it's probably worth more than $300,000."

"There's no law against being frugal, is there?" Sara admits. "I mean, being intelligent and seizing the opportunity to invest in art and possibly writing it off as an expense? I think that's just being smart in business."

"When you think about it, you could have bought a Monet or Van Gogh for a few thousand dollars during the depression, but most people, including my father, were worried about putting food on the table for their family and not hanging a painting on the wall of their home," William admits reluctantly.

"Now that I'm a dealer," Mark tells them, "would you excuse me while I walk around the restaurant and have a closer look at their collection."

About 15 minutes later they're all enjoying their entrees when Mark's father unexpectedly asks him, "May I have a taste of your crab cake?"

Mark lifts his plate over so his father can use his fork to snare a portion of his crab cake.

"Thank you, son." He chews it carefully to savor the flavor and continues, "It's good, but not as good as Mom Muller's on Bond Street."

It may seem strange that he would begin talking about the food in one restaurant while eating in another, but there's no better time to talk about good food than when you're eating it.

"Haussner's crab cakes," he continues, "have mostly back fin, but Mom Muller's had back fin and a touch of claw meat. The addition of claw meat gave their crab cake its sweetness and special taste. You weren't even born when your mother and I would go to Muller's for steamed crabs and crab cakes, and occasionally an appetizer of fried oysters."

"Oh, how your father loved those oysters. Is it true that they contain lots of iron and other elements that supposedly increase your sexual potential?" asks Sara while blushing.

"Yes, my dear, you're right as usual, but the key was the seasoning of the seafood. Old Bay seasoning was not around in those days. You had to make your own seasoning. I remember talking to old man Frank 'Pop' Muller about *his* special seasoning, particularly for hard-shell blue crabs from the Chesapeake Bay."

"I bet it was a heavily-guarded secret," admits Mark.

"Pop was reluctant to talk about it, since it was his own recipe of vinegar and a dash of liquid mustard. I watched him mix and pour it into the bottom of a giant iron kettle, never measuring it, like Julia Child and Jacques Pepin. He then dumped in a bushel of blue crabs, added a sprinkle of black pepper, and covered it with an iron lid about two-feet in diameter. The kettle was then hoisted with a pulley and moved over to an open hearth of burning wood and coals."

"Before you continue, Dad, exactly where was Muller's located?"

"In *Fells Point*," he answers quickly, "but it wasn't called *Fells Point* then."

"How big a place did they have?"

"They converted two row houses, each about 15 feet wide and 100 feet long, on Bond Street, only a few blocks from the harbor where all the ships docked. At 709, he converted the row house into his restaurant with a bar in the front, dining tables and chairs in the middle, and kitchen cabinets and cooking ovens in the rear. In the adjoining house, 711, he had a cement pad covering the entire ground floor, from front to back, for his seafood alleyway where he shucked oysters and clams and steamed his crabs, and a passage way for people to order and carry out their order."

"And where did they live?"

"Their living quarters were on the second floor, accessed by climbing a flight of stairs in the alleyway. They had bedrooms over both ground floors for their eight daughters and one son. Can you imagine climbing those stairs every night after standing on your feet 10 hours or more?"

"It seems to me that you went there not only to eat but to see the Muller family, too," Mark declares.

"You're exactly right. I never thought about it before, but it's true. Pop thought I was German like him, maybe because of my slight beer belly. He had a wonderful raspy accent, and spoke always with one-half a cigar, lit or unlit, in the corner of his mouth. I think he used to suck on it, like a lollipop. He never talked much, just concentrated on his work. He was a character, only 5 foot 6, weighed about 225, with a beer belly twice the size of mine."

He pauses to take a bite of his sauerbraten and smacks his lips in enjoyment over the taste.

"Would anyone like to taste my sauerbraten? It's probably marinated in a wine-vinegar that tenderizes the meat so that it almost melts in your mouth."

When no one responds, he resumes his memories of 'Pop' Muller.

"Didn't laugh much and spoke very few words in a strong German accent. Sadly, he wore a slight scowl on his face, probably from having to stand for hours on that cold and damp cement slab in all kinds of weather, in wet shoes and pants, with no heat in the alleyway, except from the open hearth when he steamed his crabs."

"No wonder he had a scowl on his face," answers Mark.

"I remember one time," his father says while leaning back in his chair and laughing, "after he had been shucking a gallon of oysters, his wife poked her head out the kitchen doorway and yelled down the alleyway, '*Gimmee* two dozen clams, shucked.' "

"Forgive me if I begin laughing before getting to the punch line. Pop hollered back down the alleyway in a very loud and long drawn-out rebuttal, 'What the hell's wrong with the *ursers*? I'm not shucking any more clams today Let 'em eat *ursters*!'

"The old man," his father continues with nods and rolls of his head and a grin from ear to ear, "was always standing on his feet, shucking oysters and clams when they were in season, steaming crabs, and God knows what else. I learned the lessons of hard work and devotion to his family from him."

"And what about his wife?" Mark asks curiously.

"She was a character too," adds his mother while savoring a morsel of her fresh breast of goose. "Everyone called her 'Mom.' She stood only 5 foot 2 at the most, weighed probably 110 pounds soaking wet, with thin-wire glasses halfway on her nose, hair tied tightly in a bun, and always an oversized clean-white apron around her waist, hanging almost down to her ankles, with two large deep pockets in the front where she would 'stash her cash' or 'stow her dough.'

"I saw her many times," continues his mother, with increasing gusto, "barge through three drunken seaman arguing at the front bar, grab one of them by his shirt just below his chin, and pull him through the front door and into the sidewalk outside their restaurant. Then she'd give him a good scolding or a brief lecture, and when the poor sap said he was broke and needed some money to get back to his ship, she'd take some cash out of her apron and shove it into his hand."

Mark's father laughs out loud and growls, "How I'd like to do that to some of those union thugs who threaten me, except giving them money, of course."

"The Muller's are my kind of people," admits Mark. "I wish I could have known them."

"There's more, Mark," interjects his mother. "About their eight daughters and only son, only four of the daughters worked in the restaurant. Mom Muller was as tough on her children as she was on those seamen. Those four girls worked double jobs, because they were married, too. Each still had to care for their husband and children."

"Yes, the Muller's taught us plenty about hard work and the importance of family," his father concludes. "They didn't have anything fancy in their restaurant. The walls were bare. On the ceiling were tin sheets decorated in relief, like embossed printing. People primarily came to eat their wonderful crabs, crab cakes, oysters and clams, at very reasonable prices."

"Do you remember some of their prices?"

"Like it was yesterday. The big crabs, at least 8 inches tip-to-tip, cost a dollar each, from 1930 to 1950, one price that never changed. A large fry, which included six large oysters, dipped into oyster juice and cracker meal and padded in Mom Muller's or Mom Donahue's hands, and fried in lard came with 6 crackers and a cup of Cole slaw, all for 38 cents and her customers growled that it was too much to pay.

"It's funny," he recalls, "but one time I asked her about buying some art to decorate their place, like Haussner's. Mom was outraged and stubborn, and told me in so many words, 'If the people want art, let 'em go to Haussner's. If they want seafood, we've got the best seafood in *Bawlmer*!'"

Finally, Sara recalls one last characteristic of Mom Muller. "At the urging of her customers, she would whistle the *Indian Love Song* by Rudolf Friml from the 1924 operetta, *Rose Marie*. Now, isn't that the *cat's meow*?"

"That has the makings a good art film," says Mark as he almost falls out of seat from laughing.

"Are you ready for dessert?" Sara asks. "You remember Haussner's famous strawberry pies, don't you?"

"If my life depended on it," he answers apologetically, "I couldn't fit another morsel of food into my belly. I'll pass, thank you. If I don't sleep deeply tonight after eating all this rich food, it was well worth it. But you'll have to help me up the stairs to my bedroom. Remember, I'm spending the night with you."

"Then, in that case," his father answers enthusiastically, "we'll order one strawberry pie to take home with us. You may have a slice for breakfast tomorrow morning before you return to Rock Hall."

The next morning, Annette opens the front door of her antiques shop for Knute and Maureen, who enjoy helping her in the store. After Annette notices that Liz's car is still parked on the curb outside her shop, she tells them to take over the store, so that she can help her husband to move things around in their new wing. "He's still unpacking his music reference library of books," she exclaims. "I hope we don't run out of shelves."

In the front showroom, Knute talks constantly to his pet parrot, Gertie, while Maureen 'Mo' Greenspan, a retired lawyer now living on the same floor as Knute in the Senior Living Complex a few blocks away, is busy arranging some art work hanging on the walls.

"Where's Mark?" Gertie squawks in a loud raspy voice.

Knute begins laughing and looks towards Maureen.

"Did you hear what Gertie just asked me? I guess she misses him too."

"I heard every word loud and clear. That's quite a bird you have there, Knute, very astute…say, that rhymes with Knute, doesn't it? I look forward each day to hear what she has to say in the mornings. Is Gertie a 'she?' "

"I'll be damn if I know for sure. She acts like a dame: bright, witty and temperamental. Well, Gertie girl," he says while filling her trough with parrot seed, "Mark has flown the coop. He's spreading his wings in Rock Hall now and in the foreseeable future, I guess."

Knute tears a piece of newspaper headlines and places it on the bottom tray of Gertie's cage. "Here's a new word or two for you to learn today. Have a look down while I dust a few things and talk to Mo."

Before Knute can take four steps away from her cage, Gertie squawks loudly, "Oil Spill in Gulf."

"Can you beat that. Gertie can read the headlines that I laid on the bottom of her cage faster than Usain Bolt can sprint 100 meters. I'll have to get an act together like we did when we sang Irving Berlin's "Always" at the Harvest Fest and take it to the *Hippdrum* in *Balamer*."

"You were about to say something about Mark, weren't you?" Mo asks.

"Things don't seem the same here without him," admits Knute. "He was a remarkable young man that I loved like a son, so easy going, so smart, and hard working. I liked him from the moment I met him, and not because he let me move Gertie into their shop. There's not a day that goes by that I don't think about him and wish him well."

"I feel the same way, Knute," Mo answers tenderly. "He treated me better than my own son who moved to the mid-west without telling me his new address. He was so good to everyone. He gave us seniors something to be proud of when he asked us to mentor his kids, kids who were on the verge of becoming juvenile delinquents. Together, we turned them into a championship relay team. One of these days we'll have to round-up everyone, including his Betterton Breeze runners, and drive over to see him and his new farm outside Rock Hall. Did I tell you that Mark has the intention of adopting Vera's baby?"

Back at his Ridgefield farm, cloistered in the corner of his office-studio, Mark falls back in his swivel chair, and thinks about going on Wednesday to Dixon's auction in Crumpton.

"Suddenly the hunt for that elusive fox," he says to himself, "the craving to find something special at Dixon's, those Crumpton auctions are beginning to lose their appeal. Perhaps I'm through with jockeying around all those tables inside the hangar to bid for things that might be a bargain and then get damaged or stolen before you can get them to your car. Since I don't have a shop like Annette, and no interest in owning a shop like hers, the excitement of plowing through all that junk, the *quest-to-possess,* is losing some of its attraction. It's becoming 'old hat.'

"There has to be more in life than battling those dealers and collectors and rifling through the piles of stuff everywhere. For six months it was my way of life with Annette. Now it's time to switch gears. Maybe I'm spoiled by finding the Edelfelt, and a big payday ahead of me. Perhaps enough is enough, and I should concentrate on being a private dealer and build something special at Ridgefield."

While Mark is contemplating a shift of efforts, news about his move to Rock Hall has certainly aroused the interests of solicitors, who phone him daily with offers ranging from manpower to help him manage his farm, nannies looking for employment for the care for Jaime if his petition for adoption is approved by the court, and finally agents offering investment opportunities in real estate and small businesses.

One caller, however, strikes a chord with him. A company in Wilmington, on the cutting edge of green technology, asks him to consider a partnership. They're interested in building and installing wind turbines on his farm to generate electricity that could be sold to a power conglomerate in Delaware. Such a partnership would benefit him immensely, as Delaware has no state tax. He makes a note and places it in a file marked 'Pending Action.' To say he's very concerned with reducing his tax burden is an understatement. It's foremost on his mind, because the more money he can earn and save, the more he can spend on worthy projects.

Abigail telephones Mark to tell him she's on her way to see him and give him a progress report on his plans to adopt Jaime.

After arriving at Ridgefield, she suggests his filing an affidavit to determine, if possible, the identity of the child's father through DNA testing.

"The court," she discloses, "may order Bud Wayne, who is currently serving 22 years in prison, and Pretty Boy Floyd to submit blood samples to compare with Jaime's blood. At least it will determine if either of them is the true birth father." She mentions also that she has had extensive phone calls with Mo Greenspan, and that Mo should be compensated for her time and advice.

"Make out an invoice," he tells her, "and I'll write her a check from my personal account. At this stage, my plans to adopt Jaime is a personal matter and not a business expense. And hold off any further steps in the adoption process. We should give the court the opportunity to determine, if possible, the birth father of Jaime, and how Vera's estate will be probated."

Mark is excited when he tells her about his discovery of a painting by Edelfelt, and watches her eyes sparkle at the good news.

"There's only one of his paintings in an American museum that I know of," she gushes, "but I could be wrong here. The Met in New York has a beautiful portrait that I've seen on exhibition there. The face of his model is something you never forget."

"Here's my camera," says Mark. "I'd like you to download the photos of the Edelfelt, select a good one, and send it to experts at Sotheby's and Christie's in London for their opinion on a possible consignment in one of their upcoming impressionist-painting sales in January. I foresee a big payday for us. Maybe I can make a name for myself and our team at Ridgefield."

Mark sneezes twice in succession, the second louder and longer than the first. He's been nursing a dripping nose for several days and decides a quick drive to Walgreens in Rock Hall would be a good idea to get some advice from the pharmacist.

The trip from Ridgefield to the parking lot at Walgreens normally takes only five minutes. But halfway along Eastern Neck Island Road, Mark spots one of the largest motor homes he's ever seen, bigger than a Greyhound Scenic-Cruiser, blocking both lanes of the road.

"What the hell's going on here?" he exclaims. "Looks like the driver is trying to make a turn into the Bay Shore Campgrounds, owned by Fred Wick Jr. If he backs up another foot, he'll be in the drainage ditch."

As Mark slows down and shifts his motor into idle, he notices that it's a Gulf Stream Motor Coach, about 42-feet long and 8-feet wide, with "Yellowstone Luxury Class A" stenciled on the side.

The driver puts his head halfway out the window to look down at the clearance between his left front wheel and the shoulder of the gravel road leading into the campgrounds.

"I don't believe it," he remarks with a gasp. "Just when I've telling everyone that no one comes to towns like Rock Hall, there in living color is a Justice of the Supreme Court. At least, that man looks like him, or am I dreaming?"

About a minute later, the driver of the motor coach finishes jockeying back and forth and proceeds into the campgrounds that caters mostly to campers with mobile homes and trailers and a big appetite for fish and crabs freshly caught at their doorstep. It's a popular destination for those who want to vacation for up to six months on 30 acres, situated directly on the Chesapeake Bay.

When Mark looks up at the shinning sun and blue skies, a gaggle of geese flying in a *V* formation seems to be leading him into town again and on his way to Walgreens.

When he finally arrives at their parking lot, he notices that all the parking spaces directly facing their building are occupied, except for two spaces on either side of the front door, which are reserved for handicap persons. He parks his BMW in the middle of seven empty spaces parallel to the building and perpendicular to Route 20, the main road into the Walgreens complex.

He looks to his right and left, then proceeds to walk across the driveway large enough to accommodate two lanes of traffic. There are no cars moving anywhere in the parking lot.

Suddenly, without any warning, a cream-colored Jeep cuts in front of him, so closely that the driver's side mirror brushes against his shirt. A step closer towards Walgreens would have been fatal. The Jeep must have been traveling over 45 mph.

Mark is stunned and frozen in his last footstep. A few seconds later, after he regains his senses, he walks with a stutter step quickly over to the Jeep that screeched to a halt and parked in the handicapped spot on the left side of the front door.

In the passenger seat is a heavy-set woman, perhaps 30 years old, wearing a light-colored checkered flannel shirt and facing forward in her seat. She doesn't bother to look to her right through her open window to see Mark approaching her window.

"What in the hell are you doing?" he shouts. "You almost killed me!"

The driver hesitates a few seconds, leans forward with his hands still gripping tightly the steering wheel, then turns his head toward Mark.

"I thought you saw me," he answers nonchalantly.

"Are you crazy, man?" shouts Mark furiously. "You're supposed to watch out for me, for people walking in the driveway. People have the right of way here. You must've been going 45 miles an hour or more, in a walkway for people and children, too."

The driver turns his head back again, with no further display of emotion. He continues to lean slightly forward with both hands gripping the steering wheel, staring straight ahead as if occupied by another thought bouncing around in his head.

Mark is trembling and angry enough to pull him out of his car and beat him to a pulp, but realizes that's not going to accomplish anything. On the contrary, it might put him in jail.

He walks into Walgreens and heads towards the pharmacy in the back of the store. Halfway there, he pauses in the aisle, takes out his cell phone, and dials 911.

"Is this an emergency?" the dispatcher asks.

"A jerk almost ran me over with his car," he screams into his cell phone. "He could have killed me. Something should be done right away before he ends up killing someone else."

Marks words are overheard by several people shopping in a nearby aisle, who freeze and listen closely to his remarks.

The dispatcher explains that the sheriff has no authority in the private parking lot of Walgreens.

"That's their responsibility," the dispatcher tells him. "You have to take it up with Walgreens. Outside Walgreens' property is another matter. Take it up with the sheriff in Rock Hall. Maybe he can assist you."

Mark hangs up abruptly, pauses, and speed-dials Lieutenant Morehaus, Chief of Police of Rock Hall.

"Officer Morehaus, it's Mark Hopkins. Remember me when you helped to catch Vera's murderer about six months ago? A jerk almost ran me over in Walgreen's parking lot. The 911 dispatcher said you have no authority on Walgreens property since it's private property. Can you bend the rules and help me out? Sooner or later, this guy's going to hurt or kill someone, and I don't want it to be anyone I know in Rock Hall."

Mark walks to a far corner of Walgreens where he can talk without being overheard by customers.

"I'm in my patrol car, in the parking lot of the Village Hardware Store, across the street from Walgreens," Morehaus tells him. "I'll keep an eye out for that Jeep coming out of Walgreens and see what develops."

A minute later, neither occupant has left the Jeep to go into Walgreens. The driver shakes his head from side to side and says in a loud voice, 'Shit." Then he turns on the ignition and backs out of his parking spot, and drives out of the lot so fast that his wheels screech in two quick turns to the right, followed a few seconds later by another turn to the right onto Route 20, without stopping at the stop sign there.

He accelerates his vehicle for the next three blocks and passes under the blinking yellow traffic light at the intersection of Route 20 and Route 544.

Following about 100 feet behind the Jeep, Morehaus flips a switch on his console to record the speed of the Jeep.

"It looks like Mark was right," he tells himself and turns on the siren and flashing red lights of his patrol car.

The Jeep pulls to the right shoulder, and the driver slams the gearshift into the idle position.

Morehaus approaches the driver's side cautiously with his right hand close to his pistol in its holster. He bends his upper body downward and looks directly into the driver's face.

"Turn off the motor," he orders the driver sternly.

After looking more closely into the driver's eyes, he tells him to step out of his vehicle. He leans further forward to look at the lady in the front passenger seat.

"And that means you too," he bellows. "Both of you, out of the car."

After the driver steps out of his car and closes the door, he looks up slightly into the Lieutenant's face.

"What's this all about?" he asks with a stone face.

"*Probable cause,*" he bellows while removing a small flashlight from its holster attached to his police belt.

When Morehaus shines the light into the eyes of the driver and his passenger, he orders them to walk over to the shoulder and put their hands behind their back. He applies handcuffs, tells them to sit down on the shoulder, then telephones his aide at the municipal building a few blocks away, requesting his back-up for a possible drug-related incident.

Seconds later, he reads both handcuffed suspects their Miranda rights.

"It started out as a traffic violation, perhaps two violations," he announces with conviction in his voice, "when you failed to stop at the stop sign along Route 20 and Walgreens parking lot, then you were clocked at 52 mph going down Route 20 at the blinking yellow light at Route 20 and Route 544. The speed limit is 35. But that's only for starters. I don't like the look in your eyes."

Both suspects in handcuffs seem unaffected by the arrest. They're not angry, nervous, or frustrated. On the contrary, they're almost oblivious and seemingly accustomed to being handcuffed.

Three minutes later, after the backup police officer arrives, both policemen put each one into the back seat of their respective patrol cars and attach a second handcuff to a fitting on the floor to restrict their movement during transport to Kent County police headquarters in Chestertown.

Before leaving the scene, however, both officers make a thorough search of the Jeep and eventually find hidden, under the driver's seat, a small packet of cocaine.

Morehaus has seen this situation before and suspects that they probably were rushing to meet an addict and arranging a sale in the parking lot of Walgreens when they almost struck Mark walking in the driveway. He shakes his head from side to side in frustration.

"Those bastards," he admits, "are ruining a good life for good people living in Rock Hall, plus ruining their own lives too. Drugs eventually find their way into the middle school."

Two days later, only the driver, shackled and dressed in an orange jumpsuit, stands beside the public defender inside the Circuit Court of Kent County in Chestertown.

"*Oy-yay Oy-yee*," the bailiff yells out, "The Circuit Court of Kent County is now in session, Judge Henry Wohlfort presiding. Case number 233."

The judge opens a folder, begins to read its contents and says, "Hmm, another narcotics case."

The prosecutor, District Attorney for Kent County, Winfrid Strong, interrupts and advises Judge Wohlfort that a plea bargain has been reached. In exchange for a guilty plea for possession of narcotics, with the intent to sell or distribute them, prosecution will suspend the traffic violations, and the defendant will accept a sentence of two years' incarceration without the possibility of parole, and have his driver's license revoked for a period of five years following his release from prison.

Judge Wohlfort turns a few pages of the court brief and lets out a sigh.

"I'm not convinced that the penalty is sufficient for the crime," he remarks in the direction of the DA, "that it will deter him, too. From the records handed me, this is his second occurrence. What's the purpose behind your rush handling of this case?"

"There are children involved, your honor," answers Strong, with a touch of compassion, "and we're concerned about their welfare. If we prolong the case, their kids will be at risk without their father's supervision and probably be placed in a foster home. At the moment, his live-in girlfriend has accepted custody. She was arrested, but released temporarily on her own cognizance."

"Supervision? Are you kidding me?" queries the Judge. "On the contrary, this is one individual that should not be permitted to supervise anyone, especially his children, or have any influence on his kids, at least not in his current state. Was he ever tested, with a blood test, to determine if he had ingested a narcotic on the day of his arrest?"

"May we approach the bench, Your Honor?" asks Strong.

When the public defender and the DA confer with Judge Wohlfort, the DA tells him apologetically, "I don't have all the answers yet, but it appears that the arresting officers left the testing up to another section of the police department, and subsequently the lab misplaced the samples of blood taken on the day of his arrest. It's in our best interests to get him behind bars as soon as possible, rather than take the chance of losing the case on a technicality. With the public defender's consent, we'd like to have you confirm our plea agreement now, rather than wait to resolve an embarrassing problem later."

"Very well, then," answers Judge Wohlfort, "will the defendant stand and state his name?"

The defendant answers, "Jayson Jacobson."

"And where is your domicile?" asks the judge.

"My what?" asks Jacobson.

"Where are you currently residing, your address?"

"On Skinners Neck Road in Rock Hall," answers Jacobson.

"And are you prepared," Judge Wohlfort asks, "without any coercion, to accept the sentence about to be handed down by the court?"

"What's coercion?" asks Jacobson.

"Simply stated," the judge explains, "it means you are not restrained or constrained by force, law, or authority. No one is forcing you to make this decision. You are doing it on your own recognizance."

"What's recognizance?" asks Jacobson.

The judge ignores his question and bellows out, "In that case, your plea is accepted. The sooner you're behind bars, the better for everyone, and see that the defendant is furnished with a dictionary, courtesy of the court. He'll have plenty of time to study the definition of words while in jail."

The judge turns to the prosecutor and tells him, "I want you to insure that his kids are properly cared for. Please keep the court advised about their welfare."

"Thank you, your honor," replies Strong as he slaps the file folder closed, then continues, "and we would like to acknowledge the outstanding performance of Lieutenant Stephen Morehaus of the Rock Hall Sheriff's Department for his efforts in this case."

After the judge pounds his gavel and walks away from his bench, Lieutenant Morehaus approaches Strong.

"Much of the credit should be shared by Mark Hopkins of Ridgefield," admits Morehaus, "whose diligence set a good example of how people can get involved and take responsibility when they see something wrong. Each citizen, like Mark, can make a difference: *We can be better than we are.*"

Chapter 7

Meanwhile, at the state penitentiary, renamed the Patuxent Correctional Institution, at Jessup, Maryland, Bud Wayne is alone inside his small prison cell, laying on a cot with metal springs for a mattress. With no cell mate to talk to, he spends most of his time gazing up at the cracks in the plaster ceiling and shaking his head sideways, back and forth, like the pendulum of a clock. He's still bewildered but reconciled to the fact that he will be spending the next 22 years of his life behind bars. the sentence handed down by the court for perjury in the murder of his wife, Vera.

He begins muttering one word and repeating it over and over, as it echoes off the concrete walls of his cell. The single word is *Damn.*

He replays the events of two trials over and over in his mind like a series of flashbacks, starting with the first time he met Mark at his Swan Haven Marina. Bud tried to make the best of a bad marriage with his frustrated and oversexed wife, Vera, who had an affinity for military men. He decided to marry her when she becomes pregnant and told him he was the father.

Bud recalls every detail of her telephone call to Mark Hopkins, a SEAL working at Annette's Antiques in nearby Betterton, who was selling a model ship *Gratitude*, a replica of a ferry that docked at their marina 75 years ago. Under the pretense of buying it for her marina, Vera telephoned Mark and persuaded him to bring it to Swan Point Marina for her husband to consider buying for promotional purposes.

Inside their marina office, while Vera inspected Mark, Bud studied the model and, minutes later, was handed the jeweled dagger that Mark brought back from Iraq and used to repair some parts of the model. Bud, having acquired a few knives over the years, had never seen anything like it before.

Bud, eventually, was driven into a state of rage by his wife when she flaunted herself at Mark during a dance at the Saloon in Rock Hall. After being pushed over the edge and looking for an opportunity to do away with her, Bud followed them out of town, to a secluded spot, where Vera intended to seduce Mark.

When Mark remained incapacitated, almost comatose, in the passenger seat of her car, Vera was frustrated for not realizing the potency of the drug she put into his beer stein. She collapsed from exhaustion, which created a perfect situation for Bud to cut her throat with Mark's dagger and implicate him as a possible suspect.

After killing his wife, Bud hid the murder weapon immediately in high weeds and phragmites growing near the shoreline at the Eastern Neck Wildlife Refuge.

Three months after the first trial in which he was found not guilty, Bud was tricked into retrieving the weapon. After being apprehended, he was confined behind bars while a second trial was being prepared by the District Attorney. This time he was charged with perjury for lying about having no knowledge of the missing weapon, which, when recovered by him and tested, had traces of Vera's blood still embedded in the jeweled handle.

The dagger that Mark brought back from Iraq was confirmed as the murder weapon, and after its retrieval by Bud, linked him to the case as the sole murderer. Hoping for some leniency, he pleaded guilty and threw himself on the mercy of the court, but received a sentence of 22 years imprisonment, the largest sentence for perjury ever handed down by the Circuit Court of Kent County.

Bud's flashback is a repeating nightmare, when images and words of the judge are played over and over in his head, especially the scene in which he pronounces a sentence of 22 years. The thought of 22 years keeps bouncing around in his psyche and is beginning to drive him crazy. His only relief is when he massages his temples and cries out, "Damn. Damn. Damn. Make it go away. For God's sake, make it go away."

A steel door in the hallway leading to Bud's cell opens with a loud clang. The guard tells him to get up. He has a visitor.

Attached to his hands and feet are chains that dangle and clank while he walks slowly to a secure reception room. He takes a seat as an attractive 30 year-old woman, Rachel Able, walks in from the other door and sits opposite him, separated by a glass window.

He motions for her to pick up the phone on the ledge in front of her.

"People have contacted me about selling the marina," Bud admits, "but I will never sell it as long as I'm alive. We've known each other for a long time, long before I married Vera. I probably should've married you, but Vera had a way of enticing me into her..."

He pauses to think of the right word here.

"Womb? Inner sanctum?" she answers with some disgust.

"Call it what you will," he replies. "A lot has passed through my mind lately, and I'm worried about my marina. I can imagine it going to the dogs, with Bonnie in charge. I've known you before I married Vera and regret the day I asked her to be my wife, but you know the circumstances and predicament. I was enticed into doing what was best for her pregnancy, even though I may not be the real father of Jaime, after all. But that's another story. That's water over the dam."

He takes a deep breath, looks completely around his surroundings, then back to stare directly into Rachel's eyes.

"Would you be interested in managing the marina while I'm in here?" he asks slowly with reluctance, desperation and bitterness in his voice. "Bonnie is not qualified to run it and has enough to do, being pregnant and all, plus trying to scratch out a few bucks in the soft crab business with Pretty Boy Floyd. I'm in this bloody concrete hole for 22 years with rats running around at night. Hey, as I said before, I'm not even sure that I'm the father because of her sessions in the afternoon with Floyd. This is one *fucked up* mess, isn't it?"

Rachel has bounced around with watermen in Rock Hall for 12 years after graduation from Kent High. She's well-seasoned and hardened, and clever enough to recognize an opportunity when she sees one. Up until this moment, her life is simple and she enjoys being independent and has no objections to working odd jobs to tide her over. For Rachel, it's her way or no way, so there's no one to blame when things go wrong except herself.

She takes a few minutes to digest and weigh the importance of Bud's proposition. Eventually, she looks at him, inhales a deep breath, and answers, "Did you ask if I would be interested in running the marina while you in here? If so, I might be interested in managing your marina, under certain conditions."

"What conditions?" he asks.

"You shouldn't be too shocked if you hear me say it again, because I've asked you before about getting married. So this time around, here's the deal: We will sign a pre-nuptial agreement that stipulates: First, if I marry you, I'll be paid a salary of $1,000 a month for managing your marina during your incarceration; Second, after you're released from prison, assuming your sentence is 22 years, I will divorce you and be paid a 'golden parachute' payment of $250,000 for keeping the marina in an operating condition. That's about $12,000 a year over my monthly salary, very reasonable I think. That's it in a nutshell. Take it or leave it."

"Get a lawyer to draw up the necessary papers, and arrange for a Justice of the Peace," he replies. "The sooner we're hitched, the sooner you'll be at the helm of the marina, putting everything back in ship-shape."

The following week, Rachel and Bud stand before a Justice of the Peace inside a secure reception room of the correctional facility. They sign the prenuptial agreement, and are married faster than Nick Markakis can circle the bases on an inside-the-park home run at Oriole Park.

Two days later, at 8 in the morning, Mark checks his inbox and notices that he's received emails from Sotheby's and Christie's regarding his Edelfelt painting. Estimates from both auction houses are precisely the same: $300,000 - $400,000, less a commission of 15%, with a reserve price of $250,000. He rubs his hands together furiously, like Butch Cassidy hearing about a sweet bank vault without any guards.

He jots down a plan of action, something he always does from his training as a SEAL. He loves plans and planning because he remembers the axiom, "Plan your work before you work your plan."

He telephones both Sotheby's and Christie's in New York, and learns through their consignment office that the painting should be delivered or shipped to their New York office, where it will be packed with other paintings consigned to London, in one large wooden container. It's called "consolidation," because combining consignments into one container reduces costs and handling mishaps.

"Based on what they've told me," he tells himself, "I'll wait a week until I get back to Baltimore and take the painting to a professional packer or drive to New York to drop it off, avoiding the possibility of a packing company inflicting any damage on the painting or telling me it was already damaged when they received it from me."

The news from Sotheby's and Christie's is exhilarating and Mark's confidence soars upward once again. He's on a roll.

Feeling chipper, Mark logs off from his computer but accidentally pushes the Rolodex off the top of his desk. When he picks it up from the floor, the card with Lois Carnegie's name suddenly pops up.

"Could it be fate? he asks himself. "I haven't heard from her in a while. Who knows, maybe she's interested in my Edelfelt painting and if not, she might know someone who is. It was only a month ago that I discovered that lowboy at Crumpton, bought it for $3,000, and immediately sold it to her three days later for $77,000. She told me to keep in touch and advise her if I uncover something special for her home. Now I have a good reason to call her."

Within the next few minutes, Mark manages to speak directly to her and learns that she would enjoy having a candlelight dinner with him in Annapolis at the Blue Heron Restaurant.

"Would 7 o'clock suit you?" he asks.

"Perfectly, my dear," she answers buoyantly. "I look forward to hearing more about you and the world of antiques."

During the drive to Annapolis over the Bay Bridge, Mark sits in the driver's seat of his BMW and inhales the scent of Lois' perfume.

"Is it *Shalimar* that you're wearing over your gorgeous *Maison de Givenchy* suit?" he inquires knowing already the answer.

"Right, as usual," Lois answers with a beguiling smile. "Nice of you to call and invite me for dinner. It is *Shalimar* and *Givenchy*. They go well together, don't you think? Bring me up to date. What's new in the art world and what have you been doing with your life lately?"

Over the next 40 minutes Mark explains his split from Annette, ending his affection for Sandy, buying Ridgefield Farm and plans for its development. He explains his ideas for the creating a scientific institute to study the Bay, along with an R&R Refuge for Red Cross veterans and their families, and finally the construction of a sound stage for making films.

"If I need any exterior shots, we'll use Rock Hall as it is since it's unchanged for 75 years," he tells her. "We won't have to recreate a movie set of a waterman's town. Rock Hall will do just fine. But enough of me already. What's going on at Heavenly Manor? What's new in your world?"

Lois gives him an update on her life, especially about spending more time in Pittsburgh, on the board of US Steel.

"They keep me on the board primarily for appearance purposes," she boasts. "But I often manage to stir up things after reading about unfair labor practices, union bosses wanting a four-day work week, more vacation time, more union inspectors designed to get a tighter control of production, and finally foreign governments subsidizing their companies so they can produce steel and sell it at lower prices than we can, which ultimately will drive us out of business. Then they can raise their prices to whatever level they want."

"That's almost word-for-word what my father told me recently," he remarks, "and the pressure is really taking a toll on his life. He's aged considerably in the past four years."

When they arrive at the Blue Heron Restaurant, they are greeted by the maitre d' who recognizes Mark and exclaims in a baritone voice, "Hello Mark, nice to see you again. Would you like your table at the Nest?"

"Flattery will get you everywhere," replies Mark while laughing. "One date here, and they're already naming a corner or table after you.

"At least they didn't strike up the band and play 'Hail to the President.' I'm impressed, Mark. You must have impressed them, too."

After placing their order for a magnum of *Dom Perignon* and a compote with caviar resting on a bed of crushed ice, Mark asks her about the lowboy that she bought from Annette's Antiques.

Lois acknowledges that the curator at Winterthur made it a priority for his personal investigation.

"He contacted me again last week," she admits confidentially while enjoying a morsel of caviar, "and told me it was 18th century, between 1780-90, and then surprised me by tracing its ownership all the way back to a family from Rittenhouse Square in Philadelphia. If you don't see it on my face, I'm thrilled that everything turned out even better than I expected. It was good timing and an opportunity of a lifetime."

"That pleases me immensely," Mark admits. "It was my instincts that lead me into buying it in the first place, at Crumpton, at 8 a.m., when not many dealers had arrived for the auction that Wednesday. And Lois, if your lowboy is lonely, I have another gem that you might want to consider adding to your collection. It's a wonderful painting by Albert Edelfelt, the great Finnish impressionist."

"I've been to Helsinki on business years ago," she discloses, "and remember seeing some of his portraits in the national museum there. Once you've seen the faces of his models, you never forget them."

"I shouldn't be surprised to hear that from you," he replies. "Anyone who graduated from Northwestern and told me when she visited Annette's Antiques in Betterton that she had the leading role in *Dance of the Seven Veils,* in a production of the *Arabian Nights* and furthermore, recognized a Philadelphia lowboy of museum quality when she saw it, has my admiration and respect."

When it comes time to order their entrée, Lois and Mark decide the hour is getting late, and there's still the long drive back home. Mark pays the bill, and twenty minutes later, they are looking out at the moon casting its romantic light on the Chesapeake Bay Bridge as he drives over it.

When they reach the other side of the bridge and enter Queen Anne's County, Lois opens her purse to remove a small mirror that reflects the moonlight into her eyes.

"This was a childhood prank or quirk that my brother and I would play on each other. We would look up at the moon over the Bay, then talk to the image in the mirror, like talking to the man in the moon. Silly, really. Some habits are hard to break, aren't they?

"If it makes you happy, Lois, never let go of those childhood habits."

"Speaking of talking to the man in the moon in my mirror, I got a glimpse of you driving your car, and I'm curious as a cat about your Edelfelt painting. I hope you won't think too poorly of me for not bubbling over with enthusiasm when you first mentioned it at the Blue Heron. You're aware that I'm always looking for fine art and antiques for Heavenly Manor. What would you say if I asked you for permission to see it?"

"That can easily be arranged, except it's at Cylburn Park in Baltimore."

"Well, they have roads leading from Rock Hall to Baltimore, don't they? Let's drive over tomorrow morning or afternoon. I have the entire day free."

"It's a date," answers Mark. "I'll pick you up after church tomorrow, around noon, if that's convenient with you?"

"I'd like Clowie to go with us, so you can leave your car at Heavenly Manor. I'll drive my Bentley over to Baltimore, and you can drive it on the return leg. And one last word here. Kindly leave out all those sevens in the price if I buy it, please."

"If you're referring to those sevens in the $77,000 price tag of the lowboy, they certainly brought you luck, but I'll keep everything you've said in mind. Always want to keep the customer happy."

At noon the next day, Lois is seated in the driver's seat of her 1957 burgundy Bentley, with her close friend, Clowie Bankhead, in the front passenger seat. Mark has the entire back seat to stretch out and can't help but notice the pullout tables covered with burl wood and chrome.

"This is a classic Silver Shadow," Lois tells him, "built entirely by hand in Crewe, England, and purchased in 1957 by the original owner for $35,000. I'm the second owner."

Through the rear-view mirror she notices Mark as he pulls out one of the collapsible tables attached to the back of the front seat.

"They were designed for picnics at the horse races at Ascot," she explains. "This beauty is meant for touring on the freeways. It weighs almost 4,500 pounds, and hugs the road. The suspension system makes you feel like you're sitting on a Posturepedic cushion."

"I feel like I'm floating. Your Bentley *is* something special, including the odor of old English leather," he answers while feeling the softness of the leather skins, perfectly cured without any evidence of cracking after 50 years of use.

"I bet these magnificent motor cars," he continues, "are no longer built entirely by hand, are they?"

He doesn't get an immediate answer from the front seat area.

"First, she buys the lowboy and serves me the check on a sterling silver platter," he says to himself. "Now, I'm being chauffeured to Baltimore, with the possibility of selling her a very expensive painting. Am I dreaming? Is it too much to expect here? If she buys the Edelfelt painting, I wouldn't have to worry about packing and shipping it to New York."

Lois concentrates more on the driving, with an occasional glance at the GPS that Clowie turned on and entered the address for Cylburn Park, leaving Clowie and Mark to engage in light conversation.

Clowie is the daughter-in-law of Tallulah Bankhead, who enjoys impersonating the famous actress who's buried in a cemetery outside Rock Hall. She speaks with the same accent and theatrics, wears vintage clothes like those Tallulah wore in her films, and does everything with speech and gestures of her mother-in-law.

As the Bentley's tires suddenly create a hum as they roll over reinforced concrete lanes of the Chesapeake Bay Bridge, Mark gazes out at the Bay below him and sees a flotilla of sail boats, probably a typical weekend boat race.

His mind switches momentarily to Lois, who, at 30, is a vision of beauty, charm, and intelligence. But any idea of his becoming smitten with her is out of the question. She and Clowie are a gay couple enjoying life at its fullest. Nevertheless, Mark continues to harbor the qualities that they have in common, such as education, wealth, love of fine art, and origins in the steel business.

"Sometimes you want something that you can't have," he admits to himself. "We respect each other, so, for now, I should be content with having her as a friend and client."

After they arrive at Cylburn Park in Baltimore, a maid welcomes inside. Afterwards, Mark introduces Lois and Clowie to his mother, Sara, who is holding a book of poems by Sir Walter Scott in one hand.

"He's one of my favorite poets," admits Lois as she notices the author's name and grasps the arm of Clowie. All three women beam brightly.

"Can I offer you some refreshment, perhaps a glass of champagne or fortified fruit juice?" asks Sara.

"Perhaps later, thank you. We're anxious to see Mark's painting that he's hiding here," answers Lois. "Do we need a password?"

"No password or pass key, Lois, but I believe the long drive will be worth it," Sara mentions while politely taking hold of Lois' arm to escort her down the grand hall with a cathedral ceiling.

Mark intentionally lags five paces behind to give the women a chance to get more acquainted.

"I'm not trying to show off but that looks like a Munnings painting hanging at the end of the hall," Lois boasts while nodding in the direction of a large portrait of Mark's grandfather mounted on his gray hunter.

"You're perfectly right, Lois, but wait until you see what Mark discovered recently in Baltimore," Sara tells her as they turn to their left and enter the drawing room.

On an easel in one corner of the drawing room, Mark removes a small portrait of the hunter *Alert,* also painted by

Alfred Munnings, and sets it on a shelf about waist high, in front of a row of first editions.

He turns and walks over to the antique Dutch armoire, and opens its large door.

Moments later, he places the Edelfelt on the easel and steps away so that Lois can examine it freely.

"What do you think, Lois? Isn't it one of his best works or am I just whistling *Dixie*?"

Lois' face glows as her eyes seem to brighten and sparkle. No words are spoken for at least 30 seconds.

"Uh oh, I think I saw a light go on and a sparkle in someone's eyes," Clowie admits with a Tallulah Bankhead accent. "This is going to be the fastest deal you ever made in your life, Mark."

"You're supposed to be working for me, not upping the price because you noticed a change in my complexion or disposition," boasts Lois with a giggle. "Unfortunately, I've never been able to hide my emotions when it comes to art. I make a bad player in poker because I can't bluff or fake it."

She smiles a long time as her eyes move around every square inch of the canvas.

"I know I should not be telling you this, but it surpasses my wildest expectations, and it looks to be in original condition with a light layer of old varnish and hardly any craquelure."

Lois' exam of the painting is interrupted momentarily when William Hopkins II tries to tip-toe into the room, but one of his shoes squeaks on the hardwood flooring.

"Kindly forgive my intrusion, dear," he tells her. "I certainly never intended to disturb your concentration of the Edelfelt painting. I am so delighted to meet at last. Mark told me a little about you, enough to whet my appetite and curiosity. Speaking of appetite, would you like a cocktail or glass of champagne?"

"All in due time, thank you, sir" she answers and turns to face Mark. "Well, what's this gem going to cost me?"

"I'll be honest with you," he replies, "I believe in full disclosure, so here goes: Before I thought of offering it to you, little did I know that you might even be interested in it, I sent photos to Sotheby's and Christie's in London to get an estimate if consigned to one of their upcoming auctions in January. Their estimates are a matter of record, and both were identical, $300,000 to $400,000. I would settle for the middle, so the price is $350,000."

"It's tempting, Mark, it really is. Would you mind if I sat down? I'd like to think it over."

"Tell you what I'm going to do, Lois, because time is of the essence. I would prefer to sell you the Edelfelt and keep it in America, instead of selling it at auction in England. If you can make your decision while we're here, I'll pay the sales tax, which amounts to $21,000 if the Maryland sales tax is 6%. Your net cost will be $329,000, and there are no sevens in the price tag, per your request."

"Thank you, Mark. I'm ecstatic inside, with even greater feelings than those when I first saw the Chippendale lowboy in Annette's shop. It's the unexpected reality that I have an opportunity to enjoy looking at a beautiful painting for the rest of my life, and making an investment that I can pass on to my heirs. We have a deal, Mark. And Mr. Hopkins, I *will* have that champagne now, if you don't mind."

She extends her hand to Mark to shake on the deal, and turns to Sara and says, "You have quite a son in Mark. Did you notice how debonair he was in convincing me to buy it, without having to twist my arm?"

William, in an unusually quiet tone, tells her, "I should be a little disappointed that he didn't offer it to us. But I'm terribly delighted that it will stay in the family, our extended family, since my grandfather was a partner in the steel business with your great-grandfather in Pittsburgh."

On the return drive from Baltimore to Rock Hall, passing again over the Bay Bridge, everyone is somewhat giddy. Mark sits comfortably in the driver's seat of the Bentley that hugs the road, without any sounds of the engine running. He concentrates on responsibilities as chauffeur and reflects briefly again on Lois' reaction to seeing the Edelfelt painting. He dwells momentarily on the reality that he has successfully completed his first sale and a big payday, all on his own.

Lois has a treasure to enjoy for the rest of her life, Clowie has Lois, and Mark has a big check in his wallet, plus the sensation of knowing it was his first big sale as a private dealer. He can't seem to grasp how smoothly everything developed and wants to pinch himself, thinking it might all be a beautiful dream.

"The Edelfelt painting now resting in the trunk of the Bentley," he says to himself, "will soon have a new home at Heavenly Manor, with lots of eyes to appreciate and admire it properly. Life is good. And thanks to whoever invented the Rolodex. If it hadn't accidentally dropped off my desk and Lois' name popped out, the Edelfelt painting would be on its way to London."

Back in Rock Hall, through a friend working in the courthouse in Chestertown, Pretty Boy Floyd gets wind of Mark's attempt to adopt Jaime. He manages to convince an attorney in Chestertown to represent him, with a small deposit from money generated from the soft-crab business.

Previously, Vera owned the business and ran it independently, with the help of Floyd until she caught him in bed with her baby-sitter, Bonnie Bratcher, who is now pregnant and about four months away from delivery. The father could be either Bud or Pretty Boy since Bonnie slept with both of them during the past year. To complicate things even more, Vera stipulated in her will that, in the event of her death, all of her assets should be sold and proceeds added to the trust for her baby.

During a court hearing, the executor informs the judge that this is not the time to sell any real estate or a business because of the downturn in the economy and failure of the banks to make a loan to a potential buyer. Conversely, she feels it would be better to have Pretty Boy and Bonnie continue to live in Vera's home and run her soft-crab business.

While waiting to testify in the hearing, Floyd, being ambitious and cunning, thinks mostly about Jaime's inheritance of $500,000 from his mother's life insurance policy. Despite its being frozen in a trust at the bank, he hopes to convince the court that if he wins custody of the baby, he would be entitled to money "for reasonable care and welfare" of Jaime.

During the hearing for adoption, Floyd is questioned by Judge Henry Wohlfort after reading very slowly each paragraph of the legal brief twice. He shakes his head as if to say 'this motion should never have been filed in the first place.'

"Tell the court about your current financial status, your current employment and any arrests," orders the Judge after asking Floyd to stand at attention and stop fidgeting.

While standing, Floyd combs his hair, smiles at the judge and is not the least embarrassed when he declares, "I have no assets, own no property, no money in the bank, and no job other than working with Bonnie in the soft crab business."

When Bonnie testifies to help Floyd win custody of Jaime, she admits that she's pregnant and infers that Floyd is the birth father. She hides the fact about her interludes with Bud Wayne before he went haywire and murdered his wife. Bonnie never could quite understand the difference between promiscuity and fidelity.

The executor, nevertheless, seems content to let Bonnie and Floyd rent Vera's home next to the soft crab shed because it will generate a few dollars for Jaime's trust, and will give Bonnie some employment and an opportunity to get her life turned in the right direction.

The executor emphasizes that Vera always tried to watch over Bonnie, better than the way Bonnie watched over Jaime, so it was and is the right thing to continue to help her out.

The executor repeats her earlier convictions to the judge, with the admission that if everything were sold at auction, it probably wouldn't bring much anyway because of its rundown condition and forecasts of a continued weakened economy. She concludes her testimony by acknowledging that Vera's home and soft crab business should continue to remain part of her estate and will be absorbed eventually into Jaime's trust after probate is concluded.

Based on the evidence heard during this hearing, Judge Wohlfort rules that, before proceeding further, Bud and Floyd shall give blood samples to test for DNA to determine if either one is Jaime's birth father.

When the hearing reconvenes a week later, the results of the DNA testing reveals that neither Floyd or Bud are the birth father of Jaime, leaving everyone in limbo. Vera must have had an affair with another male whose identity remains unknown.

In this reconvened hearing, Floyd tries to digest the findings of the court while sitting between Bonnie on his left and his attorney on the right. His reaction is what one would expect under the circumstances.

As most of the spectators leave the courtroom, Floyd leans over to hear his attorney's advice being whispered in his ear.

A few seconds later, Floyd nods his head and agrees to drop his request for adoption.

"You'll have your hands full running the soft crab business," Bonnie tells him, "and helping to take care of my baby. This could be a new beginning for us."

Aware of Bonnie's exploits in bed with him and Bud, Floyd now suspects that Bonnie's baby due in a few weeks may not be his, either. But he'll have to wait until it's born and undergo another round of DNA testing.

"Does promiscuity run in your family, or does it gallop?" he asks her facetiously.

"I don't know the meaning of the word. Is that good or bad?"

"I guess it depends on your perspective."

"What's perspective?" she asks with a glare across her face.

"Bonnie, you've got a great body for a 17-year old, but dropping out of school sure left you with a deficiency in your brain."

"What's a deficiency? Is that contagious? Is that something I can pass on to my baby?"

"I sure hope not," he answers with a smile while combing his hair again. The grease that gives his hair a sheen is his own concoction. Also, he seems to relish when anyone refers to him as "Pretty Boy." All his life he's never had any trouble getting a date with women of all ages, but finding the right partner was always out of his reach.

In the meantime, Jaime has been transferred to a foster home in Chestertown while Mark's petition for adoption is being prepared by his attorney.

Chapter 8

Back at Bethlehem Steel in Baltimore, William II, gets a telephone call around 5:45 pm from his son at Ridgefield, who wants to know if he has cut down on his workload.

"They won't let up, Mark. As I tried to explain to you and Sara, there are two suitors who are pressuring me to sell them the mill. The first is Robert Lewis Stackhouse, better known as RL 'Give 'em hell' Stackhouse, President of the Steelworkers Union. The second is Salvi Solomeni, executive VP of Mittal, the world's largest steel maker and a conglomerate based in London."

"Those bastards will end up killing you, Dad," he advises. "They'll never give up until you take a different tack with your sails, a different course of action. Can Mike Bloomburg help out, perhaps file a lawsuit for sexual harassment or something to switch the pressure onto them, perhaps bring the case to the attention of the government?"

"Good ideas, son," he responds. "I'll take it under advisement. I'm going to meet them in a few minutes and will let you know the outcome tonight or tomorrow. All the best. God watch over you."

Fifteen minutes later, RL and Salvi arrive at the President's Office. When they find that his long-time secretary, Miss Potts, is not at her desk, they barge into William's office without even knocking.

William politely asks them to follow him to a section of the plant where no one can hear their discussions. He's increasingly paranoid and obsessed with the notion that spies are everywhere, even inside the woodwork of his office walls.

Before he leaves his office, however, he opens a bottom drawer in his desk and removes an oxygen bottle attached to a feeder line with a mask.

"This is what you two buzzards have forced me into using with your demands," he tells them. "Even my wife doesn't know that I keep it near me for emergencies."

He leads them down a flight of stairs into a dark secluded area near an idle Bessemer blast furnace. It's so quiet here you can hear drops of water dripping out of rusty corroding pipes and leaky valves. The odor is putrid, worse than the smell of a garbage dump. The overall look is one of desolation, disintegration and deterioration.

A single 12-inch round light fixture with a curved housing on top focuses the light from a single bulb downward, casting just enough luminescence over a spot about five feet in diameter. A surveillance camera 20 feet away records only shadowy silhouettes of three men. If they were positioned in a row as in a police line-up, William would be the smallest at 5 feet 8 inches, Salvi at 6 feet even, and RL at 6 feet 3 inches.

However, despite their differences in height, viewing them from a distance can be misleading. For example, the tallest one, if standing farthest away, might appear to be the smallest of the group. It has something to do with "depth perception."

William begins first by turning to face RL directly.

"We hired three more union inspectors last week against my better judgment," he explains, "but they're not acting as inspectors. They're interfering with our production line, getting some workers to slow down so that overtime will be required to fill our orders on time. You've got to call off these thugs and give them new orders.

Furthermore, you're demanding an increase in vacation time and reduction of the work week. These three factors will cut heavily into our profits, that make it almost impossible to compete with foreign sources."

William turns and walks a few steps to face Salvi.

"And that brings me to you and your conglomerate, Mittal. What in the Hell do you want with a little firm like Bethlehem Steel when you're already the biggest in the world? Do you want to own the world and all that's in it?"

He steps away from both of them and coughs up some phlegm that he spits on the ground in disgust.

"Are you both blind? Can't you see what you are doing to me? You've pressured me almost to the breaking point. We might have to lay off some good people or possibly declare bankruptcy. I'd rather kill myself than sell the mill to you, and if you think I'm tough, wait till you have to face my son, Mark, a former Navy SEAL Lieutenant. He'll show you how the military fights a war. You'll wish you were never born if you have to go up against him."

"Are you finished? If so, you didn't have to bring us down here to tell us something we already know," RL tells him, disregarding entirely everything William just uttered. "You may want to reconsider our offer to buy your mill after you look at this."

RL hands William a large manila envelope.

When William opens it, he finds several 8- by 10-inch glossy black and white photos of him sitting on the edge of a bed with a nude woman reclining behind him. He throws the photos to the ground and stomps on them like someone grinding out a cigarette. He shakes his head disgustedly, then raises his fists, anxious to take a punch at RL.

"This is blackmail," he shouts. "You know it's not true. The images in these photos are *doctored*. But the implication would crush my family, friends and the reputation of the mill. This is ludicrous, incredulous, fabrication, falsification, **extortion**!"

"Big words from a big man in big trouble," Salvi acknowledges with a devilish smile on his face.

"It's simply not true. You must know it," William cries out with his head bending backwards and looking upward for help from God. He runs his fingers through his hair and tries to inhale a breath of fresh air. His head falls to his chest after realizing there's no fresh air here, only the stench of this abandoned furnace area. He spits out more phlegm onto the photos crumpled on the ground beside him.

His fingers grip tighter the oxygen cylinder now dangling at his side as he pauses to look around for some help and semblance of reality, then continues, "I never expected this crisis, a collaboration, a gang of ruthless cutthroats. I don't know what else to call it other than a nightmare. There's not an ounce of truth to it."

"From your viewpoint," Salvi replies, "it may look like blackmail, but there's an easy way out of this situation. Before you blow your top, let me take care of RL and the union, and these photos will disappear permanently. Sell me the plant. I'll make you richer, appoint you to the board at a million a year, an emeritus honorarium, or whatever the hell it's called in your country, for doing nothing."

"You are very desperate and stupid men," vows William for the last time, "who will never get the mill as long as I'm alive."

Suddenly, William grabs his chest, tears open his shirt, and falls to the ground. His body is crumpled until he manages to squirm and stretch himself out. However, he's now lying on top of the oxygen line and mask, and doesn't have the strength to roll his body one way or the other.

"God, help me, please," he cries out.

Both men look at him as he squirms on the ground. Suddenly, the overhead light goes out in this section of the mill. Only maintenance lights way off in the distance weakly light the area now. Mostly through shadows, it appears that the shorter of the two men rolls William over onto his back, which allows him to utter, "Help me, please."

One of the men pulls out a shiny flask from inside his suit pocket, bends down and tells William, "Drink this. It'll make you feel better. It's nitroglycerine, something you need for your heart right now."

William's hands are shaking too much, so the man pours it directly into his mouth,

About 20 seconds later, he is out, permanently.

RL gathers the crumpled photos from the ground while Salvi opens his cell phone, and calls 911.

Within 10 minutes a rescue vehicle arrives. Two attendants check William's vital signs which indicate he is dead. They transport his body to the coroner's office for an autopsy.

An hour later, as Sara is reaching for the phone to call her husband at the plant, it rings and as she holds it to her ear, she is informed of his fatal heart attack. She drops the phone to the floor, and screams at the top of her lungs, then collapses on the thick Sarouk rug covering the hardwood floor.

A maid rushes into the drawing room after hearing her loud scream, and finds Sara sobbing uncontrollably on the floor. She tries to lift her body, but Sara is too heavy for her to move. So she places a pillow under her head, and telephones Dr. John Durocher, their family doctor.

About 10 minutes later, Dr. Durocher arrives and, together with the maid, manage to move Sara to a settee. He checks her vital signs, and hands her a glass of water and some pills to calm her nerves.

"It does no good for me to say it," he tells her tenderly, "but I bear some responsibility here, because I could not get him to slow down. He really didn't need the pressures of running the mill at his age. I told him many times, 'it will kill you,' and now it's all come true."

Sara tells him to advise the coroner that he has her permission to donate his organs to help save lives.

When he finishes his telephone call to the coroner, she asks for the phone, and calls her son with the bad news.

"I should have helped him out in the mill when I was discharged from the Navy, but no, I wanted to carve out my own career, and now Dad is gone," Mark tells her as he is immediately overcome with guilt.

"There's not much anyone can do now, Son, so be careful while driving. Watch the speed limit. We will, I mean I will be waiting for you," she advises him.

Still in shock and devastated by the news, he listens to his mother carefully and finally tells her, "I'm already in my car and on my way to you. I should be with you in about two hours. Who's with you now?"

"Dr. Durocher is here. I'm in good hands, Mark. Not to worry about me," she tells him before hanging up the phone.

With his cell phone mounted on the dashboard and set for automatic speed dialing, he telephones Abigail and leaves a message about his father's passing. He advises her to assume control of everything at Ridgefield until further notice.

Three days later, a funeral Mass is celebrated for William Hopkins II at the Lady of Angels Church in Baltimore. Among the attendees from Baltimore City and the state of Maryland are: the governor, the mayor, the chief of police, two senators and four congressmen. From Bethlehem Steel and others in the steel business: members of the board of directors of the mill; RL Stackhouse; Salvi Solomeni; workers from the mill who were given the day off to attend at their own discretion; and Annette, Sandy, Abigail, Liz, Reggie, Lois, Clowie, Knute, the Breeze track team, Manny Meyer, Mo Greenspan and Jack Johnson, and Stash and Elle.

The outpouring of sympathy is overwhelming, but Mark and his mother were prepared for this day, or at least it seems that way by their demeanor

During the Mass, after a reading of the gospel, the priest nods to Mark, who makes his way to a pulpit to deliver the eulogy.

Mark pauses about 10 seconds to survey all the people attending the service, and removes his eulogy from his inside suit pocket.

"My father told me many years ago that a man is measured by the number of friends he has in life. As I look out at the great number of people gathered here today, I realize that my father truly was a rich man. Although he measured only five feet eight inches, he stood tall in the presence of bigger men. He was a servant, a faithful servant, to his family, his community, and fellow workers in his mill. He had the will power and strength to steer the ship in the right direction, and stay the course, through good and bad times.

"He was always as sensitive to the needs of his workers as he was to the needs of his family. Often there were powers greater than his, and he relented, regrettably, when his decisions were overturned by forces beyond his control, like being overruled by a board of directors or group of managers who wanted things done their way, or else, usually for their own personal profit.

"He seized the opportunity to study metallurgy at Johns Hopkins, and his education served him well in succeeding years when he joined his father in helping to run Bethlehem Steel, particularly in inventing new processes of refining the ores. He brought honor to Hopkins, where he put the lessons he learned there to good use at the mill.

"Because you are invited to join the company and work side-by-side with your father, a direct descendant of the founder of Bethlehem Steel, doesn't mean you'll automatically be successful. You have to prove yourself worthy every day on the job. Maybe some of you know how difficult it is to work for your family, where you are constantly judged to see if you measure up to your father. I know firsthand because he confessed it, with considerable urging, which lead to my decision to pursue a life away from the mill.

"He brought joy and honor to his family by balancing his love for family and love for the company, an obligation turned into happiness when things went as planned. He carried his family on one shoulder and the company on the other, like a plunging fullback. If he had any complaints, he let you know up front, never behind your back. He often said, 'Time is precious and costly, and waste of time is unacceptable and intolerable.'

"The Good Lord said, and I'm paraphrasing here, 'Husbands, love your wives, as you love yourselves, and fathers, love your children, as you love me.' In this regard, my mother and I benefited from his love and devotion. We have no regrets. But all things must end. And in the end, when God calls you, you answer, 'Here I am, Lord. Do with me what you will. I am your faithful servant.'

"We pass through life only once. My father answered God's call, but he leaves behind his spirit, filled with memories that will last for a lifetime, memories of when and how and where he touched our lives. He died on the job, perhaps something that God wanted to impress upon us, the importance of work and doing something that you love so it doesn't appear to be work. To whoever said, 'No greater glory has man than to lay down his life for his country,' I add these words, passed down from my grandfather: 'Man grows on earth, but flourishes in heaven.'

"On behalf of my mother, Sara, and I, we cry out now," Mark pauses to gather strength and increase the volume of his upcoming words, and grips tightly the paper from which he reads his eulogy to keep his fingers from shaking, "Lord, take care of your good and faithful servant, William Hopkins II. He heard you calling him. He's on his way to you. He's the lucky one. He is with God."

Everyone's eyes swell up from Mark's stirring eulogy, and all his friends let a tear roll down their cheeks. As the Mass continues, a parishioner in the second row leans over and whispers to her husband, "William would be very proud of his son today."

At the conclusion of the Mass, the priest announces, "The burial will be private at the request of the family."

After Mass, selected friends and associates of the deceased have already been invited, RSVP, to a reception at the Hopkins home in Cylburn Park, so that they can enjoy the Hopkins hospitality and pay their respects.

About thirty minutes later, guests begin to enter the enclosed vestibule and step into the main hall. Among the first guests to arrive are Lois Carnegie and her friend, Clowie Bankhead, both dressed in the latest fashions imported from the *Maison de Givenchy*. When they reach the reception line headed by Mark and Sara, Lois leans forward to give each one a slight kiss on their cheek.

"I thought your eulogy was heart-rendering," she tells Mark with compassion in her voice, "with words that I will never forget. We are very proud of you and Sara. Let us know if we can help in any way."

Because of some gentle pushing from the crowd gathering behind them, they offer their condolences and politely move towards the center of the hall.

Minutes later, the main hall is filled with over 100 guests who are seen raising a toast, their glasses producing a high C. It is by all respects an elegant reception and celebration for a respected businessman and his family.

At the far end of the hall, two of Mark's friends offer to play background music for the reception. Seated on a stool beside the baby grand is Stanley 'Stash' Piotrowski, Mayor of Rock Hall who cups a Horner chromatic harmonica with both hands while his wife, Elle, plays the Bosendorfer piano, hand-made in Vienna, with the delicate touch of a classical pianist and a jazz riff thrown in occasionally.

Stash usually plays the melody, with a little improvising reminiscent of Toots Thielemans. He enjoys the opportunity, whenever possible, of adding a tremolo by flapping the fingers of one hand wildly to produce the necessary quiver of the sounds as it leaves the reed chamber of the harmonica.

Elle, on the other hand, enjoys her role as accompanist, and her fingers glide over the piano keys, evidence of her Master's in piano from Penn State where she studied under maestro Giuseppe Paterno Jr., promulgator of the flutter-finger technique, invented by George Gershwin for his *An American In Paris.*

The duo of Stash and Elle set the tone for marvelous background music to complement the elegance of delicacies displayed on tables in the main hall.

Each table has a centerpiece sculpted from a chunk of ice in the form of an enlarged fish, goose and terrapin. The chefs who prepared these centerpieces are not only master chefs, they are master ice sculptors. From a distance each centerpiece looks as if it could suddenly come to life.

Always looking for publicity that will help in their re-election, the governor, mayor, senators and member of congress stand in line, eager to have their pictures taken, posing first in front and behind each centerpiece.

Standing beside his mother near the entrance to the hall, Mark watches the flashbulbs of cameras and whispers to her, "It must have been a politician who said, *Corpus Diem, Tempus Fugit.*"

It doesn't take very long before each guest is holding a glass of *Dom Perignon* in one hand and an hors d'oeuvre in the other. Everything is beautifully created and catered by Feinkost Kaefer (F.K.), based in Munich. They are renowned the world over for creating and serving the most exquisite food for customers who spare no expense. Their symbol is a *kaefer*, the German word for "Ladybug," with its small head turned downward, nearly hemispherical in shape, like one-half of a pea, and always six black spots on their reddish-orange wings that rest on their back. F.K. adds one black spot to make the number seven, for good luck.

For the Hopkins reception, although food is arranged at three large tables, hors d'oeuvres are served on sterling silver platters by hostesses who roam among the guests. They are seven of the most gorgeous girls, called Kaeferettes, all about 19 years old and of German ancestry, in special costumes designed to resemble a Ladybug. Their costumes are anatomically correct, except Ladybugs have short legs, and these beauties have the longest and shapeliest legs in the world.

Starting with reddish-orange high-heeled shoes, each Kaeferette wears orange-colored mesh stockings, a reddish-orange mini-skirt, resembling a ballerina's tutu, trimmed in black lace that angles out at about 45 degrees from their waist, a tight-fitting blouse of reddish-orange with black lace covering her stomach and bodice like a German dirndl. In their hair just above their forehead is a small tiara with the letters "FK" and two miniature black ping-pong balls attached to three-inch long coiled wire, to give the impression of antennae. Whenever the Kaeferettes move their heads, the black balls wobble at the end of the coiled wire, which always evoke a big smile from guests being served an hors d'oeuvre.

In the far corner, huddled together to the right of the large Munnings painting, are the two adversaries of William Hopkins II: RL Stackhouse and Salvi Solomeni. Both are still set on buying the mill at any cost, and neither will let up their fight as they huddle in a corner; the expressions on their faces are like two poker players trying to bluff the other one.

"It would be better," whispers RL, "if one of us takes the lead, buys the mill from the family, and then we can work out a deal between us, instead of bidding against each other."

"Like they do at the auctions," whispers Salvi. "But which of us will take the lead?"

"Let's get together tomorrow morning," RL tells him. "The sooner we plan our work, the better we work our plan."

They shake hands and turn just in time to take a glass of champagne from a hostess carrying the last two glasses on her tray. When they remove their glasses, an unusual light reflects off the tray, temporarily blinding them.

Finally Salvi, after consuming his champagne, places his glass on a shelf nearby, and reaches inside his dress suit.

"I've got to have something stronger.," he says to himself." He turns to the wall, and takes a quick swig out of a sterling-silver flask, and quickly returns it again to his inside pocket.

For the entire first hour, Mark is positioned always beside his mother. Despite the solemn occasion, he can't help himself by watching one of the girls serving the hors d'oeuvres.

"I can't believe it," he whispers to mother. "Look at those legs. They have to be the most athletic-looking girls I've ever seen."

His mother turns her attention momentarily from watching the guests to admiring the figure of each Kaeferette.

"I think I'm reading your mind," she whispers back. "If Florenz Ziegfeld Jr. were still alive, he'd have them in one of his fabulous shows on Broadway."

"Who's Florenz Ziegfeld?" asks Mark with some curiosity.

"Just about the greatest showman in the world in the 1920's," she answers. "We never saw his shows in person, but always watched movies and documentaries about his life. He really had an eye for beauty and glamour."

"Speaking of beauty, have you seen Lola yet? asks Mark.

"The last time I saw her, she was around the ice sculpture of the swan," she tells him. "Why don't you show her your Renoir? She's been such a dear, looking in on me every day, on her way to and from work, eager to help in anyway. Furthermore, I think she likes you and would like to get to know you better."

"Well, if you'll excuse me, I'll take your advice." Mark begins to meander through the crowded grand hall and stops occasionally to speak to whoever approaches him. Eventually he finds the Betterton and Rock Hall crowd huddled together in one corner, everyone except Judy Ridgefield, who was not feeling well enough for the two-hour drive from Betterton to Baltimore. He exchanges quick stories and memories but withholds his ideas about Ridgefield for another occasion.

It's clear that he made a good impression in such a short time on each one of them, especially Annette and Sandy.

"And you gave this up to come to Betterton?" asks Sandy. "I can't believe it."

"My mother and father liked art and invested in art. I like people and intend to invest in people. We all have a calling from God and should let him guide us. If we use our God-given talents, we can strive to make America a better place for everyone. You've lost Tommy, I've lost Rusty and my father, and we can never bring them back, but we can honor them by adhering to my motto: "You Can Be Better Than You Are."

"We did so much together in such a short time," admits Annette, "but now I realize it was only the prologue. I hope you'll include us in your plans, Mark, whatever they are, wherever they may take us. You'll always be in our hearts."

Sandy, Annette and Mark hug each other with Mark in the middle of the threesome, in the same way they hugged each other after the New Bay Belle docked at Betterton Beach after Sandy's rescue in the Bay.

"Reggie, my pal, good to see you," Mark says to him as he joins the huddle too. "Would you mind playing a song or two? I know everyone would enjoy it, especially my mother and father."

"Under these circumstances," replies Reggie, "how can I refuse you? Actually I was hoping you'd ask me because we've been rehearsing a song for family gatherings and special occasions. I assume you have a guitar handy?"

"As a matter of fact, a Paul Reed Smith acoustic guitar, all hand-made in Stevensville, Maryland, is upstairs in my bedroom, waiting for a good workout. Meet me at the stairway to the second floor in about five minutes, please."

Mark turns in the direction of the stairs and bumps into Lola, who tells him, "You're always on my mind, Mark. Remember our sleigh ride? I was hoping you would call me."

"I remember everything that we said that day. You've been on my mind too," he replies. "It must be telepathy." He pauses and leans over to whisper in her ear, "Would you like to see the Renoir hanging in my bedroom?"

"Now, Mark, I've heard that line before," she replies with a laugh, "but it was always a man asking if I wanted to see his 'etchings,' I think."

"Lola, I'll level with you. I can't thank you enough for the way you're looking after my mother. Wish there was some way for us to be a little more patient, and let loose of the reins, so each of us can run freely for awhile, without serious attachments like an engagement leading to marriage." He pauses to look directly into her eyes and continues, "Now, what in the world made me say that?"

He starts to laugh and takes her arm, ushers her up the stairs, down a short distance of a balcony overlooking the grand hall, and into a bedroom.

Once both are inside, he switches on a spotlight that illuminates only a painting of a voluptuous nude, by Auguste Renoir, painted around 1880, in a wood-carved, gold-leafed frame.

"I found it in an estate sale in Homewood," he tells her, "and talked my father into letting me bid and buy it at auction. It's a museum piece, don't you think?"

"Oh, Mark, it's heavenly. I could gaze on it for the rest of my life, and never grow tired of looking at it. It's magic. She looks so real, yet Renoir gave it the impression of a dream, like something to admire, but never to be possessed. Does that make any sense?"

"Well put, Lola. I couldn't have said it any better."

"I feel an impulse coming over me again, one that I can't quite control, like on our sleigh ride," she confides without any hesitation in her voice.

"You should always follow your impulse."

"Well, here goes," she tells me and kisses him tenderly on his lips, a kiss that last about 20 seconds. "I'm sorry, Mark. I should be ashamed for acting this way, so close to your father's passing, but I've wanted to do that since we took that sleigh ride with Nellie, around Betterton, in the snow."

"The pleasure was and is all mine," he answers without hesitation.

"This may not be the right time and place," she continues, "but I forgot to ask you why you're not married? I've met Sandy, Liz, Lois, and, need I go on, all beautiful ladies, who speak affectionately about you."

"Tell you what, Lola," he answers while adjusting his tie. "I think you've got me there, and you better be careful how you interpret that response. For now, I better deliver this guitar to Reggie, before he comes looking for us, and I wouldn't want him to get the wrong impression if he finds you in my bedroom."

He laughs as he removes the PRS acoustic guitar hanging on one wall, and takes Lola's arm again, and escorts her back to the grand hall.

Mark hands the guitar to Reggie, who's waiting at the bottom of the stairs and immediately holds it to his ear to see if it's in tune.

"If you don't mind," he asks, "would you play over the balcony where everyone can see and hear you?"

Reggie suggests a place with better acoustics would be at the end of the grand hall, near the piano, with the beautiful painting of William I on his jumper as a backdrop.

"Good idea, pal, whatever makes you comfortable."

He finds an empty bottle of champagne, climbs a few steps up the stairs, faces the grand hall, and strikes the bottle several times with a knife to get everyone's attention.

"Good friends," he begins, "I want to introduce you to Reggie Perdue, the man who rescued Sandy and me in the Chesapeake Bay. Although you may think of him as a lifeguard, patrolling the Bay, he's one of the top guitarists in the country, and you'll find his name on recordings of vocalists that reads like a Who's Who in Music in America. I've asked him to play a song or two, in memory of my father. I guarantee you that his music will strike a chord in your heart as it did in our hearts. So if everyone will kindly turn towards the piano, Reggie's music will close our reception. My mother and I thank everyone for coming, and for your expressions of sympathy."

After the audience gathers in a semicircle with the women standing in front of the men.

"To start us off," Reggie says with the distinct accent of a southern Marylander, "I'd like to play a ballad that is close to my heart because of the lovely way the melody was recorded by a little girl from Winchester, Virginia, named Virginia Hensley. She's better known as Patsy Cline, and the song is *Crazy,* written by Willie Nelson."

Reggie begins alone with a slow and deliberate pace, with his special way of introducing dominant 7th and augmented 9th chords.

After playing the first chorus, he takes a step backward and swings his arm over to introduce Stash on the harmonica and Elle on the piano who play the song while he lowers his guitar and sings the words to the music. But it's not really singing, more like speaking the words slowly with a southern drawl.

"I don't believe it," he whispers in Sandy's ear and puts his arm around her to show that friendship still exists between them. "He must have been practicing his vocalizing. That song is now one of my favorites. The melody is buried in my subconscious because it's the last song I heard over the juke box at the Saloon before Vera died."

He gazes back at Sandy and asks her, "Now, why in the hell am I thinking about Vera at a time like this? Just being crazy, I guess."

When the applause dies down after the first song, Reggie steps backward away from the microphone, looks down at the floor and then up to the ceiling.

"I'd like to dedicate this next song to Mark and Sara, two of the nicest people in the world," he pronounces slowly, pausing between each word. He beckons to Liz and Sandy, who walk forward and stand on each side of him.

"By the look on Mark's face," he remarks, "I can see how surprised he is, so with the addition of Sandy Welles and Liz Carter, along with the back-up duo of Stash and Elle Piotrowski, we'd like to play our rendition of a ballad from Stanley Kubrick's 1964 film, *Dr. Strangelove*. The song title is *Try A Little Tenderness*, written in 1932, by the team of James Campbell, Reginald Connelly, and Harry M. Woods, but with words modified slightly for this occasion. I hope you'll like it."

Reggie begins strumming his guitar with a series of single notes, played slowly without chords, to emphasize the melody and set the stage for Liz and Sandy's vocalizing.

Both young ladies, still in their middle to late 20's, are wearing dark, long-sleeved blouses and trousers, with an iridescent gold-colored silk scarf over their shoulders and tied in a large knot near their bodice.

During this song, each plays with the scarf by running their fingers slowly up and down the edges, all to give a special meaning to the words being sung. The overall effect is very sensuous.

After Reggie's brief instrumental intro, Liz and Sandy begin singing along with Reggie, as secretly rehearsed, in perfect harmony, starting with the chorus:

> *"We may be weary, people do get weary, mired in the same shabby mess,*
>
> *and when you're weary, try a little tenderness.*
>
> *You know we're waiting, just anticipating, things we may never possesses, when we're without them, try a little tenderness."*

Reggie, Stash, and Elle join Liz and Sandy in singing the following refrain:

> *"It's not just sentimental, everyone has some grief and some care, and a word that's soft and gentle, makes it easier to bear."*

As the refrain ends, all five motion with their hands to invite everyone to sing-along as the chorus is repeated.

> *"We won't forget it, we cannot forget it, love is our whole happiness, It's not so easy, try a little tenderness."*

After the last word *tenderness* is sung, there's not a dry eye anywhere, only silence until Reggie takes the microphone and whispers, "That was special and memorable. Thank you, Sandy. Thank you, Liz."

Everyone leaves Cylburn after paying their last respects to Mark and Sara, who eventually stand alone in the grand hall, with their arms around each other.

"We pass through life only once," she tells him. "You're now the head of the family."

"No one can ever take Dad's place, but you know I'll do my best," he tells her with a goodnight kiss on her lips. "I won't let you down."

"The thought never entered my mind. No one really knows what they can do until the times comes to do it. We'll probably feel much more pain in the days ahead than we do now, all because we couldn't get your father to slow down."

"It's been a long day. Let me know if you need anything during the night. Whoever gets up first can brew the coffee. If I'm late for breakfast," he whispers, "send up one of those kaefer hostesses if you find one lingering around."

During breakfast the next morning, Detective Louis Cain of the Baltimore City Police Department telephones Mark at the Hopkins mansion.

"Your father's death was not entirely the result of a stroke," he tells Mark. "We suspect foul play, since he was lying in an awkward position at the mill, positioned on top of his oxygen line and mask, and in the presence of two men with him at the time of his demise. Based on separate interviews with these individuals, we can't figure out why one or both of them failed to come to his aid."

"Who were these two men?" Mark asks with disgust.

"Stackhouse and Solomeni," answers Cain. "Do you know them?"

"I may have heard my father mention them at one time or another."

"Furthermore," Cain continues, "there was a special element in a drug found in his body that sedated him. We can't figure out why he would have taken such a drug voluntarily. There was no capsule of medicine of any kind found on his body. We're thinking that this specific sedative may have prevented him from reaching his oxygen bottle. It simply put him at rest, permanently. That's not to say he would have recovered from the stroke. It's something suspicious. Why would he ingest that drug, and for what purpose? We're going to interrogate those two witnesses again later today. As I just mentioned, both of them were known to be with your father at the time of his death. We'll also check the surveillance camera at the mill."

The next day, Detective Cain phones Mark again with an update.

"Salvi Solomeni told us about his meeting your father and Stackhouse at the mill around 6 in the evening, on the night of your father's death. He said they were all in a deserted area of the mill, then mentioned something about photos of your father in bed with a nude woman."

Cain waits a moment to get a response that doesn't come, and follows up with another question, "Do you know anything about these photos?"

"That's news to me," Mark answers, "shocking news. On the surface, it could be blackmail. I hope you'll keep my mother from hearing about it. The thought of it, true or false, would devastate her."

"Well, so far, Mark," reveals Cain, "it's only Salvi's words, and strange that he would tell me about it. Maybe he has a reason, perhaps challenging us to dig deeper. Things are muddled at the moment. I haven't seen any photos of any kind yet, but if I do, I'll keep you advised. I can't stretch my neck out to far, if you get my drift."

Chapter 9

A week later, at precisely five minutes before 9 in the morning, Mark walks into Bethlehem Steel, through the main gate, climbs the stairs, double-stepping, to the first floor executive office of his father. He soon finds a sign painter, a 35-ish, short and heavy-set, prematurely bald-headed man, adding the last two letters of his name under "Office of the President."

As Mark approaches the door, the sign painter greets him with a smile and removes an artist's *Slimline* paint brush protruding from one corner of his mouth like a cigarette.

"You must be the president," he declares. "I've asked that question to six men already this morning and none admitted that *this* is his office, although it seems as if each one wished that this was his office. A few minutes ago I overheard the secretary say 'everyone is here, except for the president.' So, by elimination, you must be the new president. You must be Mark Hopkins, right?"

"Right. This is my office, but not by elimination," answers Mark with a smile. "It's mine by right of succession."

"I'm sorry for not having the sign finished by 9," replies the sign painter. "My kid was sick with the flu the past few days, and I've been back and forth to see the doctor."

177

"In that case," Mark tells him, "pack up your paint brushes and gear, and get back home and take care of your family. That's what's important, not completion of this sign. The sign can wait."

"Well, sir, I'll only be another five minutes," answers the sign painter, "but thanks for your consideration."

He moves aside and opens the door for Mark.

Once inside a small reception-anteroom, Mark is greeted by Miss Virginia Potts, his father's long time and attractive 50-year old secretary, whose figure always draws a whistle and smile from male workers whenever she walks through the plant.

"Is everything in order, Miss Potts?" he asks.

"Everyone is waiting in your office, sir," she answers politely.

"Good. Thank you, Virginia," he replies with a confident smile. "Follow me, please. The curtain is going up on a new production of Bethlehem Steel at Sparrows Point."

Once inside the president's office, somewhat cramped with the board of directors seated around an oval conference table, he pulls the chain to turn off the electric fan humming in one corner, and reads a sign that his father copied from the one in John Wooden's office at UCLA: *IT'S WHAT YOU LEARN AFTER YOU KNOW IT ALL THAT COUNTS."*

He shrugs his shoulders under a black and blue tweed sport coat and looks down quickly at the black and blue stripes on his tie, Johns Hopkins athletic colors, and tells himself, "This is a different race that I'm entering this morning."

He smiles broadly while examining the expression on the face of each board member. He purposely decides to hold his first board meeting of three directors and three managers, all in their 60's, in his office because he likes the acoustics here.

"Gentlemen, every Thursday and Friday at 9 a.m., we will meet here for briefings. This first one is your chance to get acquainted with me and see how I intend to run the mill. It was always my father's wish for me to work my way up and eventually take over the operation. Unforeseen circumstances have made it mandatory that I assume the role of president beginning today."

"It's good to have you aboard, Mark, or should I call you Mr. President?" asks his Vice President of Operations, Dr. Joost de Wal, who holds a doctorate in metallurgy from the University of Delft in the Netherlands.

"You can call me 'Your Highness,' 'Your Eminence' or 'Your Majesty,' but never call me late for an emergency," he answers facetiously with a laugh.

His response seems to put everyone more at ease, at least temporarily.

"I trust you won't be dragging me down to those Bessemer furnaces, like your father did, whenever he needed confirmation that his procedures were followed precisely as he engineered them," admits Dr. de Wal.

Mark shrugs his shoulders as if to acknowledge his remarks and smiles because now he knows how and where his father got those rust and singe marks on his suit.

"You're the one they call the "flying Dutchman" because you can scurry quickly around those furnaces without getting your suit singed, unlike my father," he kids him with a brief burst of light-hearted laughter.

He then gazes down at some 3- by 5-inch index cards in his hand.

"My father always told me, 'If you remember anything, be impeccably honest in all your dealings,' a principle I'm passing on to you. With your support, the ownership will remain in the hands of the Hopkins family, and the mill at Sparrows Point will not be sold or splintered.

"You may have seen me wondering around in the mill at odd hours, talking to various people, trying to get a feel for the mill and our employees. You can learn a lot by listening to what they have to say and what's on their mind. This wandering was a way to size up the mill as quickly as I could, not to make any waves, but to insure that we'll keep the ball rolling, with no interruption in our production and way of doing business.

"I've come to the following conclusions: Bethlehem Steel has a good blast furnace and is accessible to a major waterway for exporting our products all over the world. It also comprises valuable land in which to expand our current capacity, such as adding a plate mill. According to land records, we are still the largest tidewater steel plant in the United States, a fact we should publicize more.

"As we begin a new era of leadership, it's imperative that everyone will continue to meet or exceed the standards established by my forefathers. Everyone has their way of running things. Changes will not be made for the mere sake of making changes. I'm not interested in putting my imprint on Bethlehem Steel. But if change is needed to stem the tide of decreasing profitability, we'll make those changes together. We've got to find a way to level our ship and, with your help of course, tackle the day-to-day pressures in a way that will not begin to torment you as it did my father. It was a dose of daily torment that took his life, much too soon.

"Whatever I do and you do from this moment forward will be overseen by my forefathers, so I ask you to think about them peering over your shoulder and ask yourselves, 'Is this what William I and II would want me to do?' For your sake, I hope the answer is *yes*."

He pauses to swallow a glass of water and watch several of the men become fidgety and squirm in their seats.

"No one has ever fallen asleep in my briefings in the military, because we were all at war," he tells them. "Well, gentlemen, we're at war here too, a different war for survival against adversaries like Stackhouse and Solomeni who want to buy the mill, against foreign producers who get subsidies from their government, and even against our own government who refuse to extend a helping hand when we ask for it. The conclusion here is simple: We have to do it on our own. You cannot expect to get any outside help."

He pauses momentarily to examine an organization chart, takes a deep breath and lets it out slowly.

"Accountability is the key word," he continues. "My first order as president is directed at the Process Control Manager, John Donnelly. Within the next seven days, I want a report, no longer than four pages, on the breakdown of man-hours and expenses to produce everything on our product line. Your report will be studied by everyone here to see if it's worth keeping the product line as it now exists, or if we should decrease or increase certain product lines. Sentimentality will not play a factor in keeping a product line alive when it should have been eliminated long ago. Any questions or comments so far?"

His board of directors all nod in agreement and acceptance of his briefing, for the time being.

"It is not my intention to lay off anyone," he pronounces with distinction. "On the contrary, if it appears that a particular product line should be eliminated or reduced, we will re-train those employees affected, give them a boost in their education, along with a raise in pay. You can call it 'a growth in spirit' that should lead to 'a growth in production.' We must put pride back into everyone's heart and mind."

Mark notices the expressions on the faces of his managers gradually change from doubt that he could take over the mill into confidence, realizing he's exciting to be around, like a fresh breeze of ideas about to blow through the mill.

"Any questions?" he asks again while perusing the room.

Heads move from side-to-side, and no questions come forth.

"In that case," he looks at Miss Potts and tells her, "make a note that I want suggestion boxes repainted in gold-colored paint and placed in prominent places around the plant, with easy to fill-out forms. We're going to have continuity and be a team, and often the best ideas come from the lowest workers on the mill floor. We have to include all workers and let them know how valuable they are to the team. If we're all pulling together in the same direction, we can face the union, domestic and foreign customers and competitors and come out on top.

"Whether or not you like it, whether or not you know it, we can only survive if each person carries more of the load that my father carried alone on his shoulders all those years. I cannot and will not let him down again. If you want a personal meeting with me, it has to be on Thursday and Friday, because that's the only days I'll be available at the mill. Each of you are being paid well and have job security, until you show me otherwise.

"Is that a threat, Mark?" asks Thomas Szymanski, Vice President of Finance. "You don't have to raise your voice with us. We wouldn't be here for over 20 years if we weren't doing a good job for your father and the mill."

"Sorry, no threat intended," he apologizes slowly with sincerity in his voice. "My father occasionally muttered something about moving further into the computer age and upgrading production through digital automation. In this regard, I want our Personnel Manager..."

He pauses to study a personnel list on the table.

"Richard Parlow?" he asks.

"Right here, Mark, under your nose," answers Parlow with a laugh.

"You're the second one to get a direct order. Check with Thyssen-Krupp in Essen and with Siemens in Frankfurt, Germany, to find a computer whiz who can join our firm and install new software into our product line, starting with Automatic Gauge Control (AGC) and Power Line Communications (PLC)."

"What makes you think you can pry away a computer whiz from Thyssen-Krupp?" asks Parlow.

"Call it intuition. The timing is right to hire a computer whiz because there's consolidation going on in Germany, with layoffs and terminations. Thyssen-Krupp already has digital systems operating in their plants, and no longer needs many of these highly-qualified, highly-paid people on their staff. We might get lucky and find another Bill Gates or Steven Jobs anxious to relocate to Sparrows Point, with new challenges ahead.

"That concludes our meeting, except that I want each of you to take a copy of *Psycho-Cybernetics* to read. You'll find them on Miss Potts' desk. The book contains some axioms that will benefit you, such as 'plan your work before you work your plan' and 'turn stress into success.' But I disagree strongly with 'fake it before you make it.' At Bethlehem Steel, we are not faking anything. What you see is what you get."

After the board meeting is adjourned, each man parades single file and extends his hand to congratulate him on succeeding his father and for conducting a beneficial briefing, his first at the mill.

As Mark follows Miss Potts out of his office, he finds Stackhouse and Solomeni pacing the floor of the outer office. Both realize that something is brewing, possibly the heir-apparent is ready to cash-out and enjoy his inheritance. Both also relish in the thought of going up against the 27-year old successor who has never run a business before, especially a complex business like Bethlehem Steel.

RL and Salvi are asked by Mark to follow him, down the stairs, leading into the belly of the mill, near an idle Bessemer blast furnace, almost exactly the spot where his father died, with the same dim light overhead. The putrid stench is still there along with a dripping sound of water coming from rusty corrosive pipes with leaky valves.

He asks them to stand in front of him, about four-feet apart, and tells them, "From what I've been able to determine, I'm standing in the exact spot where my father died."

Suddenly Mark reaches into the waistband of his trousers and removes a sheath. He slowly opens it and removes the shinny dagger whose blade reflects in the overhead light.

"Have either of you ever seen one of these blades?," he asks them. "It's tempered steel, like the blade of a Samurai sword. It can cut any bone in your body. If you didn't already know it, I was trained as a SEAL, one of the best fighting forces in the military, trained to kill people who deserve to be killed. I'm not telling you this because I like to tell you this. But your days of doing business the old ways with my father are no longer acceptable. You're not going to send me to an early grave like you did to my father.

"RL, you're going to back off with your aggressive behavior and union thugs meddling with and slowing up our production. You know what I'm talking about, and you must change your tactics. What I want from you is a willingness to cooperate with our managers, so we can continue to give America the best steel at the best price with the best union workers in America.

"Salvi, for the last time, the mill is not for sale. Get it through your thick skull, once and for all. If you attempt to intrude again with your offers, you will find yourself tied to a shovel and tossed alive into one of these blast furnaces. If Mittal wants to form a partnership with Bethlehem Steel, a partnership where both remain independent yet cooperative, we're willing to discuss a deal.

"If either of you fail to adhere to my words, the blame will be on you, not me. As I said before, you're not going to drive me to an early grave like you drove my father to his grave. Now, gentlemen, I want you to remain exactly where you are for the next minute until you hear the sound of steel striking steel, and see the overhead light come on again. I'm sure you can find your way out of the mill."

Ten seconds later, there is an incredible clang of a furnace door slammed shut, which echoes throughout this particular area and sends pigeons resting in the rafters scattering everywhere.

Moments after the overhead light comes back on, a security guard blows his whistle and yells, "Hey, you two guys, what are doing over there?"

"It's none of your business," RL shouts back, then turns to face Salvi.

Both men appear to look unafraid, with a face full of anger and resentment.

"Who the hell does he think he is?" RL says. "In my business, I'm the one that does the threatening."

"Yes, you can shove all you want," mutters Salvi slowly, almost chewing on each word, "but do you want to end up on the end of a shovel? Is buying the mill worth your life or both our lives?"

Both men walk slowly and carefully out of the secluded area to ponder their next moves.

A few days later, Mark meets Abigail inside her condo in Homewood overlooking the campus of Johns Hopkins in Baltimore to discuss the possibility of her taking over more responsibility of Ridgefield while he assumes the presidency of his father's steel mill.

"Whatever makes you happy will make me happy, too," she tells him while handing him a glass of chilled Chardonnay. "You'll have your hands full but you can do anything you put your mind to. We'll take everything one step at a time, one day at a time. Remember, Rome wasn't built overnight. If you want my advice, follow your instincts as you've always done. You've made a lot of friends, so don't hesitate to reach out for help when you need it."

"My first priority will be the care and welfare of my mother to make sure she has all the support needed to carry on with her life. I expect to get to know her all over again by spending more time at Cylburn."

"From what you've told me about your father's dedication to the mill and work schedule, Sara probably expected the day would come when he would no longer be at her side. But his death, nevertheless, is a major blow. As for Ridgefield, I can be there on days when you're in Baltimore to oversee everything. We'll both have to adjust our schedules but, as I've told you many times, I enjoy the challenge and working by your side."

"Later this afternoon," he advises her, "I'll be meeting Mike Bloomburg and Lola Albright to file the probate documents for my father's estate. Mike's been a friend, and a highly-trusted member of the Hopkins family for as long as I can remember. And his junior partner, Lola Albright, provides considerable comfort to my mother by dropping in to see her, to and from her office at Mount Vernon Place. I wouldn't be surprised if she sleeps overnight at Cylburn. They've become good friends."

Before leaving her condo, Mark surveys her small living room to see what art she has collected, then asks, "Do you have a favorite piece of art that you could never part with?" He pauses and laughs, "There I go again, ending a sentence with a preposition."

"As a matter of fact I do. It's the portrait "Little Boy in Green Jumper," painted by Camelia Whitehurst (1871-1936), who studied under William Merritt Chase in New York and Cecilia Beaux in Philadelphia, and became one of Baltimore's best known artists in the 1920's and 30's."

She walks him over to a wall where the portrait hangs above a Federal-style bow-front chest.

"The brushstroke reminds me of the paintings of Robert Henri," Mark admits after spending a minute or two to admire and study it carefully. "It looks as if it was painted yesterday, instead of the late 20's, because the pigments look wet and fresh. The child's facial expression is one of innocence, curiosity and hope that the artist will finish soon so he can get back to having some fun instead of holding the pose."

"Whenever I look at it, my heart breaks a little," Abigail tells him.

"I'd love to know why, but not if it puts you through any pain for telling me more about it."

"I don't mind because it inspires me to take very day as a blessing from God and make each day count.

"The child is Paul Wayland Berge, the third and last son of the Baltimore sculptor Edward Berge (1876-1924)."

"I'm familiar with his works which are in the collection of the Walters Art Gallery. In fact, we have a cast of his 'Wildflower' bronze at Cylburn. Did you know he studied with Auguste Rodin (1840-1917) in Paris?"

"Yes I did. We should make it a priority to learn as much as we can about Baltimore, our home town, and all its painters and sculptors.

"Paul was born around 1921 and named for the great Philadelphia sculptor, Paul Wayland Bartlett, a close friend of Edward, whose wife first commissioned Whitehurst to paint a double-portrait of her twin sons, Henry and Stephens, and thirteen years later, this portrait, provided she teach Paul his school lessons while he was posing.

"According to Henry Berge (1908-1998), from whom I bought this portrait a year before he died, Whitehurst would pick up young Paul in a chauffeured car and take him to her studio on Eutaw Place, where she drilled him on his studies while painting his portrait."

"I get the feeling that you're about to tell me something painful, aren't you?

"Very perceptive of you. According to Henry, Paul was about 6 when he posed for the portrait. and later, around 1940 at the age of 19, enlisted in the Army Air Corps. He was stationed at a military flight school in Alabama, and during one of his early training missions, around 1942, he and his co-pilot were attempting a landing when the plane suddenly flipped over and both were decapitated. Henry was ordered by his mother to go to Alabama to identify Paul's body and bring it back to Baltimore for burial."

She pauses and continues, "If you're wondering how he was able to identify his brother, Henry said 'Paul had a scar on his ankle from a childhood injury.' "

She pauses, let's her chin fall to her chest for a few seconds as tears swell up in her eyes, then after gathering her strength, looks into Mark's eyes and says, "I can't tell you in words what this painting means to me every time I look at it. It goes way beyond owning a work of art for the simple pleasure of owning a work of art, if that makes any sense to you."

"That's a story I'll never forget as long as I live," Mark declares. "Another story of a young man who died for his country. Thank you for sharing it with me."

Later that afternoon, Mark is seated inside Mike Bloomburg's office in a brownstone row house at Mount Vernon Place. While various probate papers are passed to him for review and his signature, he manages to flirt with Lola and thank her for everything she's given in the way of encouragement and solace to his mother.

"I often wondered what it would be like to spend the night with you, and now I know," she replies facetiously while leaning her body in his direction. "Recently I had the pleasure of sleeping in your bed and gazing again at that marvelous nude by Renoir that hangs across the room. It seems as if she was whispering to me and asking, 'Where's Mark tonight?' Surprisingly, your mother has not drifted into deep depression."

"You and I must do whatever it takes to see that she remains steady," he says sternly as if he's still giving advice to his men in a military briefing.

"Obviously," confides Lola, "she was fully was aware of her husband's work habits, and his refusal to back away from the heavy workload he faced every day, including weekends."

"She was reconciled that she had a competitor, a rival, for his love."

"Apparently he loved the steel business almost as much as he loved her. I hope that doesn't happen to you, Mark."

Around 5 o'clock, Mark is seated in the kitchenette, having a cozy dinner with his mother and the smell of sour beef and dumplings, marinated in a light gravy with ginger snaps, permeating the air.

"Would you consider moving to Ridgefield, or at least spending several weeks with me there?" he asks while smacking his lips and drooling a little over her special recipe. We would be together, and help each other gain a new perspective in our lives."

"But you have so many things on your plate right now. I wouldn't want to be a burden."

"Are you kidding? I'd love to have you near me. I'll build an addition or separate cottage next to the main house, so you can have your privacy and still be close to us every day, and let Mother Nature take over, with views of the Bay, geese overhead and in the corn fields, and plenty of peace and quiet for reflection. You'll have free reign to do whatever pleases you. And there's a small library inside the Municipal Building in Rock Hall, only five minutes away."

"Let me think about it. I appreciate your offer more than you'll ever know."

Sara was shielded from money worries, and is not surprised when, a day later, Mike hands her a check for $1,500,000 as half of her husband's insurance coverage.

"I'd trade it and all the money in my bank account for one more day with my husband," she tells Mike with sadness in her voice. "Looking back, though, it was an incredible love we shared. And we were blessed to have a wonderful son."

"Speaking of Mark," he tells her, "I have a similar check for him, since your husband's life insurance totaled $3,000,000."

"In that case, Mike, give my check to Mark, too. Tell him I want to invest in his projects at Ridgefield. It's better that you tell him instead of me because it's a business decision, not personal."

"By the way, Lola and I have been invited to Ridgefield on Saturday," Mike tells her, "to look over his plans and see the Wildlife Refuge nearby. I think Mark may be smitten with Lola, and needs a chaperon. Why don't you come along with us too?"

"I'm not surprised at Mark's attraction to Lola. She's been a dear to me, and I would like very much to see Mark's farm."

Back at Ridgefield, Mark is usually up at the stroke of dawn, with calisthenics and running wind sprints along the sandy beach or back and forth from the shore to Eastern Neck Island Road, all accompanied by his new dog, Jen, short for Jennifer, a six-month, short-haired golden lab. After a workout that usually last about

30 minutes, he's ready for a cup of coffee and one of Judy's just-baked muffins.

This particular morning, while Mark is finishing his last sprint, Judy gazes out a window to watch and enjoy Jen outracing him and often cutting in front of him, like a speedy driver cutting between cars on the highway. She decides to move a heavy arm chair and reposition it in the living room. As she tries to pull it a foot closer to the fireplace she grabs her heart and falls forward. It's an instantaneous fatal heart attack. She never had a chance to push her medic-alert on her key chain, kept in the front pocket of her denim trousers.

After Mark opens the front door and begins to walk into the living room, Jen races over to Judy and barks as she always does to greet her. Mark finds her body deposited in the arm chair. He checks her vital signs and calls 911.

Fifteen minutes later, the rescue squad is administering to her, and carries her body to their ambulance for transport to the coroner.

Three days later, a funeral service is held at St. John's Church in Rock Hall, first a Mass of celebration, immediately followed by a ceremony at the cemetery behind the church. A large number of neighbors, acquaintances and friends unite in a big outpouring of affection for one of the last grand dames of Rock Hall. Judy was very active and well-liked in the community, and could trace her ancestry back at least 150 years in Kent County.

Because Judy never spoke about any relatives, the pastor asks Mark to give the eulogy.

"Two people who have given me so much in my life are gone from this earth," Mark begins solemnly. "First, my father who died at the age of 60, and now Judy Ridgefield who died at the age of …"

"Over 39," echoes a voice in the crowd.

"She was a good soul," continues Mark, "one of the pioneer women on the Eastern Shore. To some, she appeared feisty, to others, grouchy, but inside, her heart was pure gold. I knew her only a few months, and frankly, there should be others who knew her much longer than me to speak here today. Is there anyone who would like to join me now?"

Typical of the people of small farming communities similar to Rock Hall, where everyone is laid back and lets the other person do their thing, no one moves a muscle to come forward and add something about her life.

"Let it be said, then," Mark resumes, "quoting from scripture, 'Come back to the Lord, with all your heart, leave the past in ashes, turn to God with tears and fasting, for he is slow to anger, and ready to forgive.' It truly is the end of Judy Ridgefield, as we know of her life with us. But we have the satisfaction and consolation of harboring memories that will last us an eternity."

Mark scratches the brow of his face, stretches his neck from side to side to remove a kink, and continues, "I don't know who said it, but certainly it applies here: 'To know her is to love her.' She opened more than her home when she sold Ridgefield to me. She opened the doors to opportunity. She always believed in my motto: 'You Can Be Better Than You Are.' She was special and will be missed."

The funeral Mass ends with the final blessing by the priest, who then proclaims, "Go in Peace to Serve the Lord, Our God." He pauses and concludes with, "The burial will be private."

Following the Mass, a reception is held at the church hall next door where a small buffet is catered by Capt'n Chucky's Crab Cake Company of Newtown Square, Pennsylvania. Owner Nancy and Chuck Wojciehowski, 'crabby' owners who are parishioners of St. John's Church, bring a selection of their famous crab cakes and home-made soups, especially their popular cream of crab along with oyster and clam chowders. These were particular favorites of Judy, who would help out in the kitchen during parish receptions.

At least 50 parishioners attend the reception and form a line for the hot buffet whose odors of highly-seasoned seafood fill the air.

"People always turnout for a free buffet, don't they?" Mark asks Sandy while both are standing at the end of the line. "I'm disappointed that not one of them made an attempt to add a few words to my eulogy about Judy Ridgefield. They pretend that she was such a good friend, yet they contributed nothing at the burial site."

"Small town mentality? We can't change what's inside them or what's not inside them, can we? But I love the flower arrangement on each table, a single rose that looks so real inside a glass pulpit vase. I had to touch it to realize the pink and red petals were silk and imported from Czechoslovakia."

"The entire arrangement," Mark replies, "was hand-made by Antoinette 'Toni' Calibey of Swan Point. She's a talented artist, like you, good with her hands and mind. But unlike you, she a little over 39, a senior member of the Rock Hall Garden Club, who always provide very creative and original works of art for occasions such as this one."

Near the end of the reception, Mark is surprised and pleased to see members of the Breeze track team looking so athletic and upbeat.

"The last time I saw you," Mark tells Jesse, "you were stretching out your chest across the finish line as the last runner of the relay team. Are you still working out at the Senior Park?"

"We're learning a trade by helping Jack Johnson in his construction projects," answers Jesse. "You probably didn't realize that we were actually working and getting paid during Judy's addition. She gave us muffins to eat and even take home. It's good that you didn't see us at Ridgefield, otherwise we'd be talking to you about sports instead of hammering those 2-by's into place."

"You may not have seen me, but I was watching you, all of you, like a hawk. After all, if you're going to be successful in business, you have to watch how and where your money's being spent."

One of Jesse's teammates, Max Speedie Jr., whose grandfather played for legendary coach Paul Brown and the Cleveland Browns of the 1950's, steps forward to say, "Sir, you mentioned several months ago the possibility of training us as a swim team. We're ready to take the plunge on your offer, if it's still possible."

"Max, your father and grandfather, if they were still alive, would be very proud to see how you've matured. I remember that you ran the first leg of the relay at the Harvest Fest, against five of the fastest sprinters in Maryland, and gave us a little edge. That was something you all should think about too. Winning or achieving something special is not about the final sprint to the finish line. It's about how you start, the beginning, middle and ending. Each and every moment is important. And there's no place for quitters or anyone who wastes time. How many times did I stress that when I was coaching you in Betterton."

"But coach, you didn't answer my idea, actually it's our idea, about training us as a swim team," repeats Max.

"As much as I'd like to see you form a swim team," Mark tells Jesse and Max as the remaining two members of The Betterton Breeze team huddle closer together, "I have a better idea. Jack told me how much you've learned about construction and how well you work together as a team. If you continue on this path, I'm ready to sponsor you in junior college. Each of you will have tuition and books, paid by me, for the first two years of a junior college of your choice. "There's a growing need for contractors, inspectors and specialists who can advise home-owners of ways to increase the efficiency of their homes. I trust your grades at Kent High meet the college entrance requirements. And after graduation, you'll always have a job with Jack and me, since we expect to build something special at Ridgefield."

They're all stunned and momentarily stone-faced, despite digesting Mark's offer to pay for their first-two years of college. Each one tries to respond but words fail to come forth.

"No one has ever given us anything before," Jesse admits after swallowing his gum. "I don't know what to say."

"All we've ever heard," utters Max, "was that we'll never amount to anything."

Finally, Mark puts his arm around Jesse and Max and looks at the other two members of The Breeze team, and says, "From my standpoint, you're now men. It pleases me to invest in you and tell you something you may not be aware of.

"Always remember that each of you is something special because you have 'resolve,' which is very hard to measure or detect. What other people think is not important. You've heard the cliché, 'Actions speak louder than words.' We're a team and we'll work as a team. And never forget: *You Can Be Better Than You Are.*"

After he finishes talking to The Betterton Breeze, Mark turns to Sandy and tells her, "I think I just gave the Mother of all pep talks. Maybe it ranks up there with Knute Rockne's 'Win One For The Gipper.'"

About a week following Judy's funeral, Mark is shocked by a telephone call from the Kent County Register of Wills in Chestertown. Mrs. Nancy Lee Jewell. "In her recorded 'Last Will and Testament,' Nancy discloses, "Judy Ridgefield stipulated that all her assets pass entirely to you as the sole beneficiary, to be applied, if possible, to your project for the Red Cross R&R Refuge. Those assets include her bank account, life insurance, along with a request for her decoy collection to be exhibited in a wing named for her and her husband."

Mark files all paperwork as beneficiary to all assets from Judy Ridgefield's estate, which amounts to over one million dollars in two bank accounts: Peoples Bank and PNC Bank, both in Rock Hall, Maryland.

A few days later, Mark attends a board of directors meeting of Bethlehem Steel where each officer admits to carrying more load or responsibility due to Mark's previous directives, with a status report 'still in the works.'

Afterward, Richard Parlow, Vice President of Personnel, remains alone inside Mark's office and tells him about telephone calls from Salvi Solomeni that were intercepted and recorded. "Salvi Solomeni," Parlow declares, "has tried to hire your secretary to eavesdrop on administrative activities in the mill. He must have heard a rumor that you are thinking of replacing Miss Potts with a younger secretary."

"That's nonsense. Where did such a rumor start?"

"Where? Who knows. That's not the point," Parlow tells him while grabbing his arm. 'Hot under the collar' fits the description of Parlow as veins begin to protrude from his neck and his face turns red. His hands tremble as he waves them around to describe the enormous impact on the operation and administration of the mill. To emphasize his anger and distain, he pronounces Salvi Solomeni's name in six distinct syllables.

"He's got to be stopped now before he gets a foothold inside our plant," he declares.

Mark is stunned and shocked, seemingly caught off guard, and doesn't know exactly how to react, so he bites his tongue and waits to hear everything Parlow has to say..

"If I were you," Parlow advises, "I'd invite him to go horseback riding in Hunt Valley and see that he has a fall and breaks his neck!"

"Not a bad idea, Richard, but that's why we have attorneys on the payroll." He pauses then places his hand on Richard's shoulder and says, "Correction. I was not inferring that the attorneys will go horse-backing instead of me."

After a good laugh, a meek attempt to get Richard to calm down so he won't have a heart attack, Mark tells him, "It's time to turn the case over to Mike Bloomburg and Lola Albright."

Mark turns away from Richard and presses the intercom on his desk.

"Miss Potts, get Mike Bloomburg on the phone and tell him it's urgent, that I must see him as soon as possible, about a problem at the mill. Arrange for me to meet him at his Mount Vernon office anytime today or tonight."

At 7 in the evening, Mark arrives at Mike Bloomburg's office and is greeted by Lola Albright, who escorts him into a small conference office with a view overlooking the Washington Monument.

"First," Mark begins after handing Mike and Lola a brief on the situation he's about to explain, "Detective Cain and the coroner discovered a special drug in my father's body, during the autopsy, and are ruling his death "by suspicious means."

"Secondly, Detective Cain said that during interviews with two men, RL Stackhouse and Salvi Solomeni, both admit to being with my father when he died near an idle blast furnace. Both of these men have been relentless in trying to buy the mill. RL, union boss, has exerted a great deal of pressure on my father, including harassment at the mill by RL's union thugs that Dad was forced to hire as inspectors but who infiltrated some workers in an attempt to get them to slow down their performance, so that overtime would be required to meet orders that were backed up.

"Thirdly, Salvi, during an investigation and interview with Detective Cain, mentioned something about black and white photos showing my father sitting on a bed with a nude woman behind him. But the whereabouts of such photos is unknown so far. It's only the testimony of Salvi at this point.

"Finally, Salvi has attempted to hire Miss Virginia Potts, my secretary, to eaves drop on administrative decisions at the mill. My VP of Personnel said I should invite Salvi to go horse-back riding in Hunt Valley and arrange to have him fall and break his neck.

"That's it in a nutshell, and I've written it all down for you so we can discuss our course of action."

"I know what I would do," answers Lola, "but I work for Mike and will let him have the first word."

"Off the top of my head, let me say that I think it will take some time to sort everything out properly, but we can tackle each point one at a time. Being an eternal optimist, I want you to pay attention and remember the law is the law, and don't do anything foolish, like going horse-back riding with the intent of breaking someone's neck.

"Let's examine your statement about your father being in bed with a nude woman. A nude woman? I don't believe it and neither should you. Those photos must have been doctored."

"The problem," Mark interjects, is that even if these photos are never found, the news would devastate my family and friends and even affect the image of the mill. So far it's just the word of Salvi, one of my father's adversaries, who wants to buy the mill for Mittal and will do anything, moral or immoral, to get his way, including trying to hire my secretary."

"Adversaries are bastards," answers Mike, "worse than rattle snakes because they don't always rattle before biting you."

"I have a suspicion," Mark roars, "who might be the blackmailer with the photos and intend to deal with him in my own way. You may think it's entirely out of character to plot revenge, but I'll do whatever it takes to find and expose him, in the same way I helped to find Vera's murderer."

"You've given me an idea, Mark," echoes Bloomburg. "This is a case for Virgil Tubbs. I've represented clients being blackmailed and, as soon as we were ready to begin court-proceedings, the blackmailers dropped all charges and disappeared. It was all a scam, a shake-down, a swindle to get honest and wealthy heads of families and businesses to fork over a bundle of cash, fast."

"Time is of the essence here, Mike," says Mark as he brings his clenched fists up to his chest.

"I'll have Tubbs look into it immediately and do everything possible to keep those photos, which must be doctored, from being published or circulated."

"In recent years," Mark admits, "Dad spent a lot of time riding his jumper in fox hunts, in the fields and woods around Hunt Valley. You know, riding a horse, whether it's simply for a walk in the park or a fox hunt, can be a dangerous thing. Look what happened to Christopher Reeve. I have a suspicion about who may be the blackmailer, and I'm going to arrange to meet him for a casual ride together. In case I don't get back in one piece, tell my mother that I love her."

"What did Mike just tell you, Mark?" Lola tells him while grabbing his arm. "Please don't do anything foolish or dangerous to compound the problem. Remember the law **is** the law, and stay closer to your mother to monitor her mail and intercept these photos if they turn up. Between you, me and the maid, we should be able to intercept these photos if they come through the mail or special delivery."

On the following Saturday, Mark has arranged to meet Salvi alone at noon in Hunt Valley, under the pretext of discussing a possible sale of the mill. They've agreed to ride their horses together in a heavily wooded private reserve on the edge of Hunt Valley, away from the fox hunt territory.

When Mark arrives on time at the designated spot, he finds Salvi lying on the ground, below the head of his horse. His jumper tries to nudge him with his wet nose, but Salvi doesn't move a muscle.

After Mark checks the carotid artery at his throat, he realizes that Salvi is dead and immediately calls 911 on his cell phone. He watches over Salvi so nothing is disturbed in a possible crime scene and waits for the police and rescue squad to make its way through the forest.

His body is transported to the coroner for an autopsy.

A week later, Detective Cain telephones Mark at his Ridgefield office.

"Salvi's death is ruled 'by suspicious means,' and possibly related to your father's death," he discloses. "We've gathered a lot of information on the case and thought you should know how the early investigation is proceeding, so here goes: Clues gathered at the crime scene, including footprints and lack of forest debris in his riding habit, lead us and the coroner to conclude that he did not die as a result of being thrown from his horse, but had been dead for several hours, and possibly moved from a previous site. That's all I can tell you at this time."

"That good news and bad news. Good that you've uncovered things that our private investigator Virgil Tubbs will appreciate, and bad for the person or persons involved in Salvi's death."

Within minutes of ending his telephone conversation with Detective Cain, Mark is on the line with Mike Bloomburg, who tells him, "I've hired Virgil Tubbs. I also heard about Salvi's death in Hunt Valley. I hope you didn't have anything to do with it, Mark.

"No, Mike, someone beat me to it, thankfully. And I just got off the phone with Detective Cain who told me that his death may be related to my father's death. Furthermore, Salvi may have died at another location several hours before I found him and his body moved to Hunt Valley."

"I'll have Virgil get in touch with Detective Cain," answers Bloomburg, "because they've worked together before and respect each other. After all, we're trying to piece this puzzle together and will need everyone's input and talents."

"About your hiring Virgil Tubbs, it pleases me immensely that he can jump right in, like he did in managing the case to find Vera's murderer. It's true what they say about him, that he has the instincts of a bloodhound and the tenacity of a bulldog in never letting go until a case is solved."

Chapter 10

After two weeks on the case, Tubbs suspects that RL Stackhouse had devised a plan to kill Salvi and implicate Mark, an attempt by him to kill two birds with one stone. By removing a rival who wanted to buy the mill for Mittal and implicating the owner's son who had revenge as a motive, RL would be sitting pretty and in a better position to buy the mill for the union.

While Virgil Tubbs is driving to Hunt Valley to examine the area where Mark found Salvi's body, he gets a phone call from the coroner.

"A strange coincidence has developed," the coroner tells him. "According to our pathologist, an expert in the field of cardiac pathology, both William II and Salvi had trace amounts of the same special anesthetic in their blood samples. It was popofol, an anesthetic that was sufficiently diluted to sedate them but possibly not enough not to kill them."

"That's the same drug that Michael Jackson took, but overdosed on," Tubbs answers.

"In the case of Mark's father, William Hopkins II, ingesting it certainly could relax him sufficiently so that he would lose all strength in his muscles, and prevent him from reaching for his oxygen tank or from taking a nitro pill."

"Interesting development, Sir," Virgil discloses. "I know Mark will be eager to hear more about it."

"Hold off a minute. Here's a little more info for you. This anesthetic contained a special additive element, an herb imported from China, intended to give the mixture a sweet taste if administered orally. Because one of the side effects is hallucination, the import of this herb is restricted and controlled by the Food and Drug Administration. When distributed by the manufacturer in Canada, each sale is carefully documented, to avoid the possibility of misuse. The anesthetic with the special additive herb can only be sold to specialists who place an order through a licensed pharmacy."

"A little more info did you say? That's an incredible amount of news to digest, all due to today's technology and skilled people who know how to use that technology. Thank you very much, Sir."

"Finally," the coroner concludes, "we've traced the records and discovered that only one pharmacy in the Baltimore area ordered it especially for Dr. Wassily Vasser, personal physician to RL Stackhouse."

"I can hardly hold in my breath any longer," Virgil replies. "There's definitely a connection here, because he was a suitor trying to buy the mill from William Hopkins. Please keep me posted and a million thanks for all your good work."

The following day investigators repeatedly telephone Dr. Vasser and get only an automatic recording on his answer machine.

Ultimately, Detective Cain and his staff decide to question him at his home office. When no one answers the front door, they realize a search warrant is not necessary for entry into his premises. Using a pass key, Detective Cain and his staff enter Vasser's home.

Detective Cain is shocked when he discovers his body slumped over the desk in his home-office. Beside his head is a small bottle of propofol and a signed confession, admitting that he may have been seduced and capitulated to RL Stackhouse's demands for the drug imported from Canada.

The wording of the confession is concise and in Dr. Vasser's hand-writing. The last sentence is an admission and apology, a painful regret for not realizing how the drug would be used by Stackhouse.

A few days later, when Detective Cain and his staff descend on Stackhouse at his country estate overlooking the Severn River, they find charred photos in his fireplace, but no negatives. The photos are damaged but enough fragments are pieced together to form a reasonable composite that shows William in bed with a nude woman.

Armed with the belief that they have "probable cause" to link Stackhouse to the death of Mark's father and Salvi, Detective Cain confronts Stackhouse who is unemotional, with the face of a zombie, seemingly unaffected by all the ruckus going on inside his mini-mansion. That is, until Cain reads him his Miranda rights, then his faces changes to one of dejection.

"Ambition has 'done him in,' Detective Cain tells Virgil who's standing nearby and witnessing the arrest.

After the last words of the Miranda rule echo through the hall, a police sergeant slaps handcuffs on Stackhouse, and leads him down a short hall, through a foyer, and into the back seat of a police car.

Later that week, Tubbs has a hunch and manages to get a list of Stackhouse's body guards and henchmen. He decides to comb all the local dry-cleaners to see if any clothes were turned in by people whose names appear on that list. He suspects that blood and soil may be imbedded in the fabrics of suits worn by those who may have participated in Salvi's death.

"It's not a perfect science," Tubbs tells himself while sitting at his desk and poring over the names of dry cleaners in the telephone book. "More like my personal theory. Blotches of blood are hard as hell to remove from a fabric, especially if there's a time lapse. Let's call it "retention of evidence," something that never goes away."

Virgil's reputation for using his instincts and for being relentless in following up on all leads and hunches is well-earned. He's also one of the highest paid private investigators in the state of Maryland

After several weeks of investigating dry cleaners, the soles of Virgil's shoes have holes in them, and the bottom edge of the cuffs of his trousers become tattered as they drag along the ground. Over the past week he may have lost a pound or two from all the leg work in walking six hours a day, with nothing to show for it so far. He neglects to tighten the size 52-inch belt around his waist, and when his pants begin to slip below his waistline, Virgil begins to look like one of those rich Wall Street brokers who's fallen on hard times.

Almost at the end of his rope, so to speak, he gets lucky when he pays a visit to a small shop, formerly a hot-dog joint, on a side street close to a liberal arts and science college, about three miles from Stackhouse's estate on the Severn River.

Tubbs shows the owner his list of names and a check is made of clothes waiting to be picked up. The cross-checking process is about to pay dividends when the owner stops scrolling the list with his finger and pounds the counter with his fist.

"Ah, yes, now I recall two men who brought in their suits for dry cleaning," he exclaims while using both hands to scratch his head furiously the way Johnny Cammareri (Danny Aiello) did in *Moonstruck,* to stimulate the memory cells of his brain.

"It seemed more than a coincidence here," continues the shop owner, "especially because both suits had blotches that looked like blood and shit, pardon my language. I explained that there would be no guarantee that the stains would come out after dry cleaning, and they both looked strangely at me and began laughing, like gangsters in an old 'Edward G. Robinson' movie."

"Astounding," Virgil remarks. "I think we're on to something."

"I just love those old movies, don't you?" the shop owner pauses to admit with a big smile covering his face.

"If you don't mind, forget those movies and please get on with the blotches of blood and, what did you call it, shit?" Virgil asks with a touch of disgust as he begins to get hot under the collar. "The suspense is killing me."

"It was a bizarre incident," resumes the owner, "but I remember it well because there were **two** men. I suspected that they may have fallen off a tractor or something like that. But then again, I realized that two men would not be on a tractor wearing dress suits, would they?"

Virgil leaves the shop faster than Alan Ameche taking a handoff from Johnny Unitas for the overtime win by the Colts against the Giants at Yankee Stadium on December 28, 1958, in the greatest football game ever played. (The reader can look up more details about the game, such as Raymond Berry's 12 receptions, so that the pace of *ROCK* HALL is not slowed up too much here.)

Armed with this information, Tubbs meets with Detective Cain at police headquarters. Together, but with Cain taking the lead, they begin interrogating these two personal bodyguards of Stackhouse.

Under heavy interrogation by both Cain and Tubbs, enough pressure is applied to break the entire case wide open, as both bodyguards admit to their involvement in Salvi's murder.

Threatened with the possibility of a seat in the electric chair, the two bodyguards confess to being accessories who acted under orders from Stackhouse, and lay all blame and responsibility for planning Salvi's murder in RL's lap. They admit that they were accomplices, present at Stackhouse's estate on the Severn River, posing as a cook and butler, and watched Stackhouse pour the anesthetic drug from his sterling-silver flask into a cocktail for Salvi, which instantly sedated him.

Then, under immediate orders from Stackhouse, they carried Salvi's body to the garden behind the house and dropped it over a stone ledge, snapping his neck. Knowing that Salvi had an appointment an hour later to meet Mark in Hunt Valley, they transported his body and horse to the rendezvous location.

Despite the success here, Tubbs and Cain are not ready to close their investigation. The flask containing the dangerous drug is still missing. It's a link, not a critical link, in this case that still bugs them, until Tubbs gets approval to tag along with Detective Cain and his staff who decide to re-examine the premises of Stackhouse's mansion.

Inside a small library at the end of a hall, Tubbs is intrigued by RL's collection of first editions, including works by Edgar Allan Poe, who's buried in Baltimore. Almost all the books have pristine tan leather-bound bindings. His eyes notice something unusual as he points his right index finger at the titles of the books and moves his body along the bookshelf.

Midway along a bottom row, he finds an oversized book with no title. After removing it from the shelf, he discovers that it's not a book at all. It's a box made to look like a large book, with an old, tan leather binding.

When he opens the box, he discovers a sterling-silver flask in a cardboard cutout, covered with black felt, shaped to hold the flask firmly in place.

He immediately transfers it to detective Cain, who closes the lid, and places the box inside an evidence bag.

Several days later, when the flask is examined by the forensics lab, traces of the anesthetic propofol, with the additive herb, are still deposited at the bottom of the flask. Also, Stackhouse's fingerprints are the only ones that appear on the flask, which has a fox hunting scene, engraved by a gifted silversmith, on the front and back surfaces.

When experts in the forensics lab examine the box further and the cardboard cutout is completely removed from its location, they discover some negatives hidden between the inside back of box and the insert to hold the flask in place. When prints are made from the negatives, the resulting photos are images of Mark's father in bed with a nude woman.

When Detective Cain is informed about the discovery of the negatives, he telephones Mark immediately.

"We have good news and bad news for you," Cain tells him. "The good news is that we've found the negatives of your father and the nude woman, and experts have determined that they are doctored. The bad news is that the negatives will remain as evidence in this murder case and probably will be sealed until the case is resolved.

"At this stage, there's not much I can do to suppress this evidence. Sooner or later, it might be a good idea to talk everything over with your attorney and decide if your mother should know something about these photos, which I'm happy to tell you again, according to experts in our photographic lab, are doctored."

Cain pauses to gather his breath and next suggestion, and tells him, "Or, you can take a chance and perhaps these negatives will disappear from our files. I've seen that happen before."

After the district attorney for the city of Baltimore meets with lawyers for Stackhouse, a plea bargain is reached for him to plead guilty to second-degree murder, and throw himself on the mercy of the court to avoid the death penalty.

During the ensuing court proceedings inside the Criminal Court of Baltimore City, Stackhouse is sentenced to 40 years of hard time without the benefit of parole and no time off for good behavior. Stackhouse will most likely be incarcerated for the remainder of his life.

A few days after sentencing, the new union president, Franz Beckenbaur, is invited to the mill to meet Mark, and discuss ways for them to work together in harmony instead of as adversaries. When they meet inside Mark's office and exchange pleasantries, Mark asks him to follow him down to an abandoned blast furnace.

"If that makes you happy, it makes me happy. Please don't let me fall and break my neck or yours if I fall on top of you," Franz tells him facetiously. He follows behind Mark for the next thirty seconds, as if both are walking down into the bowels of an abandoned battleship.

"That musty odor, as if no breeze ever found its way here," Franz utters with words that echo off the walls of this idle section of the mill, "reminds me where I started five years ago, at 22, working at a blast furnace in a steel mill in Germany, where everything was rusty, decaying, with a stench of stale air that turned your stomach upside down. It's something you never forget. I never expected to face those conditions again until now."

After they take a position under a dim, blinking light, each begins to size up the other.

"I don't like the way you're looking at me," Franz becomes edgy and utters with disgust. "Tell me what's on your mind. I don't have all day for you to study me. And you won't find what you want on the surface anyway. You didn't see any bodyguards with me, did you? What you see is what you get."

"I'm sorry, Franz," answers Mark. "It's a habit of mine, sizing up a situation or an opponent."

"I'm not your opponent," advises Franz, "so get that notion out of your head. The stench down here is beginning to turn my stomach. It's something that rats are accustomed to, not a place for two executives to talk things over. Couldn't we discuss whatever's on your mind inside your office?"

"I wanted to show you the exact spot where my father died, after spending 25 years in the mill, and giving his life for his men, mostly men from your steelworker's union," Mark discloses with passion in his voice. "He believed in compromise and so do I. But you could never ever compromise with RL. He played hard ball. It was always his way or no way. He killed my father not with one fatal blow, but gradually over a period of years with his demands. And what did it get him? A life behind bars."

"I'm a different man," admits Franz. "What RL did is in the past and had its way with him. Let's get off that track."

"That suits me fine," Mark answers. "I'm 27 and I'd like to live to be 28, and work with the freedom and respect for everyone. We're both new in the job and eager to do the right thing for our people. Today, I'd like to forge a new bond between Bethlehem Steel and your union. One of the things I learned in the military was the fact that an officer always takes good care of his men. The same conduct applies here."

"There will be no more '*Give 'em hell*' from RL," Franz replies. "You have my word on it. From this point forward, we'll do things in the most humane way possible to guarantee that there's a long-term future at Bethlehem Steel, a bond of fairness and mutual respect. We want you to produce the best steel in the world, with the help of the best union workers in the world."

Finally Mark pauses to take a last look around the idle blast furnace and tells him, "One more thing here. If any of your men have a grievance, tell them to bring it to the attention of their boss. We don't want it to fester. The same goes for you."

The two men shake hands, and each places his left hand on top of the other, as a sign of a new partnership.

The next morning at Ridgefield, Mark is finishing the last jog on the sand, with Jen running at his side. He inhales the fresh air of the Chesapeake Bay again and feels rejuvenated. He's more at peace, seeing the Bay Bridge on the horizon with blue skies above and hearing the gaggle of geese who fly overhead in a *V* formation.

Minutes later, after fixing himself a cup of 'Chock' coffee, he's seated comfortably in his office chair and gazes at a large chart pinned to the wall behind his computer. It's a monthly planner with his work schedule.

Thursday and Friday are days set aside for tending to business at the mill, and Saturday is reserved for a full day with his mother and an occasional date with Lola.

Sunday is a travel day from Baltimore back to Rock Hall.

Monday, Tuesday, and Wednesday until 3 in the afternoon are devoted to Ridgefield, conferring with Abigail, who has moved some of her things from her condo in Baltimore into Judy's portion of the house to be closer to Mark and handle administrative details at Ridgefield.

On the two-hour drive to and from Baltimore to Rock Hall, Mark always gets his best ideas and records them on a miniature portable recorder attached to the console of his BMW. It's located next to his mobile cell phone, rigged up so that it's voice-activated and he can make or receive calls all with voice commands.

The next Sunday, while Mark is driving his BMW on Route 95 in a northerly direction, half way from Baltimore back to Rock Hall, he gets a call from Abigail.

"Don't be shocked if you see a 65-year-old lady working inside the house," she discloses with a laugh. "Her name is Gabby Hayes, a spitfire of energy and fun to be around. I hired her for light cleaning, but she's really a marvelous cook. She lives in my condo complex, and her husband died recently. Temporarily, she'll be living in one of Judy's dressing rooms that I've remodeled for her."

"A dressing room, the kind that stars in Hollywood have?" He enjoys some kidding and continues, "Can't wait to meet her. A spitfire did you say? Just what Ridgefield needs."

"You'll love her because she has the gift of gab and moves around like the Energizer Bunny."

Mark continues laughing and tells her, "Hold off telling me anymore about Gabby. I better concentrate on the road, but I'm looking forward to meeting her later tonight. Tell her not to be shocked if she finds a short stocky man in his 50's with the Wall Street Journal hanging out the front pocket of his suit wondering around the premises."

"Don't tell me you hired another senior?"

"Why not. When you spot something special in someone, especially seniors who bring years of experience with them, you don't take much of a chance in hiring them. Anyway, his name is Womble Weinstein, a former wrestling coach from one of the inner-city high schools in Philly, who went back to college at the age of 45, graduated from Wharton School of Business, and worked on Wall Street where he made a fortune dealing in derivatives and credit default swaps and lost it twice as fast."

"Derivatives? Swaps?" she asks. "I don't know much about derivatives and swaps."

"Apparently, neither did he, but he's one of the brightest and funniest men I've ever met. Over a cup of coffee at Java Rock, I hired him as our financial advisor and sort of father figure since he reminds me of my Dad. I guarantee he'll keep everyone on their toes and in stitches."

A minute after ending his phone call, Mark tells himself, "Can you picture Gabby Hayes, Knute Runagrun, and Womble Weinstein meeting each other for the first time? Now, that has the makings of a good low-budget art film, like *Marty*."

The next morning, Mark settles again in his high-back swivel chair, and surfs the Internet for updates on the government's reluctance to subsidize steel manufacturers in America and for updates about the health of Chesapeake Bay.

Abigail walks into his office, hands him a cup of herbal tea, and takes a seat in the Eames lounge chair.

"Anything special brewing in your mind this morning? she asks.

"As a matter of fact, I'm feeling a little like Paddy Chayefsky when he wrote *Marty* many years ago. Last night I got to thinking about Gabby, Knute and Womble, three *Marty*-type characters, interacting in a short art film to publicize Ridgefield."

"Fascinating," she responds. "Do you have a storyline yet?"

"No, but possibly an opening scene."

"I'm all ears. Don't keep me in suspense."

"Picture an empty hallway on the second floor of the senior complex in Betterton, where the sunlight streams through a window at the end of the hall onto polished floors. Now, I know you're going to say 'seniors shouldn't have polished floors because they'll slip all over the place,' but I need the floors waxed for my film."

"All right, so they're waxed. Gone on, Mr. Spielberg."

"The door to Knute's room opens and he pokes his body halfway out the doorway and shouts down the hall, "And tell those seniors to stay *outa* my drawers!"

"That doesn't make any sense to me."

"Allow me a little latitude here, please. It'll make sense because, when Knute steps into the hallway, he's naked, except for his tugboat-captain's hat that he's holding in front of his private parts."

"Who wants to see the wrinkles of an 80-year, five-foot tall, tugboat captain standing nude in the hall of a senior complex?"

"That shot lasts only two seconds and fades immediately to a scene 40-years earlier, with a close-up of him inside the wheelhouse of his tugboat which is pulling a cargo ship into the crowded harbor at Bergen, Norway. He tilts his cap back to reveal his handsome face while getting some kinks out of his neck. With one hand on the steering wheel, he uses the other to turn on the horn to spell out the name of his tug, *CHESSPEAK* in Morse code. He named his tug after the Chesapeake Bay, but that's another story."

"That's it? That's the opening? You better go back to the drawing board or hire a screenwriter, otherwise you and I will be the only ones dumb enough to want to see such a film."

"Maybe your right. You usually are," he tells her while turning back in his swivel chair to glance at his computer monitor.

"Scheisse!" he bellows out.

"What did you say?"

"Not meant for your ears. I was releasing my frustration at those foreign governments who subsidize the production of steel and try to put us out of business. Not much we can do, since our government is brain-dead and refuses to get involved."

He logs off and swivels his chair to look again at Abigail who is adjusting her body so that her eyes are about level with his.

"Speaking of hiring someone to help you with your art film, I could use some help," she remarks. "I'm not as young as you, and frankly can't keep up with you anymore. I want your permission to hire our first Member of the Technical Staff (MTS)."

"Have you contacted or interviewed anyone?"

"I've interviewed four candidates," she acknowledges while unrolling and handing him a scroll, "and decided on a gorgeous package of beauty and brains that will take your breath away. Frankly, I'm hesitant to hire her, because you know how sensitive and lively those Italian imports are. She's top of the line, a dynamo perfect for Ridgefield. I only hope that she'll stay after we bring her over from Rome. Her name is Kimberly Bozzetti. She told me to call her simply 'Kim'. I'd like to make her an offer she can't refuse."

"Simply Kim? he asks. "An unusual name. I wonder if she can type and take dictation?"

"No, and she's not hired to do that, funny boy," Abigail remarks. "For starters, we're hiring her to establish a lab for research of the Bay, write proposals to get government contracts, and perhaps produce a small budget science or art film. You know, those Italians have a long and distinguished tradition and are very good at film-making."

When Kim finally arrives two days later at BWI Thurgood Marshall Airport outside Baltimore, Abigail and Mark meet her at the arrivals platform and are overjoyed to see a stunning lady, about 27 but looking 21, that literally takes your breath away. Her face with sparkling eyes resembles Halle Berry. In fact, she easily could be Halle's twin sister.

"Bellissimo," Mark tells her."That's the best word I know to describe you. It's also the only word I know in Italian. You're too good to be true. Welcome to America and Ridgefield."

"*Pro-fess-sore-ree?*" she asks him

"Huh?"

"Professor?" She begins laughing and teasing him. "You look like one of my professors at the University of Rome."

"Thank you, but academia was or is not for me," he responds with a chuckle. "However, Abigail and I intend to run things like a university, and let eager and creative minds like yours run freely and see what develops at Ridgefield. We want you to feel like this is your home away from home."

After a pause, he tells her facetiously, "But you may address me as *Your Highness*!"

On the two-hour drive back to Ridgefield, Mark and Abigail explain where she will live and work. Kim is uncharacteristically reticent until they finish with their spiel, then she renders an inkling of her talents and ideas. Mark has to grip tightly the steering wheel of his BMW to keep from gushing over with excitement of her joining their team.

"Wait until Sandy meets you," he tells her. "She'll want to capture you in clay and cast you in bronze."

Kim is puzzled by his remarks, and for the next hour, he explains that Sandy is a sculptor in Betterton, an ascending star in the world of art.

"I was led to believe," she acknowledges, "that you weren't hiring me for my looks, but for my technical skills and research abilities in science and engineering."

"There's nothing wrong in getting both, is there?" Mark answers with a broad smile across his face.

The day after Kim arrives at Ridgefield and settles into a luxury trailer behind the main house, Mark receives a phone call from one of his former SEAL buddies, Dave 'Monty' Montgomery, who has fallen on tough times in Los Angeles.

Mark books a flight for Saturday morning and flies to LAX for a weekend visit with Monty, who's living in an apartment in Venice, only 15 minutes from the airport. He rents a car and drives to Monty's one-bedroom pad, which is in a multi-unit complex about ten blocks from the beach, an easy 20 minute walk.

He leaves his luggage in the trunk of his car, climbs the outside metal stairs to Monty's second floor apartment, and is greeted by his buddy, who has been looking through the curtains, waiting anxiously for his arrival.

Since they are both former SEALS, Mark suggests a walk to the beach, so he can stretch out the kinks in his neck and body after a five-hour plane ride.

During the casual walk, Monty explains his recent job loss.

"I had it good, Mark," he begins slowly and happily, "working for an older, somewhat eccentric, couple. The husband, Harry Crown, was a machinist, first for Douglas Aircraft during the war, and then left them to build a machine shop on his large property in the San Fernando Valley. He continued doing specialized work for them, but as a sub-contractor. He was a precision machinist, with a hobby of restoring two classic cars, a 1952 Mercedes gull-wing, and a '56 Stingray."

"Those were automobiles on the cutting edge of technology," replies Mark, "but require a lot of maintenance to keep them running in top condition."

"That's where I came into the picture. I helped him take apart those babies, lubricate parts that needed lubrication, replace parts that needed replacement, and if any of the metal components were broken, he would machine new parts right inside his shop. As I said before, he was a genius and a perfectionist. There wasn't anything he couldn't do. If a part was machined originally by a machinist at the factory in Germany, he could duplicate it with the same precise tolerances. He was a nut for making sure everything would be original in the repairs. Do you get my drift?"

"Same old Monty. I get your drift. Go on."

"Well, like all good things, everything changed when he had a heart attack and died about six months ago. And then the craziest thing happened. His wife died within a month after her husband."

"How long did you work for Harry?"

"Two years, continuously."

"And then what?"

"Well, unbeknownst to anyone, especially me, he left his entire estate to his wife, and when she died, she left everything to a Mexican maid that cared for them for over 20 years. When I say 'cared,' I mean taking care of all the house-cleaning, running errands, shopping in the markets, and most of the cooking. There were rumors that she sometimes accommodated Mr. Crown's sexual needs, inside the trailer that she lived in, at the far end of the property. It was secluded there, and hardly anyone would even know that someone was living there. But the few times that I was inside the Crown main residence, it really smelled awful from two distinct odors.

"And what were they?"

"Mexican tortillas, Chili-Relleno, burritos, you know, all those delicious Mexican dishes with refried beans covered with cheese, and plenty of hot peppers. The Crown's loved those hot peppers."

"I can smell the odors of that Mexican cooking just from a description of your words, Monty. Now, what was the other thing?"

"A possum, the Crown's had a pet possum, and it would pee all over the house, especially on their beautiful Sarouk rug. At least it was beautiful at one time, until that possum urinated on it when the Crown's weren't looking. I think the Crown's must have lost their sense of smell in their elder years. They were both in their mid-80's when they died."

"Monty," he replies while laughing, "you would make a good investigator if you ever think of changing jobs."

"Would you believe," Monty replies dejectedly, "the maid inherited everything, including the ranch home, about 2,500 square feet, sitting on an acre of prime property in the middle of three-story apartments everywhere, plus a valuable rental property the Crown's had in Hollywood, one of those three-story mansions, like in Billy Wilder's *Sunset Boulevard,* that they converted into small apartments."

Fifteen minutes later, Mark and Monty arrive at Venice Beach, where gorgeous girls of all ages, mostly from 16 to 36, in bikinis and see-thru swimwear, are roller-skating along the concrete boardwalk. After pausing to admire and dodge some skaters, they remove their shoes and socks and walk barefooted onto the sandy beach until they reach the shoreline. They plop down to enjoy the peace and quiet of gentle waves coming ashore.

Mark looks at his watch and says, "In Rock Hall, it's 3 o'clock, the middle of the afternoon, according to my trusty Rolex, but with the time change here, it's noon in Venice."

"Are you getting hungry? The salt air of the Pacific will do that to you," answers Monty.

"Actually, I'm enjoying the story about you and the Crown family. The food can wait, if you don't mind. The Pacific, when I see it, I always think about Monterey and Carmel, the Big Sur area and the Nepenthe Inn, all my favorite places in the world. But I have to confess that my life on the Chesapeake Bay is special, too. We have thousands of Canada geese there, and that's something that you don't have here on the Pacific coast."

"Well, Mark, do you have beautiful girls roller-skating in bikinis there?"

"Are you kidding? I guess we'll have to import some from Venice Beach. But let's get back to the main order of business."

"I hate to bring it up, but I have to raise some money to pay this month's rent, due today, otherwise I could be evicted from my apartment. That's where you come into the picture, Mark.

Remember the maid who inherited the Crown home? Well, it was or is full art that might interest you. She's selling everything and moving to Mexico. Perhaps, if you buy something there, it would bring me some money, as a commission or lead, at least enough to pay my rent."

"I won't let you down, Pal. How much do you need for this month's rent?"

"The rent is $500."

"No problem, even if you can't get me in the door to see the art. I'm glad to help you out, pal."

"Well, Mark," he continues, "the Crown family had their home cluttered with art and antiques. In their main house, a rancher, the entire residence looked very unassuming from the sidewalk, since it was fenced in with old wooden planks attached to 4- by 4-inch posts, and hidden slightly behind large mature trees. If you didn't see an old rusty mail box out front, you'd never know that people lived on the property. It really was secluded, with the main house set back about 150 feet from the sidewalk, so that you hardly noticed it behind those trees. Do you get the picture?"

"I get the picture, Monty. Go on, please. It's very intriguing."

"Inside their home is an amazing assortment of porcelain vases, especially cobalt blue with painted portraits of beautiful women, probably Royal Vienna or Sevres, with bronze ormolu. It's the kind of stuff you showed me in books when we were in Iraq. Do you remember those pictures? I learned a lot from being around you, especially an appreciation for paintings and stuff like that. But I never caught the collecting bug like you. Anyway, you told me to be on the lookout for nice things, didn't you?"

"Monty, you're right on the money," he says while laughing. "Please continue."

"Well, on the walls of the Crown's living room are some very interesting paintings. I always remembered looking at the frames, too. Anyway Mark, one of the paintings is signed 'Winslow

217

Homer,' and I was shocked when I noticed it. As I said before, when we were in Iraq, you often talked about your home, going to auctions, getting the collecting bug, always looking for good paintings. So I thought about calling you to see if you might find something good here, and I could get a finder's fee. I hate to repeat myself and ask that of a buddy, but it's just good business."

"Monty, you're a gem, but you can stop repeating yourself. I said I'll take care of your rent for starters. If I buy anything, your commission will go up accordingly."

Monty finally realizes that the pressure is off temporarily, but he is a guy who always repeats himself. Mark refers to this condition as a reassurance syndrome. Such terms are not recognized by the scientific community or published in any journal of psychology. It's just Mark's way of naming a condition, based on his experience in the military, where he is forced to repeat important steps about to be taken by members of his squad.

"Let's find a café," Monty suggests, "and grab some lunch, and I'll tell you more about the Mexican maid."

They leave the sandy beach and settle down on the patio of a sidewalk café along the Venice boardwalk.

"She's about 40," continues Monty, "a little on the plump side, five foot eight, good disposition, very accommodating, most of the time. But since the Crown's have died, her girlfriend has moved into the house too. They could be lesbians. As soon as we get back to the apartment, I'll call her for an appointment to see the house. It might be better to pretend that you're interested in buying the house since she wants to sell everything and return to Mexico."

Back at his apartment, Monty makes an appointment in the next hour for Mark to see the property in San Fernando Valley, about 40 minutes away by car, and an easy drive on the freeway.

An hour later, Mark and Monty arrive at the Crown property and are greeted by the Mexican maid, Maria Montez, who welcomes them inside and promptly introduces them to Delores Hines, her close friend who's now living with her.

"Would you like a cup of coffee," Maria asks, "while you have a look around the house?"

"I'm fine, but give Monty a cup," answers Mark. "He's driving today and has to stay alert at the wheel."

"Everything's for sale, including the house which we're selling "For Sale By Owner," admits Maria. "We also have a property in Hollywood, an old three-story residence that was converted into apartments by the Crown family years ago."

In the next five minutes, Maria gives them a quick tour of the house, pointing out some details of the interior features, such as tile flooring in the bathrooms and granite countertops that match the color of newly-installed cabinets in the kitchen. At no time during the tour does she point out any of the antiques, including the art work, inside the ranch home.

Mark discretely pauses in front of each painting and, with a coin, taps a large metal bust of Abraham Lincoln resting on a pedestal to determine whether it's bronze or pot metal. When he passes in front of the Homer painting, there's no doubt in his mind that the quality of the oil on canvas represents the artist at his best. It's signed at the lower left hand and dated 1869, and depicts an empty room with an attractive woman, perhaps a young widow, dressed in a long black dress, gazing out an open window with a geranium in a clay flower pot on the window sill.

"Are you selling any of your art, such as this painting?" he asks despite knowing full well her intentions.

"As I said before, everything's for sale if the price is right," she answers. "We're moving to Mexico and money's much easier to carry than all this stuff."

"Maria, would you give us a few minutes alone to talk things over?" asks Monty.

"Why not. Delores and I will be out back in the shed, sorting some things out for a garage sale. Give a holler if you need us."

Mark looks at Monty and smiles. "By leaving us alone, she doesn't have a clue as to the value of some of these things, especially the Homer painting."

"Yes, that's true but she does know me and trusts me," answers Monty.

Mark grabs his arm and walks him into the middle of the living room, then says, "There's no feeling in the world that's better than walking into a place, not knowing what to expect, and suddenly magic happens, such as having a great piece of art drop before your eyes. I don't know how to describe it in words. Unless you've experienced it yourself, you have no idea of the sensation."

"So you're telling me that the trip was worth it?" asks Monty.

"Absolutely, but now the hard part is deciding how to proceed with Maria. It's a little like our mission in Norway where we had only the moon for light over the fjord," Mark tells him. "I've dreamed of moments like this one. From what I've been told, it'll happen once in a lifetime, so we want to make sure we complete the mission successfully. Find Maria and tell her we have a few questions to ask her."

"There's so many nice things you have here, reminds me when I was a kid walking into a candy shop. For starters, do you have a price in mind for this painting?" he asks her while pointing toward the Homer painting.

"No, I don't. Would you make me an offer?" she asks politely.

"I'll have to think about a price," he replies, "but will tell you that I like it, otherwise I wouldn't ask about the price. I want to make sure that it's an original painting by the artist. Can I take a photo of it, and get back to you in a few days?"

After getting her consent, Mark spends the next 10 minutes taking photographs of several paintings and bronzes and making some notes.

As he completes the last shot with his digital camera, he extends his hand and tells her, "Thanks a million for letting me see everything. I'll definitely get back to you in a few days. Do you have a business card?"

"Sorry, no cards," Maria tells him, "but Monty has my number. You can call me anytime, day or night."

On the 30-minute drive back to Monty's apartment, Mark is relatively quiet as he ponders in his mind the next steps to take here. Monty is pleased and somewhat relieved that he was able to get Mark admitted to the Crown residence with such a quick notice.

By the time they arrive back in Venice and step inside Monty's apartment, Mark looks at his watch and tells him, "It's 6 o'clock. Although I planned on spending the night here, investigating the authenticity of the Homer takes top priority. I better get cracking and catch a flight back to Baltimore. Here's a check for $500 for the lead, but you're entitled to more money if I buy it. There's a lot of work that I have to do, and do it now, from my office at Ridgefield."

He hands Monty his check, and tells him to keep him advised if he might consider relocating to the east coast.

"We don't have any fancy cars yet in Rock Hall," he tells him, "except for my BMW, but if I get my project off the ground in the next six months, we will need someone with mechanical skills to keep our buildings running efficiently. And you have a knack for keeping everything running like a Timex. Perhaps a mechanic's job may be waiting for you at Ridgefield."

Mark takes a few steps outside Monty's apartment and takes a moment to gaze around the area and inhale the salt water of the Pacific Ocean.

He turns back to him and stuffs three $100 bills into Monty's top pocket and says, "Here's a little advance on our next deal. I can't wait to get back to sunny California, even if it's just to see those beauties on roller skates on the Venice boardwalk."

Mark shakes Monty's hand, wishes him better days ahead, then double-steps down the iron stairway and races to his rental car for the drive back to the LAX airport.

About an hour later, he's attaching his seat belt in his first-class seat aboard an American Airlines flight from Los Angeles to Baltimore.

Much to his surprise, he looks up at the stewardess serving the first-class section and stares into the face of Ruth Wayne.

"I don't believe it," he exclaims. "Is it really you?"

"In living color," she answers with a big smile, and turns in a complete circle like a model at a fashion show, so Mark can get a good look at her. "What are you doing on an American Airlines flight this evening?"

"Seeing an old friend and checking out a painting that I might buy." He looks her over from her toes to her head, pausing at the best places of her fit figure, and says, "You're looking like a million dollars. How do you keep yourself so trim and gorgeous? How's your life in the air nowadays?""

"You've asked too many questions. But I'll answer your last one first. All right, I guess, still looking for the right man. It didn't work out with Reggie. We got along fine, but we were going in opposite directions. I was flying east to west, and he was driving north to south. I didn't want to give up my job with American, at least not right now, so we're just good friends. He's a super guy, and I thank Sandy and you for introducing him to me. We had a really good time at the Harvest Moon Fest in Rock Hall. And I love his new yacht, *Finger Lickin' Tenders*. Now, isn't that the *cat's meow* for the name of a luxury yacht?"

"Well, if you haven't heard it through the grapevine," Mark discloses, "Sandy and I have split up too, but we're still good friends. I bought myself a farm outside Rock Hall, near the Wildlife Refuge, the old Ridgefield spread that Judy Ridgefield and her family owned for 150 years. You'll have to come down and see it, spend a day...or night."

"Are you hustling me, Mark?"

"If that's what you call it, yes I am. You're a dream girl, Ruth, a vision of beauty, every inch of your six feet. Guys anxious to have a date with you would say, 'You're ripe for the picking.' "

"You're awfully fresh tonight, or maybe 'refreshing' is a better term," she answers. "I'll take you up on that, Mark. I'd like to unwind this weekend. I have a few days off, so the timing is right for me."

"And for me too," he admits, with a devilish smile on his face.

"Can I give you a lift home from the airport?"

"No, Mark, I have my own car at the airport. You'll have to excuse me. Passengers are coming aboard, and I have to go to work. If I don't get a chance to talk to you during the flight, here's my number. I'll be waiting for your call."

Mark is feeling a little giddy over the thought of a date with Ruth Wayne. He says to himself, "Without a doubt, she is movie-star caliber, with a body like Rita Hayworth, fully packed in all the right places, mature, sweet, sensitive, and easy to talk to. What else would a guy want from a girl? Who cares if you find out later that she can't boil water or spell *promiscuous.*"

The next morning, a beautiful brisk Sunday, Mark rises early to attend church in Rock Hall. Afterwards, he telephones Ruth and invites her for dinner nearby at Osprey Point, a romantic quiet three-star inn with early American antique reproductions, on 100-year-old wood plank floors transplanted from an old war ship that was about to sink in the Chesapeake Bay during the Revolutionary War.

Around 6, Mark is having a glass of wine at the three-seat mini-bar when Ruth prances in, with a touch of swagger and confidence. They exchange kisses on the cheek and the waiter finds them a quiet corner with a view of a pond surrounded entirely by grass sloping downward, cattails around the perimeter and old bird houses scattered everywhere.

"It's fate that we met on that flight," says Mark.

"I feel the same way, Mark. I still remember when I first met you outside Java Rock, and you said something about wanting to see me in a bathing suit. Well, if you play your cards right, you may get your wish."

"After dinner, would you take a walk along the shore of Ridgefield, if it's not too cold?" he whispers.

"Lead the way. I trust you won't take advantage of me, will you?"

"Not if your life depended on it. I'm looking for something permanent, not just a fling."

"I love your frankness and sincerity, Mark. You always say what's on your mind. You get right to the point."

"Time is important, and it's a shame to waste it needlessly by flirting, or saying something just for the sake of saying it."

After dinner, they drive their own cars out of the parking lot, and Ruth follows Mark in his BMW, three miles from the restaurant down Eastern Neck Island Road, until he turns right into his farm. He escorts her inside his home, and he suggests that they exchange their formal dinner clothes for cool-weather apparel: sweat suits and tennis shoes.

Ruth glances at a framed sign that hangs on a wall in Mark's bedroom. It reads, 'Never Complain. Never Explain. Do It Right The First Time.' She smiles and nods her head in agreement.

Within five minutes, they're holding hands while sitting on the sandy seashore and gazing out at the magnificent sunset of the Chesapeake Bay, with the Bay Bridge far off on the horizon. Mark turns to Ruth and says, "It's moments like this that I dreamed about when I was in Iraq, and the reason I bought Ridgefield from Judy."

"It's heavenly, Mark. I was born and raised here, and never grew tired of seeing those sunsets. From Swan Point Marina, I became mesmerized by the image, and never grew tired of seeing them, because each one was different. I never studied art, but whenever I had a layover after one of my flights and some spare time, I was always inside a museum, looking at art. I've never forgotten the fabulous skies in paintings by Albert Bierstadt and Thomas Moran. You just never grow tired of looking at their paintings. And you never grow tired of looking at beautiful sunsets."

"How remarkable to hear you speak about the same things that I love."

He reaches over and gives her a long, passionate kiss that seems to last a lifetime.

"I feel good in your arms, Mark. And I love your embrace. It's comforting. Would you do that again?"

"I feel something special stirring inside. I know it sounds crazy since we hardly know each other, but it feels good and it's real." He holds her much closer and kisses her even more passionately.

After a few minutes, he asks her, "Would you like to spend the night with me?

"Only if I can have breakfast with you in the morning."

"How do you like your eggs?"

"Fresh, just like you."

Chapter 11

Early Monday morning, Mark is dressed in his Turkish bathrobe and seated at his computer in the room next to his bedroom. He tries to be as quiet as possible while Ruth is still sleeping in his bed, or at least pretending to be asleep. She's simply reminiscing about their affair last night, and enjoying every moment that flashes across her mind.

"I can't imagine," she says to herself, "how it can get any better than that." She finally crawls out of bed, rummages through a closet, and puts on a pair of his SEAL fatigues. While glancing into a mirror, she declares, "It feels comfortable inside his sweatshirt. Hope I don't put any bulges in the wrong places."

She opens the door and walks to the adjoining room where she surprises him by impersonating a ballerina's pirouette.

He pulls her gently onto his lap and kisses her tenderly.

"Would you like to start over again," she asks, "like we did last night, with a short walk along the sandy shore?"

"I'd walk wherever you want to walk or play, but I need about 30 minutes of computer time. Try not to disturb Gabby, who's still new on the job. Would you mind making breakfast for us? I think you'll find everything you need in the kitchen."

While Ruth showers quickly, dresses, and prepares breakfast, Mark is busy setting up an appointment with the Homer expert in New York.

A few minutes later, he's on the phone with Miss Priscilla Banks, the Homer expert in New York, explaining the possibility of finding a lost work by the artist. In these situations, most experts are thrilled to hear the news and become involved, since details of the painting will add to their data bank.

She agrees to change her schedule to accommodate meeting him at noon on Tuesday at the National Academy in New York, where most of the artist's files and archives are stored. In the meantime he agrees to email her a digital photo, so she can also do some research in her archives on the artist beforehand.

Miss Banks is one of several recognized experts on Homer, who has published numerous articles on the artist. However, little money ever comes from such publications. Most of her income is generated by writing a Certificate of Authenticity, called an "expertise," on the artist.

It is her good fortune that auction houses, particularly in New York, acknowledge her as one of the foremost authorities on the artist too. When she gives her stamp of approval in the form of a Certificate of Authenticity for a Homer painting scheduled for auction and writes a glowing commentary in the auction catalog, a sale at auction is virtually assured; it also increases the competition among bidders, who are more confident when bidding on an authentic Homer painting. Naturally, the size of her appraisal fees are commensurate with the importance of the Homer painting.

At no time, however, does she ever declare the painting's value in terms of dollars. She is not an appraiser and is careful to restrict her writings only to a description of the painting and the degree of authenticity. And these degrees can be classified in the following categories:

1. An original work by the artist, solely by his own hands;

2. Attributed to Homer, which means a work that is probably by the artist, but the expert feels less certain than degree 1;

3. Studio of Homer, which means a work that is executed by an unknown hand in the studio of the artist, which may or may not have been executed under the artist's direction,

4. Circle of Homer, which means a work that is executed by an unidentified artist, but closely associated with the identified artist, but not necessarily his pupil,

5. Style of or Follower of Homer, which means a work that is executed in the artist's style, contemporary or nearly contemporary, but not necessarily his pupil;

6. Manner of Homer, which means a work that is executed in the style of the artist and of a later date;

7. After Homer, meaning a work that is executed as a copy, by an artist from a known work by the identified artist.

After Mark finishes his work and logs off from his computer, he's excited at breakfast, and tells Ruth about the Homer painting.

"I wish your eyes would light up like that when you're thinking of me," she tells him with an enticing smile.

"You may not see my eyes light up when I'm thinking of you, but if you could look into my heart, you'd see it light up. Isn't that much better?"

"If you keep that up, I'll be falling in love with you," she replies tenderly.

"After breakfast," he asks, "what would you say about a sail on the Bay right now? If we can find ourselves a boat, we'll let the wind take over and take us wherever..."

"Good timing. I have the entire day free, time to relax from the grueling schedule of a stewardess. Everyone thinks it's a glamorous job, when actually it's very hard work, especially being in different cities, temperatures, clothes and foods."

"I get the picture, Ruth. Now, where can we get a boat?"

"Well, Mark, we keep a small 25-foot motor-sailboat at our marina. It's available for our use, and it looks like a beautiful day to be sailing on the Bay."

About twenty minutes later, Ruth is releasing the tie-lines from an outside slip of Swan Point Marina, of which she is still a part owner with her sister and brother. She yells out, "Ready to cast off, Captain."

Mark, at the helm of a motor-sailboat, starts the inboard engine and steers the boat easily out of the marina and directly into the Bay. He seems quite at home behind the steering wheel, as if he's experienced with this type of vessel.

"I'd like to show you where Ridgefield is located," she replies. "Stay at least 300 feet away from the shoreline because there's not much draft here. It's probably only about 10 feet deep. You can admire the beauty of waterman's homes, if you want to call vinyl-siding beautiful. From here, you'll see the rows of crab grass below those cliffs along the shore."

Ruth takes a position directly behind him, then extends her hands so that four hands are now gripping the steering wheel.

Mark rotates his body slightly, gives her a quick kiss, and says, "Better not disturb the helmsman. We don't want to run aground."

Ruth moves to the bow of the boat and says, "I'll watch for debris floating in the water. Five years ago, we hit a tree that was submerged. We sure don't want to run into anything floating or submerged."

"I've noticed, along the shoreline," he remarks a few minutes later, "that there are long stretches where the crab grass is abundant, and the next farm has nothing growing at the shoreline."

"Farmers who plant rye and barley reduce the runoff of their fertilizers because these crops absorb nitrogen, otherwise dead zones are created here nitrogen runs into the Bay and depletes oxygen in the water, creating algae and dead zones," answers Ruth. "This is the problem that has been plaguing the Bay for years. It's undoubtedly the runoff of fertilizers and insecticides that, in rain storms and high winds, kill everything growing there. That means crabs, fish, geese, ducks…all the wonderful bounty living in these feeding grounds. That's also why our business at the marina is way down each year. The crowd from Pennsylvania and Delaware, looking to fish and crab, read about the decline in fishing and crabbing, and prefer other marinas where the water is cleaner and the fish and crabs are more plentiful."

"Amazing, when you think how hard it is for watermen to make a living, and then consider the people who own marinas, which depend so heavily on owners who haul their boats here. It's like a vicious cycle."

"And finally here is *your* Ridgefield," Ruth tells him boastfully. "You have a short sandy beach along your shoreline, and some shoals with lots of eelgrass and sea lettuce, good feeding grounds for crabs. They go there to hide, eat and feel the warm rays of the sun. In those shoal areas there's plenty of oxygen in the water that flows over them with every tide. Doesn't look like any pollution from your farm because your land slopes inward towards Eastern Neck Road."

"That's good news, Ruth."

"Bet you didn't know," she discloses, "there was once a racetrack for sulky races directly in front of your property. Over the years, hurricanes and storms gauged more and more of everyone's shoreline and deposited it right where we're sailing. The depth is probably 10 to 15 feet here."

"I love the peace and quiet," he replies. "There's something special about being *on* the water, *near* the water, *in* the water. That's why I became a SEAL."

"I could see that in your eyes," she answers. "Whenever we talked about the Bay, you seem to light up and glow. But as much as you love the water, I prefer standing on *terra firma*. I like the security of being on a solid floor, on land or in the air." She pauses as they continue to motor in a southerly direction, then asks, "I bet you don't know what else is *in* the Bay?"

"Sounds like a trick question, but I'll take a guess and say 'your bikini,' right?"

"Wrong, for once in your life. Everyone who lives and works around here knows what's *in* the Bay, in the way of seafood, but very few know about the buried treasures, in the form of shipwrecks."

"Shipwrecks? I never gave it a thought, but it seems logical, with all the naval battles, especially those fought in 1812, and all the vessels going into all the tributaries of the Bay."

"Not to mention all marine disasters starting with the English colonies being founded up and down the coast, disasters from running aground, disasters from hurricanes and storms that suddenly swept up the Bay with winds over 80 miles an hour and waves over 20 feet high."

"Fascinating."

"When you have time, we can make some inquiries and perhaps go scuba diving, and add some adventure to your dull life on the Bay," she tells him facetiously. "I'll loan you a good book by Donald Shomette that tells you everything you need to know about shipwrecks. You can browse through it between trips to the auctions."

"And let's not forget," Mark answers, "all the American Indian tribes who lived along the Bay and set traps for waterfowl. I'd like to set a trap for you tonight."

"Can't you tell that I'm already in your trap?" she asks with a sincere smile and pauses to throw him a kiss from the bow. "While we're here, we should explore further along the shoreline. You've seen the Wildlife Refuge from a point on the ground, but you should see if from the water. It really is a hidden treasure on the Chesapeake Bay. It's also known as *Honeymoon Haven* for Canada geese to nest."

"Are you suggesting," Mark asks with a lustful smile on his face, "that we pay a visit there too?"

"It's close by. Why not take advantage of the good weather?"

Twenty minutes later, their boat is offshore and parallel to Eastern Neck Island when a school of about 100 Canada geese suddenly spring out of their nest hidden in the high grass and fly directly over them.

Ruth retrieves a pair of binoculars from a storage chest and hands them to Mark, and says, "Have a look at the sparrows with a single color on their breast like it was painted in colors from an artist's palette. You might be lucky today and spot a bald eagle. If you get real lucky, you might see whistling swans, also called Tundra swans, with their black bill and all white plumage, and a wing span of 66 inches. They fly when the winds are in their favor, annually all the way from Alaska at heights of 10,000 feet, to their winter vacation at *Honeymoon Haven*."

"You astonish me, Ruth. "How is it that you remember 66 inches?"

"By association. When I see one, I imagine they're flying from Alaska part of the way on Route 66."

"I know that you've lived here all your life, but obviously you've retained a good deal of the history of this area."

Ruth continues to point out other features of the Refuge that was first discovered by Captain John Smith during his voyage up the Chesapeake Bay in the 1700's.

Mark listens closely to the words coming from her mouth and tries to pay attention to his boat while glancing as much as possible in her direction. He says to himself, "I never realized that there's such a beautiful mind inside that beautiful body. Maybe Ruth *is* the girl for me."

Finally, Ruth takes a deep breath, sighs and tells him, "I'm not trying to impress you, Mark, but our geography teacher at Kent High drummed something into our minds that she wanted us to remember about the Chesapeake Bay since we were born on the Bay."

"And what was that?"

"She told us that Captain John Smith said, 'Heaven and earth never agreed better to frame a place for man's habitation.' "

The thought of marrying Ruth now crosses his mind as he turns the steering wheel of his boat towards open waters.

The winds shift and increase in intensity, and together they raise the sail. The last two hours are spent cruising leisurely to within a mile of the Bay Bridge and back to Rock Hall harbor, all with Ruth on the bow watching out for debris. It's a glorious way to conclude an outing, without a care in the world.

After returning to Ridgefield, Ruth discovers, along a wall in the living room, a small shelf of CD's. She selects a recording of the Funk Brothers' *I Heard It Through The Grapevine,* followed by Bobby Darin's *Dream Lover,* and they begin dancing together with hardly any noticeable gyrations. They swing and sway their bodies seductively, almost like foreplay.

When they close the door to their bedroom, the next melody, David Sanborn's *Try A Little Tenderness*, begins playing softly in the background as both become surprisingly quiet and contemplative, thinking about where their love affair is headed.

The following morning, Mark is inside his BMW on the 95 expressway as he heads northward, passing Wilmington, through New Jersey. Four hours later, he arrives in New York for his appointment with Priscilla Banks at the National Academy.

At 12:15, both are huddled in a private room to examine archival material on Winslow Homer. Like two detectives on a murder case, they carefully examine his diary, personal letters, notes, records of sales, even notes of payment for various models who posed for his paintings, searching for evidence that will prove that Homer actually painted Maria's painting.

After four hours of tedious, nerve-racking study, Priscilla declares that, without some hard copy or concrete evidence, she will not give her Certificate of Authenticity for Maria's painting.

The four-hour drive from New York back to Rock Hall seems like an eternity because he is exhausted, bitter and depressed. He's furious and totally frustrated that Miss Banks has depended entirely on her finding concrete evidence in the form of notes or records in the Homer archives and has failed to give any credence to the quality and workmanship of the painting itself.

"I can smell it and taste it," he shouts in the direction of the windshield of his BMW, to release the tension building up inside. For this moment in his life, there doesn't seem to be any other options tossing around in his head.

After a night of restless sleeping to the point where even Jen comes to his bedside to comfort him, he finally makes himself a cocktail and sits outside on the porch to gaze at the moon over the Bay Bridge.

"Damn it, who can I turn to for advice?" he asks himself. "I don't even have a plan of action, of what my next steps should be, and that bothers the hell out of me. I'm stymied."

At noon, Mark decides to bite the bullet and telephones Maria in Los Angeles, where it's 9 in the morning.

"Would you consider selling me your Homer painting for $50,000?" he asks her nervously.

He waits for a response, and when none is forthcoming, he asks again, "Are you there? You haven't fainted, have you?

"Yes, I'm here, Mark, and I haven't fainted although I am a bit flabbergasted."

"Of course, you would have to give me 30 days, after you cash my check, time for me to consult with experts because I'm buying your painting for my private collection and not to resell. I don't want to keep it 20 years and find out later that it's a fake or forgery. If an expert proves, beyond reasonable doubt, that the painting is a fake or forgery, then I will return it to you and you would be obligated to return my money. Is that clear to you?"

Mark now has in mind the notion of buying it from Maria and arranging for experts at Sotheby's and Christie's to examine the painting, with a disclosure about Miss Banks' decision too.

After Mark makes his offer, he hears Maria's friend in the background tell her, "Don't do anything until we can show it to my friend in Pasadena who knows something about paintings. He's a senior member of the American Society of Appraisers, specializes in 19th Century American and European Paintings. His name is Joseph Szymanski, and he's been in the art business for over 30 years. He'll tell us what's best to do with your painting. We should contact him before he moves to Rock Hall on the east coast of Maryland."

"Let me think over your offer," she tells him with assurance, "and I'll get back to you in a few days."

Over the next two weeks or so, Mark waits to hear back from Maria but there is nothing coming in the way of a telephone call or letter from her. Although the Homer painting is always on his mind, he is reluctant to call her, thinking she would misinterpret his eagerness and suspect that the painting is worth considerably more than $50,000 if proven to be a genuine work by the artist. He is somewhat despondent and retreats into an unusual state of melancholy and isolation.

For the time being, he is unable to visualize another option, such as being her representative or agent for the sale of the painting to a private collector or a sale at auction in New York. In the back of his mind, he has the intention of keeping the Homer painting for himself. After all, how many private collectors or dealers have a Winslow Homer painting hanging on the walls of their home? Mark is in a situation where he is torn between being a dealer and a collector, and in such cases, things are difficult to reconcile.

For relaxation, he gazes at one wall in his office where black and white photos of his Betterton Breeze track team are displayed.

"Will you look at the expressions on their faces as they won the state relay championship at the Harvest Fest?" he asks himself. "Manny captured something hidden inside each one. He timed the shot to reveal the excitement in their face. That's a special talent that takes instincts. You don't learn it in a photography class. Maybe we should hire Manny to document everything in the beginning stages of Ridgefield's growth, for records of 'before' and 'after' development. Perhaps he'd like to join our team. I'll have to give him a call."

Within the next five minutes, Mark is talking over the telephone with Manny and explains, "We're still in the developing stages, but I was wondering if you would like to pay us a visit, with the intention of being our photographer. You'd be assigned to the research lab and working under Kim Bozzetti. If you have the inclination, you're free to help Gabby in the kitchen, too. But I don't like the idea of a senior, like you, driving back and forth to Betterton, 26 miles each way, in the winter months, so we'll provide you with a nice trailer in which to live, as part of your salary. What do you say?"

"I'm floored, Mark. I was getting bored and heard about Jack Johnson, who built your addition there. I couldn't drive a nail into a piece of wood if it meant saving my life, but I'd sure like the idea of being with your team and working as a photographer and part-time cook. That certainly would be fun."

"I'll leave it up to you," he answers enthusiastically, "as to when you're available to come here and see our operation. If I'm not here, see Abigail and she'll know where to find me."

Abigail is usually around to cheer him up and tells him that she's learned from Sandy that Reggie and Liz are getting serious and considering marriage. She tells him, "From what you mentioned to me over the past few months, Liz is one sharp lady, with a Hopkins degree in metallurgy and experience in surveillance at the Pentagon. I'm assuming that she'll eventually be moving to Betterton. What would be your feelings about interviewing her for the job of heading up your Red Cross R&R Refuge?"

"That's music to my ears," he answers with a clap of applause, too. "Their romance certainly went on the fast track to the altar. You probably didn't know that I first met Liz outside Penn Station after being discharged from the Navy. She was incredibly packaged in a five-foot seven-inch frame. We had a lot in common too, since we both graduated from Hopkins.

"That makes three of us; you, me and Liz," interjects Abigail with pride.

"She was in the top 10 percent of her graduation class," Mark continues, "and rose swiftly after enlisting in the military, who recognized her talents and assigned her to the Pentagon. I'm not surprised that she and Reggie have hit it off together. They'll make a fabulous pair and will be good friends to have around here."

"I'll feel her out, Mark," Abigail replies.

"I'm glad you said that and not me 'cause I would get a slap across my face if I said it," he responds. "Maybe even be accused of sexual harassment. We have to be so careful with our words and action today. Not like it was years ago."

"Let's get back on track with Liz. Where or how do I contact her/"

"Call Sandy. She'll have her number. And on second thought, you have my permission to hire her if she wants to come aboard. I wouldn't want to have someone else beat me to her doorstep. She'd be a great asset to Ridgefield provided, of course, that she'll want to work after marriage."

Seconds later, Abigail hands her cell phone to Mark and tells him, "Here's Liz."

"Congratulations, Liz. I'm very happy for you and Reggie, two of my favorite people in the world. Where do you stand with your decision to leave the military?"

"My boss, Colonel J. R. Spencer, is not happy but understands my frustration. He is accustomed to battling the political forces at the White House. But I can't take the stress as an analyst of crisis management and losing sleep at night trying to come up with innovative plans to fight the Taliban, only to have everything filed away or suspended indefinitely. It's hard enough fighting the Taliban, but impossible to fight them and the Defense Department at the same time."

"Their loss will be our gain," echoes Mark, "although it comes with some degree of sadness as the Pentagon needs all the talent it can beg, borrow, and steal with personnel like you. Keep Abigail advised, please, and I'll look forward to talking to you again."

Mark hands Abigail her cell phone just as his desk phone rings.

"It looks like it's going to be a very busy day at Ridgefield" he tells her while lifting the receiver to his ear.

On the other end of the phone is a female voice who asks, "Did you say 'it looks like it's going to be a very busy day at Ridgefield?' "

"Sorry, but you weren't supposed to hear that," answers Mark with a laugh.

"In that case," she bellows out, "maybe you could use some help at Ridgefield. This is Greta Howell. Do you remember me?"

"You caught me off guard," he remarks. "Can you give me a hint?"

"I was Vera's hair stylist. I operate a small salon in the back of my home in Rock Hall. My business has really soured lately, like many small businesses, and I was hoping that you might have a job for me at Ridgefield."

"You know, Greta, I seem to remember meeting you at the Saloon on the last night of Vera's life. Can you give me a quick rundown of your education, talents and interests?"

"Mark, I graduated from high school, took a course in hair-styling, remodeled a room in my house for customers like Vera who wanted a cut and shampoo or whatever. I'm a quick learner, trustworthy, a good listener and kibitzer, with a good deal of experience with the horoscope. Right now, I'm willing to take any job, whether it's cleaning up the house, scrubbing floors, or doing laundry. I simply have to find a job fast in order to pay my bills, especially my life and health insurance premiums."

"In that case," he tells her with a touch of encouragement while running his fingers through his hair, "we'll find a place for you, perhaps helping Gabby, our housekeeper, for starters."

"I don't care where I start," Greta answers. "I need a steady job and I'm reliable and a quick learner on the job."

"And I like the idea of having someone around who knows something about the horoscope. After you get settled here, remind me about an idea that's in the back of my head. It involves someone like you, on the radio for 15 minutes, answering callers who have problems in their families. We might call it 'Shooting the Breeze with Greta Louise' because it's catchy and rhymes. We also may want you to write a short piece each month for our newsletter, maybe title it 'Horror-scope, From Aries to Pieces,' with a touch of wit and satire."

She's speechless and begins to cough and sob at the same time.

"Greta," he interjects quickly with an order, "I'll expect you to start on Monday at Ridgefield, so report to Gabby at 9 in the morning, please."

He doesn't wait for confirmation as he ends the call abruptly. He's used to giving orders and expects them to be obeyed.

Greta is early by 30 minutes when she arrives on Monday morning and greets Gabby at the front door. Both seem delighted to be working together, especially Gabby, who can use a little help in her housekeeping chores, which would leave her more time to prepare meals for everyone.

Around 10 am, Abigail walks into Mark's office and finds him at his computer.

"Liz has Reggie's consent and will join us," she tells him, "provided she can bring Sandy along too. I wish I had thought of it myself. Sandy is creative, sensitive, and very talented in more ways than just as an artist. For starters she'll make a good assistant to Liz. In the few times we were together inside her studio, I came away very impressed with her talent as a sculptor.

But Liz mentioned that she is a good listener and very good with people, especially in putting them at ease, perfect for military veterans who would spend R&R time at Ridgefield. Moreover, she's trustworthy, diligent, someone who pays attention to every detail, and follows through with everything she starts, with good results."

"I could not have said it any better. You and Liz are absolutely right about Sandy," he answers. "I never realized it before, because I had my mind on other things, like the Crumpton auction and Howard Street. Sometimes the best people are right outside your door."

When he returns to the computer, he surfs the Internet about upcoming auction sales in New York of American paintings. He almost falls out of his chair when he accidentally discovers that Maria's painting by Homer is catalogued in an upcoming Christie's auction in New York. The painting is scheduled for auction in a few days.

After he studies the catalogue entry more closely, the text makes no mention of any comments or opinions written by Priscilla Banks. Christie's, on the other hand, simply declares in their opening description of the painting, 'Newly discovered lost work of the best period, 1869.'

There are two other Homer paintings in this Christie's sale: each one contains the statement, 'The authenticity of this painting has been confirmed by the Homer expert, Priscilla Banks,' along with a verbose description of the special attributes of Homer's peculiar talents in the creation of that specific painting.

When Maria's painting is auctioned by Christie's, it fetches $680,000, plus a 15% buyer's premium of $102,000, which brings the total price to $782,000.

Mark is distraught and jumps out of his seat. He pushes his swivel chair backwards, sending it rolling across the room until it crashes against a wall of photographs framed in glass. The force is so great that one of the smaller photos pops off its hook and plummets to the ground, with glass splattered everywhere. He walks over to spot where the frame fell off the wall, and, with his fist, pounds the wall so forcefully that he drives it through the 5/8-inch thickness of drywall.

When he realizes the size of the hole, he looks at it and says, "I'm going to put a frame around you, as a reminder that I should never give up the battle. When everything seems hopeless, I must find a solution somewhere, somehow."

Without knowing it, Ruth suddenly appears out of nowhere.

"I was in the neighborhood and dropped by to see you, then heard a loud bang. What's going on?" she asks.

"I just lost $680,000, damn it," says Mark with disgust. "That Homer painting I told you about in California should have been hanging right here in my office. I knew it was genuine Homer, of his best period, but couldn't prove it, and wasn't able to pry it away from Maria."

She tells him, "I'm feeling the same as you too. You're disappointed and upset, but it will pass. You shouldn't feel discouraged. You were very courageous and willing to take the risk. You used your instincts to ferret out a Homer painting that was hanging for years in a modest home. Should I go on?"

"By all means."

"You should appreciate your discovery and not dwell on factors beyond your control. You can't win 'em all. You don't need the money. There'll be other opportunities. It's not the end of the world, is it?"

"You sure know all the clichés, Ruth," he laughs and pulls her close enough to give her a passionate kiss. The embrace lasts at least 30 seconds. Afterwards, he whispers carefully, "We should always follow our dreams, and never give in or give up."

"I know what you need right now," she whispers into his ear, "and it's the same thing I need." She licks his ear lobe.

He looks closely into her eyes, and asks, "Are you inviting me for a roller-coaster ride?"

"If you can spare the time," she answers coyly.

"I'm all yours," he says facetiously, "but you're supposed to say that to me."

"Whatever you want to do, Mark. I **am** all yours. I have the entire day and night free."

As they walk from his office into his bedroom, Mark says, "I hate to think about losing all that money when I had a chance, albeit a slight chance, to buy it. That's one deal that got away."

"Can't you forget the money? You'll have other opportunities. That was a good experience for you. It's not the end of the world," she whispers.

"Another cliché, but you're right. It's not the end of the world. It's worse."

"Come on, Mark. There must be something that will cheer you up," she replies while removing her sweater and stretching her arms into one of his big-and-tall double X flannel shirts.

He reaches to his right and throws two switches on the wall. The first switch turns on the track lighting, while the second powers his supersonic-surround system.

He places a "Do Not Disturb" sign on the door handle, then quietly closes the door. Seconds later, out of the Bose speakers comes a recording of David Sanborn's *Try A Little Tenderness*.

The haunting sounds from Sanborn's alto sax, accompanied by Frankie Toy on the piano and Luis Jaramillo on the guitar, softly fill the master bedroom. The playback sounds are low-key, like it was recorded deep inside a cavern in Tennessee, instead of in a studio in New York. This is one of Mark's favorite songs, since it was released in 1995.

His eyes grow moist and he admits to himself, "I'm about to find out where life begins. It's the perfect music, for the perfect time, with the perfect girl."

Ruth is already hidden inside the covers of his bed, and reaches for his hand, and quietly asks, "You are thinking of me, aren't you?"

"Only you, Ruth. I'm a man who has everything in the world, except what he wants most, and now I have you."

The idea of proposing marriage crosses his mind momentarily, and he says to himself, "I must be the luckiest guy in the world."

Suddenly, his mind seems to go flighty for a moment, like a kaleidoscope with images of Sandy, Liz, Lois, and now Ruth flash across his eyes. He returns to reality as Ruth touches his hand. After he slips into bed and pulls the covers overtop, he says to himself, "Perhaps I am a Monarch butterfly after all, but I certainly don't want to be a butterfly. I simply want to be monarch of Ridgefield."

A few hours later, around midnight, one of the worst winter storms of the year crosses the Bay one day ahead of forecast, and strikes like an arrow directly into the heart of Rock Hall. It's a thunder and lightning show that produces bolts of lightning and winds never before unleashed over the Chesapeake Bay and funneled into Rock Hall. Light flashes are followed seconds later by tremendous cracking and thunder that recalls bombs bursting in wartime. The shutters on the windows on all sides of the house unfasten and begin slapping back and force in no particular regularity or rhythm. The sounds everywhere are loud enough to wake up the dead buried in a cemetery.

The thunderstorm begins as a straight-line wind storm originating somewhere near the intersection of the Atlantic Ocean and the Chesapeake Bay, with gusts measuring over 80 mph. High winds continue for about eight minutes, until there is one incredibly-loud burst of energy, like an F-16 breaking the sound barrier directly over the top of Mark's home.

This gigantic blast is quickly followed by winds howling outside that soon find a crevice in the vinyl siding. When the air is channeled through the crevice and into the interior of Judy's home, the sound changes from nightmarish howling to strange whistling, discordant and improvised jazz-like musical notes. Then a heavy downpour of rain falls vertically then swept horizontally, when whipped up by the high winds. The wind speed of 80 mph classifies this hurricane as category 1.

For the next twenty minutes, cloud-to-ground lightning strikes continue, due to invisible positive and negative charged particles on the ground and in the atmosphere. The surprising phenomenon here is lightning starts on the ground and not high in the sky. The bolt begins when particles of energy collect near an object on the ground, are excited to form a powerful surge of electricity. Instantaneously, the surge moves off the ground and flashes upward to a cloud, producing visible pathways that can be seen over 30 miles away by the naked eye.

Twenty-two minutes after the storm first strikes Rock Hall, a nightlight resting on a small table beside a two-seat sofa in the middle of the living room flickers for about five seconds, then all power in Mark's home goes out.

The inside is suddenly pitch-black, and the place becomes eerie. The silence inside the living room is broken when the overgrown toe nails of Jen are heard as she moves across the wooden floor. Lightning darts through the front double-hung windows, bounces off the floor and illuminates the action of Jen in a staccato series of flashes and shadows as she reaches Mark's bedroom door. She manages to grip the door handle with her teeth, pulls it downward to open the door, and immediately races across the bedroom and leaps over the footboard onto his bed.

She lands comfortably between Mark on the right and Ruth on the left side of the bed. Jen's action startles Ruth, but Mark is used to bodies being tossed about and to hearing sounds from bombs bursting everywhere during his four years of combat in Iraq. However, he is not accustomed to Jen leaping onto his bed.

He reaches up to turn on the swivel light above his headboard and realizes that the power is out. He turns 90 degrees and reaches between the mattress and bed spring to retrieve a flashlight placed there for such emergencies.

As he grabs Jen's collar and begins to lead her out of the bedroom, a bolt of lightning flashes through a bedroom window to shine momentarily on Ruth who is sitting up in bed with her bed sheet and blanket covering only half of her body. Her long-sleeved pajama top is open wide enough to resemble a décolletage that exposes the cleavage of her breasts.

Mark lets go of Jen's collar and bends down to give Ruth a kiss and reassurance that everything is under control. To his surprise, she is unaffected by the thunder and lightning strikes outside.

"I'm used to it after living all my life on the Chesapeake Bay," she tells him. "But it's entirely a different situation when we're flying at 30,000 feet and the pilot suddenly tells everyone to fasten their seatbelts, because we're flying around a storm." She laughs and squirms down again into bed and pulls the blanket up to her shoulders.

"In that case, I'll let you take care of me, rather than *vicey-versey*." Feeling relieved, he continues, "But I better check on Abigail to see if she's all right."

"Be careful and hurry back," she responds tenderly as he walks out of the bedroom.

Using his flashlight, he stands motionless for a moment to survey the living room like a light-house beacon. Hanging from the ceiling on wires and displayed on the shelves of the living room are over 200 wood-carved decoys, and as Mark slowly moves through the room, shadows from the duck and goose decoys play tricks with his imagination. When light is reflected off the glass eyes inserted into their faces, the duck and goose decoys appear anxious to come to life.

After he shines his flashlight to a top shelf, he discovers a Persian cat licking its paws which are then moved to the sides of its face to wipe its whiskers. The licking continues for about 10 seconds and ends when the cat lets out a big yawn, begins to purr, and turns its head curiously 45 degrees to the right in the direction of the flashlight.

When the thunder and wind outside diminish, Mark says to himself, "I thought I heard Lena Horne singing *Don't know why there's no sun up in the sky…Stormy Weather,* or is my mind continuing to play tricks with me?"

The words and music of the song fade away when the rain falls straight down and Mark suddenly hears a strange ticking sound that reminds him of an antique clock that should be adjusted by a clockmaker to keep it running properly. Jen's ears perk up too, but she doesn't bark. He realizes that there are actually two intermittent ticks, one slightly alto followed by one more baritone.

He walks slowly across the living room to a far bedroom, where the sounds seem to originate. He notices that Abigail's bedroom door is halfway open. After he pushes her bedroom door fully open and shines his flashlight inside, he first sees two metal buckets on the floor, catching water dripping out of two holes in the ceiling.

Using his flashlight like a cinematographer on a dolly shooting a Hitchcock movie, he shines it in a panning motion from the floor upward to the ceiling, then completely around the bedroom until he finds Abigail in bed, huddled up on top of a stack of pillows.

Her back is pressed against the middle of her headboard, in a far corner of her bedroom, with a long woolen stocking pulled down to her ears. She's holding a small lit candle in one hand and umbrella in the other. It's a scene straight out of the acclaimed painting, "Der Arme Poet" ("The Poor Poet"), by the German story-telling artist, Carl Spitzweg, painted in 1839. However, the poor chap deflecting the rain drops from a leaky roof is Abigail and not Spitzweg's old cloistered poet.

Suddenly, power is fully restored to the house, and Abigail sneezes twice, the second much louder than the first. In a raspy tone, like trying to talk with a clogged nasal passage, she blurts out, "Don't laugh, Mark, but I heard some loud flapping. I think the wind blew part of our roof away. I don't know how long I can hold this umbrella to deflect the raindrops. At least now I know where the expression *coming down in buckets* originates."

"Since you were director of a museum, I'm sure you're familiar with the story-telling paintings of Spitzweg, aren't you?"

"Where," she answers promptly with a laugh, "do you think I got the idea of using an umbrella for this emergency?"

"You know, Abigail, when I saw those raindrops, something just clicked in my brain, and I think you know what I'm thinking, don't you?"

"Raindrops keep falling on my head," she begins singing softly and slowly. "If I weren't nursing a slight cold, I'd be laughing at myself, but under these circumstances, I must confess that it's an interesting experience, one that I should write a short story about later."

Mark suggests, "If you'll kindly remove your lovely body, I'll move your bed into another corner, but you'll have to listen to raindrops falling until the rain stops. According to the weather forecast, it is supposed to blow quickly through the area, in a north by north-westerly direction."

"So much for weather forecasts," answers Abigail, "in which I have not the slightest faith. This storm was forecasted for tomorrow afternoon. It's 12 hours ahead of schedule."

He shakes his head from side to side and apologizes. "I never noticed the condition of the roof when we made the addition to Judy's house. We'll get Jack Johnson out here as soon as possible to repair the roof or install a new one. In the meantime, would you like a nice cup of hot chocolate or herbal tea?"

"Now that the power is back on," she tells him, "I can look after myself. Can I make a cup of tea for you too? That's odd. I think the song is *Tea For Two*, not 'Tea For You Too,' isn't it?"

"Abigail, I think the storm brings out a comedic element in all of us tonight. I hate someone who panics under stress, don't you? I'll take two cups of tea, please, one for me and the other for Ruth, if you don't mind."

Chapter 12

Mark walks back across the living room and, after entering his bedroom, finds Ruth resting in bed with her body enclosed in his SEAL fatigues. She tells him, "I've been looking forward to his moment ever since our flight together from LA...*Je t'adore*."

"Shut a door?

"No, darling, that's not what I said although it's a good idea to lock the door. *Je t'adore* is an expression I picked up in Paris, which means 'I adore you.' I love that expression and have waited a long time to use it."

He crawls into bed, reaches over to the dimmer switch to turn down the lights and says, "This night is *on* me!" (Picture her body *on* top of his.)

Early the next morning, Mark rises as quietly as possible, quickly showers and dresses in flannel fatigues, everything done in a manner that won't disturb Ruth who appears to be sleeping.

After greeting his dog Jen who meets him at the door of his office, he plops down in his swivel chair and, as a matter of routine or habit, turns on the computer to check his emails.

"After an evening with Ruth," he tells himself, "I feel rejuvenated, invigorated, whatever. That thunder and lightning last night never scared either of us. Wasn't Ruth cool and hot?"

After discovering that there are no messages in his mail box, his eyes drift away from the monitor toward a large pad hanging on an easel besides his desk. It's an organization chart of people and their responsibilities at Ridgefield.

A few seconds later he pushes his swivel chair over to a corner table, on which rests a 20 by 20-inch topographical layout of Ridgefield, all to scale. Off to one side of the layout are miniature replicas of buildings and lead figures of personnel. He begins to arrange them, like a kid playing with toy lead soldiers on a battle field. On the Red Cross R&R Refuge building, he places a figure of Liz. On the two story building for the production of art and science films he places one of Sandy. Over the replica of the marine lab, he installs a figure in a white smock, and says to himself, "That's Kim Bozzetti's lab for the study of the Bay."

He hesitates for a moment, turns his swivel chair around and moves again to his computer, and says, "To pull everything together, we'll need to hire a designer-architect, and the sooner the better."

He surfs the Internet to find the best architectural schools in America, and in a few minutes, discovers that the University of Pennsylvania is ranked Number 5. It's also closest to Ridgefield, only two hours away by car.

An hour later, he smells freshly-brewed coffee in the kitchen, as Ruth hustles up a continental breakfast of croissants, assorted jams and fresh fruit to go with the coffee. After she invites him to the cozy corner table near the front bay window, he looks directly into her eyes. He feels complete contentment. No tension, frustration, or anxiety. Perhaps Ruth is the girl for him at last.

While she pours him a second cup of coffee, Mark tells her that he has to find and hire one of the most important persons for Ridgefield.

"The key," he exclaims, "is the designer-architect."

Within the next few minutes he's back inside his office and on the phone with Dr. Michael McGrath, Dean of the School of Architecture at Penn.

"I had a most unpleasant task over the past weekend," Dr. McGrath tells him. "I had no choice but to expel a brilliant 27-year old student going for his Master's who refused to adapt his thesis to the principles of established designs, precedents and traditions of architecture taught by our esteemed professors. His buildings looked like mushrooms sprouting up out of the earth, a mini-Disneyworld."

Mark persuades Dr. McGrath to reveal his name, York McGuffin, and phone number, so that he can contact and console the student. But he has in mind a scheme to get this student to visit Ridgefield. Mark has a hunch that York could be the exact person to design Ridgefield Village.

Minutes later, Mark is on the phone with York, the youngest of a prominent family from Newtown Square, a small village that oozes with wealth, referred to as 'mainline' people. Mark assumes that he is qualified as an architect and decides to find something about his character that would give him a path in which to entice him into coming to Ridgefield. Consequently, he begins by asking about his current activities, and learns that he is one of the youngest Masters of the Hunt, and oversees a small lab for stem-cell research on his family's 1,200-acre estate.

York admits that he was the favorite grandchild of his grandfather, who changed his name because he was the black sheep of the distinguished Strawbridge family of Pennsylvania. Several minutes later, York agrees to spend the weekend at Ridgefield as Mark's guest, to meet him and his people and ascertain exactly what he's looking for in the way of a designer-architect.

Mark has four days in which to lay out his plans and get Abigail, Liz, Sandy, Kim and others on site to meet York.

"Get your ideas down on paper," Mark advises them, "keep it simple and concise and be prepared to meet with him individually to give him your ideas and requirements, so we can find out if he's the designer-architect we need to make Ridgefield a success, with buildings you'll be proud to work in."

On Thursday afternoon, Mark finds Gabby humming in the kitchen as she arranges some copper pots on the stove and various fresh vegetables scattered on the counter top.

"Tomorrow," he tells her, "a VIP will be arriving for a weekend at Ridgefield and your cooking could be an important factor in whether or not he joins our team. What would you say to making a pot of your special home-made Chesapeake Bay crab soup?"

"You must be a mind-reader, because that's what I was thinking too. Instead of using fresh Maryland back-fin crabmeat, I'll cook some vegetables with the crabs split open so all that fat from inside the shell can do its thing, good for the flavor but bad for cholesterol. My mouth is watering just thinking about it."

"I won't tell a soul about the cholesterol," he tells her. "I can't wait to taste it. Those crabs couldn't have a better ending than inside your copper pot. We'll probably have eight to ten people for dinner tomorrow night."

On Friday at 3 o'clock in the afternoon, York drives his Jaguar past the Ridgefield sign and up a muddy road leading to the main house. When he closes the door to his car, he looks around at nothing but puddles of mud everywhere, as far as the eye can see, all the way to the water's edge. There's not a goose anywhere in sight. It's a gloomy landscape dominated by gray skies overhead, similar to the Dutch coast at Scheveningen which overlooks the North Sea. That's where the noted artist Hendrik Willem Mesdag painted his best paintings, in which the landscape views appear wet and marshy.

York climbs four steps onto the front porch and notices to his right, a row of muddy shoes, placed perfectly under a bay window with the smallest pair nearest the front door, as if their ready for a military inspection.

As York is about to push the doorbell, Mark opens the door and takes a moment or two to size up this lanky 6-foot 4-inch 27-year old architect.

"Dr. Livingstone, I presume?" York asks with a laugh.

"Yes, and I feel thankful that I am here to welcome you. You are Mister Stanley, Henry Morton Stanley?" responds Mark with a bigger laugh.

"Where have you been, in Setswana, seeking the source of the Nile?" asks York.

"I know the Nile River doesn't flow into the Chesapeake Bay like 150 other rivers. Do you speak Setswana?" Mark asks while continuing to laugh.

"Like it's my second language!" York bends over with an ache in his belly from laughing so hard.

Sandy and Liz overhear them and are puzzled until Abigail joins them and says, "They're do their best imitation of Livingstone and Stanley, and enjoying a little play-acting. The air around here does wonders for your brain so ladies, inhale and fill your lungs with the spirit of the Bay."

Mark shakes York's hand and puts his arm on his shoulder to welcome him to Ridgefield.

"Looking for a job, one that'll challenge your abilities?" asks Mark while handing him a pair of Under Armour casual shoes.

"According to Dr. McGrath at Penn, I'll never make it as an architect because I refuse to adapt to the current trend," he answers.

"Well, what does Dr. McGrath know? He's only the dean. Anyway I have a hunch that you'll fit right in here. And speaking of fit, try these size 13's on for size and leave your muddy shoes on the porch."

York finds a comfortable patio chair to sit in while changing his shoes and rises to meet Sandy, Liz and Abigail who are waiting in a short reception line and eager to meet him.

"Welcome to Ridgefield," Sandy tells him slowly and with emphasis on each word."Did anyone ever tell you that your resemble Frank Lloyd Wright?"

"Yes, but that's where the similarity ends. I don't accept rejection like he did, but that may change if I don't get a job soon," replies York.

"Let me introduce you to Liz Carter," Sandy says and passes his hand over to Liz.

"A pleasure to meet you," Liz remarks and passes his hand finally to Abigail.

"Yes, York, it *is* a pleasure to meet you. We're all anxious to know more about you. Come inside and get comfortable. Would you like some refreshment?" Abigail asks like a hostess in a country club.

After York takes a seat on a settee in the middle of the living room, Mark's golden lab, Jen, walks up to him and brings her right paw up as if to say, 'Welcome' too.

After a round of cocktails, Gabby proudly announces that dinner is being served near the bay window where everyone can watch the sun setting over the Bay Bridge.

During dinner, Mark throws a log into the fireplace and lowers the temperature setting on the thermostat. When he gazes towards the dinner table, he is reminded of the paintings of Norman Rockwell, especially those subjects about Thanksgiving. Everyone is interacting and completely at ease

"By nature, I'm normally quite reserved," York explains, "since I was the youngest of four who never got a word in edgewise at the dinner table. If I appear a little quiet, it's because I'm a better listener. If I have something important to say, I'll squeeze it in somewhere, like complimenting Gabby for her delicious crab soup."

"By the looks of your slender frame," Mark admits, "you look as though you were squeezed out at the dinner table, too."

"Your physique will change once you get a helping of Gabby's linguini Alfredo over baked rock fish," Sandy tells him. "Just before serving, she adds a sprinkle of Old Bay Seasoning and touch of cherry-herring liquor from Sweden, pronounced *Schvee-din,* to enhance the flavor and add a wonderful aroma that you can smell all over the house."

"The smell reminds me of my mother's homemade sour beef and dumplings, with ginger snaps," Mark admits. "You could smell it simmering a block away from our home when the wind was blowing in your direction."

"None of you show any effects of Gabby's rich cooking," responds York with a smile. "It must be exercise that keeps you all in shape."

"It's Mark's fault," Abigail retorts. "He keeps us moving with his grand ideas for Ridgefield and the Bay."

"When you stand on your feet like I do, sculpting a life-size figure in clay," Sandy concludes, "you're constantly moving around, bending up and down, almost without thinking, and the workout doesn't seem like a workout at all. I think all of us agree that living close to the Bay, whether it is Betterton or Rock Hall, is good for the soul. I haven't seen your work yet, but Mark mentioned that you might be the designer-architect we're looking for."

"Well, Sandy," York answers, "you never know what's around the corner of life until you turn the corner. Pardon my boldness for getting personal, but you might be the person I'm looking for, too. I can't remember being inside a home with so many lovely and friendly ladies, like being stranded on a muddy deserted island with native girls, all wanting to show me a good time."

"It may look like mud outside and seem like mud, but it's clay." Sandy is quick to correct him and continues, "It goes down 20 feet in some spots. Whenever we have a heavy rainstorm, the water doesn't seep into the ground. It runs off into the Bay. And the clay is bad for septic systems, but good for sculptors."

Sandy pauses, gathers another thought, and leaves her seat to walk towards York.

"As the local folk around here say, is there anything I can do you for?" she asks with a laugh. "I got the distinct initial impression that you were a shy guy, but the way you're talking with us, it's nice. Very nice."

"Maybe," he answers, "just maybe it's the informality, letting everything run its course, casual, no pretences, no egos."

For dessert, in honor of York, Gabby has designed a special pumpkin roulade that resembles a tree limb, about one foot long, and three inches in diameter, covered with snow and two holly leaves. The illusion ends when Gabby cuts and folds the first slice neatly onto York's plate. It's a delicious pumpkin-ginger cake, made from a batter of all-purpose flour, eggs, ground cinnamon, baking soda, nutmeg, granulated sugar, with a filling of imported Italian mascarpone cheese (instead of Philadelphia cream cheese), and crystallized ginger.

The snow effect is the result of confectioners' sugar sprinkled unevenly on the surface to give the illusion of snow on a tree limb. Gabby's creation is topped with several green-colored marzipans shaped like holly leaves.

When someone asks about the recipe, Gabby says, "There is no recipe. I've been making it for ages. It's simply a dash of this and a dash of that, just like Jacques Pepin and Julia Childs. And tomorrow, the Good Lord willing, I'll bake 'Poulet-Chateaubriand.' You can brush up on your French and find out for yourselves precisely what that is. When you find out, let me know so I don't leave anything out."

Gabby has a good laugh at herself as she slices her pumpkin roulade, and says, "Good to the last slice."

After dinner, everyone gathers around the fireplace. Mark hands York a key and tells him, "Your lodging for the weekend will be inside a luxury mobile home behind the main house. It has four blue stars with your name on the door, like those trailers for movie stars. We're hoping to spoil you a little even though we haven't a clue about your talents and achievements so far. And there's a phone inside if you need anything. Sleep well, my friend. We'll see you in the morning for breakfast, with some award-winning muffins from Gabby's kitchen."

The next morning, after breakfast, Mark is huddled with York in his office, going over his organization chart and topographical layout of Ridgefield. Mark explains his vision of a village where the pace is slow but sure, a place to reflect and contemplate: a science lab for no more than five people, including Kim Bozzetti, to study marine life; a building for the production of art and science films, with Kim as an advisor and manager to be named later; and a building for Red Cross veterans and their families, an R&R, under the direction of Liz, with Sandy as an assistant. The R&R building will have a separate room to display decoys collected by Judy Ridgefield and her husband, as stipulated in her will.

On the second floor of each building would be housing and living quarters for personnel working at Ridgefield, if they choose to live there.

"The entire concept," explains Mark, "is flexible and still evolving in everyone's mind and subject to change, so you're free to offer your ideas. In fact, we encourage your input. And one final factor here: all profits from my salary at Bethlehem Steel and my art business are funneled into Ridgefield. It's important to do something special for Red Cross vets who served in Iraq and Afghanistan, and never made it back home all in one piece."

When York asks about the Wildlife Refuge nearby, Mark suggests that Sandy give York the million-dollar tour, exactly like the one she gave him when he first came to Betterton six months ago.

While Sandy drives Mark's BMW, with York relaxing in the passenger seat, down the dirt road from the main house to Eastern Neck Road, a 'Big Brown' UPS truck is coming up the opposite side of the road. It's a delivery for Mark, who meets the driver on the front porch of the main house. He notices that the package is something mailed from Ruth Wayne.

After he removes the outside wrapping, a note inside reads, 'Dear Mark: Here's a house-warming gift I found in an antiques shop in San Francisco. I'm on my way to London. Hope to see you next weekend. Love, Ruth.' It's attached to a framed print from the 1880's, with the inscription: *Dear Lord, Help me to win, and if I fail, help me to brave the consequences.*

"How about that," he tells himself. "Very thoughtful of her to think of me during her flights. I'll find a good spot for it inside my office."

A few minutes later, Sandy is driving across the rickety wooden bridge onto Eastern Neck Island then, after a quarter of a mile further, turns right onto a dirt road leading to a small parking lot with an 8-foot wide, wood-planked main walkway that runs about 200 feet directly to the shoreline.

Eventually, Sandy and York mosey down the main walkway until it connects to a short 4-foot wide walkway, leading to a small three-sided shed where spectators can observe birds, geese and egrets at work and play.

As both are walking slowly and York is digesting nature's beauty, something happens between them. It's not love at first sight, but more like a magnetic field that attracts two people with similar talents in art and architecture.

While each peers through a knothole in one wall of the shed, York whispers, "It looks like a bald eagle resting on top of that tree, about 45 feet up, probably a tree that was shattered during the recent hurricane. How proud that eagle looks."

Sandy is surprisingly reticent and seems as if she's meditating on the beauty and harmony of God's creation here.

On the walk back to her car, halfway along the dirt and gravel pathway, she takes his hand and tells him, "I never get tired of seeing this place. I've wanted to paint it on canvas but afraid I won't do it justice."

"You'll never know until you try it, Sandy, so why not give it a try?" he remarks.

"I haven't seen your work yet," she tells him, "but if Mark offers you the job of designing and building Ridgefield Village, I hope you'll take it. His ideas will never materialize until he gets the right designer-architect, and that might be you. I can also tell you this: There's no pretending with Mark. What you see is what you get. I should know. I thought we'd be a twosome, but it didn't work out."

"Where do you think I could put my hands on some Whatman paper?" he asks. "I'd like to get my ideas down on paper before I forget them."

"I have some watercolor paper in the trunk of my car. I keep it there for unexpected occasions. You're welcome to use my watercolor kit if you need one."

"Actually I have everything I need, but like to have lots of paper around me when I'm sketching. I probably tear up 80% of everything I draw until I'm satisfied."

"By the way, I thought of one more bit of information," she tells him with a gentle tug of his arm. "You might consider it a word of advice. If you decide to come on board, remember that Mark admires a good effort and despises a quitter. From his standpoint, just because something may have failed before doesn't mean it will fail the next time. He likes people who keep plugging away. And don't ever tell him that 'it can't be done.' He takes it personally. His motto is: 'You Can Be Better Than You Are.'"

After he opens her door and she takes her position behind the steering wheel, he walks around her car and settles into the passenger seat.

"Thanks for the advice," he tells her, then stretches one hand over to stop her from turning on the ignition.

"Whenever I start a project," he admits, "I would never have the audacity to tell someone, 'it can't be done.' I have no right to make such remarks, even if I've known that person a long time."

He leans back into his seat and sighs. "I enjoyed our walk here but have to confess that it's not new to me. I've been to the island many times as a teenager with my grandfather on his hunting trips. He stopped inviting me after I entered college because I always missed shooting a geese, intentionally. Everything here seemed so idyllic. I even hated to fire my rifle."

When they return to Ridgefield, York abruptly tells Mark that he won't be able to have dinner with them.

"What did you say to him, Sandy?" Marks asks her.

"Not to worry, Mark. It's nothing she said. I feel the urge to get some ideas down as soon as possible so I don't forget what everyone's told me. There's a lot of work ahead and I'm not sure what to do first. Most of the time, my best work is done on an empty stomach, anyway."

"We can send over a nice hot plate if you get an appetite," Mark tells him. "Just pick up the phone and let us know, please. Also, you're free to use the kitchen and help yourself to the leftovers. They're tastier when you're real hungry."

Before York leaves the main house, Mark asks him to consider adding a cluster of twenty wind turbines for the generation of electricity, if you can fit it in without disturbing the geese.

"It's a shame to waste all that energy when we can harness the winds blowing day and night across the Bay and convert it into electricity," he tells him. "A manufacturer in Wilmington wants to form an alliance with us. We have the land and the wind, and they have the wind turbines. Perhaps you can place them in a spot where they won't interfere with the geese.

Mark asks everyone if there's anything else they want to 'unload' on York's shoulders, which brings a good laugh but no further words at this time.

"Well, in that case, let me end this historic evening by saying, 'in conclusion,' we'll see you in the morning." Mark raises his hands high above his head and drops them forcefully onto York's shoulders and continues, "Sleep well tonight. May all your dreams be pleasant ones."

The next morning, a brisk Sunday with light winds blowing 15 mph in a northeasterly direction, Mark is seated at his computer, tapping the keyboard as he skims his emails, while his left hand is scratching the forehead of his golden-haired lab sitting by his side.

He discovers an email from Richard Parlow, advising him that he has found two men, 27-year-old twins and computer experts who set up one of the most advanced systems in automation in Essen, Germany.

'Their names are Michael and Philip Wew, nicknamed Ying and Yang respectively, and both are looking for new challenges and willing to join Bethlehem Steel, with your approval,' the email reads.

Mark immediately sends Parlow his authorization to hire them and adds, "If you encounter any problems with immigration and work permits, classify the application as 'critical employment,' which often puts it on a faster track through governmental bureaucracy."

After Mark logs off from his computer, he notices that everyone is huddled around the dining room table where platters of assorted sausages from an Amish deli in Lancaster, eggs Benedict and pancakes are passed around the table, family style.

The conversation is light-hearted, and everyone wants to know more about York's research lab in Newtown Square.

"It's no secret that everything I make as a designer-architect gets funneled into a stem-cell lab," he tells them. "I provide the funding for two bright young doctors who are experimenting with crippled horses, especially their spinal-cord and leg injuries like those that ended the career of *Barbaro,* the 2006 Kentucky Derby winner, a few years ago."

After breakfast, York invites Mark to his trailer to see the sketches and renderings he produced well past midnight.

"If it were 9 o'clock in the evening, under a bright moonlight," he tells him, "I'd ask Sandy if she'd like to see my renderings, not you, Mark."

Inside York's trailer, six 18- by 24-inch sheets are scattered around the interior. Each sheet is a rendering, a quick pencil and charcoal sketch, heightened with watercolor and gouache to give the layout and design concept of each building.

Mark's eyes shift from one rendering at eye-level, then to one at waist-level where he has to bend his body over to examine it carefully and finally one high above his head where he has to stand on his toes to see it close up.

York scattered them wherever he could find an open space, in no particular order of importance.

Mark is uncharacteristically silent and patient, conserving his breathing like a SEAL on a mission when his tank is running low on oxygen.

"Fantastic," he blurs out. "You've transformed everyone's ideas into fabulous fantasy-like buildings, each one different yet complimentary. No building is larger than two stories, and …"

Mark pauses again to gather his thoughts and continues, "I'm floored. It looks like these buildings sprung up out of the wet clay. The only thing missing is the yellow-brick road and Judy Garland singing *Somewhere Over The Rainbow*."

As York turns deftly silent, Mark faces him squarely and continues, "I know you have more experience in the principles of structural engineering, but wouldn't it be gratifying if you and Liz could put your heads together and invent a new building material that we could use in the construction, something strong like titanium blended with graphite? Instead of a Stealth Bomber, which uses tons of graphite, we'd have Stealth Buildings. Maybe, if we all work together, we can find a way to save the Bay after all."

"Any talk about materials should come later, much later. We've got to make sure the design is what all of you want."

"Before you head back to Newton Square," he orders York, "get together with Abigail, give her an indication of what sort of salary you'll need to come aboard. You can transfer your stem-cell lab here if you want to. We've got 50 acres, and if you need more for your work, we'll buy it for you. Your research lab and our lab might be able to work together and share information."

"I'll take your offer under consideration," York answers.

"I'll need a few minutes with Abigail alone to bring her up to date," Mark admits. "In the meantime, show your renderings to Kim Bozzetti to get her reaction and then to Liz and Sandy. It's important that we're all on the same page here."

"A word of advice," York declares. "You cannot design a project like Ridgefield by committee. Remember the expression, 'The Buck Stops Here?' Well, you and I will have to make the final decision, otherwise things get complicated."

"By the way, York, I know a bright young man, Tony Wanderer, of American-Indian descent, who's working for the Bureau of Indian Affairs in Washington DC and studying architecture at night. He might assist you like a paralegal in a lawyer's office, if need some help."

"I'll make a note of that."

"While it may seem to be a collaboration or team effort, once you're on the payroll you will have the final word on the location, internal and external design, and the intended function and purpose of each building."

"Have you given any thought to the problems associated with building permits and zoning restrictions? York asks.

"We expect problems with the Planning and Zoning Department of Kent 0County, in Chestertown. But Dan Sanderson, an attorney who gets $250 an hour, has had good success in this field and may be persuaded to represent us. There's not much new development going on in Kent County."

"I'm well aware of the attitude of Kent County officials and inhabitants, who would prefer to see geese instead of people living here."

"We're probably looking at six months before we get permission to put a shovel in the ground. There will be open meetings with townspeople, politicians, Department of Health and Sanitation, Department of the Environment, soil and erosion, water resources, almost everyone on God's green earth, yes, even the Green party who want eco-friendly buildings and developments. It's enough to drive you crazy, and wonder why I would want to drive down that road of helping to restore the Chesapeake Bay and more importantly, helping military personnel and their families."

York waits patiently to get a word in edgewise, and tells him, "I have a bit of bad news for you, though."

"Oh, no, everything was looking so upbeat," Mark exclaims. "Better give me the bad news now, otherwise I won't sleep tonight."

"The bad news," he declares, "is it will cost you about $350,000, but money well spent. If you want to keep Ridgefield from being continually eroded by the Bay, rip-rap must be installed along your shoreline. You probably have a shoreline of at least 1,600 feet My guess is that you or the previous owner already lost 300 to 1000 feet of land due to erosion and storms that gouged your shoreline. It's called a washout. I'm surprised that you're surprised by this news."

"Perhaps," Mark answers quickly, "you should make that your first order of business, getting us the government regulations and requirements or specifications. In the meantime, I'll find out from other property owners in the area what they've done to resist erosion. Well done, York."

"When you think about it, that's really not bad news. It's good news, in that you're correcting and preserving Ridgefield for future generations to enjoy."

Mark feels as though he's floating on air as he and York walk from the trailer to the main house.

Once inside, Sandy tells them, "I could see from the window that both of you have a bouncy step which means you're flying high today."

"York has agreed to join our team," Mark boasts, "and here are some of his preliminary renderings. Don't all ask your questions at one time. Try to digest and picture in your mind what it will be like for you to live in one of these buildings for the next five years, at least. This is the start of our five-year-plan for Ridgefield and the Bay."

While Abigail huddles with York and looks over his drawings, Mark takes Liz and Kim over to his office and tells them, "An idea crossed my mind last night that I'd like to toss at you. We know that large amounts of nitrogen from fertilizers and pesticides are creeping into the bay from property owners, especially farmers, whose land is situated along the shoreline. This is a given, and it dawned on me that if we had a litmus solution to test for pollutants, civil authorities may be able to prosecute these owners under the latest 'Cleanup the Chesapeake Bay Act.' How about putting your heads together and see if you can invent a low-cost, easy-to-use litmus test? I realize it's just a start, but everything has to start somewhere."

Kim and Liz smile at each other, and Liz asks, "How much sleep did you lose last night thinking about this idea, Mark?"

"Actually, you might be on to something here," Kim remarks. "Perhaps we could take a common bell buoy and install an electronic sensor that detects harmful chemical agents such as nitrogen. The information could automatically be transmitted to a control center that monitors all the buoys anchored in the Bay."

"Of course," interjects Liz, "the buoys would have to be anchored and designed so that they're not an obstacle to navigation, especially to watermen who are making their living on the Bay. With your permission, I could make some inquiries with various government agencies to see if they have an interest or anything already in the works. If they don't, we could write a proposal, and remember, there are 150 rivers that flow into the Chesapeake Bay. This idea could lead to a major undertaking for us, and I wonder if we're ready, willing and able to handle your idea if it should take off. For starters, we'll need some time to develop the concept of a floating electronic sensor, with good accuracy and inexpensive to manufacture. "

"Take all the time you need," Mark declares as he loosens the belt on his trousers. "I think that Gabby's roulade with ginger that we had for dessert last night must be good for the brain. Crazy ideas kept popping up in my mind during the night."

"One last thought here," Liz advises. "It wouldn't cost much to have some shirts silk-screened with our emblem, *R for Ridgefield*, and around the outside, "Be a Buoy. Protect the Bay."

Mark gives Liz and Kim a big embrace as he leaves his office and tells them, "Your fantastic."

"I bet you tell that to all the girls," Kim answers while laughing.

Mark spots York gazing out a bay window as the sun sets over the Chesapeake Bay and puts his arm around him.

"I can't begin to tell you how good I feel at this moment, due in part because you're aboard our ship. Look at yourself. You're 27, 6 - 4, the same as me. You're 'mainline' and I'm 'main stream.' We've come from different walks of life, yet we share a common goal, free to do something special with our God-given talents. Look outside. What do you see on the horizon?"

"Sounds like a trick question," York answers quickly. "What do you see?"

"A spirit rising but can't make it out because it looks like it sticks it head out above the waves, then drops back down into the Bay. Maybe my imagination is playing tricks on me, but can you imagine what we can do together over the next 5 to 10 years?"

"Imagination is one thing," York answers confidently. "Challenge is another. You can count on me to do my part for vets and their families, and whatever it takes to protect the Chesapeake Bay."

Abigail, Liz, Sandy, and Kim join York and put their arms around each other as cheerleaders and gaze at the setting sun.

Mark moves to the front door and notices his golden retriever, Jen, barking halfway between him and the shoreline. Seconds later he's baffled and more than curious by her actions as she dashes towards his farmhouse.

"That's strange," he says to no one in particular while moving out of the house and plopping down on the front steps. "I've never seen her run, stop to drop her head and bark, and run again...can't make it out from 50 yards, but looks like she's got something in her mouth."

After Jen reaches within 30 feet of the house, she runs to the back door and leaps onto the porch which wraps all around the house.

Mark watches her until he's distracted by the distant sun as clouds begin to move over it. Its rays manage to stream downward through the clouds, creating an optical illusion, similar to a sky after a rain storm where clouds suck water out of the Bay and store it for the next rainfall.

"It's looks like a picture-postcard, a magnificent sunset with the Bay Bridge on the horizon," he says to himself. "God never created anything better. This is what led me into buying Ridgefield in the first place."

Meanwhile, Jen walks around the porch, takes a position behind him and begins to shake the water off her body in a movement so vigorously that the spraying action gives him a quick shower.

He begins to laugh until he realizes that Jen actually has something in her jaws. His suspicions were right.

While holding her in place, he discovers that she's gripping a green-colored metal canister seven inches long and one inch in diameter, about the size of a fat hot dog, like the one served in a potato roll bun from either Polock Johnny's on Washington Boulevard or Attman's on Lombard Street, in Baltimore.

In a quick flashback he recalls his days at Johns Hopkins and biting into one of those delicious dogs at these landmarks. The flashback ends when the image of one dog (his hot dog) fades into another (his dog Jen).

"Jen, let go, girl," he hollers. "What in the hell have you found?"

Jen swings her head from side to side, then bends her head downward and opens her jaws to put the canister directly on the ground in front of him, an action repeated many times when Mark and her played games with a stick on the sandy beach.

After Mark picks up the canister, he looks at Jen who simply sits in an upright position and nods her head twice towards the shoreline, as if to tell him 'that's where I found it.'

"Do you know what this is?" he asks with trepidation in his voice. "Unless my mind's playing tricks on me, it's a can of Nitrogen Mustard gas, and not very old. No corrosion that I can see. The markings read 'ECBC...APG...HN1.' It weighs less than a pound. I don't believe it. We had these in Iraq, to get those suicide-bomber bastards out of their holes and caves."

He puts the canister in his front pants pocket, removes a towel hanging over the railing and bends down to wipe her wet body.

When she stands up and puts her front paws on his waist, he gives her a big hug.

"Good girl, good girl" he tells her with a few seconds of pause between each word. "Now, go inside and dry yourself off. You've earned a few extra dog biscuits before we hit the sack tonight."

Since Mark doesn't want to alarm anyone inside, he walks along the porch toward the back of the house.

"I bet that terrific storm," he says to himself while looking again at the canister, "the one that funneled up the Bay a few days ago tore into Aberdeen, lifting and churning debris into the Susquehanna and eventually all the way down the Bay to our shore."

With one hand gripping tightly the canister, he uses the other to scratch his hair furiously, the way Johnny Cammareri (Danny Aiello) did in *Moonstruck,* to stimulate his brain cells.

"I guess I'm back in the saddle again as Gene Autry would say, military-wise," he continues talking to himself. "I'll have to get my SEAL Lieutenant's uniform out of mothballs and meet the brass at Edgewood Chemical Biological Center (ECBC) in Aberdeen as soon as possible. After all, I'm still a reserve officer, which carries a little weight with the government. If Jen found one canister, there must be more scattered around the Bay."

He grabs the porch railing with both hands and leans slightly over it, then adds, "Is finding this canister a coincidence or Devine

Intervention? Is God trying to tell me something, making me think about mustard gas? Yes, now I recall reading in the *Sun* a story about a patent issued for a sorbent to decontaminate toxic elements like Nitrogen and Phosphorus. Perhaps farmers can use this sorbent to lower the toxicity in their fertilizers, and eventually help with the runoff into the Bay. I'll definitely have to arrange for Kim and Liz to go with me to Aberdeen, to speak with the people at ECBC. Wouldn't it be nice if we can get involved as a subcontractor for R&D?"

Mark returns the canister again to his pocket and rubs both hands together in an action as if he just hit four 7's on a slot machine.

Suddenly, Jen appears next to him, stands on her hind legs and grabs the top of the railing with her front paws, gazing out at the Bay, too.

"You always had a mind of your own, didn't you, pretty girl?" he asks while massaging the back of her neck. "I thought I ordered you inside the house."

Seconds later, from somewhere in the middle of the Chesapeake Bay comes a thundering voice that causes him to freeze momentarily.

"Moses? Can you hear me?" booms a man's bass voice.

"There's no Moses here," Mark shouts out in the direction of the Bay.

"I want to talk to Moses," the voice echoes with increasing intensity.

"I'm trying to tell you there's no Moses here," Mark shouts at the top of his lungs and cups his mouth with his hands to form a megaphone. "Can you hear me?"

"I can hear you. A deaf man could hear you," answers the image. "Who are you?"

"Who am I? My name is Mark. Who are you? Are you God?"

"No, I am not God."

"Then, are you the Lord?"

"No, I am not the Lord. I am the spirit of the Chesapeake Bay."

"Wonderful. Can you shorten your name, so I can address you easier?"

"You can call me the *Almighty One.*"

"And what would you have me do for you, *Almighty One?*"

"You can begin by giving your dog a pat on the back for helping to clean up the Bay, and by telling everyone: 'You Can Be Better Than You Are.' "

"Yes, *Almighty One*, I will do what you say," replies Mark with assurance. "I've been preaching that for years."

Moments later, the image of the spirit is completely above the water and resembles the figure of a white-bearded Rabbi, dressed in a long iridescent Tiffany-blue robe.

As it continues to ascend slowly upward into the sky, a loud gurgling sound is heard. After the spirit's mouth is cleared of Bay water and the gurgling sounds fade away, there is a moment of complete silence, as if the whole world suddenly stops to listen and see what's going to happen next. Not even a goose is anywhere in sight.

"*Diss is not dee end,*" the spirit cries out, "*Diss is not even dee beginning of de end. Diss is only a little past dee middle of dee beginning and dee end* (66% of the trilogy)...*Next and last stop:* ***ABERDEEN*****!**"

(For readers who have reached this point with the end in sight, the reason for the spirit speaking with two distinct voices is simple: The spirit speaks with a forked tongue; he talks one way when in the water and another, out of the water!)

THE END

Pronunciation and Glossary Guide

(Credit to Gordon Beard who published "Basic Baltimorese" in 1979, '90, '99)

PRONUNCIATION (SLANG)	CORRECT SPELLING
Aba-deen	Aberdeen
quairyum	aquarium
amblanz	ambulance
Naplis	Annapolis
Anne-Arunnel	Anne Arundel
anythink	anything
apt-tight	appetite
Ay-rabb	Arab
rown	around
arthur	author
orning	awning
Bawlmer or Bawlamer	Baltimore
baffroom	bathroom
bootiful	beautiful
bin	been
Betterin	Betterton

bob-war	bobbed-wire
burn	born
beero	bureau
Blair	Belair
Bethum Steel	Bethlehem Steel
keerful	careful
Cha-lee	Charlie
Chesspeake	Chesapeake
quarr	choir
Clumya	Columbia
complected	complexioned
curup	corrupt
curyus	curious
curyusty	curiosity
Curt's Bay	Curtis Bay
doll	dial
Droodle Hill	Druid-Hill
Dundock	Dundalk
igger	eager
iggle	eagle
eht	eat
ee-light	elite
excape	escape
Yurp	Europe
zackly	exactly
Fillum	film

Far	fire
Faloo	flu
Furd	Ford
Fur	for
Fert Mckenny	Fort McHenry
Furty	forty
jografee	geography
Goff	golf
Glenin	Glyndon
Goldie	goalie
Guvner	governor
Greenmont	Greenmount
Harber	harbor
Har	hire
Harred	hired
Harrid	Howard
Harrid Street	Howard Street
Hoss	horse
Harble	horrible
yewmid	humid
yewmity	humidity
Hippdrum	Hippodrome
i-deer	idea
ig-nert	ignorant
Inna Harber	Inner Harbor
inner-rested	interested

inner-restin	interesting
Arn	iron
jiggered	jagged
Jools	jewels
Kroddy	karate
kidney garden	kindergarten
Lig	league
lie-berry	library
Liddle Itly	Little Italy
Luck's Point	Locust Point
Lumbered Street	Lombard Street
moran pie	meringue pie
mezz-aline	mezzanine
Murlin	Maryland
Mare	mayor
neck store	next door
Noh	no
Notink	nothing
Orning	awning
Oryuls	Orioles
urshter	oyster
Patapsico	Patapsco
payment	pavement
pa-lease	please
po-leece	police
Patomac	Patomac

plooshin	pollution
pawtrit	portrait
Plaski	Pulaski
Corter	quarter
Recerstown	Reisterstown
member	remember
rower skates	roller-skates
Roolty	royalty
Sagmor	Sagamore
sec-er-terry	secretary
Sore	sewer
Sigh-a-neye Hosbiddle	Sinai Hospital
Zinc	sink
sil-lo-kwee	soliloquy
somethink	something
spicket	spigot
Sparris Point	Sparrows Point
Tulla	Tallulah
tarpoleon	tarpaulin
Dare	there
Tink	thing
tuhmar	tomorrow
Talzin	Towson
twunny	twenty
Umpar	umpire
Uhpair	up there

Vandabill	Vanderbilt
Vydock	viaduct
Vollince	Violence
Dubya	W
warder	water
Warshtin	Washington
Westminster	Westminster
Whataya	What do you
winder	window
Wit	with
Wuff Street	Wolfe Street
Whirl	world
Varse	worse
wrench	rinse
x-lint	excellent
x-raided	x-rated
Yella	yellow
yesterday	yesterday
Ya	you
Yur	you're or you are
Yursell	yourself

Glossary and Pronunciation Guide

(Credit to Gordon Beard who published "Basic Baltimorese" in 1979, '90, '99)

SPELLING	PRONUNCIATION (SLANG)
appetite	*apt-tight*
Aberdeen	*Aba-deen*
aquarium	*quairyum*
ambulance	*amblanz*
Annapolis	*Naplis*
Anne Arundel	*Anne Arunnel*
anything	*anythink*
Arab	*Ay-rabb*
around	*rown*
author	*arthur*
awning	*orning*
Baltimore	*Bawlmer or Bawlamer*
bathroom	*baffroom*
beautiful	*bootiful*
been	*bin*
Betterton	*Betterin*
bobbed wire	*bobwar*
born	*burn*

buoy	*boe-way*
bureau	*beero*
Belair	*Blair*
Bethlehem Steel	*Bethum Steel*
careful	*keerful*
Charlie	*Cha-lee*
Chesapeake	*Chesspeake*
choir	*quarr*
Columbia	*Clumya*
complexioned	*complected*
corrupt	*curup*
curious	*curyus*
curiosity	*curyusty*
Curtis Bay	*Curt's Bay*
dial	*doll*
Druid Hill	*Droodle Hill*
Dundalk	*Dundock*
eager	*igger*
eagle	*iggle*
eat	*eht*
elite	*ee-light*
escape	*excape*
Europe	*Yurp*
exactly	*zackly*
February	*Febrarie*
film	*fillum*
fire	*far*
fireaway	*farway*
flu	*faloo*
Ford	*Furd*

for	*fur*
Fort McHenry	*Fert Mekenny*
forty	*furty*
geography	*jografee*
golf	*goff*
Glyndon	*Glenin*
goalie	*goldie*
Gough Street	*Guff Street*
governor	*guvner*
Greenmount	*Greenmont*
harbor	*harber*
heard	*hoyd*
hire	*har*
hired	*harred*
Howard	*Harrid*
horse	*hoss*
horrible	*harble*
hospital	*hosbiddle*
Howard	*Harrid*
humid	*yewmid*
humidity	*yewmidity*
Hippodrome	*Hippdrum*
idea	*i-deer*
ignorant	*ig-nert*
Inner Harbor	*Inna Harber*
interested	*inner-rested*
interesting	*inner-restin*
iron	*arn*
jagged	*jaggered*
jewels	*jools*

karate	*kroddy*
kindergarten	*kidneygarden*
league	*lig*
library	*lie-berry*
Little Italy	*Liddle Eitly*
Locust Point	*Luck's Pernt*
Lombard Street	*Lumbered Street*
meringue pie	*moran pie*
mezzanine	*mezz-aline*
Maryland	*Murlin*
mayor	*mare*
next door	*neck store*
no	*nope*
nothing	*nothink*
awning	*orning*
Orioles	*Oryuls*
oyster	*urshter, arster*
Patapsco	*Patapsico*
pavement	*payment*
please	*pa-lease*
police	*po-leece*
Patomac	*Potomac*
pollution	*plooshin*
portrait	*pawtrit*
Pulaski	*Plaski*
quarter	*corter*
Reisterstown	*Ricerstown*
remember	*member*
rinse	*rench or wrench*
roller-skates	*rower-skates*

royalty	*roolty*
Sagamore	*Sagmor*
secretary	*sec-er-terry*
sewer	*sore*
Sinai Hospital	*Sigh-a-neye Hosbiddle*
sink	*zinc*
soliloquy	*sil-lo-kwee*
something	*somethink*
spigot	*spicket*
Sparrows Point	*Sparris Point*
Tallulah	*Tulla*
tarpaulin	*tarpoleon*
there	*dare*
thing	*tink*
tomorrow	*tuhmar*
Towson	*Talzin*
twenty	*twunny*
umpire	*umpar*
up there	*uhpair*
Vanderbilt	*Vandabill*
viaduct	*vydock*
violence	*vollince*
W	*dubya*
war	*wah*
water	*warder*
Washington	*Warshtin*
Westminster	*Wessminister*
what do you	*whataya*
window	*winder*
with	*wit*

Wolfe Street	*Wuff Street*
world	*whirl*
worse	*varse*
excellent	*x-lint*
x-rated	*x-raided*
yellow	*yella*
yesterday	*yeserdy*
you	*ya*
you are	*yur*
yourself	*yursell*